VAN BUREN DISTRICT LIBRARY
DECATUR, MICHIGAN 49045

# Many Rivers to Cross

# MANY RIVERS

# to

# CROSS

**a novel by**

**Thomas Zigal**

Fort Worth, Texas

2/15
B+T

Zig

Copyright © 2013 by Thomas Zigal

Library of Congress Cataloging-in-Publication Data

Zigal, Thomas.
Many rivers to cross : a novel / by Thomas Zigal.
p. cm.
ISBN 978-0-87565-569-7 (alk. paper)
1. Hurricane Katrina, 2005--Fiction. 2. New Orleans (La.)--Fiction. I. Title.
PS3576.I38M36 2013
813'.54--dc23
2013008551

TCU Press
P.O. Box 298300
Fort Worth, Texas 76129
www.prs.tcu.edu
*To order books:* 1.800.826.8911

*Designed by Barbara Mathews Whitehead*

*For the people of New Orleans*

*Those who survived,*

*and those who perished*

*This is a work of fiction*
*inspired by actual incidents that took place*
*during the first three days after Hurricane Katrina made landfall*
*in late August 2005. As sources of this story, I relied on fieldwork*
*in New Orleans, personal interviews, email exchanges, blogs,*
*online written and video reports, documentary films,*
*and many hours of television and newspaper coverage.*
*I am indebted to the authors of several outstanding books and articles*
*about the hurricane, especially those by*
*Douglas Brinkley, James Lee Burke, John Burnett,*
*Joshua Clark, Michael Eric Dyson, Dave Eggers, Jed Horne,*
*Tom Piazza, and Chris Rose.*

# Monday,
# August 29, 2005

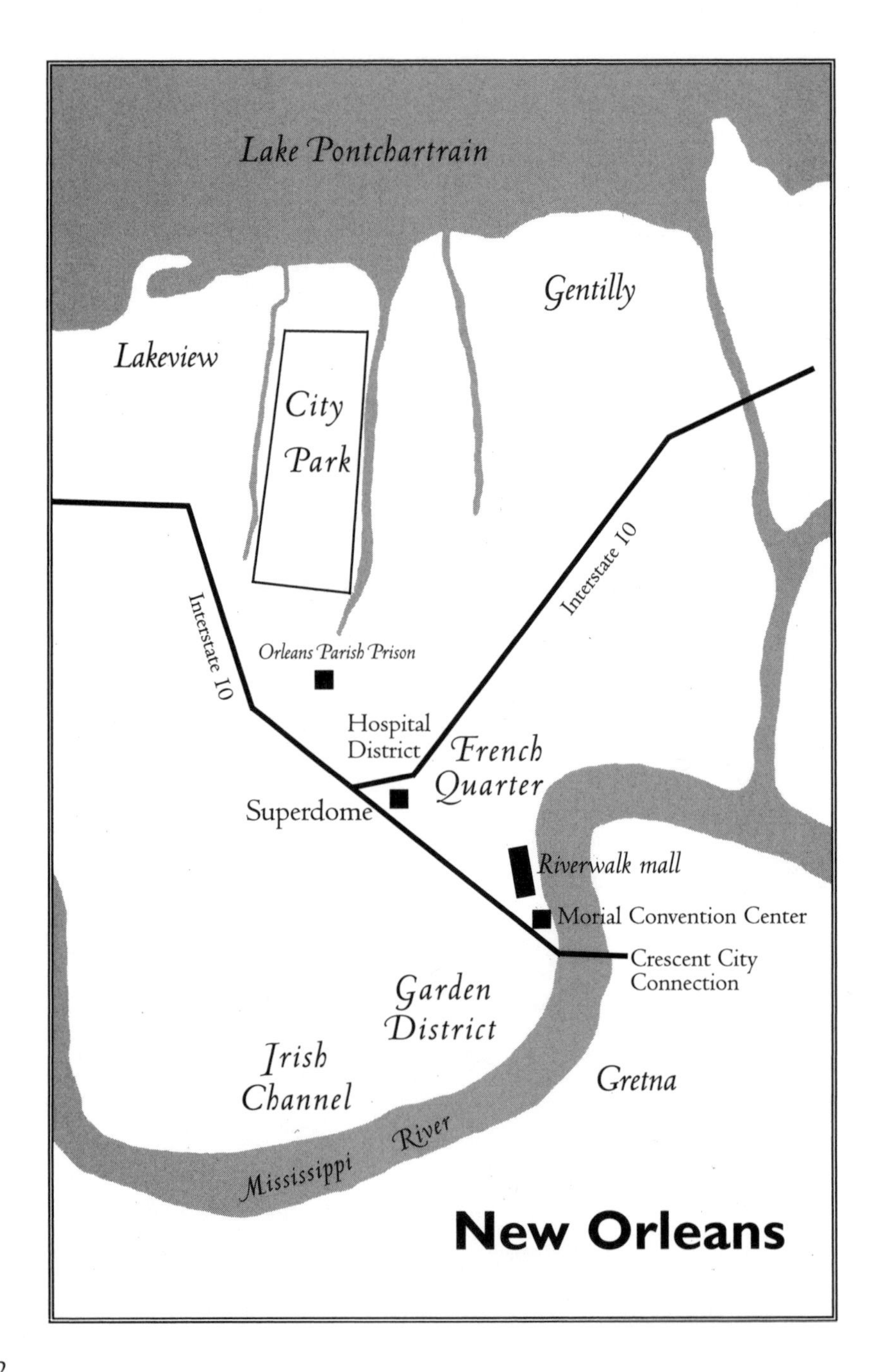

Lake Pontchartrain
Gentilly
Lakeview
City
Park
Interstate 10
Interstate 10
Orleans Parish Prison
Hospital
District
French
Quarter
Superdome
Riverwalk mall
Morial Convention Center
Crescent City
Connection
Garden
District
Irish
Channel
Gretna
Mississippi River
New Orleans

# 1

The two men expected to encounter state troopers on their way into the city. But once they'd passed through the blinding rain of Baton Rouge and climbed up onto the long elevated stretch of Interstate 10 over the bayous, they saw no traffic ahead, only an endless maze of limbs blown across the road from the tops of marsh trees still swaying in the wind. They were the only fools trying to get *into* New Orleans. National Guard, Red Cross, emergency rescue vehicles, not a trace of them anywhere. The radio was reporting that the levees had collapsed in at least three places, and the city was filling with water from Lake Pontchartrain and the canals. Citizens were being warned to seek higher ground, which meant attics and rooftops and the upper stories of parking garages. No one in their right mind would venture into a city built six feet below sea level after the eye of a category three hurricane had slammed ashore only a few miles to the east, near Slidell and the state line. But Dee had called her father in Opelousas to say that water was rising in the streets of her Gentilly neighborhood, where she lived with her two small children, and she felt trapped and desperate. She was a strong young woman, but he could hear panic in her voice.

*I'm sorry I was so hardheaded, Daddy,* she'd said on the phone that morning. Hodge had asked her to leave the city on Saturday, after the governor had declared a state of emergency. Hodge's home in Opelousas was less than a three-hour trip into Cajun country in the southwest part of the state, and he urged her and the children to come and stay. But she didn't take this storm seriously. She'd left New Orleans during hurricane alerts in years past, and they'd usually turned out to be false alarms, the eye veering down to the Texas coast or curling back on Florida. Last year, during the Hurricane Ivan scare, she and the kids were on the road for fourteen hours, bumper to bumper. All New Orleans suffered was a little rain and wind.

By the time the mayor had issued a mandatory evacuation on Sunday morning, as Hurricane Katrina took dead aim on the city, the highways were gridlocked in the somber August heat. *We were scared to be in that line,* she'd admitted during her telephone call. *I saw some thugs drag a man out of his car.* Only two vehicles ahead of her. One of them pistol-whipped the poor man as he begged for mercy. They stole his car and left him bleeding on the side of the road. When she heard another gang of loud young thugs prancing around the cars behind her, project teenagers looking for vehicles to carjack, it was more than she could bear. Her seven-year-old daughter, Ashley, was crying and couldn't catch her breath, so Dee pulled the little Toyota out of line and rutted her way across the grassy median. Speeding off down an empty lane in the contraflow, she headed back into the city.

*Don't worry, sugar,* Hodge had told her. *I'm coming to get you and the kids. Stay calm till I get there. You still have that Smith & Wesson I gave you? Don't be afraid to use it if you have to.*

Hodges Grant guided his old GMC pickup and boat trailer through the obstacle course of scattered limbs on the interstate, the bald tires hydroplaning over a slick wet mat of green leaves that unfurled ahead as far as the eye could see. It was midafternoon on Monday when they crossed over the spillway and entered the city. The rain had let up, but the sky was still gray and ominous, a cauldron of clouds boiling northward. Although Katrina had moved inland and was now battering the Mississippi pines, its tailwinds were still blowing debris across the roads here in New Orleans. Power lines were down everywhere, like a jungle of sagging vines. He could see a piece of the swollen lake off to the left, the slate-gray water as choppy as the open sea.

Duval spoke for the first time in nearly an hour. He was listening to a pocket-sized radio plugged into his ear. "Radio says the cops can gank anybody's boat they want," he said. "Only got five boats in the entire New Orleans police force." He looked at the older man behind the wheel. "Mayor says cooperate if the police want your boat."

Hodge grunted a laugh and shook his head. He was a tall, rawboned man who had shed twenty pounds since the heart attack last year and felt better than he had in a long time. He was two years shy of his sixtieth birthday and had fought in Vietnam as a Marine leatherneck, which felt like another man's life now, something that had happened to a young blood he hardly remembered anymore. All he cared about right now was his daughter and two grandchildren. They were stranded in a flooding neighborhood, and he was coming to pick them up and take them back to his farm outside Opelousas, where they would be safe. Nobody was going to stop him, not New Orleans police or National Guard or God Almighty himself. Nobody was going to confiscate that fourteen-foot johnboat strapped down in the trailer behind them.

"It might get heavy," he told the younger man, the father of Dee's children. Hodge had come close to knocking this homeboy around a few times, back when Duval first walked out on her and the kids. Player had a weakness for other women and street rock, or so Hodge had heard. But he needed Duval now. He needed a second pair of arms in case they had to paddle the johnboat. He needed somebody who'd grown up in this crazy doomed city and knew the streets. And he needed somebody with a cell phone. Hodge didn't own one, didn't have much use for it on the farm.

"Keep your head up, son," he told Duval, "and we'll make out all right."

The interstate ran as straight as a razor through the suburbs of Kenner and Metairie, where white folk had fled decades ago to live in big ranch-style homes and send their kids to safe white schools. Towering light poles along the freeway had toppled in the hurricane wind, and Hodge slowed his pickup to swerve around them and the scattered glass. He had never set foot in those shopping malls he could see from the road, their parking lots now knee deep in murky water. The roof had been ripped off a Sears department store and large sheets of plate glass hung like broken teeth in a row of nearby businesses. A huge billboard sign had keeled over onto the new cars swamped in a dealership lot. As they approached a freeway interchange where the exit ramp trailed off into a shallow lake of neighborhoods, Hodge could see a score of people stranded on the overpass, shouting and waving at the truck in desperation. They wanted out of this city by any means possible.

"Poor bastards," he said to himself. "Where the hell is the police?"

"Saving they own sweet ass," Duval said with a smirk.

A mile farther on, the long white sawhorses of a police barricade lay splintered and strewn across every lane. "I guess it's coming up," Hodge said.

"Say what?" Duval asked, removing the earpiece.

"The end of the line."

Hodge slowed down when they reached sight of an ornate old cemetery whose gothic white mausoleums rose like church spires out of the flood. Lights were flashing above a New Orleans police cruiser parked sideways in the middle of the interstate. He downshifted and tapped his wet brakes, testing them. When they drew closer, they could see that the vehicle was unoccupied. Its windows had been smashed and one of the tires was gone.

"Must be cutthroat owchere," Duval said, "if the Man cain't take care of his own ride."

Hodge stopped the truck, stepped down out of the cab, and stomped his work boots on the wet pavement, restoring the circulation in his legs. The rain had settled into a fine mist that swirled around him in the trailing winds of the hurricane. He understood now that the police car was a warning sign, like a human skull impaled on a tall spike. He gazed past the white cruiser and saw that fifty yards away, the interstate disappeared like a boat ramp into the floodwaters. Farther in the distance, the shadowed cityscape of downtown New Orleans stood grim and powerless in the rainy gray gloom. You couldn't get there from here.

He looked over at the fifteen-foot concrete safety wall that bordered the highway. It protected the nervous white people of this neighborhood from traffic noise and wandering drunks. "You know where we're at?" he asked Duval through the driver's window.

"Fucking Metry," the young man said with a weary sigh.

"Can you find Gentilly from here?"

Duval ducked his head and peered out his window, then stared at the windshield wipers sweeping back and forth. "S'pose so," he said.

Hodge had no idea if Duval was up to this, but there was no other choice. He wished to hell he knew how to find his son, PJ. *Pops Junior.* Big strapping street-smart warrior who would've watched his old man's back on this mission. But PJ was somewhere in the system now, and Hodge had lost track of where.

He opened the door and crawled behind the steering wheel. "I'm gonna drive back down the road apiece and leave the rig in that nice white neighborhood over there," he said. "And cross our fingers it's still there when we come back with Dee and the kids."

Duval folded his arms, incredulous. "That the plan?" he asked. "Leave the ride way out here in Metry?"

"Unless you got a better suggestion," Hodge said.

He turned the pickup around and drove the wrong way on their side of the interstate, in no danger of oncoming traffic. There was a breach in the lane divider where a fallen light pole had crushed the concrete wall. Hodge guided the truck slowly over the broken slabs, the cab rocking as if in rough water, scraping bottom, the trailer dragging like dead weight behind. After some delicate maneuvering, the tires gripped smooth asphalt on the other side, and within minutes they had exited into the dry suburban streets north of the freeway.

Veterans Highway was an older commercial strip, less highway than broad boulevard, the east-west thoroughfare through Metairie before the interstate was built. Veterans now sprawled with fast food joints, used car lots, drive-in banks, drive-thru daiquiri stands, and chain motels, an anywhere four-lane through an anywhere suburb. A Jefferson Parish patrol unit was parked on the side of the road ahead, its overhead light spinning in the blustery gray haze. Two uniformed deputies wearing yellow rain ponchos were standing near a drainage ditch, looking at something in the weeds. When they drew their weapons and began firing, Hodge stopped the truck.

"What the fuck they doing?" Duval said, reaching for the duffel bag on the seat between them.

"Be cool," Hodge said, grabbing Duval's hand so he couldn't get into the bag. They both knew what was in there, tucked under the grocery sack and flashlights.

"We in Jeff Parish, man," Duval said. Metairie and Kenner, white as rice. "Hope it ain't some niggah taking a deuce in that ditch."

Hodge waited, the old motor idling in a rackety rhythm. When the deputies holstered their guns, he put the truck in gear and rolled ahead, no more than twenty miles per hour, a law-abiding citizen driving cautiously through a school zone. He had heard that the cockeyed sheriff of Jefferson Parish had once tried to set up checkpoints in Metairie to stop black people from entering the white neighborhoods. This wasn't a good place for a black man to get crosswise with the authorities.

As the pickup crept past the patrol car, Hodge could see the alligator lying in the wet weeds. At least five feet long, big enough to eat your poodle. One of the deputies nudged it with his boot to see if the creature was still alive. They'd put six rounds in it, by Hodge's count.

"God dayum," Duval said, craning to see the gator. "You s'pose we gonna run into many of them bad boys out there?"

City boy, grew up in the St. Bernard Housing Project. Hodge laughed at him. He'd dealt with his share of gators while fishing in the Atchafalaya swamps. "That's what the paddles are for," he told Duval. "Swing fast enough, they won't take your arm off."

In another block they'd reached the Seventeenth Street Canal and the final boundary of dry land. Hodge hit the worn brakes and the pickup skidded to a halt. They sat in silence, watching the current flow from north to south across Veterans Highway, rushing downhill toward the bottom of the bowl, somewhere miles away in Mid-City. Earlier that morning he'd listened to reports about this canal on television. Surging storm waters had broken through the earthen levee up near the Old Hammond Road bridge and the marina, only two hundred yards from Lake Pontchartrain, and the lake was pouring into the well-to-do Lakeview neighborhood.

Hodge realized he was clenching the steering wheel so hard his hands had lost color. He let go, dropping them into his lap. They were parked on a slight bank above the canal, watching debris swirl in the floodwater ahead, tree limbs and driftwood and bobbing garbage barrels and what looked like jagged sheets of aluminum siding. Off on the right, a radio tower as tall as an oil derrick had tumbled into the stream, its satellite dish clinging by a long cable. There was water as far as he could see. And somewhere out there, his daughter and her children were fighting their own battle to survive the rising tide.

"See if you can reach Dee on the cell phone," he said to Duval.

Duval pulled the phone out of his baggy shorts and speed-dialed the number. To his surprise, the call went through. "Dee!" Duval shouted, his small wedge of face showing signs of life for the first time on this trip. "You okay, baby? How the kids?"

"Give me that," Hodge said, ripping the phone out of his hand. "Dee, honey," he said, "tell me what's going on. Are y'all safe?"

"It's bad, Daddy," she said, her voice warbling the way it always did when she was fighting back tears. *Hide the fear* was something her mother had taught her. God bless that fine woman. *Be strong, girl. Hold your head up and don't let them see you thisaway.* "The street's flooded and water might come in the house," she said. "We might have to go up in the attic."

"You have an ax, darlin'? Or a baseball bat?"

She was still his baby girl, thirty years old or not. This was tearing his heart out.

"LaMarcus has that bat you gave him for his birthday," she said.

"Take the kids and that bat and a water jug and the Smith & Wesson with you up in the attic. Do it now, sugar. The water's rising awful fast."

"I've got to go check on Tante Belle next door," she said. "Poor old lady can't get around anymore."

"No, Dee, take care of yourself and the children. Don't worry about nobody else right now. You hear me? Get up in the attic right away!"

"Where are you, Daddy? Do you have your boat?"

"I've got the boat and we're fixing to put in. I don't know how long it'll take us, baby, but we're coming. You can count on that. We'll be there before you know it."

"I love you, Daddy," she said.

He could hear her catching her breath, fighting the tears, and his own lungs burned now, he hurt so bad for her.

"Stay strong, girl," he said. "Do like your Momma always told you. Keep your smarts and everything will come out all right."

In that moment he saw a terrible image of them drowned in their attic because he hadn't got there quick enough.

"Before you hang up," Duval said, angry that Hodge had taken the phone from him, "let me talk to my kids."

"Make it quick. They don't have time to waste," Hodge said, handing him the cell. "We gotta get this boat in the water."

Hodge was angry, too. If you love those kids, he thought, why aren't you there with them? Why did you treat their mother like you did and walk out on them when they were babies? He was angry, but he couldn't let the anger own him. They had a job to do.

While Duval was talking to LaMarcus and Ashley, telling them to be brave and listen to their Momma, Hodge swung the truck over to the Wendy's parking lot and backed the trailer down to the churning water. When he got out of the cab, he noticed the Jefferson Parish patrol car approaching slowly through the blowing mist, its spotlight trained on the pickup. "Get off the phone and give me a hand," he said, tapping the glass. He didn't have a good feeling about that patrol unit. He thought it best to get busy and launch the boat as fast as they could.

He and Duval were standing in ankle deep water, sliding the long johnboat off its rollers, when he heard car doors slam.

"Hey, there!" one of the deputies shouted at them. "What y'all up to?"

Hodge looked up and waved at them with his free hand, smiling friendly. He didn't want trouble. "Afternoon, officers," he said, hanging onto the guide rope as Duval loaded the duffel bag into the boat. "Helluva storm, ain't it? Saw that gator you bagged. Wonder how it ended up way out here?"

"I was about to ask you the same thing, chief. Can I see some ID?"

The two deputies were white men who looked to be in their late thirties. Dark blue caps, water dripping off their bills, yellow ponchos streaked with rain. Hodge couldn't see their hands, which made him uneasy.

"Just drove in from Opelousas," he said. "My daughter and her two kids are in trouble over by Gentilly. House is flooding. We're gonna go pick 'em up and take 'em back home."

"Lot of water between here and Gentilly," the deputy said. He was a short stout man with a thick neck and ruddy complexion. He had no eyebrows, or so it appeared to Hodge, and that gave his eyes a crazed and piercing intensity. "I need to see some ID," the deputy said. "Just wanna make sure y'all are who you say you are. We've had reports about looting in the city, and we don't want it to get started out here."

Hodge glanced at Duval and saw what these white cops saw. A young hip-hop niggah wearing baggy basketball shorts and hundred-dollar Nikes, his black face hidden in a hoodie. *Banger* written all over him. Duval stared back at Hodge with a slight shake of the head. *Don't let them run my ID.*

Fucking Jesus, Hodge thought. Outstanding warrants for God knows what, the dumbass. He tossed the guide rope into the boat and leaned close to Duval, speaking in a low voice with his back to the deputies. "Push off and crank the motor," he said, "but stay close in. I may have to swim for it."

He turned and walked up the wet pavement toward the officers with a broad smile on his face, reaching into the back pocket of his camo fatigues to produce his wallet. "Gentlemen, I don't want to be rude," he said, handing his driver's license to the deputy who had asked for it, "but we're in a hurry to find my daughter and grandchildren. They're not but seven and nine years old. I'd appreciate it if you'd let us be on our way."

The deputy gazed up at the cap Hodge was wearing. Marine Corps insignia, VIETNAM VETERAN embroidered below the eagle and globe. Hodge had worn it on purpose, hoping it still meant something in this country.

"We've got a serious situation in Old Metairie. Seniors trapped in their homes," the second deputy said as he wandered over to cup his eyes and peer through the pickup's passenger window. He was nearly as tall as Hodge, maybe six-feet-two, and sported a well-trimmed black mustache. Olive complexion, Italian heritage or a Cajun from out Hodge's way. "Boss says we need more boats. He's given us an order to go out and find some."

Hodge knew about Old Metairie, the wealthy folk on the other side of the interstate from here. Manors hidden in live oak lanes, country clubs, long green fairways, lawn jockeys painted pink so they wouldn't offend the help.

"I'm sorry, officer, I cain't give up my boat," he said. "I built that thing with my own hands when I come back from the Nam."

Took him a month to get it right. Fourteen feet of fir plywood, a handful of galvanized screws, fiberglass tape, and Epoxy glue, not much more than that. Except for the planing and sanding and three coats of deck paint. Fishing was his solace in those early months after the war.

"We're really not asking for your permission, chief," said the deputy holding Hodge's license.

At the sound of the first crank, the three of them turned. The johnboat was floating aimlessly a dozen yards out in the floodwater, Duval kneeling over the motor. He gave the rope another yank and the old Mercury outboard sputtered again.

"Yo, *dawg!*" the tall deputy shouted, jogging toward the water with his hand gripping the pistol holstered underneath his poncho. "Bring that boat in!"

Duval didn't look up. He pulled the rope again and the motor coughed. Hodge could smell gasoline in the air. Homeboy had flooded the engine.

"Me and my son-in-law need to be going," he said to the deputy standing beside him. *Son-in-law* was far from true, but it sounded better than *baby daddy crackhead that knocked up my daughter twice.* "Can I have my license back?"

The deputy reached under his poncho and withdrew a pair of handcuffs. "You can step over here by the cruiser, chief," he said, "and put your hands behind your back."

# 2

Dee and her children lived in Gentilly Terrace, an older neighborhood of modest California-style bungalows and English cottages. What was once a shallow swamp during the plantation era had become a surprisingly organized grid of streets east of the oak forest of City Park. Gentilly was the middle-class black stepsister to the mostly white Lakeview district on the west side of the park. And like Lakeview's Seventeenth Street Canal, which drained the city's heavy rainwater into Lake Pontchartrain, Gentilly had its own London Avenue Canal to serve the same purpose. Around daybreak on Monday morning, the swollen lake had forced ten feet of water back into the canals, buckling the concrete I-walls on top of their grassy levees.

Her given name was Deidre, but everyone had called her Dee since she was a little girl. She worked as a teacher's assistant at a local elementary school and lived in a one-story, rented bungalow with her children, LaMarcus and Ashley. They had been good soldiers and, for the most part, remained calm overnight, huddling with their mother on a mattress in the closed-off hallway. Rain hammered their roof and wind shattered two windows in the living room. They could hear transformers exploding nearby and tall trees crashing through the fence in the backyard. LaMarcus loved math and nearly drove them crazy with his ceaseless accounting of things. *That's the fourth car alarm, Momma. . . . One Mississippi, two Mississippi, three Mississippi—hey, that lightning was only three miles away.*

Ashley was worried about the landlady who lived next door with her dog. *I bet you Tempo is hiding under a bed,* she said after thunder had shaken their house. *I hope Tante Belle is safe, Momma.*

Dee was concerned about Tante Belle, as well. The elderly

Creole woman seemed to be the only other person on their block who didn't evacuate. At first sign of daylight, when Dee opened the hall door and ventured into the living room to sweep up the glass, she noticed Tante Belle waving from her window, the miniature collie cuddled in her large pillowy breasts like a docile child.

"Are you and Tempo okay?" Dee shouted through the broken window frame. "Do you need anything?"

"We'll be just fine, baby. I think the worst is over. A few trees down, that's all. You and *les enfants* holding up all right?"

Tante Belle was seventy-five years old and well over three hundred pounds, a grand light-skinned woman with copper-colored hair who could *passe blanc* anywhere else in the country. She had lived in that gingerbread cottage since her childhood and had taught scores of young girls from all over the city how to play piano and speak French. She let Dee's children walk Tempo up and down the sidewalk every day after school.

"You need something, you shout, okay?" Dee said.

"I'm pretty well fixed," Tante Belle said. "Preston made groceries for me before they left town. I've got more cans on the shelf than Schwegmann's, doll."

The beloved music teacher didn't drive anymore and relied on her nephew and the neighbors to bring her groceries and medicine. She limped around her cozy old maid's cottage with the aid of a cane, listened to opera at full volume, baked cookies for the entire block, and played bridge and bourré with anyone who cared to learn. Her nephew and half the neighborhood had pleaded with her to leave with them in the caravan out of town, but Tante Belle had stubbornly refused.

*Tempo's too fussy, and I'm too fat to go very far nowadays,* she'd told everyone. *This has been my home all my life, and if it goes down, I'll go down with it.*

By midmorning the levee had given way on both sides of the London Avenue Canal, sending a torrent of water and mud into the streets of Gentilly. When Dee stepped out on her raised front porch and noticed water eddying around the Babineau's house across the street, washing garden tools and sandbox toys across their lawn, she phoned her father in Opelousas to tell him that something had gone wrong. Her battery-powered radio was saying that the city had survived the worst of Katrina's fury, but there were isolated reports about London Avenue and breaches in the Industrial Canal to the east of them. By the end of her call, a steady stream was pouring into their neighborhood from two different directions, and she realized that the reports were true.

She went back inside and told the kids that their Pawpaw was coming to get them in his fishing boat. "Okay, math wizard, this is what I want you to do," she said to LaMarcus. "You see those bricks on the side of Tante Belle's house? Keep an eye on the waterline, and tell me how fast it's rising up that wall." She wanted to know how much time they had.

He looked at his mother and smiled. "You mean how many bricks per hour?"

"That's exactly what I mean, Einstein. You up to the assignment?"

"I'm all over it," he said, consulting the oversized watch on his wrist, a birthday gift from his grandfather. Like a diver's watch with all the gauges and barometers. "We will begin the measurement, shall we say . . . right . . . now," he said, slashing an index finger through the air.

Access to the attic was a pull-down ladder in the hallway ceiling. Dee jerked the rope, and the door dropped on creaking springs. She reached up and unfurled the ladder, climbing the steps to inspect that musty dark hideaway. She couldn't remember the last time she'd been up here. Maybe as long ago as New Year's Day, when she'd returned the Christmas tree ornaments to their yellowing cardboard box.

The attic was sweltering from the trapped summer heat and stank of mildew and something wild and nasty she couldn't identify. Weak daylight seeped through the louvers of a triangular air vent at one end of the pitched roof. Dee turned on her flashlight and swept the beam across the crumbled gray insulation that heaped in rows along the attic's floor. She could hear water dripping from nail holes in the shingled roof. The claustrophobic enclosure gave her the creeps, and she wondered how the children would manage up here, breathing this bad air. She had almost adjusted her mind to the fact that they might have no choice when her light revealed small red eyes staring back at her. The rats were bigger than footballs.

"Sweet Jesus," she cried, clicking off the flashlight and hurrying down the ladder.

"What's the matter, Momma?" Ashley was standing in the hall, watching her mother fly down the steps. She was a chunky little girl, like Dee when she was her age, with beaded hair she spent hours mixing and matching.

"It's nothing, babe," Dee said, folding the ladder upward and giving the door a hard shove. The rusty springs creaked and the panel slammed in place against the ceiling. "Just a little funky up there."

Dee walked into the living room on trembling legs and sat on the couch. She was feeling lightheaded and defeated and didn't know where to turn. *My God, rats!* How many were up there, searching for food and shelter from the flood?

LaMarcus turned from the window, where he'd been studying the waterline on Tante Belle's brick wall. "By my calculations," he announced, "the water is rising one brick every twenty minutes."

Dee looked over at her tall slender son, trying to wrap her thoughts around that figure. Twenty minutes per brick. "Tell me what that means for our house," she said.

LaMarcus opened the front door and walked out onto the porch. Dee watched him pacing back and forth, lost in his computations, staring into the river that had once been their street and front yard. She was proud of her nine-year-old genius with his nerdy cute box-fade haircut. LaMarcus was going to college someday on a math scholarship, if she had anything to say about it, and would not take a detour through the gangsta crowd or a basketball court.

He came back inside with a troubled expression on his face. "If it keeps going at this rate," he said like a young professor standing before his class, "the water will cover our porch in two hours."

They grabbed towels from the bathroom closet and old clothes destined for Goodwill and stuffed them against the door strips and windowsills, preparing for the worst. Dee told the children it was time to put their special things up high, and LaMarcus and Ashley raced around the house picking out toys and keepsakes and placed them on the upper shelf in the bedroom closet they shared. Dee found all the photo albums in a bureau, along with file folders containing birth certificates, medical and insurance records, and financial statements, and she climbed up onto a kitchen counter to store them on the top shelf of the cupboard.

"I'm hungry, Momma," Ashley announced in the middle of their frantic mission.

Dee realized they hadn't eaten since supper last night. She was surprised to find the dark inside of the refrigerator still cool. The three of them sat at the kitchen table and ate cereal and applesauce and finished off the milk and orange juice. To pass the time waiting for her father, they played a dice game called Farkle that required complicated scorekeeping with columns of numbers jotted on paper, and after awhile Ashley accused LaMarcus of making up the rules as they went along. Their argument had escalated into a bitter fight when Dee's cell phone rang.

"*Quiet!*" she shouted at them. "Stop it *right now!*"

It was Duval, calling from somewhere in Metairie. They had reached the city in one piece. Hodge did most of the talking, then Duval came back on the line and asked to speak with the children.

As he talked with his father, LaMarcus's face grew bright with hope and expectation. He was still in game mode and didn't fully grasp the danger they were in. "Daddy's coming with Pawpaw," he said, handing the phone to Ashley. "They're going to rescue us."

LaMarcus was the only one in the family who felt some connection with his father. He talked about him all the time, asked questions. *How come we never go over to Daddy's house? What kind of job does he have?* Dee did her best to be positive and not criticize their father in front of them. Most of the time she had to bite her tongue. Duval rarely came to see his children anymore. Sometimes he disappeared for three or four weeks without a phone call.

"He wants to talk to you," Ashley said, handing the cell phone to her mother. Ashley had spoken very little to Duval, only a few halfhearted responses. *Okay, Daddy. Sure. Thanks.* The girl's indifference toward her father was palpable. She seemed to embody Dee's own private resentment.

"Time to get your stuff together, kids," Dee said, taking the cell phone. She told them to pack a few clothes in their school backpacks and to gather up their blankets and pillows and flashlights and one toy apiece, because they might have to climb up into the attic soon.

Still listening to Duval on the line, she walked down the hall and into the living room, where floodwater was seeping up through the floorboards.

"I thought y'all were long gone, girl," he was saying into her ear. "'Sup with that? You shoulda left on Saturday when *I* did."

She'd told her father where to find him, the exact address. Motel 6 in Baton Rouge East. She wished she could've been there when Hodge went banging on doors, bellowing Duval's name in the pouring rain. She would've paid money to see the look on Duval's face when he unlatched the door and her father locked that huge paw on his shoulder, saying, *Put your big boy pants on, son, you're coming with me.*

"We ran up on some trouble, Duval." She turned to make sure the children weren't in the room, then lowered her voice anyway. "Young niggahs jacking cars all around us." She didn't like to talk street, but she was angry at him and *street* was the only way to reach Duval most of the time. "A woman with two kids can't do everything by herself. Where were you, homeboy? Fucking some skanky ho in a twenty-dollar motel room?"

"Now come on, Dee, it ain't like that," he said, his voice softening into his sweet-boy routine. This was how he'd charmed her from the first, showing that other side. "I thought you had it under control, baby, like you always do."

She was livid now and struggled to keep her voice down. "You couldn't call and see if your children needed a ride out of town?"

"I fucked up, Dee. I'm sorry, ah-ight? But I'ma straighten it out. Your daddy and me, we out here in Metry, fixing to drop his big-ass boat in the water."

Static washed through their conversation like rain battering a tin roof. Duval's voice began to break up.

"We coming, baby . . . promise you that . . . cool, ah-ight? . . . Make sure the kids . . ."

"Duval?" she said, but the line went silent. She didn't know if her charge was dead or the link had gone down. When she turned around, the children were staring at her from the hall doorway, their backpacks strapped to their shoulders, their arms full of pillows and tangled blankets. The water was already above Ashley's sneakers.

"What about Tempo and Tante Belle?" Ashley asked in a small, scared voice.

"Can they stay with us in the attic?" LaMarcus asked.

Dee glanced out the window at the dark house next door. "I'll go check on them," she said, squeezing the cell phone in her hand as if to coax it back to life. "Come on, wait for me in the kitchen. Sit on the table where it's dry."

The children climbed up on the tabletop, arranged their blankets around themselves like the walls of a fort, and laughed at where they were sitting. Dee kissed them both on the forehead and tried to smile. "This is quite an adventure, hunh?" she said, trying to put a calm face on it. "Like *Where the Wild Things Are.*" They all loved that book.

"Oh man, I remember Max sailing off in a boat," LaMarcus said with a laugh. It had been a long time since they'd read the story together.

"I remember that scary sea serpent in the water," his sister added.

"You two stay put. Don't go sailing off on your own," she said. The boom box radio they'd been listening to throughout the night was sitting on the kitchen counter and she turned it back on. A newsman named Garland Robinette at station WWL was still on the air. "Y'all check out what they're saying and tell me when I get back."

The house was warm and sultry and beginning to smell like a wet animal, the memory scent of previous lives within these old walls. Dee sloshed into her bedroom and took the one-piece bathing suit off a hook behind the door. The suit she wore two nights a week at the UNO pool, where she swam laps after her evening class. It was where she'd met Greg and his teenaged daughter. Professor Gregory Wilson, history instructor. They hadn't seen each other in a couple of months, but the hurt was still fresh. The hurt and the longing. She hoped he was safe with his parents in Atlanta.

She sat on the bed and stripped off her sweaty clothes, pulling the blue suit up over her hips. It was fitting snug nowadays and made her all too aware that she'd added a few pounds in the wrong places. The comfort food you ate after a breakup. Their clandestine affair had lasted only a year, and they'd kept it a secret even from their children and closest friends. Sometimes at night, when she was drifting off to sleep, she closed her eyes and still felt his arms around her.

Dee slipped her khaki shorts over the bathing suit and forced on a pair of wet surf walkers she'd bought for the beach in Biloxi. She splashed across the hallway to the children's room and found their Styrofoam kickboard floating in a corner next to the soccer ball. This dinged-up green and yellow kickboard was the lifeline she needed to make it to Tante Belle's house.

When she opened the front door in the living room, a warm wave poured into the house, swirling around her ankles.

"Be careful, Momma!" Ashley yelled from the kitchen table.

"Just stay where you are!" Dee shouted. "I'll be back in a minute."

She trudged out onto the raised front porch, where the mud-colored water lapped against her knees. Tendrils of ivy and red geraniums, freed from their pots, floated like water lilies near the wood-slat swing. Dee looked out over the creeping river and feared for her children. Only the roof of her Toyota was visible, the rest of it sunk like an ancient galleon in the lost driveway. Debris drifted across the neighborhood, tree branches and split-open garbage bags and household possessions that hadn't been tied down. Patio furniture, a wicker basket, long coils of garden hoses. She could hear Tempo howling in the house next door and the faint shrill melodrama of opera music wafting through the muggy air. Had something happened to Tante Belle?

She waded to the edge of the porch and clutched a support beam, steadying herself, holding the kickboard under the other arm as she peered down into the opaque water. Where were the steps? It must have been six feet deep out in the street. She inhaled, let it out, inhaled again, a little nauseated trying to visualize the plunge into this sewage dump. She'd grown up in Convent, a petrochemical town on the Mississippi River halfway between New Orleans and Baton Rouge, and she knew what was in this water and in every bayou and waterhole in South Louisiana. Her father had worked in a plant there for thirty years and had forbidden her and her brother PJ to swim in the river. He'd seen what his company dumped down their drainage pipes every night, the benzenes and chlorides and acids that would make a person sick.

Tempo was howling again, poor thing, a sad mournful sound. Dee took one final breath and let go of the porch beam. She squatted down in the water, lowered her chest against the board, and kicked off, paddling out into the yard like a surfer searching for a wave. The water was cooler than she'd expected. She was determined not to get any in her mouth and kept her head high, legs churning. Her heart was beating fast. She tried not to think about what was lurking underneath her, the nasty sharp edges that would slice her open, the Wild Things that would snatch her up.

# 3

odge heard the outboard motor roar to life and turned to find Duval signaling from the johnboat. *Time to go,* he was saying. He'd managed to start the damn thing.

With his hand on the grip of his holstered weapon, the deputy at the water's edge ordered Duval to steer the boat back to dry land. The young man turned up his palms in a defiant shrug. "What you gone do, Starsky? Cap my ass?" he said. "Better check with your boy Hutch first."

There was a *thump thump thump* sound somewhere above them in the wet gray sky and it grew louder as the Coast Guard Jayhawk appeared from the north, flying in low over the apartment complexes near the canal. Hodge walked away from the deputy holding the handcuffs and waved his cap at the chopper. "You want to cuff a Marine vet and steal his boat," he said to the deputy, raising his voice to be heard over the racket, "you'll have to do it in front of these puddle jumpers."

The Jayhawk dropped its black nose and hovered eighty feet above them, canting slowly in the stiff wind, its downdraft stirring the muddy floodwaters where Duval struggled with the boat. The cargo door was open and a crewman wearing a headset helmet waved back at Hodge. The HH-60 was in search and rescue mode, hunting for people in distress. They had probably picked up the flashing lights of the patrol car and now appeared to be waiting for some response from this strange scene below them. A johnboat idling in the water, two sheriff's department uniforms, an agitated black man waving his cap to get their attention.

Such a pretty sight, Hodge thought, that bird flying in to cover them. He remembered how sweet it had felt that time in the Delta when the Huey swooped down to pull their stranded crew out of the elephant grass. He smiled up at the young Coastie crouched in the open hatch and gave him a proper military salute. The crewman saluted Hodge in return.

"You want my boat," Hodge shouted at the deputy with the handcuffs, "you'll have to kill me for it."

He set out walking toward the water and the deputy yelled something at him. Maybe the word *Stop!* But Hodge didn't stop, not even when the other deputy, the taller one with the thick mustache, saw him coming and squared his shoulders as if to take him down. "*Back off,*" Hodge said, waving his cap at the Jayhawk cockpit again to make sure they were witnessing this. He and the deputy circled each other slowly, like dogs sizing up the fight, but the man finally stood aside and let him pass. Hodge waded out into the water, a foul-smelling concoction neither warm nor cold, until he was nearly waist deep and had reached the johnboat. Duval grabbed him under the armpits and helped him crawl aboard.

"Let's bump the fuck on out of here," he said, scrambling to the front of the boat so Hodge could take the throttle.

"You got that right," Hodge said.

His wet work boots felt like they weighed a hundred pounds, and his fatigues were soaked through to the skin. He had half expected to take a bullet in the back. When he glanced over at dry land, the two deputies were standing side by side in their yellow rain ponchos, giving thumbs up to the Jayhawk pilot. All is well here; we don't need you.

The chopper rose higher into the blustery wind and buzzed away toward the flooded neighborhood to the east. When it was gone, the short deputy smiled at Hodge and waved the driver's license victoriously, as if it were a winning lotto ticket. "You want your license back, chief?" he yelled at Hodge.

"Why don't you mail it to me, officer?" Hodge suggested without a trace of humor.

"Can do," the deputy said. "How about airmail, asshole?"

He flung the license Frisbee-style toward the boat and it sailed no more than five yards before dropping into the water. Hodge watched the card float for a moment and then slowly sink into the murk. His only means of identity, like dog tags when he was in country. What if something happened to him, how would anyone know who he was?

"We're coming back here with my daughter and her kids," he shouted at the two officers. "I better find that truck and trailer where I'm leaving them. Because if I don't," he said, "I'll pay your boss—the sheriff—a visit with my attorney. And I never forget a face."

The short deputy laughed at him. "You'll be lucky to get across Lakeview alive," he said with a snort. "I wouldn't count on making it back."

Hodge stick-throttled the old outboard motor, feeding it gas, and the johnboat picked up speed as he guided them into a brisk wind toward a row of sunken houses on the Orleans side of the canal levee. They were fighting the current, thousands of gallons of water pouring into Lakeview, and short choppy waves splashed against the flat prow.

"You our eyes and ears," he said to the young man's back. Duval had pulled the hood up over his head. "You the navigator, son. I don't know this part of town."

"What makes you think *I* do?"

"I figure we keep heading toward City Park," Hodge said. He knew that Gentilly was on the other side of the park. He slipped his arms through an old flotation vest he'd carried on this boat for thirty-five years. "Put your lifejacket on," he said. "Could get rough on up the road."

Duval glanced at the spare lifejacket and shook his head. "Drive this boat better than you drive that old piece of shit truck and I won't need that thing," he said.

A fire was burning in the West End marina near the lake, the stately old Southern Yacht Club in flames, and they could see black smoke drifting above the houses ahead. A street sign that said *Fleur de Lis* was bent at a forty-five degree angle, and a huge oak tree had fallen and crushed the roof of a nice red brick home on the corner. As they entered deeper into the Lakeview neighborhood, Hodge saw that the waterline was halfway up the windows in all these expensive houses. Mother Nature didn't pick favorites this time.

He was concerned about underwater bushes fouling his propeller and tried to keep the boat in the street, but there was no way of knowing where the lawns began or ended. A woeful, whimpering sound caught his attention, and he glanced up into a drowning pecan tree to discover a wet dog shivering in the branches.

"Yo, man, check this out," Duval said, pointing at the dog, some kind of border collie mix. "How the fuck it get up there?"

"Same way you would," Hodge said, "if high water was hosing up your ass."

Duval whistled at the dog, made a smooching sound with his lips. "Hey, boy," he said in a sweet sing-song, "Hey, now. Hang tight up there, you be ah-ight. Keep hope alive."

He turned around and looked at Hodge. "We oughta take him with us, man," he said. "He ain't gonna make it up in that tree."

"Do a little more worrying about your children, Duval, and a little less worrying about a stray dog."

Duval shot him a quick look, his eyes narrowing. "Fuck you, old man," he said, turning his back in anger. "I love my kids. Fuck you and this boat you rode in on."

This had been eating at Hodge for two days and he wasn't going to let it slide. "If you took those children with you to Baton Rouge in the first place, they wouldn't be holed up in a flooded house halfway across town, and we wouldn't be out here in a goddamn johnboat looking for them."

The way Dee told it on the phone, Duval hadn't even checked on his children. Just took off on Saturday with those homeboy losers he lived with in Gert Town and shacked up in a cheap Baton Rouge motel with their bitches and a case of malt liquor and who knows what else. When Dee finally tracked him down on his cell phone, she could hear the party in the background.

"She told me she was driving out yesterday," Duval said over his shoulder. "I figured they'd be in Opelousas by now."

"It's your job to keep track of those children, son."

Duval had a mean little laugh. "Like you some kind of Dr. Phil expert," he said. "Where the fuck is your boy at? Doing time somewhere in lockdown? You don't even know."

Hodge had to let all of that go now. He needed Duval's full attention as they traveled farther into this nightmare, where something biblical and signifying was taking shape, dark smoke coiling in the mist and dogs stranded in trees and a flood over all the earth. He listened for the sound of human voices, but the world was silent. At the next street sign he steered the johnboat past what appeared to be a garden of majestic oak trees, maybe two hundred years old, all of them uprooted and piled against one another.

Duval turned halfway around and pointed again. "You see that?" he nodded. "Over there, man."

A body was floating between houses on the other side of the street. Hodge maneuvered the boat for a closer look. They crossed an open yard and approached the house itself, a large wooden structure older than the others on the block. He cut the engine and let the momentum carry the boat toward the corpse.

He was a small white man lying facedown in the water, his limbs spread-eagle, forming an X. His body hadn't begun to bloat yet or decompose. But the air was warm and steamy, and a fetid smell surrounded him, as if he'd crapped himself. He was wearing pajamas and only one house slipper, and he looked to be in his seventies or eighties, judging by the gnarled shape of his arms and legs and the sparse silver hair on the back of his head. They bobbed alongside the body, staring in silence, Hodge struggling to keep the boat steady. He had no idea how the man had ended up outside his house. Maybe he was feeble and went looking for help. Hodge remembered the first dead man he'd come across in Nam, a VC floating facedown in a rice paddy, flies swarming all around him. No telling how many days he'd been there. Their platoon leader warned them not to fool with the body because it was probably booby-trapped.

"Hand me that piece of rope," he said to Duval.

Duval was clearly not feeling well. He looked like he might puke up that breakfast bar Hodge had given him on the road. "What you gonna do?" he asked in a tight voice.

"The current will take him off," Hodge said. "That ain't right. He needs to stay near his house here, so his family won't have to go looking for him."

"You gonna touch that dead old dude?"

Hodge lifted the bill of his cap and sighed. "Hand me the rope, Duval," he said.

He found the hunting knife in his duffel bag and cut a piece of rope long enough to tie the man to the trunk of that sturdy pine tree in his yard. He used a paddle to edge the boat up to the corpse, then knelt between benches and reached out for the man's leg, feeling the stiffness that had settled in the bone. He was tying a secure knot around the scrawny calf muscle when he heard the distinctive sound of a pump shotgun jacking a shell into its chamber. The blast came from somewhere above them and Hodge nearly fell out of the boat. He wasn't hit, but his heart was pounding way too hard and he grabbed his chest.

"Muthuh*fuck*uh," Duval cried out, his hands fumbling for the duffel bag.

A white man was standing on the roof of the house next door, staring down a smoking twelve-gauge shotgun barrel aimed directly at Hodge.

# 4

She had almost reached Tante Belle's house when she saw the snake, a thick cottonmouth water moccasin zigzagging toward her across a slick of sudsy scum. She kicked harder, pumping her legs, trying to scare the snake away with her commotion, but it kept coming at her, a waggling ribbon of deadly venom.

She'd grown up around snakes, watched her father stomp a cottonmouth to death when it dropped from a cypress tree into the johnboat out in Bayou des Glaises. The snake bit through his boot leather and Hodge's leg swole up so bad he'd almost died before they found a doctor to cut him open. *They won't bite you in water,* people had always said. But Dee had never believed that old wives' tale.

When the moccasin slithered within arm's reach, she started treading water, thrashing her arms and legs, swinging the board at it. Then suddenly she couldn't see the snake anymore. She dogpaddled full circle, panicked, searching for its olive hide and dark bands. *Could they go underwater!* She didn't think so. *Was it anywhere in striking distance?* Heaving her chest onto the board again, she kicked with renewed strength, propelling herself toward the small red brick house.

Once she arrived at Tante Belle's landing, her feet found a solid stone step and she stood up and looked back for the snake. No sign of it anywhere. She banged hard on the front door, calling her neighbor's name. At first she thought the heavy wooden door was locked, but with more effort she shouldered it open and splashed inside the front parlor. Tempo was lying on the couch next to Tante Belle. The dog raised her head and growled at Dee, then saw who she was and dropped her nose onto Belle's lap.

The good lady was sitting upright on the couch with her huge legs soaking in the brackish water that measured two feet deep throughout her house. It had already ruined dozens of books on the bottom shelves of her built-in cases and her prized LPs arranged in a stand next to the stereo. Belle's large head was tilted back against a cushion, her eyes closed, opera music blaring from the portable radio on the end table beside her.

"Tante Belle!" Dee said in a loud voice as she waded toward her. "Are you all right?"

When she touched the old woman's warm forehead, Belle opened her eyes and smiled a dreamy smile at her. "*Il Re Teodoro in Venezia,*" she mumbled through dry lips. The poor dear appeared to be dehydrated and hallucinating. "Giovanni Paisiello—1784, I believe," she said. "A very obscure recording on a small Italian label. I don't know how our radio host is able to play such sublime music at a time like this. It gives me comfort to hear one of my old favorites."

Dee turned down the volume and gazed up at the ceiling, looking for an attic hatch. "We've got to get you out of here," she said. "The water's rising a brick every twenty minutes. I'm not sure when it'll stop."

Tante Belle's laugh sounded like a wind chime tinkling in warm sunshine. "Mercy, child, it would take four strapping firemen and a forklift to hoist this fat old body up off the sofa."

She was one of those charming old Creole women whose soul was so beautiful, her smile so radiant, you didn't notice her size anymore—even if the only dresses she wore were flowery Hawaiian muumuus as wide as a pup tent.

"I'm happy as a canary right here, baby, and I'm not going anywhere," she said, feeding Tempo a dog biscuit from a box next to the radio. "If the Good Lord wants me so bad, he can have me."

Belle was certainly right that it would take more than Dee to lift that massive body. The phone lines were dead and there was no one to call on for help. She hadn't seen anyone else in the neighborhood since yesterday afternoon. "I can't just leave you here like this," she said, circling the sofa in a slow watery shuffle, searching for answers she didn't have. "We've got to do something, Belle."

The old woman laughed and shook her head. There was a tender light in her eyes and she seemed to accept whatever happened next. "You want to do me a favor, doll?" she said, biting into a dog biscuit and chewing it like a cookie. "Take Tempo with you and make sure she's safe. She's my precious baby girl, and I can't stand to see her suffer." She let the collie nibble on the biscuit. "I don't want her to see what's going to happen to me."

The little collie was shivering and knew that something was wrong. Protective and good-natured, Tempo had always been a great watchdog for the children in the neighborhood. She growled at male strangers, the postman, and anyone delivering packages from a big brown truck. More than once she'd chewed on the pants cuff of a door-to-door salesman.

"Take her with you and let the children keep her when I'm gone," she said. "Please do that for me, baby. God loves those who care for his creatures. He will smile on you."

Dee bent over and threw her arms around Belle's soft fleshy neck. "I can't leave you here without a fight," she said in a husky voice. "You mean too much to me and my children."

The old lady held her in a smothering embrace. Dee could feel the strength that still resided in those heavy arms. "Now you listen to me, Deidre," she said, pushing her away so she could look into her eyes. Tante Belle was the only person besides Dee's mother who had ever called her by her given name. "You're a beautiful young woman and you take such good care of your children. When all this is over, you need to get on with your life. God has given you the brains to be a schoolteacher and I want you to finish getting your degree, no matter how long it takes you. I know what I'm talking about. There are so many children out there waiting for someone special, like you, to turn on that light." She gave Dee a gentle shake. "And another thing," she said, "I want you to find yourself a good man and fall in love and have more babies."

Dee sniffed back the tears and laughed at the idea. What she needed was more mouths to feed.

"I'm not playing with you, child," Belle said with a stern but loving regard. "The best thing you can do for this old piano pounder is to promise me you'll live a happy life with an abundance of children and a fine husband who treats you right." She patted Dee's cheek. "You promise me that, and everything between us is settled."

Dee nodded, speechless, trapped between the darkest sorrow and the bright holy blessing of this dear woman.

Tante Belle stroked Tempo's back. "You'll have to carry her out the door," she said. "She won't go willingly. Take the leash."

Dee was trying to catch her breath. "Can she?—Can she swim?" she managed to ask.

"Oh yes," Belle said with a proud smile. "Far better than you and I."

Dee looked around the flooded house one last time. Sheet music was floating behind the couch. "Let's pray it stops soon," she said. "Let's pray this is as high as it gets."

She kissed the old lady on the cheek, then reached down and lifted Tempo into her arms. The collie fought her for a moment, squirming and whining, barking in her ear. Dee held her firmly and waded toward the door, where the kickboard bobbed near a coat tree. "This isn't goodbye, Belle," she said, her voice rising. "I'm going to find some help and get you out of here."

Tante Belle offered her a tender smile. Neither of them really believed that would happen. "Take good care of my baby," she said. "Keep those children safe."

She blew a kiss to her pet collie and turned up the volume on the radio. Static was interrupting the transmission and the opera music faded in and out. And then the static finally prevailed and the station went dead.

# 5

The shotgun's report echoed in the heavy air. Smoke coiled from the barrel. The man on the rooftop pumped another shell into the chamber and Hodge could hear the spent casing clatter down the shingles. "What the hell are y'all doing with that man?" the shooter said. "Leave him alone and get on away from here!"

Hodge felt a familiar tightening in his chest. Sometimes he wondered if those two stents were enough. "We're gonna secure this gent to that tree over there so he won't float away," he said, nodding at the tall sturdy pine rising like a pole out of the water. "Why don't you put down the shotgun?"

Duval was fumbling with the pull string of the duffel bag, cursing and trying to untie the knot, but Hodge smacked his hands with the paddle and dragged the bag out of his reach. He didn't want that young hothead to pull out the .45 and start slinging lead. He knew that the man on the roof could have killed them both by now if he wanted to, but he'd fired a warning shot instead.

"What are y'all doing in this neighborhood?" His voice was brittle and strained. "You don't look like you belong here."

He was dressed in creased slacks and a button-down shirt with a collar, his dark wavy hair cut in one of those classy hairstyles that white men paid eighty bucks for. Hodge figured him for a businessman or lawyer who worked in an office building downtown, the kind who went on a weeklong duck hunt every season with his buddies in the country club. Which is why he owned that spanking new Remington twelve-gauge he was pointing at them.

Hodge tried his best to smile. "My name is Hodges Grant," he said, "and we just drove down from Opelousas. My daughter and her two children are holed up in Gentilly, and we're headed that way. Do you know who this gentleman is? Somebody ought to tell his family."

The man squinted down the barrel of the shotgun for an uncomfortably long time, then pulled back the weapon and propped it against his shoulder. His eyes were puffy and there was a look of terror on his face. He'd ridden out the hurricane all night and his half-million-dollar home was full of water, everything he owned in ruin, maybe his wife and kids huddled in the attic. Hodge could envision this man snapping if things didn't go right in the next sixty seconds.

"That's Mr. Schulte," the man said. "He lived there by himself. Poor guy was scheduled to have bypass surgery in a couple of weeks. I didn't know he was still here. His church friends were supposed to come pick him up yesterday."

Hodge stared at the body tethered at the end of the rope. A year ago he could have been this man if he hadn't found the strength to get up out of that recliner and drive himself to the emergency room. The doctors said that sooner or later he would need a new heart valve.

"I heard him calling for help early this morning but I couldn't do anything about it," the man said. He sat down on his pitched roof and rested the shotgun across his lap. "The wind was blowing a hundred miles an hour and all hell was breaking loose. A power line fell in my backyard and sparks were flying everywhere. I thought my house was going to burn down."

He dropped his chin, brought his knees to his chest, and curled into a ball. The posture looked like something they taught you to do in a health safety class to circulate the blood to your brain. Hodge waited for him to speak again. He thought the man might be hurt or exhausted—or possibly both.

"You okay up there?" Hodge asked, finally.

The man raised his weary eyes and gazed down at them. "I don't know," he said. "Thank God my wife and boys are with her sister in Memphis." He looked out at the floodwater that surrounded them in every direction. "It's still rising, you know. This is far from over."

Duval slumped on the front bench of the johnboat, facing Hodge, his head down, buried in the hood. "Time to roll on out of here," he said to his shoes.

Hodge thought about the water inching higher in Dee's house, his grandchildren climbing into the attic. Duval was right for once. "If it's okay with you," he said to the man on the roof, "we're gonna tie Mr. Schulte to that pine tree and be on our way."

The man unfurled his legs and stood up. "I'm not sure I could make myself come down there and do that," he said.

He seemed like a decent man overwhelmed by all this calamity. Hodge said, "Times like this, you be surprised what you'll end up doing before it's all said and done." He handed the rope end to Duval and put the motor in gear. "Don't lose him, son," he said, "and don't let him turn belly up. We don't need to see his face."

Duval gripped the rope with both hands and didn't say a word as they cut a slow wide arc across what had been Mr. Schulte's yard, dragging his body like a thick branch caught in a seine net. Mr. Schulte bobbed facedown, the rope cinched to his calf, while Hodge fastened the other end around the tree trunk using a hitch knot he'd learned in the Marines.

"Mr. Grant!" shouted the man on the roof. "Do y'all have time to join me in prayer?"

Hodge removed his cap. "Certainly," he said.

"He was a nice old man. Every once in awhile he treated my family to dinner at the Piccadilly cafeteria. I'm sorry I wasn't a better neighbor."

Hodge closed his eyes and let the boat drift away from the tree. He could hear the man intoning the Lord's Prayer from the rooftop and he joined in, repeating the words in that familiar, age-old cadence. When he opened his eyes, Duval was studying him, his hands hanging loose between his knees. "We gonna pray, or we gonna play?" he said with a smirk. "We got kids to grab, Pops. Let's book."

"I hope you find your loved ones safe and sound," the man shouted from the roof. "You be careful out there."

Hodge put his cap on and swung the boat toward the wide water channel of the street. "You see a Coast Guard chopper fly over," he shouted back, "flag it down! They'll take you out of here. No telling how high the water's gonna get or when it'll go down. You don't want to stay up there for a week with no food or water."

A half block away, when Hodge turned and gave him a final wave, the man was sitting beside his shotgun on the roof, clutching his knees and staring forlornly across the dark green lagoon of his neighborhood, where an old man with a damaged heart floated like a warning buoy tethered to a tall pine tree.

They hadn't gone much farther when Duval said, "If you gonna kiss the ass of every white man pulls a piece on us, better get used to the taste."

"He was scared," Hodge said. "Shouldn't judge the man. You aren't walking in his shoes."

"You know what he saw, yo. Two niggahs robbing a dead man. Lucky he didn't shoot us in the back."

"Cut the dude some slack, Duval," Hodge said. "He wasn't thinking straight. Two or three feet of water in his house and not done yet. Probably lose everything he owns."

Duval was watching the waterlogged houses go by. He'd never been to this neighborhood before. One fine crib after another. Large, solid brick places next to those old white Southern homes with screened sleeping porches upstairs, all of them soaking in the same shit now. "Insurance companies take good care of these people out here," he said with a dismissive shrug. "Rest of us left sucking lake water."

Soon they'd reached the broad open river of Pontchartrain Boulevard, and the sound of moving water had reached a low roar. Hodge eased up on the throttle to study the torrent of deep turbulent water cutting off their direct route to City Park. The current was flowing down from the canal breach just north of them and the johnboat rocked with more force now in the undertow. The Yacht Club was still burning and its acrid smoke darkened the sky, giving the sodden, wind-gusting afternoon the illusion of a wintry drizzle. They coasted at a leaning stop sign as if waiting for traffic to clear so they could drive ahead. Hodge was trying to gauge the velocity of the river. It was strange to see whitecaps breaking across a city boulevard. All manner of debris hurtled past them—a mattress, granny's rocking chair, Styrofoam ice chests, plastic detergent bottles, long shreds of screen.

"We gotta cross this mess," Hodge announced. "It's too far to go around."

"*Day-um!*" Duval said. "Gonna be like playing *Frogger* for real."

Hodge revved the motor. "You the spotter, son," he said. "Keep your eyes peeled and let me know where the torpedoes are."

He nosed the johnboat out into the stream and picked up speed. A grassy neutral ground as wide as a football field, the divider between traffic lanes, lay beneath them like a hidden reef. On the open water, the wet wind blew in their faces at thirty miles an hour and Hodge could feel the old Merc struggling. Duval hunched into his dark blue hoodie and Hodge forced the cap down tighter on his stubbled head. They hadn't traveled more than twenty yards when something struck the port side of the boat with a jarring thud.

"Goddammit, Duval, you supposed to be watching for that shit!"

"Dead up, man. I didn't see it coming!" He searched one side of the boat then scooted over to search the other.

"What the hell was it?" Hodge asked.

"Fuckin' *Jaws*, you ax me."

"Stay alert, goddammit. We don't need a hole in this boat!"

Duval began to point out everything he could see, even the small harmless things like a child's doll and the spread pages of a newspaper and a bushel of floating lettuce. Hodge had just swerved around a screen door when Duval yelled "*Incoming!*" Hodge glanced portside and picked up the projectile movement of a round porch beam plunging toward the johnboat's plywood hull like a deadly lance. The beam was long and white and lathed with a frilly elegance, a piece of wooden lacework still attached at the end. It had probably ripped free from some old white lady's wraparound gallery.

"Brace yourself!" Hodge warned, trying to tail away from the beam. It hit the side near his bench and wood cracked like a dry branch. The boat shuddered violently. Both men grabbed the gunnels to keep from pitching overboard.

"You okay, son?" Hodge said, grasping the stick throttle to regain control.

Duval had tumbled on top of the duffel bag stowed between benches. He looked scared. "Everything cool," he said, pulling himself onto the seat.

Hodge leaned over the side of the boat to examine where the beam had struck. There was a serious fracture in the plywood but no daylight. A little harder and they'd be taking in water right now.

"What the . . . ?" Duval said, raising a trembling finger to point north. "What the . . . fuck . . . now?"

Fifty yards away, an automobile was bucking in the current like a giant silver dolphin, rising and dipping and rising again. It was headed on a collision course directly toward their boat.

Duval was hyperventilating. "Get out the . . ."

Hodge couldn't believe that two ton hunk of metal was still afloat. Honda Accord, damned good car. But he didn't want to get run over by one. "Hang onto your nut sack," he said, turning the boat to face the bucking beast. "Ride might get a little bumpy."

This was the way you did it, same way you dealt with a train coming at you down the track. Face it square on and sidestep. Try and outrun it with your back turned and it would cut you down.

Hodge revved the motor and edged forward, planning to dodge to the left but prepared for anything. The Honda dipped and splashed and pounded toward them like a Higgins Boat in the surf off Normandy, and as it drew closer he saw that someone was in the car, a young white woman banging her fists against the windshield and screaming frantically as she was tossed from side to side.

# 6

Eight thousand inmates were incarcerated in the tall gray monoliths of the Orleans Parish Prison, a county jail complex in the shadow of Interstate 10 near Mid-City. By noon on Monday, the flood had reached the rec yard, and by early afternoon there were two feet of brown lake water in the Templeman III unit—T3—where Lucien "PJ" Grant was locked in a holding cell with three other inmates he didn't care to know. The power had been dead for hours, the heat stifling, the air rank from floating islands of raw sewage. No one had been given drinking water or food since the guards had fed them bologna sandwiches on Sunday night, tossing them between the bars the way you feed baboons in a zoo. And now the guards and prison personnel had all disappeared, abandoning their posts and hiding out on the rooftops of the OPP buildings as the water surged higher inside the facilities.

When it became clear that no one could stop the flooding on the bottom floor of T3, inmates trapped in their cells began to panic and kick the bars. Somewhere down the cellblock an old drunk was pleading like a backwoods preacher. "We have sinned in this den of iniquity and Gawd has troubled the waters!" he intoned. "Gawd has troubled the waters! We throw ourselves at your mercy, O Lawd, sinners though we are."

Someone yelled, "Shut that crazy motherfucker up!"

"Set us free, O Lawd, 'fore we all drownded in this turrible place! Please, Gawd, open up these gates!"

"Somebody shut . . . that . . . motherfucker . . . up!"

PJ Grant sat on the top bunk and stared at his cellmates lounging on the top bunk opposite him in the cramped quarters. The younger one was a crackhead from the Lower Ninth Ward, popped for possession with intent to distribute, and the other dude was a badass head buster called U-Rite with a spider web tattoo covering one side of his neck, Chinese tats on his arms, and gold slugs for teeth. PJ knew U-Rite's reputation on the street. Word was he'd pulled the trigger on the late great rapper Soulja Slim. Everybody feared U-Rite. This stretch he'd been booked for shooting at a club owner in Tremé over a woman, and he'd taken out his anger on the poor young Tulane student cowering on the bottom bunk. He was a white boy with a Yankee accent from New Jersey or somewhere like that, picked up Saturday night for pissing against a wall in the French Quarter. U-Rite had slapped the boy around a couple of times for looking at him the wrong way.

And now the banger was sitting back on his bunk and sizing up PJ with a wicked gold-flashing smile, his thick legs hanging off the side in a pair of bright orange prison issue. They'd been in this cell together for a week and the tension between them was reaching a flashpoint. "What we gone do 'bout this situation, dawg?" he asked PJ. It wasn't clear if he meant the flooding or the showdown that had become personal, one too many alpha males in the same cage.

The old drunk kept hollering *Lawd, do somethin' 'fore we all drownded* and voices were echoing back and forth through the cell-block, mass hysteria brewing like the stench from the backed-up toilets. PJ had finally had enough. He dropped down off his bunk with a loud splash and gripped the bars of the cell. "Say, bruh!" he yelled to the inmates sitting on tables out in the commons area. "The man's right. We all gonna get drownded up in here if y'all don't help us out."

The men marooned on tables were from lockdown in St. Bernard Parish, the swampland and fishing villages south of New Orleans. They'd been deposited here yesterday by St. Bernard deputies for safekeeping from the hurricane, which they knew would deluge their parish first and far worse. Because the OPP cells were filled to capacity, the 350 St. Bernard convicts had been issued blankets and told to make do on the floor of the walkout area.

"Yo, somebody bring them benches over here and start banging on these bars," PJ instructed them. "Find something you can swing and come swing it! Fucking COs have all run off. Ain't nobody else can help us now."

PJ was a tall, muscular young man, thirty-two years old, with a commanding voice and enough tats on his chest and ripped biceps to give him serious street cred. This wasn't his first vacation in the Orleans House of D. He'd been here twice before, and the last conviction had sent him up north of Baton Rouge for a two-year stretch in the Dixon Correctional Institute. He didn't know what would be worse, drowning in this fucking cell or facing a parole violation and a bracelet trip to LSP Angola, where nobody came out alive.

"You go, home slice," said U-Rite with a cynical laugh. "Put these nappy-headed country boys to work."

The first men to slide off a table and pull a metal bench out of the water were two brothers from the town of Reggio, booked for DWI and resisting arrest last Friday night. Working like a SWAT team with a battering ram, they hammered PJ's cell door a dozen times before changing strategy and focusing on the key box.

"Bring it!" PJ whooped after every blow. "Come with your A game, niggah. Whup that bad boy!"

"Man, this could take all day," said one of the brothers, huffing from the workout.

"Yo, money, it's not like you going clubbing anytime soon," PJ said with his heavy laugh. The brothers laughed and made another lunge at the key box.

Others had crawled off their tabletops and were picking up submerged benches, slogging through the water to ram cell doors. The banging noises echoed like pistol shots in the ripe air. A middle-aged white man wearing a ponytail appeared out of nowhere with a steel shower rod and started prying at the door to PJ's cell.

"Where'd you come from, m'man?" he asked the white dude, whose tanned face was scabbed and swollen from a recent fistfight.

"Echuca, Australia, mate," the man said, his rugged features contorting as he pried at the bars.

It wasn't what PJ was asking, but it was worth a smile. "You talk like that cat Crocodile Dundee," he said. "Fact, you kinda resemble him, too."

The man stopped grunting and stared at PJ. "We gonna bust you out of here," he said, "or we gonna kiss and hold hands?"

PJ liked his attitude. "Slip that thing right through here," he said, clenching the end of the shower rod, "and let's gang bang this bitch."

The work went on for half an hour, the Reggio brothers smashing the key box, then stepping back to let PJ and the Australian pry at the lock hinge. The water was nearly up to their waists by then, and the chatter was loud and desperate as the men tried to break open cell doors with whatever tools they could fashion from tables and benches and plumbing fixtures from the shower room.

And then it happened. The Reggio brothers finally shattered the box, and metal springs and rusted parts scattered into the water. Using the shower rod as a fulcrum, PJ and the Aussie managed to force the door open about fifteen inches. A tight passage, but PJ wasted no time squeezing through it. When he was free of the cell he raised his arms in triumph and began to hoot and give his three accomplices the high five, hugging the bony Australian and lifting him high in the air.

"'Bout time you geniuses put the hurt on that thing," said U-Rite, hopping from his high perch into the floating shit. "Another hour and we all be gator bait."

He turned around to look at his cellmates. The crackhead had passed out on the top bunk and the Tulane boy was standing in deep yellow water next to the other bunks. He was a slender young man, nineteen or twenty, with a two-day stubble and short dark hair, mussed and greasy. "You come with me, Tinker Bell," U-Rite said to him. "We in here much longer, I might need some punk to suck my dick."

The Tulane boy turned his head away and PJ could see he was too humiliated to speak. U-Rite waded back toward him. "I'm talking to you, bitch," he said, seizing the boy by the arm. When he tried to fling away U-Rite's hand, the banger grabbed him by the neck and dunked his head under the yellow diarrhea water.

"Hey, hey!" the Australian shouted at him. "Leave that poor bloke alone!"

U-Rite laughed and pulled the boy's head up out of the water like a preacher at a river baptism. "'Sup wichew, Crocodile?" he asked with fake innocence. "You want some of this nice white cake for your own self?"

The Tulane boy was gagging and spitting water and fighting for air. U-Rite shoved him away and waded toward the bars. He was staring at the Australian with narrowed eyes, his gold slugs shining. "Maybe you the one ought to suck my dick, you old faggot," he said.

The Australian was a small wiry man and older by fifteen years, but he didn't back down. "Where I come from," he said, "that makes you a faggot too, butch."

PJ didn't want this tough little scrapper to end up with his throat slit, so he nudged him away with his forearm and said, "Yo, bruh, back off from this. It ain't your play. Let it slide and walk away."

U-Rite struggled to squeeze his thick body through the opening in the cell door. He was shorter and heavier than PJ, with a barrel chest he was having trouble wedging through the tight space. PJ thought about leaving him trapped there to drown. He waded over to the sliding door and pushed on a bar, pinning U-Rite against the metal frame. "You need some help there, slim?" he asked with a grin. Then he pulled back on the bar with all his strength and it gave another two inches, enough to set U-Rite free.

"Ha ha, standup comic," he said to PJ as they stood facing each other in waist-deep water. "You think you fucking Chris Rock or somebody?"

"Just messing wicha, man. It's all good," PJ said. He extended a fist and U-Rite hesitated, then pounded him, knuckle to knuckle.

"We out of one box and into another. Now what?" U-Rite said, gazing around the commons area at the inmates shouting at each other and slamming benches into cell doors. He seemed to be looking for someone, maybe the Australian. "You got a standup comedy plan for getting us out of this fucking flood?"

They heard the shatter of glass and both turned toward the security doors at the end of the cellblock. Three inmates had used a bench to break through a plate-glass window in the door. "There's our ride," PJ said, swinging his arms and hips as he tried to run through high water.

Inmates in the commons area were rushing toward the broken window. When PJ got there, with U-Rite and the Reggio brothers and a hundred others breathing down his back, he could see more inmates scurrying through the hallway beyond the door. There had been a jailbreak on the second floor of T3 and men in orange jumpsuits were roaming freely through the building, looking for a way out. PJ could smell something burning. Dark smoke trailed through the corridor. He wondered if some fool had set a fire and they were all going to burn to death.

He was the first to straddle through the shattered window. When he stepped down into shallow water on the other side of the door, it felt like a child's wading pool after what he'd been standing in. Prisoners had broken into an office and were ransacking the place, scattering manila folders and paperwork in a hail of pages. They were searching through drawers and filing cabinets for food and meds and drinking water and possible weapons. What caught PJ's eye was the outside window above a copy machine, where weak gray light shone through from the storm world beyond. He dragged the machine aside, found a straight-backed wooden chair, and swung it at the glass. The window broke easily, but security wire mesh covered the outside frame. PJ had to stand on the chair and kick and kick at the sturdy mesh until it began to give way. He could see the floodwater high against the chain-link fence out in the yard, maybe four or five feet deep, and he realized that busting out of this building would be the easy part.

"It's bad out there," he said to the cluster of men waiting anxiously behind him. "More fucking water."

And then he saw a motorboat patrolling the flooded yard, then another one. Orleans sheriff's deputies in their starched cream-colored shirts were watching the pandemonium behind dark sunglasses, their shotguns held aloft for inmates to take notice and fear.

"The hacks are waiting for us out there in boats," PJ said.

One of the Reggio brothers pushed closer to peer out the window. "Cocksuckers," he said. "Where they been when we needed they sorry asses?"

"Motherfuckers hoping we all get drownded inside this shithole and all they got to do is kick dirt over us," U-Rite said, joining them at the window. "Anybody make it out alive, they round 'em up for attempting to flight."

PJ stared across the dark wavering pond of the prison yard. It was maybe thirty yards from here to the sixteen-foot fence topped with coils of razor wire. More boats were trolling through the yard now, armed deputies observing silently as windows were smashed on the floors above and inmates leaned out to beg for rescue. He knew these bastards weren't going to lift a finger to rescue anybody. If you made it out, you lived. Sink or swim.

"How many boats they got?" he asked the men standing on either side of him. "They cain't take us all down."

He stood up on the chair again and kicked at the mesh with a furious rhythm until he'd kicked a hole that opened wider with each new thrust of his boot.

"My *man!*" U-Rite said with an explosive laugh.

PJ stood down and stepped aside to catch his breath. The Reggio brothers were the first ones through the mesh. They were tall and razor thin, with arms as taut as ropes, and they showed no hesitation in leaping into a world of water. They waded farther out into the yard and a sheriff's boat sped toward them, one of the deputies barking from a bullhorn: "*Stop where you are! Put your hands on your head and prepare to come aboard.*"

Two other deputies, a black man and black woman, trained their shotguns on them. The Reggio brothers stopped wading and raised their hands.

The yard was filling with inmates who had escaped through windows in T3 and were making their way voluntarily to the rescue boats. PJ moved away from the window as prisoners scuffled with one another, pushing and shoving for the chance to climb through the mesh.

*"For your own personal safety,"* the bullhorn announced, *"we will begin transporting you out of this unit to the overpass bridge. I repeat, we will be transporting you to the Broad Street bridge."*

PJ noticed U-Rite sitting on a fax machine, watching the parade of inmates with a bemused smile on his hard banger face. "How come you not taking your turn, dawg?" he asked PJ with a nod to the window. "Something else on your mind?"

PJ was thinking about hard time, maybe thirty years in the Angola pen. He looked out the window again at the sixteen-foot fence and tried to calculate how he could get over that razor wire. "Same thing on your mind," he said to U-Rite.

New Orleans police had pulled PJ over after his boy D'Wayne was shot dead by some moonlighting cop taking a smoke break in the storeroom of the liquor store they were trying to rob in the Lower Nine. PJ jumped out of the car and tried to help his running buddy, who was lying facedown in a pool of blood spurting out of the hole in his neck. The moonlighting cop was a speed-snorting crazy bastard and he waved his gun at PJ and then started shooting, and PJ was lucky to get back to the car alive. He was no more than three blocks away when the screaming police cruisers rolled up on him from every direction, like they were just waiting for him to fuck up again. After they threw him across the hood, they found three stolen guns and a bag of weed in the trunk of D'Wayne's beat-to-shit Cutlass.

U-Rite folded his tattooed arms and watched more inmates crowd into the office. "Lot of commotion. Niggahs running wild," he said. The cons were cutting in front of each other and scrapping like schoolyard bullies, fighting for the front of the line. "Boo-coos of bruthuhs in this wet-ass hotel. They gonna count every head out on that bridge?" He shrugged. "Might not miss two or three till Christmas."

PJ glanced out the window at the razor wire. "We need some blankets," he said.

He elbowed his way back through the growing mob and into the dark corridor, where men wandered about in a daze through the drifting smoke, a smell like charred mattress. Someone had finally managed to bust open that door to T3's bottom floor, and he stopped on the landing to measure the scene. All the cells had emptied out and only a dozen or so—the crackheads and lunatics and damaged fuckups who belonged in the infirmary—were still roaming around in the oil slick of human shit that covered every surface. The Australian was wading toward him with his arm around the taller Tulane boy, and PJ couldn't tell if he was protecting the young man or holding on for dear life.

"Yo, Crocodile!" PJ called out to him. "Go in that cell there and bring me all four blankets."

The two men followed his instructions without question or complaint. They were able to slip through the narrow gap into an empty cell, and within moments they were carrying out the blankets lofted above their heads.

"You plan on getting some extra sleep, mate?" the Australian asked with a tail of cloth hanging across his face.

PJ hustled the blankets into the office where U-Rite was waiting next to the fax machine. The space was jammed shoulder to shoulder with more inmates lining up to exit through the window, but PJ bumped them all aside with the bundle in his arms. "Scuse me, coming through!" he said. "*Coming through!*"

He shoved the blankets against U-Rite's chest and said, "You down, balluh? Time to bust a move."

When he crawled through the window and dropped his legs into warm floodwater, the blankets packed against his chest, PJ found himself surrounded by hundreds of desperate ward boys afraid of the water, grabbing and splashing and scrambling for the rescue boats. *Git your hands off me, niggah! I ain't your milk tit.* Scuffles were breaking out and the deputies had their hands full trying to supervise the terrified prisoners clamoring aboard their boats.

Wading toward the fence, PJ gazed back at the upper floors of T3 and noticed the crazy fuckers waving flaming bed sheets and holding a sign that said HELP US, as if somebody out on submerged I-10 could rush to their rescue. He saw that U-Rite was only a few yards behind him, slogging along with blankets in his arms, and he kept angling toward the fence like a river otter, smoothly negotiating the deeper currents. In his mind he could already picture how this would go down. He could feel it in his blood, like he sometimes felt before things happened. It was his destiny today. He was going over the wall, and in all this panic and confusion, nobody would notice.

When he reached the fence, he tossed a blanket over each shoulder and glanced around to make sure the deputies were preoccupied. He began climbing, his long fingers slipping into those galvanized steel diamonds as he scaled upward one full arm-stretch after another. He tried to find traction with the toes of his wet boots, but they were a clumsy hindrance and he wished he'd kicked them off and gone at this with bare feet. His arms were everything now. Straining, burning, they pulled his 230 pounds up the fence, the blankets draped over his shoulders like limp wet flags.

"Go, go, go." U-Rite was urging him on in a low voice just below him. "I'm all up under your ass."

PJ made it to the top without a single order shouted at him. He threw one doubled blanket, then the other, over a loop of razor wire. A hand shook his ankle and he looked down to find U-Rite heaving another blanket up to him. Once he'd secured all four blankets over the deadly sharp bands of stainless steel, he pressed his weight against the padding to see if the blades would tear through. "Solid," he said.

When he glanced down again, a knot of inmates was staring up at him from the water below, maybe a dozen in all. The Australian was quickly mounting the chain link with short, monkey-like arms.

"We gotta fly," PJ said to U-Rite, "before they bring the heat."

"Then move over, rover, and let U-Rite po'vault this motherfucker."

U-Rite climbed up to where PJ was clinging to the fence and threw a leg across the stacked blankets, straddling the flattened razor wire for an instant before slinging his other leg over and cannonballing sixteen feet into the floodwater outside the prison fence. The loud splash drew attention from half the men in the yard. Inmates began to cheer when they saw U-Rite surface without a broken neck, soaked from head to foot, wiping water out of his face. Free now, he turned and started wading toward the tall concrete pillars of the Broad Street bridge.

"*Man outside!*" a deputy hollered.

Civilians were out there, too, a long straggling trail of people left homeless by the flooding, all of them trudging through the brown water with their possessions piled on a door, a wedge of packing material, anything that would float. Silent and defeated, they were heading south toward the hospitals and the Superdome. PJ watched U-Rite blend into their grim march, seeking the cover of numbers. Who would dare fire a weapon into a crowd of innocent citizens?

"*Come down immediately,*" a deputy yelled through a bullhorn, "*or we'll shoot!*"

PJ turned and saw a deputy down on one knee in his boat, aiming a shotgun at him.

"He's bluffing, mate. They're not gonna shoot anybody," the Australian said, climbing past PJ to the pad of blankets. The Tulane boy was right underneath him.

The shotgun boomed, its charge ricocheting off the razor wire a few feet from the Aussie's head. "Fuck me, wrong again," he said, rolling agilely across the blankets and dropping deadweight into the water on the other side of the fence.

The Tulane boy was struggling to make it to the top. "Come on up out of this hell hole, college boy," PJ said, reaching down to grip the young man's thin wrist, "before one of these devils eats you alive."

The second round hit PJ Grant square in the chest. The impact knocked him backward and he fell across the draped blankets, his shaky hands groping to find blood on his jumpsuit, a hole through his spurting heart. The Tulane boy was saying something to him in a loud voice, grabbing his legs, but the pain was so intense he blacked out before plunging headlong into the deep.

# 7

Hodge saw a motorboat approaching the bucking Honda from the far side of the flooded boulevard. A white man was standing at the wheel behind a Plexiglas windshield and he pointed at the car, circling his hand over his head in a lasso motion.

"He think we cowboys?" Duval said. "Gonna rope that thing?"

As the car loomed nearer, Hodge focused on the young woman trapped inside. They made eye contact and she beat even harder against the glass. He knew the Honda could go under at any moment. He steadied his hand on the throttle, and as the car hurled past them, he opened up the gas and turned the johnboat, pulling alongside the passenger door, keeping pace with the car's rocking momentum.

He heard the other boat, a newer Evinrude motor, roaring nearby and looked back to see where it was. The boatman had closed the distance quickly and joined the chase, catching up on the driver's side of the vehicle. The two boats were locked on like protective escorts in a rain-splashed motorcade. Hodge had no idea what the other guy intended to do. He was driving solo and couldn't render much help unless the girl managed to roll down a window and crawl aboard his rig. But she was too distressed to understand that. She kept battering the passenger window with her fists and begging Hodge to save her.

"Can you kick in her window?" he shouted at Duval.

"Say what?"

"Kick in her window!"

Duval turned to look at him, his head buried in the hood. "Fuck that, man!" he shouted back. He couldn't figure dying over a white woman. "Get this boat on away from here before it take us under!"

Hodge edged the johnboat closer to the car. He stood up halfway, in a crookbacked old man's crouch, and could see murky water bubbling up on the Honda's floorboards. When the water got higher, maybe only as high as her lap, the car would deep-six and the young woman would be lost. He gave her the hand-crank signal to roll down her window. If she could do that without taking in water, Hodge would kiss the boat against the car and they'd pull her out. But the trapped woman shook her head, frantically thumbing the switch to show him that the window wouldn't open. The electrical system was dead.

"She's stuck in there!" he shouted to Duval. "Kick the damn glass and drag her into the boat."

Duval stared at the young woman pounding on the window, her long brown hair flying across her face, tears streaming down her cheeks. There was a thick streak of blood on the glass. She'd cut herself, maybe with her own nails. He didn't want to hang his ass out on the line for this bawling chick. She might fight him, rake those nails across his face like drowning people did when you tried to save them.

"Come on, son!" Hodge yelled at him. "Kick in her fucking window!"

The johnboat was bouncing along at the mercy of the choppy current and Duval rose slowly, cautiously, his arms extended to keep his balance. The plywood hull was vibrating underneath them, the screws and ancient dried glue straining to hold this old bucket in one piece. When he finally managed to stand up straight and set his feet, he tried to kick the car window. The vehicle rocked away from them and his kick fell short. He lost his balance, lurched forward, and grabbed the gunnel, saving himself from somersaulting into the narrow space between the car and boat. In that brief instant he pictured his skull being crushed as the two monster forces slammed against each other in the raging flood.

It wasn't the woman. It was the water. A fear he didn't dare show the old man, who already thought he was a coward. "You want this white girl so bad," he said, turning toward Hodge, "come get her yourself."

Hodge felt like pitching Duval's sorry ass overboard. His blood pressure was rising and he'd broken into a hot sweat. But he couldn't risk losing his temper and blowing out that weak heart valve. "Take the throttle, son!" he yelled. "Just keep us steady and close."

When Duval crawled back and grabbed the stick, Hodge brushed past him and squatted at the center of the long vessel, waiting for him to maneuver the boat within striking distance of the car. He knew that Duval had no experience at piloting a boat, but he prayed that the boy would keep his cool and not wreck them against the Honda. Lord God, he wished his son PJ was here to deal with this. PJ would have already pulled that girl out.

"*Closer!*" Hodge shouted, waving his arm.

The young woman appeared exhausted now and had given up her struggle. She was slumped back against the steering wheel, breathing hard and staring forlornly at Hodge. A paper cup floated in the pool of water below the dashboard. The car was sinking lower and Hodge knew there was little time to waste. He looked over at the white Dorado ski boat and saw the driver signaling to him and punching the air, entreating Hodge to break in.

"*A little more!*" he shouted at Duval.

As the boat swerved closer, Hodge stood up and pivoted sideways, sending a swift karate kick at the window, his heavy work boot cracking glass. But the collision propelled him backward, swaying the boat, and he tumbled onto the duffel bag, banging his head against the gunnel.

"You ah-ight, man?" Duval called to him.

Hodge pulled himself up slowly, his thoughts hazy and unfocused, and watched the young woman pound on the cracked window with renewed energy. The water was in her lap.

"*One more time!*" Hodge yelled. "*Bring us in tight.*"

When the boat drew dangerously close, within a few short feet,

Hodge motioned for her to move back and delivered another side-kick, this time shattering glass all over her. For a moment his leg was lodged inside the car and he felt a burning pain above his ankle and thought he might have sliced open a vein. He grabbed onto the slippery wet roof of the Honda to free himself and suddenly realized that the johnboat had separated on impact, bouncing away, leaving him stranded on top of the car. Spread-eagle and facedown, desperately trying to hold on, he raised his head to search for Duval and found him thirty feet away with his hood fallen back and an expression of horror on his face. He was fighting the guide stick, struggling to steady the boat.

The young woman was chattering hysterically at Hodge as she attempted to climb through the broken window. "*Where are you?*" she cried. "*Where are you?*"

He watched her long white arms emerge like bloody vines, reaching up onto the roof and searching for him. But water was gurgling into the window now, an eerie, drain-sucking noise, and the car was capsizing quickly. Just before the roof disappeared underneath him, Hodge heard the woman's frantic choking sounds. The waves were too strong and washed her back inside. She couldn't escape the car.

With one hand clinging to the doorframe of the sinking automobile, Hodge used his other to release the clips on his lifejacket and slipped free. He gripped the top of the passenger door and rode the car underwater in a storm of air bubbles, fighting to hold on against the upward pressure. Below the surface, the floodwater was too murky to see anything, so he kicked his legs and squirmed through the narrow jagged window opening by touch, groping for a limb, a snatch of clothing, any trace of the young woman. Halfway inside the car, he felt her long willowing hair and grabbed a handful, pulling her back toward the window. She clutched his arm like a tarpon fighting a twenty-pound test line and he worked hard to haul her out, knowing she'd panicked and couldn't hold her breath much longer. There was a time when he could stay underwater for nearly five minutes, back when he was a young jarhead patrolling the Mekong Delta, but those days were long behind him.

The car's roof was only three or four feet under the surface and he popped quickly into blessed air, choking and spewing rank water. His lungs were on fire as if he'd swallowed gasoline. He caught the young woman under her arms from behind and locked her narrow waist between his thighs and crotch, resting her body against his own as he labored to float on his back. She was limp now, unconscious. He suspected she had drowned.

He heard the boat's motor roaring closer and thought it must be Duval coming to fetch him and this girl. But it was the white man in his white Dorado and he cut the throttle and drifted alongside them. With Hodge's help, pushing from underneath, the man dragged her dead weight up and over the gunnel into his boat.

Hodge found a ladder aft, near the engine, and pulled himself out of the choppy current, his entire body shaking and weak. The woman was lying facedown on deck and the boatman knelt beside her, pressing her upper back with both hands. After several firm thrusts, she began to cough and gag and spit up water as dark as camp coffee. She was alive.

"Thatagirl, keep it up," the boatman said as he forced more water out of her lungs. "You're gonna be all right."

He was no more than thirty years old, a stubby fellow with small stubby hands and a round unshaven face and stringy, rust-colored hair showing bald patches of scalp. He wore a CVS Pharmacy uniform shirt. His clothes were dry but smelled as if they'd been slept in for a week.

"Man, that was a righteous thing you just did," he said, smiling with admiration at Hodge. "You okay?"

Hodge was trembling and cold, and his heart wouldn't slow down. He felt lightheaded, his left arm tingling, going numb. He needed his nitro tablets, but they were in his travel kit in the duffel bag. Where the hell was Duval? He searched all around for signs of the boat.

The young woman pulled herself onto her knees and tried to sit up, but she continued to gag and heave up water and whatever was in her stomach. She was wearing jeans and a flowery red blouse that clung to her slender ribcage. Somehow she'd lost her shoes. Hodge knelt down and rubbed her cold feet. "Better get her to a hospital," he said to the driver. "Make sure she checks out all right."

"Keep an eye on her," the man said, rising. "I'm gonna grab the wheel before we float on down to the interstate."

Hodge noticed that her hands were bleeding. He felt something sticky and warm running into his boot and knew he was bleeding as well. His ankle stung where he'd cut it on the window glass

"I borrowed this bad boy from my neighbor. He took off for Texas on Saturday and don't know it's borrowed yet," the man said, handling the wheel with a rogue's smile. "I was on my way to check on my momma's house up by Robert E. Lee Boulevard and saw this gal in the Honda. I followed her for five or six blocks. Didn't know how I'd get her out of there until you came along. Dude," he said, staring off across flooded Lakeview, "ain't this some serious shit?"

"You got that right," Hodge said, glancing up to see the johnboat motoring toward them.

"Here comes your son," the man said. "He had a rough ride after you jumped."

"Not my son," Hodge said.

"Way that old tub was rocking, I thought he might go under himself."

The young woman had stopped choking and was breathing freely now. She sat curled against the hull, her knees squeezed against her chest. Long snarled hair had fallen across her face and she was staring without focus at something on the deck.

"She might be in shock," Hodge said. He wasn't feeling right himself. The numbness in his arm was beginning to concern him. He needed to take a nitro tablet before the angina got worse.

"I'm not in shock," the young woman said in a small, distant voice. She spoke with her forehead touching her knees. "I'm cold and totally freaked out, but I'm not in shock." She lifted her head and peered over at Hodge through a mess of hair. "Thank you for saving my life," she said. "What's your name, sir? I won't ever forget what you did for me."

Hodge told her his name and that he had a daughter about her age who was holed up in an attic in Gentilly with her two children.

"Do you have anyplace to go?" he asked her.

"My parents live uptown," she said. "They didn't evacuate. I was on my way there, but I waited too late to leave my apartment. I don't know where all this water is coming from. It didn't rain that hard. The radio says the levees are falling apart."

Duval brought the johnboat in closer but kept his distance in the bobbing current. His hood was thrown back and his baby dreads were wet from the mist and splashing waves and his eyes were wide with fear.

"Stay where you are!" the driver yelled, signaling for Duval to hold steady. "We'll come to you!"

The driver guided the Dorado up next to the johnboat, cut back on the throttle, and tried to steady her, but the two vessels banged against each other in the rough swells. Duval grew more alarmed and looked as if he might turn the boat and flee.

"Y'all better head someplace safe," Hodge said. "I was you, I'd point this rig downtown, where there's bound to be some medical help. You need to get these cuts looked at, miss," he said, examining the torn skin around her nails and the ragged gash across one palm.

He called out for Duval to throw him his duffel bag. The boy let go of the stick throttle and stumbled to the middle of the boat. When he tossed the bag, it almost dropped short into the water.

Hodge rummaged through his stuff, found the travel kit, and fumbled with the cap on a bottle, his hands shaking. He slipped a nitroglycerin tablet under his tongue and waited for the tightness to ease in his chest. It didn't take long, less than a minute. He closed his eyes and inhaled a deep breath, then let it out slowly.

"Here," he said to the young woman. "Let's fix up your hands."

This was how he was trained. You helped the wounded when they went down. You didn't leave anything to chance. He pulled a small bottle from the first aid kit and poured hydrogen peroxide over her open cuts. She winced but tried to show courage. He used a clean T-shirt from his bag to daub her hands dry and applied an antibiotic cream, then Band-Aids. "Soon as you can," he told her, "find yourself a nurse to look this over. It's some dirty water we're dealing with and you don't want to get infected."

The young woman threw her arms around his neck, hugging him. "If you need a place to rest, Mr. Grant, you're welcome anytime at my parents' house on St. Charles," she said, suddenly overcome with tears.

This girl was from one of those families that lived in a magnificent oak-shaded mansion on St. Charles Avenue, where the streetcars ran.

"Bring your daughter and her children," she said. "There's room enough for everybody."

Hodge thanked her and shook hands with the driver. He stood up with his duffel bag and studied the distance to the johnboat as the two crafts danced with each other, smacking together and parting in the windblown waters.

"Get me in a little closer!" Hodge shouted to the driver. "I'm too old to jump that far. And I don't want to drink any more of this Katrina Kool-Aid."

# 8

Tempo scratched at the door to Tante Belle's house, whimpering for her owner, but Dee yanked the leash, pulling the collie away from the steps and into deep water. Resigned to her fate, the dog swam alongside Dee as she thrashed across the flooded yard on the kickboard. "Stay close, girl," she said, searching for that fat cottonmouth lurking out here somewhere, thinking maybe a huge nest of them had washed in from the lake. Unlike Dee's noisy crossing, Tempo's beautiful butterscotch nose skimmed the murky water like the graceful prow of a schooner, a gentle wedge parting the current, and they soon reached the sunken porch of Dee's bungalow, the collie obedient and submissive at the end of the leash.

The flood was rising faster now and everything was afloat near the porch railing and drifting out toward open water—the wicker chair, the plastic flowerpots, the stiff garden gloves she'd forgotten to put away. "Come on inside, girlfriend, and make yourself at home," she said, tossing the kickboard aside and lifting the small wet collie into her arms. Tempo smelled funky, in need of a bath. When was the last time dear old Tante Belle had bathed this delicate creature?

Glancing back for one final survey of the flooded neighborhood, Dee noticed someone sitting on the roof of that trashy rent house a few doors down. It was the only place on the quiet block where people came and went at all hours, a parade of pimped rides, their speakers booming bass and *booty booty up in it skeet skeet skeet,* young gangstas sliding by to smoke pipe with *they boys* in the crib. Dee considered waving to the young man, a dark brooding figure hunched over and hugging his knees, somebody who could help her move three hundred-pound Tante Belle up into the attic. But Tempo saw the man too and issued a low disapproving growl. The dog's warning drew Dee back inside herself, sobered her thoughts. In this stormy chaos, when the neighborhood was deserted and all the rules had broken down, maybe it wasn't such a good idea to be alone with some baggy pants hip-hop porch boy she didn't know.

The children hollered and cheered when they saw Tempo in their mother's arms. They were sitting docilely on the kitchen table, huddled under their blankets, the invading water nearly level with the tabletop. "Tempo, *Tem*-po!" Ashley cried, reaching out to caress the friendly collie. Tempo squealed and licked her face.

"Where's Tante Belle, Momma?" LaMarcus asked as he rubbed the dog's wet belly.

"Safe in her house. She's got plenty of food and an attic just like ours," Dee said, a mother's lie to ward off the painful truth. "So let's get our stuff together and climb on up there. Y'all stay here with Tempo while I grab my bag."

She handed the squirming collie to the children and waded down the hallway and into her bedroom. Floodwater had submersed the bed and crept up the wall, turning the room she loved into a smelly cesspool. She stared at the drifting pillows and shoes, and at the skirts of her few good dresses spreading like swamp ferns in the opened closet, and began to choke up. Would any of this be salvageable? Could you ever wash out all the stink and grime?

She waded over to her bureau. The three lower drawers were already underwater. How high would the water climb? Would it eventually overtake the perfumes and lotions and tray of earrings on her dresser? What should she do with that ornate old hand mirror passed down from her mother and grandmother? She lifted it from the dresser and examined her face. She couldn't let the children see her this way. Her eyes were puffy and all her worries were sketched in the lines around her mouth. She would have to do a better job of hiding her fear.

Wiping tears from her cheeks, she took her gym bag down from the closet shelf and filled it with underwear, socks, and shorts. There was no point in packing anything but light wear. It was the end of August and damned hot in the house without the AC working and it would get even hotter in the attic, maybe rising to a hundred degrees or more when those gray storm clouds cleared the city and the sun burned down again.

Underneath her folded T-shirts she found the old Smith & Wesson snub-nosed .38 her father had bought in an Opelousas pawnshop and had given to her years ago, when she was a freshman at Dillard. *It's New Orleans, Dee,* he'd told her at the time. *You cain't tell when this thing might come in handy.* She had never fired the gun and really didn't want it in the house, but she didn't have the nerve to give it back to him or get rid of it. She dropped the revolver and its small box of bullets into the gym bag and zipped it tight.

"Okay, kids, let's roll," she said, slogging back into the kitchen. "LaMarcus, go get your baseball bat. Ashley, hang onto Tempo until I pull down the ladder to the attic. Everybody got their assignment?"

Always the teacher's helper. Always trying to organize.

LaMarcus reluctantly crawled out from the refuge of his blanket and slipped into the water. "Uh-huh-huh," he said with a shiver, "this is some seriously nasty stuff, Momma. Did you know that the Mississippi River is two thousand three hundred and forty miles long and begins in Minnesota? This feels mostly like Minnesota to me."

"Bust a move, son," she said. "We've run out of time."

She turned on the tap to fill a pitcher with water, but the water smelled strange and quickly ran brown. "So much for drinking water," she said to Ashley, who was holding Tempo and watching from the table.

"Tempo drinks toilet water," Ashley said matter-of-factly.

"Not for awhile she won't," Dee said. "It'll make her real sick."

She trudged down the hallway again and into the living room, where the water stirred in a slow circular motion, rising above the button panel on the old JVC television set. Her stack of favorite CDs had toppled over and disappeared. LaMarcus's video game strategy guides were floating alongside *Essence* and *Ebony,* that issue with

Toni Braxton wearing a hot skimpy bikini on the cover. Dee waded to the broken window and peered out toward Tante Belle's house. The windows were dark in the dying afternoon light and there was no sign of the old lady. She imagined her sitting on that couch like a stoic nun on a chapel pew, her fingers entwined with a rosary, praying for deliverance while the water surged higher and higher. It was more than Dee could bear. Wasn't there anything she could do? Should she wade out onto the porch and call for help to that young brother stranded on his roof?

Tempo barked and Dee turned to find the dog paddling toward the front door with Ashley splashing close behind, trying to grab the slippery collie. "She got away, Momma," her daughter said with a nervous laugh. "I think she wants to go home."

Dee waded over and picked up the miniature collie as she flopped around in the water, struggling to stay afloat while clawing at the door. Tempo wriggled and barked in Dee's face, making it clear she wanted to be with her owner in this terrible hour. "I'm sorry, girl," Dee said, looking out the window at the house next door. "You're gonna have to stay with us today."

When she pulled down the panel to the attic, the children were standing beside her in water up to Ashley's waist, their backpacks strapped high on their shoulders. "Let me make sure it's all clear first," Dee said, mounting the ladder with an armful of blankets and pillows.

"Why, Momma? What's up there?" LaMarcus asked, fear creeping into his voice. "When you were over at Tante Belle's, we heard something moving around."

"Are there ghosts in the attic?" Ashley asked.

"Don't be silly. There's no such thing as ghosts," Dee said, shoving the blankets ahead of her like a shield into the dark rectangle cut in the ceiling. She had lodged her gym bag between the steps just below her feet and could get to that Smith & Wesson if she needed to. "I just want to make sure the roof hasn't caved in."

She clicked on her flashlight and took another step up the ladder, cautiously raising her head out of her tensed shoulders until she could see soft afternoon light slanting from the louvered air vent. Lifting the flashlight to eye level, she turned a slow circle, shifting her feet on the narrow step as her beam scanned the dark enclosure. Rainwater was still trickling from holes in the roof and the smell of damp rotted wood wafted through the attic's oppressive heat. *Where are you nasty ass rats?* Her stomach churned at the thought of them sharing the same tight space. But except for dripping water, it was quiet up here. Maybe she'd spooked them and they'd scurried back outside on their nasty rat feet, the same way they came in.

"What are we waiting for, Mom?" LaMarcus called out from the bottom of the ladder. Her children were staring up at her, the floodwater eddying around them. Tempo barked, a persuasive plea. Dee realized she couldn't wait any longer. The attic would have to be their refuge until the boat came to rescue them. They had no other choice. It was only a matter of time before the water surged to the ceiling in every house in the neighborhood.

"Give me Tempo," she said, stepping down the ladder to take the dog from Ashley's arms. "Come on, girl, you're gonna have to earn your keep."

The little collie whimpered and squirmed and tried to escape Dee's hold, but she pressed Tempo firmly to her breasts and mounted the steps until she'd reached the top again. "I'ma let you go, girl," she whispered in Tempo's ear. "Don't forget you're a real dog, even if you look like Lassie's tiny little cousin." She scratched the collie's head. "A real dog knows how to hunt. So do your job, killah."

She released Tempo and the dog trotted off into the suffocating attic but stopped abruptly on a flat sheet of plywood, staring into darkness like a pointer signaling game. She'd picked up a scent she didn't like.

"Hey, come on, hurry up!" LaMarcus was behind his sister on the ladder, pushing from below. "It's scary down here."

"Niggah, please!" Ashley said, kicking at him.

"Young lady, none of that ghetto talk, you hear me?" Dee scolded.

"He poked me in the butt, Momma."

Dee crawled into the attic and helped her daughter up through the opening, then reached down for her son. The poor boy was struggling to hang onto the gym bag, a flashlight, and the baseball bat.

"Where's Tempo?" Ashley asked.

Dee directed her flashlight beam into the dark empty space surrounding them. They heard a growling sound, a low snarling catch deep in the dog's throat. Suddenly the barking began, and the clatter of claws over wood. A fight had broken out somewhere in the darkness.

"What is it, Momma?" Ashley cried. She'd begun to tremble and Dee held her in her lap, doing her best to calm her.

"Tempo's taking care of business," she said, praying that that pretty little Lassie dog knew how to handle herself against huge nasty rodents.

"Holy crap!" LaMarcus said. His hand was shaking as he pointed his flashlight beam across the attic floor. Three gigantic rats were scuttling toward them, Tempo chasing and snapping at them from behind. Only they weren't rats, Dee realized now. She'd grown up around these things out in the swamps. They were nutria, fat as beavers. She pulled her daughter off her lap and reached for the baseball bat.

# 9

He was dimly aware that he was upright, on his feet, being dragged along through waist-deep water by sturdy arms on both sides of him, his legs heavy and unsteady as he waded in what felt like setting cement. The pain in his chest was so intense he could concentrate on little else. He stared into the distance and watched an orange jumpsuit disappear into the shadowy columns of the Broad Street bridge. U-Rite had jumped out ahead of them and wasn't slowing down for anybody.

What had happened came back slowly, out of a deep fog, the thudding blow to his chest and the long weightless fall. But when he inspected himself now, there was no blood on his jumpsuit and he wondered how that could be. The shotgun round had hit him flush in the sternum and knocked him over the fence. He ripped his arms free of whoever had a hold on him and unzipped the suit to feel where the breastbone was tender and bruised. There was no hole, no open wound. He withdrew his hand, expecting a palm full of blood, and rubbed muddy water between his fingers.

"Beanbag," said the voice on one side of him. "They weren't using real bullets."

It was that Tulane boy, the tall skinny dark-haired kid with the Yankee accent.

"You're damned lucky it wasn't an M-16, mate." The Australian he called Crocodile grasped his other arm, urging him toward the straggle of refugees wading for the dry bridge. "We'd've left you for the crows to pick over."

Looking back over his shoulder, PJ saw that a riot had broken out in the yard. Deputies were pulling inmates down off the fence where they'd left the blankets. "We need to get shed of these jail rags," he said, his words sounding edgy and slow.

"I wish I knew where the fuck we are," Crocodile said with a raspy laugh. "You got any clue where we are, Tulane?"

"Waist deep in duck shit," the young man said, forging ahead.

*"You men outside the yard—report back immediately!"* A deputy was standing in a boat with a bullhorn in his hand, directing his words at them through the chain-link fence. *"That is an official police order. Report back immediately or we'll shoot to kill!"*

"We got a S-O-S situation here," PJ said. "Save-our-self."

He started splashing toward the bridge, each deep breath aggravating the ache in his chest. He kept his head down, waiting for the rifle shot that would tear through his spine, this time a real chunk of lead.

"You know where you're going, mate?" Crocodile shouted, splashing along behind him.

The Calliope Housing Project was just beyond the bridge and the railroad tracks and that industrial freight yard on the other side of the interstate. His dawg D'Wayne had grown up in CP3—Calliope projects, Third Ward—and PJ had hung with him sometimes when D'Wayne rolled back around to throw dice with the porch boys he'd grown up with.

"Y'all cain't follow me," PJ huffed. Three men wearing orange jumpsuits was two too many. "Where I'm going, it ain't safe for white people."

The Australian and the Tulane boy caught up with him in a spray of churning knees. "We just saved your bloody ass and we're not bloody good enough to pass a skin test?" Crocodile said.

The three of them merged into the caravan of displaced people who had abandoned their flooded homes and were making their way to higher ground. PJ looked back toward the prison yard and knew they wouldn't shoot at them now. They were wading among children clinging to inflated inner tubes and plastic buckets. Nearby, a shirtless man with a weightlifter's build was pushing his elderly neighbor in a wheelchair, the spokes spinning underwater.

*"Fault the man!"* the chair-bound old gentleman kept yelling to the heavens. Brown water was lapping at his chest. *"Fault the man for doing us like this!"*

Others marched along in shock and confusion, teenagers in baggy shorts toting the one thing they needed to save—a basketball, a dented tuba. Although the rain had stopped hours ago, a white-haired woman carried a silky parasol opened over her head as she held the hem of her loose cotton dress above the waterline. They were all homeless now, their few possessions in ruin. PJ believed the old man in the wheelchair. This was somebody's fault, somebody other than the folk who'd been washed out of their homes, and nobody was going to save them from this misery but themselves.

"Hey, bruh, you better put the pedal to the metal," the shirtless man shouted over to PJ. His shoulders and biceps flexed like a pro linebacker's as he pushed the wheelchair through grimy water. "Case you haven't looked lately, Five-O is on your tail."

PJ turned and saw three Orleans Parish deputies wading after them with shotguns braced against their chests. They were forty yards away and gaining. How did those bastards get outside the yard so fast? He started running again, weaving his way through families, his knees pumping as he struggled to sprint in high water.

"I'm not going back inside that shit hole," Crocodile yelled, trying to keep up. "They'll have to shoot and skin me first."

PJ could hear the deputies shouting at them to stop and put their hands on their heads. He didn't like his chances against three trained shooters in open water. Maybe if he ditched these white guys he could manage his own escape. He wasn't going back inside, either. Better to die out here belly-down in the flood than to face a long violent stretch at LSP Angola.

"Every man for hisself!" he yelled to the others. He was swinging his elbows, finding a rhythm. "We split up, they cain't take us all!"

Tulane was keeping stride with him, step for step. "Don't dump me, man," he pleaded. "I go back, you know what'll happen to me."

PJ sucked air, the pain sharp in his chest. If he let this boy run with him, sooner or later they'd feel buck shot in their backsides. He had any sense, he'd knock this kid down right now and let the hacks have him.

"Stay clear of me," PJ said, his lungs burning as he tried to lengthen his stride and lose the kid. "We make it under the bridge, you head on down the tracks and find yourself some street threads."

When they reached the shadows underneath the Broad Street bridge, PJ knew they had only a few frantic moments to choose their destinations before the deputies arrived in pursuit, shotguns shouldered, eager to take them out now that there were no witnesses. "Thataway!" he shouted, pointing south toward downtown.

A shotgun roared behind them, the boom echoing through the cavern of huge concrete pillars. "Don't follow me!" PJ hollered. "We got to split up!"

He scrambled toward the chain-link safety fence bordering the interstate, its traffic lanes deep in floodwater. He could see newspaper trucks sitting in water over their tires in the *Times-Picayune* plant on the other side of the freeway. The Calliope projects were only a few blocks farther on. If he made it past the interstate, these fucking uniforms didn't dare follow him into the projects.

He reached the fence and began scaling the chain links in boots that felt like fifty pounds of cable tangled around his ankles. A shotgun fired again and heated voices echoed high off the underside of the bridge, but he kept climbing and didn't look back to see what was going down. This fence was half as tall as the one at the yard, with no razor wire along the top. He figured the climb would be easier, but pain seized his chest every time he stretched an arm. When he finally reached the top bar and straddled it, doubled over in agony, he saw a hack wading toward him with his shotgun raised.

"Come down from there or I'll shoot your sorry ass!" the deputy barked.

PJ slung a leg over the bar and plunged feet first into the lagoon on the other side. He surfaced quickly but couldn't find sure footing, only slippery mud that sloped down into the interstate itself. The deputy had reached the fence and gave him another command, and when PJ ignored him, forging his way into deeper water, the bastard stuck the shotgun barrel through the chain links and fired at him.

PJ dove head first and tried swimming out across the submerged lanes, a good strong confident swimmer from his youth and the big muddy river that ran through his hometown. But his boots were weighing him down, making it impossible to kick, and the pain twisted in his chest like a broken bottleneck. Halfway across the interstate he stood up in neck-deep water and fought the undercurrent as best he could, moving frantically toward the fence on the far side, another forty yards. The hack fired another round at him, splattering the surface a few feet away. A third round followed quickly, then another, and he realized that the other deputies had joined the shooting gallery.

Vehicles had been abandoned out here where they'd flooded out, their roofs peeking above the waterline. A small Ford Taurus drifted along with its doors wide open like a sleek sea creature with dorsal fins. He lunged ahead toward the car, working his arms underwater, one slow motion stride after another. He could hear the men laughing as they reloaded. When they began to fire again, a deadly volley of buckshot ripping water all around him, he swam around behind the floating car, keeping its solid body between him and the shooters. This only encouraged them. They began to blast what was visible on the Taurus, its roof and narrow strip of windows. PJ could feel every shock reverberate through his hands as he clung to the open passenger door. When the firing grew more intense, he closed his eyes and dipped his head underwater and held his breath as long as he could, then slipped quietly to the surface again, waiting for the next round to commence. But the car had drifted farther south and the deputies had stopped shooting because it was either out of their range or they'd run out of shells.

He heard a distant voice say, "Did we get him?"

"Hey, shiteater, you hear me out there?" One of the deputies was wading along the fence line, shouting at him. "You can run but you cain't hide in that shiteater suit! We gonna bring your ass back in, dead or alive. You make it hard on us, we ain't gonna forget that."

After a long silence, the first voice said, "We mighta got him, man. I don't see him no more."

PJ hugged the car door for what seemed like hours, waiting patiently for the deputies to retreat. He wondered what had happened to Crocodile and Tulane—and to that head buster U-Rite. Had these sick bastards shot them down?

The Taurus floated closer to the interstate fence on the far side. PJ shoved off from the door and frog-paddled quietly until he was able to grab the chain link and hold on, his hands nicked and softened by the dark water. He didn't know if he had the strength to climb over one more goddamned fence. He rested the side of his face against the galvanized steel diamonds, catching his breath, wondering if that beanbag bullet had broken bone, it hurt so bad.

Another round of shotgun blasts shook him out of his daze and he thought they were shooting at him again until he looked up and saw an orange jumpsuit swimming across the interstate about fifty yards farther south, the pellets spraying water all around the swimmer. He couldn't tell if it was Crocodile or Tulane or U-Rite, but somebody was swimming for his life.

"Go, motherfucker, go," he muttered. Whoever it was, he'd drawn the hacks away from him and it was time to move before they spotted him again. He gathered all his strength and pulled himself up out of the water, climbing the fence with numb and bleeding hands. His waterlogged boots and jumpsuit felt like a dozen tugging arms trying to yank him back down. But if he could get over this fence without taking buck shot in the back—if he could make it to the projects—they'd never catch his big black ass again.

# 10

Hodge throttled the old Mercury outboard toward the row of houses on the east side of Pontchartrain Boulevard. The water appeared less turbulent there, between those stucco apartments and sturdy brick homes that looked like houseboats resting on a placid lake. "Damn good thing that other boat was close by," he said to Duval, who had mumbled only a few scattered words since Hodge had reboarded. "Where the hell were you when I come up out of the water with the girl?"

Duval sat facing him on the front bench. "Looking for this," he said, tossing Hodge the Marine baseball cap he'd lost in the rescue. "Couldn't find the lifejacket. It floated off somewhere."

Hodge offered an apologetic smile. He'd been too hard on this boy. "Might let it dry out a bit before I put it on," he said with a tired laugh. "Had this thing since the Nam. I'm much obliged you fished it out."

Duval stared at him solemnly. "Listen, man, I mean no disrespect for what you did, y'understand," he said, his face buried in the hood. "But you gotta forget about all these people. The dead ones, the fucked up. We got other considerations. It's real up in here, yo. We cain't save 'em all."

Hodge was hurting too much to argue. His chest, his ankle. He slid up the pants leg of his camo fatigues and unlaced his work boot. The sock was bloody, but it was only a scratch. The high-top leather had prevented the Honda's glass from severing an artery.

He noticed Duval looking at the L-shaped scar on his calf. He'd won a Purple Heart for that wound. Fragments of a VC Claymore mine had killed a Tech 3 from Cotulla, Texas, named Ernie Garza and chewed into Hodge's calf and hip.

"See if you can get Dee on your cell phone," he said, digging into the duffel bag for the first aid kit.

"Be surprised if anybody's getting through in a hundred miles."

"Try again," Hodge said firmly, splashing hydrogen peroxide over the cut and flinching from the sting. He was in no mood for disagreement.

While Duval waited for a connection, that little drug-dealer phone pressed to his ear inside the hood, Hodge maneuvered the johnboat between houses, searching for clear passage to City Park, the grand old forest they would have to cross before reaching Gentilly. He followed a tall wooden privacy fence rising out of the water and entered another block of modest brick bungalows, their windows dark and silent. The angina had returned, gripping his chest like a tight fist, and he needed another nitroglycerin tablet and a quiet moment to catch his breath. That rescue business was more than his heart had bargained on. He released the throttle and let the boat coast while he settled another tab under his tongue and closed his eyes, praying for longer relief this time. The doctor had warned him to take no more than three tabs in fifteen minutes. If the pain wasn't gone by then, it was time to call EMS.

"Cain't get through," Duval said, snapping his cell phone shut. "Might not hear from them again till we see they faces. You gonna be ah-ight? You don't look too good."

"Give me a minute," Hodge said, bent over, massaging his chest.

"You want me to drive this bitch?" Duval said. "'Cause I'll drive this bitch like Sulu drives the fucking Enterprise."

Hodge raised his hand impatiently, signaling for quiet, and slumped back against the warm motor to rest a spell. He remembered when all this first came on, maybe a year after Rochelle had lost her battle with bladder cancer in that downtown hospital. After she passed, he retired from the plant in Convent, the town where they'd lived for thirty years and raised their two children, and he returned home to the piece of land his folk had left him outside Opelousas. He was settled there but a few months when he began to struggle with his breath, growing winded whenever he went out to feed his Catahoula hound or tend to his vegetable garden. Dee and the kids had come to visit him one weekend, and she noticed he couldn't walk thirty feet without stopping for a blow. She was used to seeing her tall old pine tree of a father endure every hardship. He was a man who'd never run across anything he couldn't open, fix, or whip with those powerful hands and arms. *Something's not right, Daddy,* she'd told him with a concerned frown. *We need to get you checked out.* But he was stubborn and thought it would pass, like every trial and tribulation on God's green earth. And yet it wouldn't go away, the fatigue and shortness of breath, and one night it hit him like a timber log square in the chest when he was watching television from his recliner. They sent him to Lafayette for the stents, but the doctor said his heart valve was weak and getting weaker and he would need to have it replaced before long. It wasn't something Hodge wanted to think about, the way they split you open and spread your ribcage like a field-dressed deer. But as he slumped against the motor, waiting for the chest pain to go away, he told himself that when he made it out of this godforsaken storm water with his daughter and grandchildren, he owed it to them to make that trip to the medical center in Houston.

When he was able to open his eyes and take the throttle again, he saw that Duval was eating another power bar Hodge had tossed in a grocery sack at the last minute. He'd packed a jumbo bag of chips, a six-pack of soda, a jar of peanut butter, crackers, cookies, power bars—whatever he'd found lying around in his pantry. "Save some for the kids," he said. And then he noticed something farther up the street, a man lying on the roof of a half-submerged car parked in a driveway. Duval hadn't seen him yet, and Hodge didn't want to ruin the boy's appetite. He gave the engine some gas and they surged ahead over the smooth tea-colored water.

"Oh *hell* no," Duval said when he turned and saw the body. They were swerving past a tall spreading ash tree in what appeared to be the man's front yard. "What the fuck he doing on top of that car?"

"'Spose he's like that girl in the Honda," Hodge said. "Thought he could make it out of here but waited too late."

"Yeah, but the man is on top of his car. It don't make good sense, why he didn't go back to the house."

He was a large white man, maybe three hundred pounds, wearing a nice Sunday dress shirt and tie and pleated khaki pants as big as a parachute. The gloss still shone on his polished wing tip shoes. Except that his tongue was hanging out of his mouth and his slack face was contorted by the final spasm of whatever had killed him, he could have been asleep on that roof, curled on his side, his hands clasped between his knees as though keeping them warm and dry.

"Musta had a heart attack, a stroke or something," Hodge said, seeing himself in that man, alone and desperate to find help, his heart valve failing to open when it counted. "I don't know what he's doing up there, either, but he won't stay put for long."

The water was less deep here than out in the boulevard, only partway up the car windows, but the flood line was rising and it would soon wash this fellow off the roof. Hodge looked back at the sturdy ash tree in the yard. "Hand me the rope," he said, slipping the hunting knife out of his duffel bag.

"Un-unh. Oh hell no you don't!" Duval said, disgusted by what he knew was coming. "I am fo' sho not gonna bust a sweat over this fat bastard. Let's get the fuck on up the road, man! We got some other place to be."

Hodge sometimes wished they would bring back the draft. Young blood like Duval, he could use some serious boot camp training and a couple of years tromping around in the desert with badass Arabs shooting at him. Might make a man out of him.

"You never leave a man behind like this," Hodge said. First thing you learned in basic. Always bring your buddies back with you, don't leave them behind for Charlie or the jungle. "Like I told you before, son, he's got people that care about him and they don't need to go looking all over town for his body. A man deserves a proper burial by his kinfolk. What if it was your daddy laid up like that? You want him to wash off somewhere?"

"I ain't never met my daddy," Duval said. "I'd let the motherfucker rot in the sun, it was up to me."

That was his problem, Hodge thought. Never had a daddy to teach him respect and the ways of the world. "Hand me the rope," he said. "I'm not gonna ask you again."

Duval stared at him for several tense seconds. What was the boy going to do? Climb out of the boat and swim away?

"This is some serious bullshit," Duval said finally, flinging the rope at Hodge with an angry grunt. "Don't expect nothing out of me, man. I ain't handling that fat old faggot."

Hodge measured a long length of rope and cut it with the hunting knife. "Do me a favor, hotshot," he said, making a slip knot to tether the man's ankle. "I croak out here in this goddamned flood, tie me up somewhere so Dee can find me when the time comes."

Duval laughed like Hodge had never heard him laugh before, deep in the throat like an old smoker with a bad lung. "You die on me," he said, "I'ma feed you to the sharks they say is out there in the lake nowdays."

Hodge tied one end of the rope to a cleat on the side of the johnboat and angled the vessel up to the sunken Volvo. He reached over to slip the knot around the man's leg, but rigor mortis was setting in and he was forced to pry those huge ankles apart, a sound like breaking a chicken wing.

"Fuck me, this is some Negro work," Duval said, turning his back to Hodge and the dead body on top of the car.

Hodge revved the engine and pulled away from the vehicle, the rope stretching taut, the motor straining to haul its load. "Better hold on, son," he said. "When he comes off that roof, this old boy's gonna make quite a splash."

# 11

Tempo chased two of the nutria up a rafter, but the third one veered away and scrambled blindly toward Dee and the children. Ashley screeched, "Don't let 'em get us, Momma!" and Dee popped the nutria hard with the baseball bat and it rolled into the crumbled insulation and scurried after its companions. She said, "Shush now, calm down," but she herself was shaking and held her children close with the skinny bat handle still gripped in her hand. They heard a noise above them in the rafters and LaMarcus pulled away from his mother and shined the flashlight at the pitched roof and they saw the fat rodents crawling across a thick four-by-four out of Tempo's reach.

"They're going to jump on us, Momma!" Ashley cried.

Dee squeezed her tight and said, "I don't think so, honey. They're just as afraid of us as we are of them."

Tempo kept barking and leaping and tumbled into a pile of insulation, but she sprang up quickly and trotted over to sit on the sheet of plywood with Dee and the children. "Good girl," Dee said, patting her back and brushing insulation out of that lovely golden coat. The collie raised her eyes and growled at the nutria on the rafter above them.

"It's okay, everybody chill," Dee said. "They're up there out of our face and Tempo won't let them come down anytime soon."

"They look bigger than rats," Ashley said.

"They're nutria, honey. Your Uncle PJ used to shoot at them whenever we went boat riding in the swamps when I was a girl."

LaMarcus said, "Nutria came from South America. Mrs. Cox says they brought them here for their fur." His third grade teacher. "But they escaped and went wild and started eating up all the plants in the swamps."

"Thank you, Doctor Dolittle."

"Do they eat people?" Ashley asked in a tiny muffled voice.

"No, stupid, they're herbivores," her brother said.

"Don't call me *stupid,*" she said, punching his arm.

"Oww, *Momma!*"

"He called me *stupid!*"

Dee gave them both a firm shake. "Now listen, you two. We're in a jam here and I don't want you fighting. We've got to stick together and help each other out. You understand me?" She was using her serious mother's voice. "This is no time for squabbling or talking trash. You see that down there?"

She grabbed LaMarcus's wrist and pointed his flashlight into the open hatch a few feet away. The swirling water had risen farther up the ladder. It was over the children's heads now.

"We don't know how high this flood is gonna go," Dee said. "It might come all the way up here in the attic. So we've got to be prepared. We've all got to be brave. Is that clear, Ashley girl?"

Ashley lifted her face and stared into her mother's eyes, trying to read her expression in the dim light. "Are you mad at me, Momma?" she asked in a hurt voice.

"No, darling, I'm not mad," Dee said, leaning over to kiss her sweaty forehead. "I just need you to be strong. We might have some tough times ahead of us before Pawpaw gets here."

"Yeah, Ashley, stop being a wuss."

She swung at her brother again, but Dee deflected the punch. "Now that's what I'm talking about!" she said, raising her voice. "Stop dissing each other or I'll send you both to time out over there in a corner." She pointed into the darkness.

The children sat for several minutes in petrified silence. The entombed attic air was stifling and hard to breathe. It had to be one hundred degrees up here in the August swelter. Dee could feel her lungs laboring and sweat breaking out underneath her tight bathing suit. Tempo was panting now, too. It was the kind of drowsy summer heat that numbed your brain and brought on sleep.

LaMarcus unzipped his backpack and took out a small football that whistled when you threw it. His daddy had given it to him for his last birthday. Not to be outdone, Ashley unzipped her backpack and fished around for her favorite stuffed animal, a weenie dog named Otis. She clutched the dog to her chest and rested against her mother's shoulder. "Do you think Pawpaw will get here before the water reaches us?" she asked.

"Of course he will," Dee said with a bright smile. It was the right thing to tell her anxious daughter. But she had no idea how bad the weather was out there. It wouldn't be easy reaching Gentilly with water rushing through the levees and the wind still blowing hard.

"I'm glad Daddy's coming with him," LaMarcus said, tossing the football up and catching it, tossing it again. "He can show Pawpaw how to get here."

Dee arranged the blankets and pillows into a walled pallet that enclosed them like cupped hands, then sank back into its soft familiar folds, the children nestled beside her. In spite of everything else on her mind, she kept thinking about her son's need for a father he could believe in. She had once believed in Duval and depended on him, as well, but that illusion had disappeared long ago, after she'd discovered the drugs and other women and the posse he couldn't give up from his old life in the projects.

There was no love between them anymore, but there had been, in the first year or so, and the promise of a decent life together, maybe even marriage. She'd first noticed him in the library at Dillard University, her sophomore year, where he was reading a worn paperback of *Soul on Ice*. Her father had owned a copy of that book when she was growing up, but she'd never read it. She was sitting across a polished oak table from Duval and got up the nerve to lean forward and ask with an ironic smile, *Are you some kind of Panther revolutionary?*—because of the book and his faded jeans and denim work shirt and scraggly goatee and the cool baby dreads he wore with pride. She didn't realize this was his custodian's uniform and he was on a lunch break. He didn't tell her for at least three weeks, and by that time they'd already made love in her dorm room when her roommate was out of town for the weekend. It didn't matter to her that he'd concealed the truth. She was in love for the first time and love hadn't come easy for a small-town college girl carrying extra pounds and the Word of God Sunday Bible Study in her innocent heart.

Duval was twenty years old at the time but still living with his mother and two aunts in their all-female stronghold in the St. Bernard Housing Project, within walking distance of the university. Love had blinded her to all of that. She was smitten by his good looks and intelligence and tenderness when they were alone. Unlike the broad, muscled men she'd grown up around, the plant workers and cane cutters of St. James Parish, Duval was small and slender, with delicate bones and a smile as handsome as Tupac Shakur's. Who wouldn't want to wake up to that smile every morning for the rest of her life?

But her parents hadn't liked the sounds of him and they liked him even less when Dee got pregnant and Duval disappeared for awhile, frightened of what it would mean to be a father, the tied-down life, an anchor around his neck. Her dad had threatened to skin his hide and her brother said he'd kick his ass if he ever saw him on the street. But PJ had troubles of his own with the law and couldn't be counted on for what big brothers do.

Dee gave birth to LaMarcus and dropped out of college, and Duval would come and go, making groceries when he could, no money in his pockets, losing job after job. Counter man at Popeye's, custodian's assistant at one of the schools, parking attendant at the Hotel St. Marie in the French Quarter. There were other women, too, she knew for certain. But weighing 180 pounds with a squalling baby at her breast, how could she keep him at home? Her mother admonished her to move back to Convent and live with them again, and raise her son in a small town surrounded by family. But Dee was determined to make it on her own and began an odyssey of odd jobs herself, mostly secretarial work at insurance companies and a veterinarian's office. She found an old nanny who took care of children at her place in the St. Thomas Housing Project and was happy to welcome LaMarcus into the fold.

Dee had graduated near the top of her high school class and had always wanted to be a schoolteacher. But she'd ended up shuffling paperwork in a dentist's office, picking up her baby every day at 5:00 and going home to an empty house to make supper and fall asleep by 8:30.

One cold rainy night, when she was especially lonely and tired and disappointed with what she'd made of herself, Duval showed up in her life again. He beat on her door in the downpour and begged her to let him in. He was sorry and lonely, too, and wanted to see his son. He promised her he'd been clean for two months and would never touch the pipe again. There was no one in his life but Dee. *I love you, baby, and I want us to be together,* he'd cried out, hammering hard on the screen door. *Come on, sugar, open up this door and let me talk to ya. Let me hold my boy and make this right.*

Like a silly fool, miserable and broke and exhausted, she'd let him in. They made love again and tried to mend the wounds. He could be such a sweet man with baby LaMarcus, singing songs to him in his bath. *People get ready, there's a train a-comin'. Gonna lay down my sword and shield. Get away, Jordan.* Gospel songs and Motown he'd learned from his mother and aunts when he was a boy. Some evenings he would come back home with an envelope full of cash he'd earned singing backup loops for the rappers at a studio on Banks Street. Life was good for awhile. He was gentle and loving and told her his dreams about making it as a rhymer, maybe starting his own label. But he was gone in another month and the drugstore test showed she was pregnant again. This time she didn't bother to track him down. He didn't find out until he knocked on her door another cold rainy night when she was large with their second child. He accused her of sleeping with other men and she screamed *Get the fuck out of my house, Duval Webster* with a forceful shove. He kicked the screen door off its hinges and banged out into the dark winter chill and didn't show his face again until Ashley was born. Dee remembered looking up from the hospital bed with her baby girl feeding at her breast and there he stood with a dozen red roses, beaming with pride and wearing that drop-dead handsome smile.

"Momma, look at this!"

Dee had drifted off to sleep in the suffocating heat and woke in confusion. LaMarcus was shining his flashlight into the open hatch. She rubbed the sweat from her face and saw that one of his PlayStation magazines was floating near the top of the ladder, only two feet below the attic floor where they were camped out.

"It's coming up here real fast," he said, and for the first time since the hurricane had struck, she feared they might not make it out alive.

"*What*, y'all?" Ashley moaned. She was sitting up now, rubbing her eyes, working her tongue in her dry mouth. "I'm sweating all over, Momma. Did we bring any Diet Coke?"

Dee unzipped her gym bag and rummaged through the clothes until she found her cell phone. Where the hell was her father? How close was he in that damned old boat? She dialed Duval's number but the beeping began immediately. The system was down. "*Damn!*" she said, throwing the phone back into the bag.

There was a long awkward silence in which Dee struggled to compose herself. Ashley said, "You told us to be strong, Momma. So be strong."

The three of them held each other in a desperate embrace. Dee could feel the tension in their small restless bodies. She was afraid and alone with two precious children stranded in an attic in the middle of a flooded city. What was she going to do now? How was this going to end?

"Where we gonna go when the water gets up here in the attic?" Ashley asked. She was trying her best to show courage, but she needed answers first, assurances.

"Maybe the water will stop right there," LaMarcus said, shining his light into the hatch. "It could happen, Momma. Really it could. It's mathematically certain that the flood will stop someplace, and maybe that place is right there."

Dee couldn't live with the idea that her children might slowly drown up here in this death trap, clinging to rafters as the water surged higher and their skinny arms finally gave out and they sank crying into the depths, begging their mother to save them. The image terrified her, left her trembling. She had never felt more desolate and helpless.

*Dear God of mercy,* she prayed with her eyes closed, *give me strength.*

She bent over the gym bag and ran her hands through the cotton T-shirts until she felt the cold steel grip of the Smith & Wesson. She located the box of bullets, snapped open the pistol's cylinder, and began filling the chambers with the short deadly .38 caliber shells she'd never touched before.

"Wow, Momma, is that a real gun?" LaMarcus asked, training the flashlight on her nervous hands.

"I'm afraid it is," she said, dropping a bullet onto the pallet and retrieving it quickly.

"What are you going to do with the gun, Momma?" Ashley asked.

The cylinder was fully loaded now, five rounds. Dee snapped it shut and glanced at the hatch in the attic floor, wishing she could close it. The floodwater had bubbled up to the frame of two-by-fours bolted around the opening and was seeping over the studs like a bathtub slowly overflowing. A rivulet of water raced across the plywood and washed against Ashley's outstretched feet.

"Here it comes, Momma!" the girl cried. "I can feel it."

"Put your hands over your ears," Dee said, cocking the hammer on the Smith & Wesson. "Both of you."

LaMarcus stared at the gun in his mother's unsteady hand. "Why do you want us to do that, Momma?" he asked, his voice cracking.

# 12

He waded farther into the inland sea he knew to be a big play yard at the center of the Calliope projects, the beige brick buildings all the same, like military barracks with battered AC units sagging out of a thousand windows and rusted fire escapes zigzagging up their sides. The clotheslines had snapped loose and the stoops where he shot craps with the porch boys had disappeared under the floodwater and an unnatural quiet had settled over the entire housing project. The place felt abandoned. Had all the residents evacuated? He pumped his knees through waist-deep water and kept looking up at the windows for a glimpse of somebody at home, a little kid's face staring back at him, an old auntie waving. No trace of anybody anywhere.

PJ glanced back to see if he was being followed. No sign of the deputies and their shotguns, either, only a long oil-stained trough of dark water stretching all the way back to the rec center, where the weird curved shapes of a metal sculpture poked out of the water like the propeller of a capsized ship. He'd been right about those chickenshit key jockeys. They were too fat and lazy to climb the fence and fight their way across the interstate to track him down.

He knew if he could find D'Wayne's Grammy's place, he could shed these jailbird colors and hide out a spell. Before he was shot dead, D'Wayne had told him he'd stashed their liquor store takings in a crawl space attic up in the old lady's crib, and PJ figured he could walk off with that money and hotwire a ride and slip on out of this washed-up town, maybe head for Opelousas to crash at his Pops's farm until things died down.

He waded through the bayou-green shadows between building

courts and came out facing Earhart Boulevard and a familiar corner church whose dead neon sign proclaimed

U<br>N<br>T<br>O<br>HOLINESS<br>T<br>H<br>E<br><br>L<br>O<br>R<br>D

A burglar alarm was ringing a block farther south on Earhart, where looters were swarming in and out of a retail clothing store. It was owned by an old New Orleans white family that had traded peacefully with black people from the projects for as long as PJ could remember. He and D'Wayne had once bought themselves some fly Nikes in that place with revenue from the liquor industry.

Teenagers were emerging from the store's broken display windows, their arms loaded with merchandise. A trail of looters traipsed off toward the railroad tracks bearing large cargo boxes on their heads. PJ glanced at the church's neon sign and thanked the Holy Lord above for delivering unto him a clothing store busted wide open. Where else was he going to find himself some decent civilian threads straight off the rack?

By the time he reached the building, the alarm had gone dead and the rush had dwindled to a few slow old ladies climbing out with plastic shopping baskets full of shoes. Was anything left? Two inked-up bangers had backed a dented Ram pickup against one of the windows and were piling the truck bed with everything they could get their hands on. "Hurry up, niggah!" one of them was shouting to somebody inside the store. "Time to pack this bitch up and roll!"

PJ stepped up through a smashed display window next to the chained front doors, his heavy wet boots crunching across shards of glass. A shirtless white man was coming toward him, some kind of gnarly day laborer wearing a painter's cap, with a Nam tat fading on his scrawny bicep. He was dragging an overstuffed hiking pack by the strap. "They give you a 'Get out of jail free' card, brother?" the man asked with a whisky laugh.

"Step on out of my way," PJ said. He'd been wading too long and needed to feel solid ground underneath his feet.

"Better hustle," the man said, dragging his pack past a row of stripped and fallen manikins. "The clearance sale is nearly over."

It was almost dark inside the store and the terrazzo floor was ankle deep in water. PJ could hear stragglers still foraging around on the premises, things being knocked over, quick feet splashing down the aisles. He slogged past the shattered display cases of perfumes and cheap jewelry and the empty revolving racks of women's blouses, making his way toward the darker corners of the menswear section. The shelves of jeans had been raided and stacks of on-sale Dockers were dumped onto the wet floor, and the tie stands and underwear bins had been kicked over and left to soak in the shallow pond. Two skinny boys maybe twelve years old were laughing at something they were witnessing near the dressing rooms. When PJ drew closer, he could see one of their buddies squatting on a table with his pants down, taking a crap on a collection of plastic-sealed plaid dress shirts.

"Hey, bwah, what you doing?" PJ asked the kid. "No use'n that. Take what you want and get on out of here. You don't have to disrespect this place."

The boys saw he was wearing orange prison issue and stopped laughing and stared at him. Two of them broke away running and the squatter quickly ripped open a packaged shirt and started wiping himself as he stumbled along after them, trying to pull up his pants. "Toilet ain't working at home," he said by way of explanation.

"Get your nasty ass on out the door," PJ said.

He remembered that the sportswear department was somewhere over in this direction, right next to men's jackets, but when he got there, the entire section had been picked clean. Empty shoeboxes floated near the try-on chairs. The NBA jerseys and shorts were all gone. He wandered down an aisle advertising jogging outfits and discovered one lone pair of shiny blue nylon warm-ups with double white stripes down the legs. He leaned against the tall metal shelving and removed his soaked boots and socks and squeezed the water out of them and set them in an empty nook where scores of jogging hoodies were once neatly folded and separated by size. He unzipped the wet jumpsuit and let it drop into the sloppy water. He never wanted to wear one of these motherfuckers again.

Stripped down to his wet drawers, he tried to examine his chest in the hazy light and found the tender place on his sternum where the beanbag bullet had struck him, leaving a deep bruise blacker than his skin. It was sore when he probed at it with his fingers. He pulled off his clinging drawers and let them plop into the water as well, and then slipped into the blue warm-ups. They suited a shorter man, rising three or four inches above his ankles, but they were close enough for hurricane wear. No way was he crawling back out into that oily floodwater without something covering his legs. His Pops had told him and Dee about the poison chemicals his refinery dumped into the Mississippi every night. He pictured all that waste and sludge pouring downstream through the broken levees and into the city, and maybe that's why his skin had begun to itch and burn. Maybe this polluted water was going to make everybody in the N. O. deathly ill.

He put his wet socks and boots back on and went searching for something that passed for a shirt. The next aisle had once contained football jerseys, according to the sign, and to his surprise there were still a few scattered on the shelves. No Saints or Raiders, but plenty of Houston Texans. As he was trying one on, a pair of dark figures slipped around the corner at the far end of the aisle and splashed toward him in the faint light. A man and woman, his arm locked around her narrow shoulders. She seemed to be resisting him as they stumbled along like children kicking water in a shallow ditch.

"But you gotta front me something, y'unuhstand," the woman was saying in a slurred voice. "I got mowfs to feed. And now look at all this shit we in. What we gone do?"

"We gone take care of bidness first," the man said, tugging at her loose T-shirt, "and then we'll find you something for them kids."

PJ didn't need daylight to know who he was. He recognized the voice and the orange jumpsuit that glowed like a traffic cone on a dark road.

"Who you grittin' on, niggah?" U-Rite said, staring hard into PJ's eyes as he blew past him with the woman in tow. Then he stopped suddenly and turned around, towing the woman back with him. "Well, well, if it ain't the class clown," he said, smiling his broad gold-slug smile. The tattoo on his neck looked like a spider web in the rain. "Didn't recognize you, dawg, without our school colors on. I see you made it across."

PJ was pulling off a jersey that was way too small for him. "Still walkin' and talkin'," he said.

"You got some rock for me, doll?" the woman asked PJ. Closer now, he could see the sharp gaunt bones of her face, the lanky strands of hair. She was a strung-out crackhead, thirty going on sixty, grinding her teeth. "This motherfucker ain't got no rock," she said.

"Shut up, bitch," U-Rite said, jerking at her limp arm. He smiled at PJ. "Let me tap this hole," he said, nodding at the woman, "then we'll chirp, dawg. Catch up on old times. Don't go too far, ya heard me? I'll be done in a shake."

PJ watched him hustle the woman around the corner and out of sight. He found a bigger jersey. *Carr,* the quarterback's name on the back, above the number 8. Goddamned punk-ass Houston Texans. So lame, looters wouldn't steal them.

He could hear the woman ragging on U-Rite as their voices faded into darkness. "You gotta come up with some sugar for me, sugar, or I gotta bounce." And then a loud slap, a second one. She began to cry, begging him not to hurt her.

PJ wasn't going to wait around until that head buster was finished with the woman. He had to find a pair of dry kicks, size thirteen, and get on about his own business.

When he waded back to the Calliope projects, he discovered that floodwater had pooled chest deep around Grammy's unit, blocking the doorway to the interior stairwell, so he climbed the fire escape up the side of the building, his new Adidas squishing on solid metal steps. He and D'Wayne had sat out on this fire escape many a summer's night, burning long rolled spliffs while the noises of laughter and strife slowly dissolved into silence over the whole dark compound that sprawled for block after block, generations of poor black folk falling asleep the best way they knew how in the humid New Orleans swelter.

He was reasonably sure he'd found Grammy's window. It was locked, so he rapped on the glass and peered inside. Maybe Grammy hadn't evacuated with all the rest. She was a stubborn old bird who didn't listen to anybody. Maybe she'd recognize him and let him in. "Hey, Grammy, you in there?" he said, tapping on the window. He could make out the silhouettes of her shabby towel-covered furniture and the rabbit-eared TV in the small living room. Someone had left a Saints cap on her coffee table. PJ liked the old lady and hoped her daughters had come and taken her somewhere far away from all this misery.

He rapped again, and when no one appeared, he kicked in the pane above the latch, released it, and lifted the window. The air in her living room was stuffy and warm. Grammy's place always smelled the same, a funky brew of roach spray, bath powder, and red beans simmering on the stove. But as he stood motionless in the middle of the spooky quiet room, all he could smell now was damp Sheetrock and a sour odor like the putrid stink of sewage floating through the T3 cellblock. It was probably an overflowing toilet. He told himself he would find the money and then get the fuck on down the road.

According to D'Wayne, there was a black trash bag full of cash in the attic, the loot they'd jacked on their three clean liquor store jobs before the last one blew up in their faces. Somewhere around two *large* in that hidey-hole, by PJ's reckoning. As he moved through the dark apartment, the smell was growing worse. When he gave the door to Grammy's bedroom a cautious push, he saw why. The old woman was lying across the bed in her own excrement, a limp arm dangling over the side, reaching for the bottle of pills scattered across the rug only inches from her crooked fingers. She looked stone cold dead, and the foul smell and sight of her soiled body turned his stomach. PJ gripped his knees and gagged, dry-heaving from the odor. Poor old lady had been left up in here to survive a hurricane on her own. Where were all them grandkids she'd raised? D'Wayne wouldn't have done her thisaway. He would've picked her up in his Cutlass, come hell or high water, and taken her someplace safe and looked after her, made sure she took her meds when she was supposed to. This wasn't right, what had happened to her.

He grabbed the bottom of the frayed chenille bedspread and stretched it across her body, covering her and the loose wet shit that smeared her cotton dress. Then he bowed his head and said a quick prayer for her soul, the one his Momma had taught him when he was a child. He hadn't prayed in a long, long time, and when he raised his eyes to ask God to forgive him for the many terrible things he'd done in his life, the jacking and thugging and smoking Indonesia, he noticed a small square panel in the ceiling above her bed.

"D'Wayne, you crazy niggah," he said aloud in the gloomy silence of the room. "You hid the cheddar over Grammy."

He took a quick breath, searching for courage. He didn't want to touch the old lady's body, or drag her off the bed wrapped in that filth. So he stepped up onto the sagging mattress and straddled her draped corpse, like a baseball batter with a wide stance. His head nearly touched the ceiling. He reached up and pushed on the attic panel and it lifted with little effort. Sliding it aside on his fingertips, he grasped the two-by-four frame around the opening and pulled himself higher, until his legs were dangling and his head and wide shoulders were squeezed into the narrow dark crawl space above the bedroom. The sealed heat of the attic blew over him like a flaming wave and he broke into a sweat. He couldn't see anything in the absolute darkness, but he hugged the flooring with his forearms and wriggled his long body halfway up into the tight hatch. What he needed was a flashlight, but he wasn't going back down to look for one.

With his ass resting on the wood framework and his legs hanging free, he raked his hands across the gritty attic floor, searching for the plastic trash bag full of dead presidents. It wasn't far away. He dragged the bag toward him and fumbled with it until he found the drawstrings and opened it up. He ran his hands through rustling paper that could've been dry leaves, for all he could tell in this darkness. When he found the gun at the bottom of the bag, he smiled. It felt like the heavy 9mm Ruger that D'Wayne had boosted from a pawn shop.

PJ cinched the drawstrings tight and dragged the bag toward the attic opening, planning to swing it down onto the bedroom floor, away from the body. But the plastic snagged on a raised nail head or something, maybe a bolt he hadn't felt in the dark, and the bag ripped wide open as he swung it, scattering bills like green confetti over Grammy's shrouded corpse below.

"Fuck me!" he cursed aloud, watching the money flutter and settle on the bed. He pounded the hatch panel with his fist. God damn it, now what? He'd have to fetch up all those fucking bills that had fallen on the shit-smeared old lady.

Bundling what was left in the bag, including the Ruger, he lowered himself and landed astride Grammy, loose twenty-dollar bills strewn like flower petals all around his shoes. "Jesus!" he said, springing onto the floor. The bills were everywhere. He grabbed a fistful from the foot of her bed and walked back into the living room and dropped the money and pistol and torn bag onto the coffee table piled with the old woman's church bulletins.

He went to Grammy's small kitchen and found another drawstring outdoor trash bag in a box underneath the sink. The old lady had always managed to keep her kitchen clean and tidy, even when she was chopping vegetables and stewing pork chops for a half-dozen grandkids. He could hear her saying *a hurricane is no excuse for living like a heathern.* She'd left a bowl of SpaghettiOs and a can of Coke sitting on the table. He hadn't eaten in nearly twenty-four hours, if you could call a dry bologna sandwich real food, but he couldn't bring himself to eat anything in this stench.

Back in her bedroom, he began stuffing into the new bag all the bills that had drifted onto the bed, the floor, and the corpse stiffening underneath the bedspread. A brown stain had seeped through the chenille, making the paper Jacksons stick to Grammy's backside. He'd finally talked himself into picking them off the spread when he looked up and saw a man standing in the doorway, pointing the 9mm Ruger at him, the gun he'd left on the coffee table. PJ swallowed hard. The only sound he could hear now was water dripping from the man's football jersey. Arizona Cardinals. Looters didn't want their jerseys, either.

The man smiled darkly at PJ and said, "Smells like you made her shit all over herself. You do that old lady for all this green?"

PJ shook his head. "She was dead when I got here," he said.

"I saw you come up the fire escape. Figured you had something going on in the 'hood. How come you didn't hang back at the store, like I axed you to? You trying to hurt my feelings, bruh?"

"You were busy."

There was a noise outside, down below in the flooded play yard, and PJ glanced out the bedroom window.

"I heard about you and your dawg D'Wayne and them liquor

stores. A shame what happened to him," U-Rite said, cocking the hammer with a menacing click. The spider throbbed on his neck. "Looks like y'all done some serious dirt. Too bad, yo," he said, showing the gold slugs in a wide smile. "All that hard work and now it's mine."

"And all this time I thought we were friends," PJ said.

U-Rite aimed the pistol directly at the number 8 on PJ's chest and held out his free hand, palm up. "Give me the sack, cotton pickuh."

PJ glanced out the bedroom window again. "Before you do something fucked up," he said, "you might oughta take a look at what's going down outside."

A motorboat bearing four Orleans Parish deputies, armed with shotguns, slowly patrolled the play yard below. They looked fierce in sunglasses and bulletproof vests, their caps pulled low over their eyes. They seemed to be transporting a prisoner. A man wearing an orange jumpsuit was handcuffed in the back of the boat. PJ could see blood streaked across his white face. Was it that Tulane kid? They'd caught one of the white dudes.

# 13

When the johnboat angled onto Harrison Avenue, a commercial strip on the park side of residential Lakeview, they saw their first looters. The alarm was ringing as two young men waded out of a pharmacy, dragging plastic trash barrels through the water like salvaged cargo from a wrecked ship. They began waving and yelling at the boat, trying to flag Hodge down. "Yo, man, give a bruthuh a ride!" one of the looters shouted. The flood was nearly chest deep on him, and he and his partner were struggling to negotiate the whirling water and their bounty floating between them.

Duval reached into his hood and pulled the radio plug out of his ear. "Whatchall got there?" he asked with a roguish grin. "Afro Sheen and SunnyD?"

The second looter laughed. He was tall and slender, wearing a baggy white T-shirt, his shaved head growing out to stubble. "It's our town now, dawg!" he shouted back, stretching his arms wide. "The sto' is open for bidness. We got anything you want."

The other looter raised his chin toward Hodge. He could tell that the older man with his hand on the outboard throttle was the one in charge. "Give us a ride, unk," he said, splashing quickly toward the boat. "We trying to keep from going under. Give us a ride and we'll cut you in on this snag."

Hodge didn't like what he was seeing. The only two black men they'd come across in mostly white Lakeview and they were breaking into a drugstore. He gave the engine more gas, maneuvering the boat farther away from them. "We got some business to take care of ourselves," he said, "fu'ther on up the road."

"Hey, slow down, unk," the looter said. "It's real owchere. Down to the bone. You gonna leave a brutha stranded in this high fucking water?"

With the hood pulled up over his head and his small face hidden in shadow, Duval turned and looked back at Hodge. "They might have something we could use," he said. "Loaf of bread. Gatorade for the kids."

The boy didn't have a brain in his skull. "Malt liquor, more like it," Hodge declared flatly. "I don't tolerate looters. It ain't right to take what don't belong to you."

"Hey, fuck you, old man!" the tall looter yelled at him. The two of them were trying to catch up with the boat, but they couldn't move fast enough with the trash barrels in tow. "We just taking what's going to waste. Look around you, niggah. You see anybody gonna help you out of this bitch? The crackers done cut and run for they lives. This is our town now, bruh! Time to make groceries."

Hodge was keeping the boat at a safe distance, but they were still in pursuit with a threatening insistence. "You got nothing but groceries in those barrels, son?" he asked. "Food and water?" He'd seen looters on the ten o'clock news every time a city won a Super Bowl. People running wild through the streets, breaking windows, setting cars on fire. "Show me you didn't take beer and drugs," Hodge said, "maybe I'll reconsider."

The looter in front was a short, round, gap-toothed man wearing a sleeveless T-shirt that showed off the tats on his muscled shoulders. A pic was sticking out of his moochied hair. "I catch up to your sorry old country ass," the looter said, "that boat is mine, niggah. You gonna *swim* back to Mamou."

Hodge opened up the Merc and motored at full throttle down Harrison Avenue toward City Park. The looters were shouting and cursing at him but he paid them no attention, erasing their angry voices in the engine's roar. Cars were abandoned under tall palm trees on the boulevard's neutral ground. Hodge knew the collapsed levees would eventually swamp these shiny automobiles left behind by white people desperate to flee. The flood had almost reached their door handles, and rainbow colors floated on the dark water from gasoline leaking out of their tanks. A careless cigarette tossed into that spill would send this entire block up in flames.

As they carved their way farther down the street, they saw that cafés and a grocery store and corner gas station had all been shut down, their windows boarded up with plywood. The waterline was at five feet, maybe deeper, along the white stucco walls of the Whitney Bank. Hodge thought he could hear dogs barking inside the office building and wondered if some cruel branch manager had left them there to guard the money.

"Harsh, man," Duval said after a few minutes of silence. "Why you hating on them bruthas like that?"

Hodge let out an exasperated breath. "You heard what they said, son. They want to knock us upside the head and take this boat for theirselves. We cain't take chances like that. Dee and the kids are counting on us. We lose this boat, we lose everything."

Duval shook his head slowly, facing forward, staring across the bow. "Ain't nobody gonna take this beat-up old pile of wood while we strapped," he said.

Hodge was still not feeling on top of his game. The chest pain had ceased but his mind was slightly fogged by the aftereffects of the nitroglycerine tablets. "We reach Dee," he said, rubbing his neck and the side of his face, "you can find your own way back out of this mess, far as I'm concerned. See how you like sporting around outside this beat-up old pile of wood in eight foot of water."

They could see the earthen levee of the Orleans Avenue Canal up ahead, just beyond a red brick elementary school and submerged playground. As they approached, Hodge dropped the motor out of gear and stood up in the boat, looking north and south, studying the concrete I-wall imbedded atop the levee. He could find no breach or erosion or collapse of any kind. The levee seemed to be holding strong, the wall panels defiantly upright, a thought that gave him momentary comfort. What he didn't realize was that five blocks farther south, where the canal ended, the back-flowing lake water had topped the embankment, sending torrents into City Park.

Hodge knew the park was on the other side of this levee and they would have to pass through that woodland of ancient oak trees in order to reach Dee and the children. As they idled closer to the small two-lane traffic bridge that spanned the canal, he saw people gathered there on higher ground.

"You got any bright ideas how we gonna get over this bridge?" Duval asked him. "It's a damn long way to Gentilly if we try to go around."

"Then I reckon we'll have to drag the boat," Hodge said, nodding ahead.

They watched a dozen white people race to the water's edge, waving and shouting at them. "Check it out," Duval said, looking back at Hodge. "They think we're their limo ride."

Hodge let the boat coast toward the small congregation from the neighborhood. Their houses had flooded and they'd found their way to this bridge. He felt sorry for every one of them, but he knew he couldn't save them from this tribulation. Where was that Coast Guard chopper he'd seen earlier? Where were the police rescue teams and the National Guard? One old lady wrapped in a wet bathrobe was crying in the arms of her scarecrow husband. A pretty blonde mother rocked a frightened child against her chest. A white-haired gentleman wearing a starched dress shirt with suspenders leaned forlornly on his walker. Others were hurrying along the empty traffic lanes to join them. The elderly and disabled, the young and helpless, all of them confused and frantic. What they needed most was a boat—anything that would float—to carry them to safe shelter.

"Listen up, Duval," Hodge said in a low voice. "When we reach the pavement, you get out and start pulling us across the bridge with the tow rope." The one tied to the cleat on the flat bow of the johnboat. "I'm gonna be pushing this thing from behind. Don't stop for anything, just keep pulling. They're all gonna try to sweet talk us into taking them along. But we cain't take nobody on board. We gotta make room for Dee and the two kids."

Duval studied the desperate faces staring back at them from the bridge. "We dragging this fucking bathtub all the way across to the other side?" he asked. "What if these bug-eye zombies get up in our grille?"

"Whatever goes down, just keep dragging the boat, son," Hodge said, putting on his wet Marine cap. "Let me handle the talking."

There was a shoreline of debris where the flood stopped and the bridge's pavement began, blackened driftwood and a deflated inner tube, an empty ice chest turned on its side, the lid hanging open. The gawkers stood back a few yards from the water's edge, at least twenty of them now. They were shouting at the boatmen, all talking at once, making it difficult for Hodge and Duval to understand them. Duval turned around and frowned at Hodge. "How come I'm the one got to be up front?" he asked.

"Why you think I invited you to this hoedown?"

"I shoulda never left the motel room."

"Get out and pull us ashore, Duval," Hodge said. "I got your back. They're not gonna serve you for supper."

Duval grabbed the coil of rope, then stood up on wobbling legs and hopped into the shallow water, his motion rocking the johnboat from side to side. He tromped through the dark ring of debris and pulled the rope taut, waiting for Hodge to pivot the killed Mercury motor out of the water so the propeller wouldn't scrape concrete.

"Who are y'all *with?*" asked the old man leaning on the aluminum walker. He looked as if he would tumble head over heels if he moved one step closer. "Are you here to pick us up?"

When Duval splashed onto dry pavement with the rope stretched tight across his shoulder, the refugees surrounded him. Someone patted him on the back and tried to embrace him as if he was a liberating soldier. The woman in the bathrobe clutched his arm, mumbling something to him in a weak voice.

"Please give us a ride to the Hyatt," said the young mother holding her coughing child. "I'll pay you whatever you want. My boy's having an asthma attack and they say the mayor and all the nurses are in the Hyatt."

Duval glanced back at Hodge and saw him wading in knee-deep water, pushing on the back end of the boat with all his strength, his face straining from the effort. He was worried that the old man was going to have another attack, or whatever it was. The rope went slack in the strong thrust of the boat, its forward momentum hurling it onto concrete, and Duval bent his back and pulled harder, legs pumping, his wet Nikes trying to grip the slippery road. Dragging the boat over pavement felt like hauling a Buick with four flat tires up the ramp of a parking garage.

"Please!" the young mother begged Duval. She was walking alongside him now, the child in her arms. "The water's getting higher. We can't stay here much longer. Please take us to the Hyatt. I'll give you anything you want."

Without slowing his stride, Duval turned his head and stared at her through the hood. This white girl was giving him the impression she would suck his johnson for a ride in the boat. "It ain't up to me," he said, nodding toward the rear. "You have to deal with ol' massuh Hodge back there. I jes totes this bale and keeps my mouth shut, missus."

"Y'all back off, please!" Hodge said in his master sergeant voice. Canal water was splashing over the I-wall and he wondered if this bridge was in danger of washing away. "Back off and give us some room."

A score of desperate people were besieging them now as the two men tugged and shoved the johnboat's old plywood bottom across the road, making a loud scraping sound like a hundred fingernails across a blackboard. The people talked nonstop, telling their sad stories, pleading for help, grabbing at Hodge's T-shirt and Duval's hoodie. Hodge had seen this kind of thing in the Nam. Burned-out villagers begging for food scraps and a lift out of the fire zone.

"A fire truck came by and pulled us off our roof and brought us here," explained the old scarecrow gentleman holding hands with the woman in the wet bathrobe. "They told us the rescue boats would be here any minute, but that was two hours ago and I don't believe they're coming."

"The damned fire department keeps bringing people to this bridge and dropping them off," someone else complained. "What do they expect us to do? Stay here all night?"

"My wife suffers from dementia," said the scarecrow, patting her hand. "She doesn't fully understand what's happening to us. Would you be so kind as to give us a lift down to the Magnolia Club? The radio says there's no high water on Canal Street."

"I'm sorry, sir," Hodge said, huffing hard as he thrust himself against the stern, his arms outstretched as far as they would extend. Sweat was stinging the cut above his ankle. "We aren't headed in that direction."

After forty yards of pushing the johnboat, Hodge's heart was pounding and he feared he might have to stop and rest. But that wasn't a good idea, given his suspicion that at the first sign of weakness this mob would tear them apart and fight over the boat.

As they reached the middle of the bridge, an air horn blasted behind them and Hodge turned to see a large red fire engine plowing through the flood, the water nearly topping its huge tires. Everyone who had been following the boat stopped to watch firemen help the old and infirm down metal steps and deliver them onto dry pavement.

"The whole damn town gonna turn up and want a lift," Duval said. He was winded now, the rope cutting into his shoulder.

"Come on, son, pull!" Hodge said, panting like his old glass-eyed Catahoula hog dog back in Opelousas. His mouth was dry, his throat burning. "We don't have far to go."

There were fewer people on the far side of the bridge, maybe a dozen in all. Hodge saw the white boys right away, but Duval was struggling with the rope and staring straight ahead toward the flooded park and didn't take notice.

"Dude, check it out," one of the boys said. "Our ride has arrived."

"Hey, bro'," his buddy said, "where you going with my boat?"

Three others were sitting on the guard rail beside a blue cooler full of ice and beer, making a party of it. Rowdies in their early twenties, hip-hop white boys with faux-hawk hair and wife-beater T-shirts, their jeans hanging low on their scrawny asses, showing plenty of underdrawer. *Wiggers,* they called them. White wannabe niggers. Another one was standing on the traffic stripe, his face flushed from alcohol, throwing chunks of ice at empty beer bottles lined up for target practice. A piece of ice ricocheted off the rail and busted a bottle, spreading glass. His buddies laughed and threw ice at him.

The thrower slung his hands and rubbed them against his jeans. "Yo, yo. What up?" he said to Duval, his cap at a slight angle like the black bangers wore them. "You want a brew, dawg?"

Duval would have killed for a beer right now, but he shook his head. He didn't like the hostile vibe coming off these boys. "Naw, man, I'm cool," he said.

The boy in the road turned to his friends around the cooler. "C Murder don't want to drink our beer," he said. "I guess it ain't gangsta enough for his bad self. How 'bout you, granddad?" he asked Hodge. "You need a brew before you fall over and croak?"

The boys laughed again. Hodge ignored them and kept pushing the johnboat.

"Where'd y'all get this boat?" asked another boy as he stepped out into the traffic lane. He was tall and well put together, with a barbed wire tattoo around one bicep. "You take it from somebody's backyard, bro'?"

When Hodge looked up again, Duval was surrounded by four of

them. Another boy had wandered over to the boat and was looking through their gear.

"Hey now," Hodge said as a warning, shaking his head with a look that said *Step away from my rig.*

The boy with the barbed wire tattoo reached out and pulled the hood off Duval's head. "Don't play that," Duval cautioned him.

"Wanted to see who we got here—C Murder or Flavor Flav," the boy said with a snicker.

Duval stood up straight and looked every one of them in the face. Somebody grabbed the tow rope and tried to tug it away from him. "This is the boat you stole from my cousin," the boy said. "He says he wants it back."

"He says it's our boat now, dawg," another boy said.

Duval glanced back at Hodge and saw him sliding around the side of the boat, reaching for his duffel bag.

"Yo, dude, let's gank this ride and go find ourselves another party," said the boy with the barbed wire tattoo.

He shot a hand against Duval's sore shoulder, and Duval dropped the rope and shoved him back, both hands against the boy's chest. Somebody threw a sucker punch that caught Duval on the side of the head and sent him sprawling to the pavement. He pulled his knees to his chest, protecting his ribs, ready for their blunt-toed boots. A gunshot went off, loud as a cannon. A woman screamed in the distance.

"I'm gonna put a hollow point in the next peckerwood that lays a hand on this young man." Hodge was standing over Duval, the pistol raised in the air. He fired a second round. "Do I make myself clear?"

Duval raised his head and saw the white boys scattering off toward the fire truck, running for their lives.

"Come on, son, get up," Hodge said, holding out his hand. "You all right?"

Duval sat up, catching his breath. The side of his head was numb from the punch. "Fuck no, I ain't all right," he said, gripping Hodge's hand to drag himself to his feet.

"They got off with our grocery bag," Hodge said, nodding at the boat. All the food he'd packed for Dee and his grandchildren.

"Gimme that thing," Duval said, reaching for the old Colt Model .45 that Hodge had bought from a second lieutenant in Southeast Asia. "I'ma go rain on those motherfuckers." Where Duval grew up, somebody would die over this shit.

Hodge walked back to the boat and dropped the pistol into the duffel bag. A silent crowd had gathered a short distance away—the scarecrow gentleman and his sick wife, the young woman with her coughing child, others he hadn't noticed before—watching the man who had fired the gun. "Let's get this old tub back in the water," he said, "before they come down here asking for more favors."

# 14

She aimed the Smith & Wesson and pulled the trigger and the loud report echoed through the rafters. Ashley screamed and stared in horror at her mother. "What are you doing, Momma?" she cried.

"Hold your ears," Dee said, pointing the gun again. The cordite smelled like burning newspapers. "I'm making a circle pattern," she explained, firing another round into the flat wood between the roof's brace studs. Three small shafts of daylight angled into the attic from outside. "We've gotta bust our way out of here and get up on the roof."

She fired the last two bullets in the chamber, then reloaded in the dim light and emptied five more rounds, making a decent ring of punctured wood with the two final rounds cored into its center.

"Give me the bat," she said.

She rammed the fat end into the splintered circle again and again, feeling the wood crack and give until the bat finally smashed through the roof's shingles into outside air. Her arms had grown weary but she kept poking at the jagged hole, widening it with every thrust.

"Get your backpacks together and the blankets," she instructed the children. "We're climbing out."

A damp cool wind poured into the suffocating attic. She could see gray sky. Using the bat as a bludgeon, she pounded away until the hole looked big enough for her wide hips.

"Let me go first and make sure it's all right out there," she said.

She had broken through on the lower slope of the roof, not many feet above the rain gutter. Once she'd forced her upper body through the hole, it took little effort to shinny onto the wet black shingles. She set herself in a crouch, planting her feet firmly underneath her on the slippery surface, then stood up slowly to full height. Wind whipped across the rooftop, cooling her sweaty body, ruffling the small branches and carpet of green leaves deposited from surrounding trees. The pale afternoon light was beginning to fade even more and a strange menacing breath shivered through the air, the first sign of evening approaching. Katrina had wrecked all measure of nature, tricking the season into believing it was winter. Darkness would come earlier than it should.

Dee looked out over the surging flood that had consumed the neighborhood. Her car was somewhere beneath all that water. Only the rooftops remained visible, like barges docked at a wharf. She glanced over to the house where she'd seen that young man sitting on the roof, but he was gone now and she feared the worst.

"Is it safe, Momma?" Her son's brown eyes were peering out at her from the hole in the roof.

"It'll do until Pawpaw gets here," she said. "Come on, let me help y'all out of there. Ashley first."

"Why does she always get to go first?" LaMarcus asked in a whiny voice. He was standing on his tiptoes, blinking into the natural light.

"Just do what I tell you," Dee insisted. "Ashley, girl, hand me your backpack. LaMarcus, help your sister on up here."

Ashley nudged him aside with a bony forearm. "In your face," she said, tossing her backpack through the hole.

She sat beside her mother on a mat of wet leaves while LaMarcus pushed blankets through the opening and then Dee's gym bag and the baseball bat and flashlights and finally his own backpack. "What about Tempo, Momma?" he asked, ducking his head back into the attic. "I don't see her anywhere."

"Let's get settled first and I'll go find her," Dee said.

They dragged their possessions higher up the roof near the peak, where Dee spread the blankets for them to sit on. "Y'all stay put, okay?" she said, taking a flashlight from the gym bag and scuttling down the incline to the hole. She dropped her legs into darkness and squeezed into the attic. The bitter smell of cordite hung heavy in the trapped gloom. She could hear a ruckus coming from somewhere near the louvered air vent. "Tempo!" she called out, directing the light across the damp insulation. Had the collie trapped those nutria again? "Tempo, where are you?" she called.

There were three inches of floodwater in the attic as she bent low, crossing from stud to stud. The noise grew louder, a scratching, clawing sound like an animal trapped in a wire cage. She should have brought the baseball bat. She didn't like the idea of encountering those big fat swamp rats with the flashlight as her only weapon.

She found Tempo alone near the triangle of tepid light. The dog was whimpering now, and Dee wondered if she'd hurt herself. She'd pawed through the rusted screen covering the louvers and was gnawing at the wood slats. Dee shined the light on her dirty butterscotch coat. She didn't see blood and guessed that the poor thing was trying to escape this awful place.

"Hey, girlfriend, I know how you feel," she said in a soft voice as she approached the animal. "We've gotta get you out of here before this old attic fills up with water."

The dog turned and growled at the light in her eyes, barked, then backed away and continued to claw and bite at the louvers.

"Come see, girl," Dee said, making a kissy sound and holding out her free hand. "Come with me. Let's go find Ashley and LaMarcus."

She knelt down in the wet insulation and crawled closer, reaching for the dog, but Tempo snapped at her and cowered against the torn screen. "What's the matter, baby?" she asked. "Don't you recognize your old friend Dee?"

Tempo rested her nose on a louver, whimpering and peering out into the failing light. Dee followed the collie's line of sight and saw what was upsetting her. "My god!" she gasped, staring at the huge body floating facedown between houses. She recognized the flowery muumuu, puffed out like an inflatable raft. It was Tante Belle.

Dee sat back in the insulation and began to weep. Everything she'd been holding onto for the past three days came rushing out in a torrent of tears she had no power to stop. Her dear old landlady was dead. All their belongings were dissolving in foul water, the photographs and mementos and precious keepsakes. She thought about the videotapes she'd shot of the kids with a borrowed camera, their school field trip to the Audubon Zoo and Easter time at her parents' home in Convent, her mother walking LaMarcus and Ashley through her prized flower garden. All was gone, the music and children's books and photo albums she'd kept since they were babies and her computer hard drive and file cabinet stuffed with records of who they were, certificates and artwork and report cards, and the many stuffed friends who lived on Ashley's bed, each a special story, and the expensive action figures LaMarcus had collected and hoarded like a miser. It was all destroyed and she had no renter's insurance to cover their losses. They would have to start over with only the clothes on their backs.

Struggling to catch her breath, Dee leaned over to hug the whimpering dog for comfort. Tempo fought her embrace, squirming and squealing, but Dee held her tight and said "Hush, girl" and stroked her small head and wouldn't let her go. The animal's warm stinking body and beating heart were the only things that felt real in this terrible moment.

"*Momma, where are you?*" It was Ashley, shouting into the hole in the attic. "*Did you find Tempo yet?*"

The fear in her daughter's voice tore its own hole through her. Dee knew she had to stay strong for them. She couldn't show fear or weakness or doubt. Not now, not ever again. Wiping away the tears, inhaling a deep breath, she collected herself and set out duck-walking across the attic, carrying the wriggling collie back to daylight.

Once Tempo was outside on the roof, she leaped and danced about, happy for her freedom and the open sky. She dashed from one end of the roof to the other, skittering and sliding on the wet leaves, her claws scratching against the brittle shingles. The children laughed at her antics. Dee laughed, too, but she couldn't erase that image of Tante Belle from her mind.

"We shouldn't wander too far from our camp," she said. "It's awful slippery up here."

She didn't want the children to roam over to the side of the house where the body was floating.

"Can't we play with Tempo, Momma?" LaMarcus asked.

"If we all stay here on the blankets," Dee said, "she'll come hang with us. We've got a box of Frosted Flakes she might be interested in."

She reached into her gym bag, found the box of cereal, and poured a little heap on the blanket. The collie trotted over to smell the sugary flakes and nibble at them. The children laughed at the notion of a dog eating cereal. Dee passed around the box and they all grabbed as much as they could hold and munched on the last meal they would ever share at their old home.

"It's getting dark," LaMarcus said with a mouth full of Frosted Flakes. "Are Daddy and Pawpaw going to get here before it's nighttime?"

Dee pictured the old johnboat out there somewhere, breaking apart in the vicious storm waters, her father and Duval scrambling for their lives.

"I bet they get here before too long," she said, bluffing her way through her fear. "They should be pretty close by now."

Ashley craned her neck, staring at the flooded houses across the street. "I think I see them coming," she said.

"Where?" LaMarcus asked, rising quickly to his feet, looking.

"They're out there by the high school," his sister said wistfully, "and they'll be here in less than one hour."

"You're such a liar," LaMarcus said, shoving her shoulder.

"Oww!" she said, swinging at him.

"All right, knock it off," Dee said, insisting that LaMarcus move to the other side so she would be in the middle. "Do you think you two could leave each other alone until we get out of this mess, for God's sake?"

"He pushed me," Ashley whined, kicking at the baseball bat lying on the blanket.

"It's over, okay? Settle down and keep your hands to yourself, both of you. And start thinking about how you can help our family instead of picking on each other all the time."

"She's a liar," LaMarcus said.

"Okay, that's enough! I want dead silence for the next five minutes. You're both in time out."

Dee was beginning to feel exhaustion. She lay back on the blanket and rested her head against a folded pillow. The air up here felt dense and oppressive, as if some invisible pressure was still weighing on them in the aftermath of the hurricane. Tempo had finished eating the Frosted Flakes and wandered off toward Tante Belle's side of the house, and the children sat upright like secret lookouts, watching vigilantly for signs of the approaching rescue boat. Dee needed to close her eyes for a few minutes. Darkness was coming soon and she didn't know how they would manage with only two flashlights on a rooftop in flooded Gentilly. She had to figure out the next step, plan ahead, devise some strategy that would save them if the flood kept rising and swallowed up their entire house, roof and all. Where would they go if that happened? High into the thick-limbed oak tree in their backyard? She was too tired to puzzle through all the possibilities. She needed a few minutes of precious sleep. Just a few minutes and she'd be able to protect them again, find a way out.

At some point she was vaguely aware that the children had nestled against her and were resting peacefully with the covers pulled around their shoulders. There was a deep thuttering sound somewhere in the distance and it may have signified something approaching, but she was too settled and snug to rouse up and look, even if it was her Daddy's johnboat coming to save them. When she heard soft footsteps shuffling through the leaves, she was lost in that long-ago time she'd gone fishing with her Daddy and PJ in the bayous of St. Martin Parish and they'd brought new water skis for her to try out. The swamp was thick with knobby cypress trees and choking vines and small islands of lily pads, not enough open channel to ski in. She was floating in the water without a lifejacket, waiting for her father to straighten out the ski rope, when that water moccasin came slithering for her through the green slime. Its cotton mouth was opening wide, revealing long gleaming fangs, and she cried *Go, Daddy, go! Pull out!* But when the sharp fangs sank into her tender throat, she realized she wasn't dreaming anymore.

"Don't say nothing. Be cool, ah-ight?"

She felt his hot breath in her ear, menacing and real. His hand was cupping her mouth; a knife blade pressed against her Adam's apple.

"I been watching you a long time," he said in a breathy whisper, "long before this storm. I seen you coming and going. Walking around in them tight shorts. You got back, girl. You get up next to me—we kick it awhile, get better acquainted—you'll like what your boy do."

She began to tremble. It was nearly dark now but she could see the man kneeling over her. He had a young voice and lean build, and his arms were dripping water. She knew who he was. The homeboy sitting on the roof of that rent house.

"Come quiet with me," he said. "We gone take care of this private like."

The knife was at her throat and she was so scared she could do little more than blink her eyes. A drop of blood was trickling down her neck. He lifted his hand from her mouth. "Come on before them kids wake up," he said. "They don't need to see they mommy stretching her back."

The Smith & Wesson was in her gym bag. Could she get her

hands on it? "Please don't hurt my children," she managed to say in a quavering voice.

"Then get up, bitch," he said, pulling on the strap of her bathing suit. "We gone have our own little picnic on the other side of the roof."

# 15

U-Rite lowered the gun to his side and backed along the wall, halting at the edge of the window to peek through the open blinds. The Orleans Parish deputies were talking to one another in the boat below. "Muthafuckuhs," he said, raising his thick eyebrows. "I didn't figure they wanted us that bad."

PJ shrugged. "Like you said before, lotta niggahs running wild in this water. How they gonna know it's us if we're not wearing orange?"

U-Rite stepped away from the window and pointed the Ruger at PJ again, reaching slowly for the trash bag in his hand. Even with a 9mm in his face, PJ was reluctant to give up the money. He watched the man's eyes narrow and a wicked smile tug at the corners of his mouth.

"Long as I can stand the stank, I'm gonna sit up in here and chill," U-Rite said. "Count my money. Figure how I'm gonna spend it." His grin had turned vicious. "Crib ain't big enough for boaf of us, dawg. You gonna have to take your chances out there," he said, wagging the gun at the window.

"I don't want to fuss around with you, bruh," PJ said. "Let's split this grip and leave it at that. You can have D'Wayne's half. He won't argue with you."

U-Rite laughed a hard cruel laugh. "Yeah, you right," he said, his trademark tag. "And you won't argue, neither, if you hugging the rug with a cap in your head."

PJ glanced out the window. The flat-bottom motorboat was slowly cruising toward the gap between buildings, its crew standing with shotguns raised, their eyes searching in every direction. "You don't wanna do that," he said. "You pop one off, the heat's gonna be all up in this place."

He didn't see it coming. U-Rite swung the pistol at his head and the blow knocked him against the wall. He slid to the floor with a moan, struggling to figure out what had just happened. He touched the side of his numb face, ran a finger inside his mouth to check if any teeth were loose, wondering if his jaw was broken. He'd been hit harder than that once or twice and had always bounced back to handle it. But never against a man with a gun in his hand.

"Get the fuck on out of here, comedian, before I lose my patience," U-Rite said, standing over him with the Ruger pointed at the top of his skull. "Don't let me see your ugly face again, ya heard me? I didn't like your uppity ass inside and I sure as hell don't have to tolerate it out here. Go take a long swim, homeboy," he said, gesturing with the gun toward the door. "Next time I run up on your sorry ass, Five O won't be 'round to hear what I'm 'on do."

Moments passed before PJ's head cleared. He could feel warm blood on the broken skin of his ear. He rose slowly to his feet and walked past U-Rite without uttering a word and found himself in the dark living room, wobbly and staring at the Saints cap on Grammy's scarred old coffee table. He was aware that the head buster was standing a few feet behind him with the pistol aimed at his back. He took his time adjusting the plastic snaps and fitting the cap on his head. It had been one long hard goddamned day and he was at the end of his rope, with nothing but bruises and a bleeding ear to show for it. He didn't like the idea of wading back into the floodwater without the money. How was he going to blow this town now? Working the bill of the cap up and down, rubbing the side of his numb face, he considered a quick spin move, defensive lineman-style, and attacking the man, but he knew he wouldn't be quick enough. Not the way he was feeling, with everything moving in slow motion.

As he reached the window to the fire escape, U-Rite said, "They catch you, niggah, you better not dime me out. Ya feel me? 'Cause I'll find your big ass, wherever you end up."

PJ crawled through the window and stood on the rusted landing, staring back into darkness. He could make out the number 13 glowing on the jersey of the man with the gun and bag of money. "You ain't gonna live long enough to spend that cash," PJ said. "You didn't have that chickenshit piece in your hand, this show'd be over right now. Better watch your back, bwah. That sound you heard is me coming up behind you with a crowbar."

When he heard the Ruger's hammer cocking, he bounded down the metal steps to the muddy brown waters swelling in Earhart Boulevard. Wading out into the flooded street, heading toward downtown, he could feel U-Rite's eyes on the back of his neck and wondered if the bastard was stupid enough to squeeze off a round at him.

The sky had deepened into a twilight shade of gray and it was harder to see all the debris now, tree branches and cardboard boxes and long split boards ripped from houses, a steady undercurrent moving everything southward as if toward some giant drain. He'd waded no more than a block, dodging the wreckage of other people's lives, when he heard the motorboat's engine and turned to watch them speeding toward him. He gave the armed deputies a friendly wave, as if acknowledging old friends passing by in a car. Two of the deputies shouldered their shotguns and aimed them at him. The pilot lifted a bullhorn and issued an order: "*Stop where you are and raise your hands where we can see them.*"

PJ raised his arms with an easygoing smile, the only way to play this. Drawing closer, the pilot cut the motor and slipped into a soundless drift. PJ caught a glimpse of orange prison issue curled up in the back of the boat, a human body tucked somewhere in that pile of rags.

"Could use some help, officers," PJ called out, waving his arms. "My Grammy passed up in her place over there," he said, pointing toward the projects a block behind them. "Heart attack, most likely. I don't know what to do with her."

Let them climb up the fire escape and face off with U-Rite and his bag of money, he thought. See who comes out on top. Didn't make much difference to him.

The pilot of the boat was wearing sergeant stripes and dark sunglasses. "This look like one of 'em?" he asked his team.

The men with shotguns gazed silently at PJ. They wore bulletproof vests over their short-sleeve khaki shirts, all of them wet below the waist. One said, "Could be him. But how he got them clothes so quick?"

PJ recognized his voice. The first hack who'd shot at him through the interstate fence.

"Ought to pop him for wearing a Houston Texans jersey on a public street," said another deputy.

"What's your name?" the sergeant asked him.

PJ noticed the prisoner stirring in the rear of the boat. Handcuffed, slumped over from a beating. "Curtis Johnson," he said. "I stay over by Toledano Street and I come up here to check on my Grammy and found her deceased. I don't know what to do with her, officer. Can y'all take her someplace?"

"Let's see some ID, Coolio," the sergeant said.

PJ had already worked through this in his head. "Left my billfold behind," he said. "Didn't want to get it soaking wet and ruin all my cards."

The sergeant smirked and gave the other deputies a look that said he didn't believe a word of this. He shook his head slowly. "Lemme see your feet," he said. "Show me what you're wearing, Coolio."

It wasn't easy raising a leg out of chest-deep water. He had to float on his back and kick the heavy Adidas he'd scored at the clothing store. He lost his balance and plunged underwater and came up spitting and wiping his eyes, searching for the Saints cap. The deputies laughed at him, a pathetic, helpless niggah flopping around in shitty floodwater like a drowning retard. One of them said, "Coolio taken his only baff this week."

The sergeant turned and gestured toward the rear of the boat. "Drag his ass over here," he said, "and see if he can ID this clown."

The deputies seized the prisoner by the arms and hauled him deadweight toward the bow. There was a pattern of bloody pockmarks across the back of his orange jumpsuit, where twelve gauge BB shot had peppered his flesh. His face was swollen and smeared with blood, and PJ didn't recognize him at first.

"You know this man?" a deputy asked the prisoner, grabbing his dirty blond hair and jerking his head up.

It was Crocodile, the Australian. He struggled to open his eyes. With his mouth hanging slack, gasping for air, he stared at PJ and blinked wildly like a man who'd just woke from a long coma. PJ stared back at him, begging with his eyes, trying to reach him. *Don't do this, man. Don't rat me out.*

Crocodile smiled at him. It was a crazy cockeyed smile emerging slowly through the blood and pain. His laugh made a thick wet gurgling sound in his throat.

"You know this man here?" the deputy asked him in a loud angry voice, as if the prisoner hadn't heard him the first time. "He one of the shiteaters that busted out wichew?"

Crocodile laughed hard until something balled up in his throat and he began to cough and gag.

"Pull your shit together, motherfucker," the deputy said, shaking his shoulder. "This dude one of the jumpers?"

Crocodile caught his breath and raised his chin, and PJ could see a small dim light go on behind those swollen eyes. "Go ahead and shoot him if it suits you, mate," he said in a raspy voice, "but I've never seen this bloke before in me life."

"You sure 'bout that?" the deputy said, kneeing Crocodile sharply in the ribs.

The Australian doubled over in pain, holding himself and panting. "Fuck you, man," he said in a pinched voice, spitting blood. "I don't give a shit what you do to him, you fucking jackal, but he ain't who you're looking for."

The sergeant behind the wheel studied PJ through his sunshades. He seemed to be squinting at something small, maybe the raw cut on PJ's ear. In the long grudging silence, the boat quaked slightly, at the mercy of that faint dark undertow.

"Yo, sarge, you see what's going down?"

A deputy was pointing to the clothing store a block away, where another round of teenagers was crawling out of the broken display windows with armfuls of loot.

"Our boys might be down there," someone else said.

The pilot jammed the boat in gear. He didn't appear to be finished with his interrogation yet, but the action down the street had distracted him. "Stay out of trouble, Coolio," he said as the motor revved and the boat pulled away, spreading a deep wake that lapped into PJ's face.

"What about my Grammy?" he yelled after them, wiping his face.

"Fuck that old bitch," one of the deputies shouted back. "She still be dead tomorrow, when all this water gone."

The boat picked up speed, cutting a wide arc across Earhart toward the clothing store. The prisoner raised his bloody face and smiled at PJ. He wondered what they were going to do with that tough old Crocodile. Beat him to death and dump his body overboard? *Escaped prisoner drowns*. And he wondered what would happen when they searched the store and found a couple of orange jumpsuits lying in the puddle. It was all the evidence they needed to come looking for him again.

# 16

Once they had entered the flooded woodlands of City Park, the air turned thick and sluggish, the drooping oak limbs and soggy vegetation closing around them in the dark green lagoon. A million frogs were croaking, as if Katrina had spawned them overnight. For Hodge, motoring deeper into this marshy forest brought back memories of Nam—the narrow deadly tributaries of the Mekong Delta, mangroves and elephant grass and mud up to your neck. There were no street signs anymore, no landmarks to tell them where they were going, only this rambling arcade of ancient oaks rising out of the flood.

They followed an open waterway between trees, what may have been a road through the park, but Hodge was worried they'd lose their way and not find Gentilly before darkness descended over an entire city without power. He prayed that Dee had kept her head and led the children safely to the attic. He was grateful that her mother wasn't alive to witness this nightmare. Before the cancer, she would have insisted on making the trip with him, becoming a burden now in these dangerous waters. Even if he could've convinced her to stay at home in Opelousas—to sit by the phone and relay messages and get the house ready for company—she would have driven him crazy with her constant phone calls until Duval's cell went dead. He could imagine her sleepless and walking the floor until the truck doors creaked open in the middle of the night and the kids came running across the yard, yelling *Nanny, Nanny, we're here!*—like they'd always done when she was alive.

He was lost in the warm currents of memory when something snagged in the propeller. It shook the boat, a metallic twisting, crunching sound as if a drawer full of forks had been caught in a garbage disposal. The old motor stuttered and smoked and shut off with a cough, like a lawnmower blade choked by high grass. He could smell scorched valves.

Duval spun around on his bench. "The fuck was that?" he said.

Hodge had released the stick throttle and slid away from the outboard, expecting it to catch fire. Black smoke was belching into the steamy air. "We hit something," he said. "Or something hit us."

He waved his hand back and forth, blowing away the bitter smoke, then stood up in the boat and reached back behind the hot engine and pulled, his hands burning as the motor pivoted upward out of the water. "God damn," he said, rubbing his palms against his fatigues and staring at the tangle of barbed wire and driftwood that had bent the propeller and broken off a blade.

"What the hell we run over?" Duval asked, peering around Hodge's shoulder at the snarl of wire and what looked like a piece of rotted fence post.

"Something that bleeds," Hodge said, staring at the pool of blood bubbling to the surface. He knelt down and tried to untwist the rusted barbed wire that had wedged around the shaft. He couldn't remember the last time he'd had a tetanus shot. "Get on the other side and see what you can do," he said to Duval. "Don't cut yourself on this rusty shit. I cain't be running you to the ER."

The two of them worked at it slowly and methodically, and Duval said, "Wish I had a pair of fucking gloves."

Hodge said, "Wish I had my cutting torch." He knew the propeller was damaged beyond repair and the motor wouldn't crank again. From here on out they would have to use the paddles.

As they freed more coil, a jumble of fence wire floated to the surface and they spotted the bloody culprit, an animal ripped open by barbed wire and gutted by the propeller blades. Its matted gray fur had been chewed on by whatever was living under these waters. "Some kind of fat old tom cat," Hodge said. Its teeth were bared, its head nearly severed.

"You ax me," Duval said with a visible shiver, "this some bad juju, yo. Let's get the fuck on away from here."

Hodge laughed at him. "Just a damned old cat, son," he said. "You think this is ugly, you wouldn't believe what-all I've seen wash up in my day."

They were staring down at the drifting entrails of the dead cat when Hodge noticed the sudden quiet. "Listen," he said, cocking his head.

In the dead silence, the boat coasted peacefully on the serene lagoon. "What it is?" Duval said, going very still.

"The frogs have stopped. Something's down there."

"Don't be telling me that spooky shit," Duval said, frozen in fear.

A heavy ripple disturbed the water and dark jaws broke the surface, snatching at the bloody entrails and dragging the carcass down into the murky depths. The gator must have been five feet long, as big as the one the cops had shot in Metairie. Duval fell back against the middle bench, kicking his legs as if fighting off those snapping jaws. The boat began to rock back and forth and Hodge thought they would surely tip over.

"Chill, son," he said, dropping his full weight onto the terrified Duval, trapping his movement. "Stop that, goddammit." They were nose to nose, close enough for Hodge to head butt him if it came to that. "Be cool or you'll tump us over!"

He pinned Duval's flailing arms, restraining him as best he could. He flashed on that time he'd pinned his son on the living room floor in a fight the boy had started when he was fourteen, knocking over lamps and furniture. Hodge had eventually locked him in a bear hug, saying, *Son, we're not going down this road, y'understand? We're not gonna start hitting on each other. That's not the kind of people we are.*

"Where's the gat?" Duval shouted into his face. "Get the fucking gat!"

"Relax, Duval," Hodge said, holding him against the deck, their legs tangled across the middle bench. "The gator's outside the boat, you dig? It cain't hurt us if we stay calm and don't capsize this son of a bitch." He spoke slowly, precisely, trying to soothe the crazed boy. "We stay cool—and *inside* the boat—we're in our world. We don't wanna turn this thing over and end up in *his*."

Duval's eyes were closed, his entire body trembling. Hodge could feel him slowly releasing his clenched muscles. He looked into his face and saw the little boy who'd grown up in a house full of women doting on his every charming smile. What had happened to that sweet little boy his mother and aunts had loved so much? Was he buried somewhere deep inside this thirty-year-old hip-hop doper?

"Now I'm gonna let you up, and I want you to pull your shit together and help me, y'understand?" Hodge said. "We gotta finish clearing that prop so we can get on with our bidness."

Duval spoke with his eyes still closed. "I ain't sticking my hands anywhere near the fucking water," he said.

Hodge grabbed his hoodie and shook him, his limbs like loose bones rattling around in a sack. "You'll do whatever it takes, son," he said. "We're not playing out here. Time to step up your game. Nobody can do this but me and you."

Hodge let him go and crawled away, returning to the motor to try and clear the last of the debris. After a few moments, Duval slid over to the other side of the Merc. He seemed to be searching the water for signs of movement.

"He's gone," Hodge said.

"How you so sure 'bout that?"

"The bullfrogs." They had begun to croak again.

In time Duval convinced himself to reach down and grip a handful of vines and strip them free of the shaft. He kept glancing about as he worked, his eyes darting toward the mosquito hawks that dipped against the water's surface. Eventually they freed the prop, the barbed wire and chunks of fence post sinking back into the floating moss.

"Some seriously bad juju up in this place, all I'm saying," Duval said, still gazing about. "Crank this fucker and let's jam."

Hodge found the paddles lodged under a bench. "Here," he said. "Take one of these sucker sticks and get back up front. Ain't no cranking to it. The motor's gone."

Duval looked as if Hodge had smacked him across the face with the paddle. "The fuck you talking about?"

"Go on back to your spot," Hodge said, shoving the paddle against Duval's chest. "We gotta row this thing from here on in. It's gonna take us awhile longer to find Dee and the kids now, but we got no other choice."

Duval dropped the paddle at his feet, pulled back his hood, and rubbed his face. He gazed high into the trees and screamed "*Fuck ni-ggah!*" as loud as he could. A large bird fluttered off somewhere in the jungle of branches.

Hodge waited. "This is what you're here for, Duval," he said in a calm voice. "Case something like this come to pass. Now get on up there and put your scrawny back into it. We lack a long ways to go, by my calculation."

Duval watched Hodge reach into his duffel bag and remove the Colt pistol and set it on the bench beside him. "A gator jumps up and grabs your arm while you're paddling," he said, "I'll go ahead and shoot you. Put you out of your misery."

Duval took his time picking up the paddle. "Ain't nothing to joke about, old man," he said, examining the scarred and yellowing wood as if he'd never seen anything like it.

"What makes you think I'm joking?" Hodge said, sliding his paddle into the dark water and deftly pulling the first stroke. "Now turn around and get busy, son. We got some traveling to do."

Paddling the heavy fourteen-foot johnboat was harder than Hodge remembered. The last time he'd snagged something this bad, it was a mess of creepers and old cypress stumps waiting for them on a duck hunt in the bayou near New Roads when PJ and Dee were teenagers. The three of them took turns paddling back to the truck in the winter cold. But this time the truck was a world away and darkness was approaching quickly and there were children to rescue before they could head back home.

They followed a ragged channel through the trees, their leaves turning from green to black in the gathering dusk. Hodge didn't know where they were. They could have been paddling around in circles. Duval was no help. He'd withdrawn into silence and brooding and dipped his paddle awkwardly into the water like a chef stirring a vat of boiling crawfish.

"Dee tells me you can sing," Hodge said, breaking the uneasy silence between them. He was curious to know if the father of his grandchildren had any skills whatsoever. He sure as hell didn't know how to paddle a boat. "I mean, really sing. Not that gangsta hip-hop rapping shit. Old school gospel. Soul. She says you have a pretty decent voice."

There must have been something salvageable about this skinny fool. Some hidden talent or attraction that had caused his very smart daughter to give herself up to him for two precious children.

"She says you made a record with some people. Is that what you see yourself doing in this life, Duval? Making records? It's a noble calling, as those things go."

The young man paddled in silence, adjusting his awkward stroke, finding a clumsy rhythm. Hodge wasn't sure if Duval had heard him with the hood pulled up over his head and this loud frog orchestra performing all around them.

"Know any songs about rivers?" Hodge asked, using his paddle as a rudder, guiding their passage through a palmetto grove. "When I was in the Delta fighting Charlie, all these white boys could sing at night was river songs. Michael row the boat ashore. Rollin' on the river. Even the Jordan River has bodies floatin'." He laughed. "Best I could figure, the white boys were queer for rivers. Mississippi River. Jordan River. You name one, they'd sing about it. You got any river songs in your repertoire, Duval?"

Duval, sullen, dipped his paddle and refused to respond.

It was hard to reach these boy men. Hodge had tried and failed with his own son. He didn't know why.

When PJ was coming up, he was his daddy's shadow. Pops and Pops Junior, a big husky child who trailed after him wherever he went. Hodge taught him how to throw a baseball, how to bait a hook and fish for bass and bluegills and channel cats out in the bayous. He bought him those Golden Books they sold at the grocery store and read him stories before the child could read on his own. So how was it he'd lost that beautiful boy?

First came the troubles in small-town Convent, the altercations with police. When PJ was sixteen he ran away to New Orleans, where he lived who knows where, with what kind of people. Maybe on the street. Every evening after Hodge got off work at the plant, Rochelle would fix him supper and then he'd drive to the city and cruise the black neighborhoods, looking for him. Tremé, Gert Town, the Black Pearl, the Lower Nine. The St. Thomas, Magnolia, Iberville projects. He did this for months while Rochelle cried herself to sleep at night. The police gave them little help or encouragement. There were too many runaways in the N. O. They said they would contact the Grants if they needed to ID a John Doe who fit their son's description.

They had almost given up hope when PJ called one night from a precinct station near the Quarter. He'd been picked up for possession of marijuana. Hodge paid his bail and brought him back home. He tried to talk to him. Rochelle tried to talk to him. Even his little sister tried to talk to him. This was how it went, a long destructive pattern. PJ would get in trouble, Hodge would bail him out and he'd come back home for a few weeks, then disappear again. For the next ten years, Hodge would rescue him time after time. Public intoxication, shoplifting, a bar fight in Tremé. Hodge's minister counseled him to stop providing a safety net. *He won't straighten up his life until he hits rock bottom,* the minister had told Hodge one Sunday after service.

*And he hasn't hit rock bottom yet because you won't let him.*

To make his parents happy, PJ would find a job every now and again. Low-wage jobs in the tourist trade. Busboy at a hotel restaurant in the Quarter, bouncer at a strip club on Bourbon. They didn't last long. Soon he was gone again, and they never knew where.

A couple of years ago, PJ was convicted of breaking and entering his former girlfriend's place and stealing her cash and jewelry. He was sent upstate to Dixon for a short stretch. Hodge and Rochelle drove up to visit him once. Seeing her boy wearing prison issue broke her heart. She'd just begun her cancer treatments and Hodge was convinced, after all was said and done, that their son's behavior had weighed heavy on her for too long and made her recovery impossible.

The last time Hodge had seen his son was at Rochelle's funeral. PJ looked respectable in a borrowed suit and tie, his shoes gleaming like a car salesman's. He apologized to his father for not staying in touch and cried on Dee's shoulder. He hadn't realized how sick his mother was, and he didn't know she'd asked for him during her final hours.

What had happened to this entire generation of boy men? Didn't they know they were hurting everyone who had ever loved them? Or maybe that was the problem, Hodge thought now as they paddled into the menacing stillness under the oaks. Maybe there wasn't enough true love in their lives. Maybe Hodge hadn't been a good enough father and he needed to own that. He'd worked shift work at the plant when PJ was growing up. Evenings, graveyards, weekends, sleeping when he could, sometimes in broad daylight. He wasn't around for the boy when it counted. Like Duval had said back when he said it, Hodge had no business putting himself up as some kind of role model. Somewhere along the way, in spite of how hard he'd tried to always do the right thing, he had failed his own son.

"You're right, my man," he said aloud, half to himself. "I've got no room to talk. Let's stop chewing on each other and go find our children."

Duval inclined his hooded head, a partial turn in Hodge's direction, as if he'd heard something in the distance that roused his attention. Hodge thought the young man would say something, but he didn't. They weaved through the drowned forest of City Park, searching for a way to the other side. Evening was settling on the jungle foliage like a gentle mist. It would soon be dark.

After a long interval, Duval stopped paddling and turned partway again, his bearing more vigilant. "Listen up," he said, suddenly alert.

Hodge listened to the croaking frogs.

"You heard that?" Duval said.

Hodge listened harder. And there it was, carried on the dying wind. A bleating noise growing louder. Not one, but many. What sounded like a traffic jam of car horns in the distance. Whooping sirens. An entire range of alarms, all going off at once.

"Their batteries have worn out," Hodge said with a knowing laugh.

It sounded like the last desperate gasp of every alarm in the city. The power was dead and water had flooded their circuits and the systems had gone down. All the batteries were dying in one final fanfare, like wounded soldiers blowing the bugle near the bitter end of fighting.

"Gotta be a neighborhood with houses and cars," Hodge said, angling his paddle rudder to take them in that direction.

"Gentilly," Duval said, paddling harder now.

They would follow the sirens.

# 17

He was pulling her along by the strap of her bathing suit and she lost her footing in the slick wet leaves, slipping down and scraping her knees against the rough shingles. On all fours, she raised her head and tried to meet his eye, hoping to reason with him. "Don't do this!" she said in an urgent whisper. "Not in front of my children!"

He grabbed her hair and pressed the knife blade against the artery just below her ear. He had already nicked her throat and blood was trickling down her neck. "Don't fight me, girl," he said, "and we'll keep it on the down low."

He dragged her to her feet and led her over the roof's peak and into a snarl of fallen branches. She struggled to escape from him but he was quick and seized her neck, sticking the knife tip under her chin. She closed her eyes, scared and furious and panting from fear. "Why do you have to do this?" she asked in a trembling voice. "Isn't it bad enough, what we're going through?"

"This bitch Katrina gonna keep rising till we all drownded," he said, squeezing her neck. "Mize well go out of this world the same way we come in."

"My Daddy will be here any minute in his boat," she said, desperate now, saying whatever came to mind. "He's going to take us out of here. You can come with us, too."

"Don't lie to me, girl. Ain't nobody can save us. Now git on down there by that big limb and slide them pants off. Let me hit that," he said, rubbing the back of her shorts, "and you can go on back to them kids with a nice smile on your face."

She resisted him, trying to push his hands away, and he shoved her down the slant of roof toward a large ash limb that had crashed against the side of the house. He forced her to lie across the thick limb on her belly, and when she attempted to crawl away, he grabbed her khaki shorts from behind and ripped them down to her knees, running his hand over her buttocks.

"You got some serious junk in your trunk, homegirl."

He bunched the crotch of her wet bathing suit in one hand and cut it clean through with the knife, like a butcher slicing skin from a raw chicken. She felt the violent, painful intrusion of his middle finger. She was crying now, pleading. "Don't do this to me, please," she said. "We'll give you a ride out of here. I won't tell anybody."

*"Momma, what's going on down there!"*

She turned and saw her son standing on the peak of the roof, staring down at them with the baseball bat in his hands. "Go back and stay with your sister!" she yelled at him.

"Do what your momma say or I'll hurt her," the stranger told him. "Git on back away from here, bwah."

LaMarcus stood his ground. "What's he doing to you, Momma? Are you okay?"

"Go stay with Ashley!" she said, fighting tears, trying to sound in control.

"You better not hurt my momma!" LaMarcus said, raising the baseball bat and taking three unsure steps down the roof.

Dee heard the growl approaching from the far end of the house and saw Tempo dashing toward them across the slippery leaves. She was barking now, racing at full speed, and when the man stood up with the knife in his hand, the little collie attacked his bare legs, clamping her small jaws just above his ankle. He cried out, taken by surprise, and kicked at her, slashing with his knife, trying to shake her loose.

Dee pulled up her torn shorts and staggered to her feet and broke off a piece of limb bigger than that baseball bat and swung as hard as she could, cracking it against the stranger's kneecap, snapping the wood in half. He groaned and went down with Tempo all over him, her blunt old teeth biting his arm, his face. Dee watched the knife plunge into the dog's belly, and Tempo howled as blood spurt across her beautiful butterscotch fur. The man rolled over and climbed to his feet, kicking at the wounded dog, then turned to Dee with the knife dripping blood down his wrist. All she had for protection was a broken piece of limb. She backed slowly away from him, the limb gripped like a club. A moment passed when she saw him clearly for the first time. Shiny black do-rag, gold in his ears, goatee gone to seed. Tempo had scratched him badly, leaving bloody claw marks on his bare arms and a jagged bite on one cheek.

"I'm gonna cut you for this, bitch," he said, limping toward her with the knife flashed out in front of him.

The first pistol shot missed him by less than two feet and blew a hole in the fallen ash trunk, spewing bark and leaves. The stranger turned quickly to find Ashley standing next to her brother, aiming the Smith & Wesson with both hands. She fired at him again, the .38 recoiling in those small hands, and the stranger ducked low and hurried toward the edge of the roof, dragging the leg Dee had smashed with the limb. The third shot struck shingles near his feet and ricocheted into the submerged trees in their backyard. The floodwater was only a few feet below the rain gutter and the stranger leaped, making a loud splash.

Dee was running up the incline toward her daughter, shouting "Give me the gun, Ash! Give me the gun!"

Later, she wouldn't remember what had happened next. Whether she hugged the children first or not at all. Yet somehow she found herself standing at the edge of the roof, firing the gun into the murky water, the final two rounds and then a dry *click, click, click.* She didn't know where the stranger had gone but she kept pulling the trigger. *Click, click, click.* She thought maybe that was him breaking water near the sunken swing set. *Click, click, click.*

"I've got a full box of bullets!" she shouted into the trees. *Click, click,* the snap of firing pin on metal. "You come back anywhere near this house and I will cap your filthy ass, mother-fucker!" *Click, click, click.*

She realized her children were crying. She turned and saw them gathered around the wounded collie. Tempo lay on her side on a mat of leaves, whimpering and panting hard in the humid air. "She's hurt, Momma," Ashley moaned through her tears. "That man stabbed her and she's bleeding."

Blood had pooled underneath the dog and trailed through the leaves down the slope of the roof.

"She saved you, Momma," LaMarcus said in a quiet, sad voice.

Dee walked over and sat down with them and slid the gun aside. She stroked Tempo's fine hair as the children petted the dog and leaned over to hug her wheezing body.

"I wasn't afraid, Momma," Ashley said, hugging her mother, too.

"You did great, baby. I don't want you to ever pick up a gun again. But you did great."

In the last grim traces of daylight, the children snuggled against their mother and they all stroked and petted the collie's warm panting body, comforting her in soothing voices. They were waiting for the sweet dog to breathe her final breath. They were waiting for someone to rescue them. They were waiting for the night to fall.

# 18

The rundown shotgun houses were all dark and abandoned in this backstreet neighborhood, their stark shapes softening in the dying light. When he heard a boat motor approaching, PJ splashed across somebody's yard and hid beside a shadowy old garage, one of those doorless tilted shacks built for cars from an earlier time. The boat was cruising down the street only a half block away, its spotlight sweeping across the flooded landscape, and he could hear the deputies' laughter in the warm muggy air. They'd found the jumpsuits by now.

Taking no chances, he waded toward an alley whose long line of backyard fences was bowed by tidal waters, their age-old trees uprooted and flung against roofs. He banged against floating trashcans and tangled hoses and two-by-fours drifting from a lumber pile. Something nettled his knees underwater—it felt like seaweed—and he jumped and kicked until his legs were free. Fearing he'd given himself away, he looked back down the alley for the boat, but there was no sign of it. He couldn't hear their voices anymore.

A child was crying in one of the houses ahead, where a light flickered in a window. He told himself he wouldn't hurt anybody or go thugging these people unless he had no other choice. All he wanted was a dry spot to lay low until it was safe to move on.

Their picket fence was floating in sections. He worked his way across the backyard toward the fluttering light and stood on a small concrete landing at the rear door. Cupping his eyes, he peered through the glass and saw a candle sputtering on a round kitchen table, and another one on a countertop piled with dirty dishes. A young girl was sitting on cleared counter space, rocking the crying baby in her arms, saying shh shhh, hugging the child to her chest. The baby needed a milk tit, PJ thought. Where was their mother?

A jabbering little boy, maybe four years old, was stooped over a toy boat, pushing it around the kitchen in a foot of brown floodwater, making a buzzing sound with his lips. When he looked up and noticed PJ standing behind the square of glass, he smiled and waved and turned to his sister, pointing at the door. He was a handsome little boy wearing shorts and a SpongeBob T-shirt. He waded over and picked up a flashlight from the table and shined it through the glass into PJ's face. PJ tried the knob and discovered that the door was unlocked. When he pushed inside, the motion sent a small wave across the kitchen tile, nearly capsizing the toy boat. Except for the stuffy heat, it wasn't too bad in this house yet, the water no deeper than shin high on him.

"Whazzup, little man?" he said to the boy, patting him on the head and taking the flashlight out of his hands. "What they call you?"

"Edgar," the boy said in a shy voice.

"He don't talk real good," his sister said. She looked to be eleven or twelve years old, her bare legs hanging off the counter as she rocked the baby in the weak candlelight.

"Where your momma and daddy?" PJ asked her.

"My momma in the bathroom," the girl said, "but don't go in there. She sick."

PJ glanced at a dark doorway on the other side of the refrigerator. "Back there?" he asked, pointing the flashlight beam.

"Yeah," the girl said, "but she don't like to be disturb when she doing her business." She cocked her head with attitude. "Unless you be sent from Maceo."

He stared at the door. "She with somebody?" he asked her.

The girl shook her head. "Back there feeling sick, all I know."

She was long legged and barefoot, with an innocent face and wiry brown hair tied in an updo that might have looked good two days ago but was wilting in the soggy heat. Like everybody in summertime N. O., she was wearing shorts and a T-shirt. PJ could see the outline of budding breasts under the sweaty shirt clinging to her skin.

"What you go by?" he asked her.

"Jasmine," she said.

"Watch your little brother, Jasmine," he said. "Be back in a minute."

He sloshed into the dark bedroom with the flashlight aimed in front of him. Sheets were twisted on a stained mattress, clothes hanging out of a dresser drawer, flip-flops floating near the closet. He smelled crack burning in a pipe, maybe from behind that half-opened door. "Yo in there," he said in a firm voice, nudging the door wider with his shoe and shining the light on a woman slumped over on the toilet seat. Her jeans were pulled down below her knees, as if she was relieving herself, and her arms were dangling loose, her head resting in her lap. The crack pipe smoldered on the ledge of the bathtub, in easy reach.

"Wake up, woman," he said, shaking her bony shoulder. "You don't hear your baby out there bawling for you?"

The woman's limp body keeled over in the pool of water on the bathroom floor. He dragged her up onto the toilet seat and felt her neck for a pulse, checked her wet wrist. He couldn't find a heartbeat.

"This is messed up," he said, lifting his Saints cap and rubbing his slick head. What was he going to tell those children?

The woman was all bone, her hair matted with sweat, a smell of urine and the bitter chemical trace of crack oozing from her damp skin. He knew her body wouldn't stay upright on that toilet for very long, so he hoisted her up and laid her on her back in the bathtub, where she would be out of the water for a little while longer. He pulled her pants back up on her scrawny hips and then checked her pockets to see if she had any loose change. Nothing but a Bic lighter and a broken hair pic. He shined the light on her ravaged face, the bone structure like carved rock, sharp and hollowed out and washed in sweat. He wondered if this woman was the one U-Rite had dragged around the clothing store.

He sloshed into the dark bedroom, fetched a sheet, and brought it back to drape over her body and face. He didn't want her children to wander in here and see her like this. Before he pulled the shower curtain closed, he brushed the crack pipe into the dirty water that was a foot deep throughout the house.

In her bedroom he used the flashlight to search through the clutter on her dresser—bottles of nail polish, fake eyelashes, cheap jewelry and rings. He was looking for cash or something to fence. Without the bread from Grammy's attic, he needed walking-around money, enough to get him out of this fucking town. But this poor crackhead woman didn't have two quarters to rub together. He stuffed the jewelry into the pockets of his jogging pants and dug through her drawers, tossing aside panties and skinny tank tops and a flimsy silk negligee she would never wear again. Preoccupied with his search, he didn't hear those tiny legs splashing toward him until a small voice asked, "What you looking for, Mistah Man?"

"Just looking to see what I can see, little man."

"This my momma room," Edgar said.

"Go wait in the kitchen with your sister," PJ said, rummaging through a drawer filled with sex toys, a pair of handcuffs, a long pink vibrator.

The boy waded toward him and PJ slammed the drawer shut. "You heard what I say, Edgar?" He was irritated that he hadn't found a damned thing worth stealing.

"I'm hungry," Edgar said.

PJ rested a hand on his hip and turned the light on the boy. He was a sweet little kid with knobby knees and a buzz cut maybe two weeks old. His nose was running. PJ reached down and used the SpongeBob T-shirt to wipe the snot away. "Tell you what, skitter britches, I'm hungry too," PJ said with a tired laugh. "Let's go see what your momma got for us to eat."

Jasmine was still sitting on the countertop between stacks of dirty dishes. The baby had cried itself to sleep in her arms. Rocking seemed to soothe the girl as much as it calmed the baby. He felt her eyes watching him as he opened the refrigerator and studied the meager offerings. He shined the flashlight on a half-gallon of milk, some cans of Yoo-hoo, a shriveled bag of lettuce, a small carton of eggs. The dead refrigerator had begun to stink. He opened the milk, smelled it, and made a face.

"Be real with me, Jasmine. You been back there to see your momma?"

She nodded, rocking faster. Her lower lip was quivering now.

"You know what it is, then," he said.

She sniffed, nodded again. He noticed how pretty she was. Deep brown eyes, her mother's long slender build. A delicate silver bracelet around one ankle.

"You got a daddy?" he asked her. "Somebody y'all can stay by?"

She shook her head. "Maceo all I know," she said in a trembling voice. "He come around when my momma need to work. But I'm not going with him. He slap on her all the time. Spank Edgar with a belt," she said, staring at PJ through those defiant eyes. "He look at me the wrong way. Say nasty things." She wiped away the tears. "I'ma drown myself before I go with Maceo."

PJ didn't know what to do with these children. What was going to happen to them? It was only a matter of time before water rose above the kitchen counter in this shabby old house.

He was thirsty and opened a Yoo-hoo and drank it all in one breath, the chocolate liquid dripping down his chin. He searched through cabinets, desperate for something to eat, and found a half-empty jar of peanut butter and a box of Saltines. He cleaned a grease-smeared steak knife on his jersey and spread peanut butter on a stale cracker that tasted so good he savored each bite as if it was prime rib. He handed a cracker to Edgar, who licked the peanut butter off first, then ate the rest. They washed it down with more Yoo-hoo, sharing the last can. The boy dribbled it all over his shirt, and PJ laughed at him and Edgar laughed back, holding the can with both of his dirty little hands. His smooth round cheeks were smeared with peanut butter.

"Better eat something," PJ said, giving Jasmine a cracker slathered with creamy brown goo. "Gonna need all your strength before this is over."

She downed the cracker in two quick bites. PJ heaped more peanut butter on crackers and doled them out to the children, wolfing one down whenever he could.

"What's the baby called?" he asked Jasmine.

"Darius," she said. "He not a year old yet."

The baby was wearing nothing but a diaper, which was beginning to smell ripe.

"You got some clean diapers handy?" he asked. "Better change Darius here pretty soon."

She told him there was only one left in the bag.

"Whatever comes to pass, Jasmine," he said, "you make sure you keep that baby close to you and safe. Ya heard me?"

She nodded. "Ain't nothing gonna happen to Darius," she said.

Edgar picked up the toy boat floating near a trash can and waded to the back door. He made that blubbery noise with his lips. "They coming, Mistah Man," he said, holding up the toy boat to the glass.

And then PJ heard what the boy was hearing. The deep rumbling sound of a boat motor. "Y'all be quiet," he said, blowing out the candle on the countertop and splashing over to extinguish the other one with his fingers.

The house was in total darkness. "Why you do that?" Jasmine asked.

He could feel Edgar's little hand grabbing the leg of his wet jogging pants. "I'm scared, Mistah Man," the boy said.

"Hush now and don't move," PJ said, pulling the boy against his leg and clamping a hand over his mouth. He glanced at Jasmine. He could see her silhouette in the moonlight shining through the window above the sink. "Duck back," he told her. "Don't let the light catch you."

When she moved, Baby Darius woke up and began to cry. "Shut that baby up!" PJ whispered.

The boat was trawling down the alley between floating fences. The baby was crying. "Shut him up!" he said, crouching down next to Edgar.

He could hear their voices now. The spotlight blazed against the square of glass in the kitchen door, went dark where he crouched under the cabinets, blazed across the window above the sink, then disappeared altogether, the motor fading into the darkness. He waited a good long while before he removed his hand from Edgar's mouth and stood up. He realized that the baby had stopped crying. He clicked on the flashlight and found Jasmine sitting against a cabinet door, cradling the child in her thin arms. To make him quiet, she'd raised her T-shirt to let the baby suckle on her small breast.

"Somebody looking for you?" she asked. The way she said this, she sounded like a grown woman.

"Pull your shirt down, girl," he said, turning the beam away from her. "Don't light these candles again. We don't want nobody coming up to the house."

"What happen to your ear?" she asked him.

Ignoring her question, he said, "Me, I'm going into the bedroom to catch some winks. I don't know what y'all gonna do. Anything bad happens—the water gets too much higher—come wake me up. Ya heard me? That boat comes back around, you wake me up fast."

In the bedroom he took off his cap and lay down on the bare mattress, the flashlight by his side. His clothes were soaked to the skin, his Adidas like cinder blocks, but he was too tired to care how uncomfortable he felt. He was slipping into the warm grip of sleep when he heard small legs stirring the water. Edgar had pushed the toy boat into the bedroom and was making his motor sounds.

"Cut the noise, son," PJ said. "Didn't you hear me say I'm trying to sleep?"

"I'm sleepy too, Mistah Man."

"Then come over here and lay down."

The boy crawled onto the bed and curled his small body against PJ's. He smelled like pee and sweaty child funk. "Where my momma at?" he asked.

PJ didn't know what to tell him. "She had to go to the store," he said. It made no sense, but it seemed to satisfy the boy. Soon he was breathing deeply, sound asleep. PJ put his arm around him and pulled him close. He hated to think what was going to happen to this sweet little boy.

PJ dozed off, woke, dozed again. At some point in his restless sleep he became aware that another body was occupying the bed. He clicked on the flashlight. Jasmine was lying on her back, wide awake, the baby cuddled against her chest. She turned her head and stared at him. "Please don't hurt me," she said in a fragile voice. A tear was running down her cheek.

"Nobody's gonna hurt you, child," he said, clicking off the flashlight. "Now get some sleep."

He didn't know how late it was, or how long he'd been asleep, when he woke with the frightful sensation of drowning. He kicked his legs and thrashed his arms, trying to stay afloat, and realized it was only the mattress. It had become sopping wet underneath him. He found the flashlight and swept the beam around the room and saw that the bed was now an island in a dark lagoon. The water had risen another foot since he'd gone to sleep. Edgar's toy boat was floating near his face. How long until the bed was completely underwater?

He shined the light on the children and discovered Jasmine staring at him through those haunting brown eyes, the baby and Edgar crowded next to her on the mattress. "You gonna leave us here?" she asked him in a hoarse whisper.

He dropped his head back on the soggy mattress and closed his eyes. He hadn't bargained on taking care of a bunch of snot-nosed kids in this goddamned flood. He was having a hard enough time taking care of himself.

"Go to sleep, girl," he said. "I'm not leaving while it's dark outside."

# 19

Tempo's body was still warm when they covered her with a blanket and arranged broken limbs around her in a kind of primitive burial pyre. As LaMarcus held a flashlight, Ashley fashioned a cross out of two small branches, tying them together with a willowy switch and placing it near the little collie's head. Dee couldn't forgive herself. She'd promised Tante Belle she would take care of Tempo and she'd broken her promise. And now she was afraid she couldn't save her children, either.

"Momma, do you think Tante Belle went up into her attic?" LaMarcus asked in a small wounded voice.

"I hope so," Dee said, knowing the terrible truth. "Let's ask Jesus to watch over her."

The children joined her in a silent prayer. Dee closed her eyes and asked God to safeguard Tante Belle's body and not let her float away or be humiliated by the elements. And she asked God to hide the poor woman from her children's sight.

They camped in darkness on the side of the roof facing the drowned street. Mosquitoes were swarming off the water, buzzing all around them and biting. The children draped blankets over themselves and peeked out of face holes, shining their flashlights over the rippling lake that had submerged all but the roofs of Gentilly Terrace.

"Look, Momma, there goes somebody's couch!" Ashley said. The couch was drifting along, trapped in a tangle of tree limbs, its cushions missing.

While Ashley and LaMarcus played their game of identifying things in the dark water, Dee set the reloaded pistol by her side and dug around in her bag for new clothes. Batting at mosquitoes, she slipped out of her ripped shorts and bathing suit with her back to the children, watching the roofline in case the stranger decided to return. Her knees were scraped raw and the nick on her throat was still fresh and she felt a small sting where his jagged nail had scratched the soft tissue inside her. If that bastard showed his face again, she was going to put a bullet through his evil heart. Not just for her, but for what he'd done to Tempo.

She heard a *thut thut thut* in the distance and gazed into the dark sky. It was a clear starry night, despite the ragged kite-tail of Katrina's winds trailing north toward Lake Pontchartrain. The sound was drawing closer, and soon she saw lights crisscrossing the rooftops of the blackened neighborhood. LaMarcus threw back his blanket and leaped to his feet, waving the flashlight. "Here we are!" he shouted. "Here we are!"

The helicopter was three or four blocks away, cruising low over the storm-bent trees, its searchlight shifting directions, hunting for stranded survivors.

Ashley jumped out of her blanket and waved her arms, too, caught up in the noise and excitement. "Can you see us?" she screamed. "Hey, up there, can you see us?"

Dee didn't hear the second helicopter until it roared over their house from the rear, stirring a whirlwind of leaves and small branches and billowing their blankets like sails. For a brief moment the searchlight captured them in its jittering beam. Shielding her eyes, Dee rose to her feet and read the words *US Coast Guard* painted next to an insignia. The children jumped and whooped, but the chopper kept flying toward the park as if it hadn't spotted them. They fell silent and stared forlornly at its blinking taillights. "It missed us, Momma," LaMarcus said, his shoulders sagging.

And then the helicopter made a wide curving turn and stuttered back in their direction. "It sees us! It sees us!" Ashley shouted, wagging the flashlight over her head.

LaMarcus was jumping up and down again, slashing the darkness with his light. "It's coming back!" he yelled. "Hey, we're over here!"

Dee didn't know what to think. Did they need to be rescued by a Coast Guard helicopter? Or should she wave them away? Where the hell was her Daddy and Duval in that goddamned boat?

The chopper hovered high above their roof, scattering tree limbs and whipping their hair and clothes in the violent downdraft. A lone figure gripping a cable dropped down toward them, his blue helmet and neon orange jumpsuit gleaming in the shaft of light. LaMarcus and Ashley clung to their mother's side, watching in awe. When his boots met the roof shingles, he released the cable attached to his chest harness and jogged toward them. "*You're gonna be all right!*" he shouted to be heard in the squealing din. He was a tall white man whose features were obscured by the Plexiglas face guard. "*We're here to take you to safety!*"

Dee held the children close to her side. "My Daddy's coming for us in a boat!" she shouted back. "We should probably wait for him!"

The Coast Guard rescuer looked up at his cockpit crew and gave them the thumbs up. "I don't think so, ma'am. You don't know *when* or *if* he's coming. It's hell out there! He may have run into trouble. Three or four of the levees have broken down," he said. "We don't know how high the water's gonna rise. It may come up over your roof in another hour. You can't stay up here all night long."

He was right—the flood had been rising steadily the entire day and showed no signs of stopping. And the johnboat should have been here by now. Her heart sank when she thought of what might have happened to them.

The man touched the top of LaMarcus's head with a gray glove, giving him a friendly shake. "I can't let you and these kids stay up here, ma'am," he said, still shouting to be understood. "It's my job to make sure you get to safety. We'll take you to where it's dry and there's food and water and a place to spend the night."

"I appreciate that," Dee shouted back. "But what happens if my daddy gets here and we're gone?"

He looked up again. A wide basket was lowering by cable, the wire enclosure spinning in the wind. "I'm gonna put your children in the basket and take them up first," he explained. "You guys ready for a ride?" he asked LaMarcus and Ashley. "Have you ever been in a helicopter before?"

The children shook their heads silently, grimly. They burrowed deeper into their mother's hips. It was a long way up there.

"It's the right thing to do, ma'am," he said to Dee. "Your daddy will understand we couldn't take any chances."

"But how will he find us?" Dee asked.

Everything was falling apart around them. Her father's rescue plan was disintegrating. If they went with these men, she feared they would end up hostage to all the chaos, a mother and two small children wandering the flooded streets a long way from her Daddy's farm in Opelousas.

"You have something to write with?" the man asked her as he reached over his head and grabbed the swaying rescue basket, tugging it down to rest on the roof. "Leave them a message!"

Dee had no pen or paper. All their school supplies were dissolving in the house underneath them.

"Come on, kids, hop aboard!" the man shouted, holding the basket in place. "All you have to do is sit still and let my buddies take you up into the bird."

Dee hesitated, paralyzed by the idea of her two precious children suspended in the dark night high above a raging flood. The man sensed her panic and held out his hand. "Come on, young lady," he said to Ashley, "it's a piece of cake. You look like somebody who likes to ride on a Ferris wheel. This is more fun."

Ashley smiled and looked up at her mother, waiting for permission. Dee knew the man was right. They might not get another chance to leave. She took a deep breath and let her daughter go.

Ashley and LaMarcus slipped on their backpacks and crawled into the basket, sitting down and facing each other, their legs entwined. Dee kissed them both on the cheek and gave them strong hugs. Her heart was ready to burst.

"What about Tempo, Momma?" Ashley cried out as the Coast Guard crewman gave the signal and the basket began to lift. "We can't leave Tempo here by herself!"

"Tempo will be fine!" Dee shouted to her. "When Pawpaw gets here, he'll put her in his boat!"

She held back the tears and watched her children rise into the current of dark air, their small bodies borne away toward the open cargo door of the helicopter. Halfway up, the basket began to spin slightly and Dee's heart pounded. "Are they going to be all right?" she shouted to the crewman standing next to her.

"Yes, ma'am, they're in good hands," he said, patting her shoulder. "Now you and I are gonna go up together. I want you to hold on tight, okay?"

She looked at him, then upward again to watch the basket being pulled into the cargo door by neon orange arms.

"Don't worry. I've been doing this for fifteen years and I haven't dropped anybody yet."

She stepped over to collect her gym bag and he said, "You'll have to leave that here. I can't hold onto you and a bag, too."

The Smith & Wesson was resting on top of her wet clothing. She wouldn't leave it behind for that evil bastard to find. She fetched the pistol, walked over to the edge of the roof, and flung it into nine feet of floodwater. The Coast Guard crewman watched her but didn't say a word. They stood together in silence, waiting for the cable to drop back down.

"Thank you, mister," she said, finally. "Thank you for being here."

He gave her a quick two-fingered salute and fastened the cable hook to his chest harness. "You ready to rumble?" he said.

"Where are you taking us?"

"To the Superdome, ma'am." he said. "You'll be safe there."

She wasn't so sure they'd be better off in that huge place. She remembered that fights had broken out in the Dome the last time people had evacuated there during a hurricane.

"I'm gonna wrap my legs around you on the way up," he shouted. "I hope you're okay with that."

She glanced up at the hovering helicopter, where her children were waiting for her. "I've had worse offers," she said with a tight smile.

He secured an orange safety harness around her, bracing her against his body, and gave the cockpit the thumbs up sign. She had no choice but to hug this tall white man and rest her head on his chest. His jumpsuit smelled like sea salt. When they were lofted into the air, he locked his legs around her waist and said, "Here we go, ma'am. Everything's good."

The downdraft battered them in its unyielding cold wash and they twisted slightly as they ascended higher. She clutched the man for dear life. When they were almost to the bay doors, she opened her eyes and glanced back down to the spotlighted roof and saw the hole she'd smashed in the shingles and their blankets blown around like paper streamers and the branches of Tempo's pyre scattered away from the little dog whose body lay exposed where they'd placed her. Their home was gone, everything they owned. A sunken chest full of memories spilled on the floor of a dark lake. Dangling a hundred feet in the air, she felt too scared and exhausted to cry. When the johnboat came for them—if the boat made it at all—they would find the ruins of a rooftop campsite demolished by the winds, its inhabitants vanished in the tropical night.

# 20

The car horns and house alarms beckoned them toward the pitch-black neighborhood of Gentilly. They emerged from the oak-shadowed park and crossed Bayou St. John where it narrowed, trailing down from the lake, and the landscape was so dark and befuddling that Duval couldn't get his bearings in a part of town he'd known all his life. He had bungeed Hodge's big square flashlight to the prow of the johnboat as their headlamp and they paddled on, searching for street signs and corner package stores, anything Duval might recognize. They paddled past small brick houses and wood-frame shotguns, where power poles were tilted all down the street, their lines ripped loose and coiling dangerously into the water. Not a light burning anywhere, not a soul in sight.

After their long row through the park, Hodge's chest had begun to feel tight. His breath was shallow, his arms weak, and he'd broken a sweat. In the back of his head there was a little voice saying, *Pace yourself, old dog. You don't want to suck on any more nitro tablets.*

As they ventured deeper into the neighborhood, a dark undercurrent tugged at the boat and Hodge knew they had to paddle harder or be swept into the clutches of some unseen force. "Which way we need to go, son?" he asked Duval.

"I don't know where we at, man."

Hodge resisted the temptation to chew the boy out. "I was counting on you to take us straight to Dee's house," he said.

"You haven't noticed it's fucking *dark* owchere and high water up our butt cracks?"

They had reached the tree-lined neutral ground of some larger boulevard. A dead traffic light poked out of the flood. Hodge clicked on a flashlight and directed it at the green street signs. Paris Avenue. Harcourt Street. "Ring a bell?" he asked.

Duval shrugged, unsure. He knew this town by its corner stores and Popeye's drive-thrus and cheap gas stations, not by the names on street signs.

They paddled on, and in time the grainy flashlight beam penetrated a row of small bushy trees ahead. They'd come upon the London Avenue Canal. Hodge raked his light across the bulging concrete I-wall for fifty feet or more and saw it spurting here and there like a punctured garden hose.

"Let's get the hell out of here before this whole damn thing blows out," he said. "Which way, Duval? Your call. Right or left?"

Duval was trying to remember where the bridges were located. Dee and the children were on the other side of this canal and the boat would have to cross over somehow. "Mirabeau bridge," he said, pointing. "Gotta be up thataway."

Hodge angled the johnboat northward and they paddled into the current. A breach farther up, on the west side of the canal near Robert E. Lee Boulevard, was gushing lake water down into this wooded neighborhood. The two men fell into a paddling rhythm, something they hadn't done until now, quickening their strokes and fighting the flow with their backs into it. For three blocks they fended off debris streaming toward them, mostly tree limbs and gnarled stumps, Hodge doing his best to rudder the fourteen-footer away from catastrophe. In the weak beam of the bungeed flashlight he could see that houses had slipped off their foundations and seemed afloat like those houses that washed down the Mississippi River in olden days. Before long they found the bridge, a wide four-lane that spanned the swollen canal.

"This is straight up trippin'," Duval said. "We gonna have to drag this tub across another bridge?"

"Unless you can make her sprout wings," Hodge said.

They assumed their roles, Duval pulling the tote rope, Hodge heaving from the stern, the plywood bottom scraping across hard pavement. Cars were abandoned on the bridge, and they were forced to haul the johnboat around them. Hodge was breathing heavier now and grew lightheaded as they soldiered on. Halfway across, Duval stopped abruptly and said, "Dude, this is whack." He was staring into the window of an ancient bronze-colored Bonneville. "Couple of cold ones. Look like they sleeping," he said.

Hodge shined his flashlight into the driver's window. They were at least eighty years old, the man light skinned, almost white, his hair gone and his glasses hanging by one ear; the woman much darker, with a shock of gray hair pulled into a grandmother's bun. They were both belted into bulky life vests but didn't appear to be wet. Underneath the vest, the old woman was clad in a cotton summer dress from another time, and the man was wearing pleated slacks. They held each other in a tender embrace, like lovers huddled in a lifeboat, but they'd slumped over toward the passenger door and his large body imposed on hers in their final resting state.

"Ought to check if they're still breathing," Hodge said. He opened the creaking car door and discovered what it smelled like when bowels went loose for several hours in a hot closed-up automobile. His stomach turned. He gagged and backed away.

"God *damn,* old son!" Duval said, backing away as well. "How they end up like that?" he asked with a hand across his nose. "Both gone at the same time?"

"Better off this way," Hodge said. There were too many lonesome nights since Rochelle's death when he wished he could have joined her the day she flatlined in her hospice room.

He closed the car door, shutting the old couple into their metal mausoleum, and walked over to the boat and sat on the bench next to the ruined motor. Duval watched him but didn't know what to say. The old man slouched forward, head down, his elbows resting on his knees. He looked tired and played out, and for the first time since they'd shoved off on this boat ride, Duval wondered if Hodge was going to make it.

"You ah-ight?" Duval asked him.

Hodge took a long time to respond. Finally he nodded. "Just need a minute." He was thinking about that old couple in the Bonneville. He wondered who they were, what kind of life they'd had together. Would their children ever know what had happened to them?—their final moments in a car, on a bridge, going nowhere?

He was thinking about Rochelle, too. Dead at fifty-six. They were never going to grow old together and die in each other's arms. She had passed in a hospital bed with tubes stuck in her body.

They'd been high school sweethearts, and Rochelle promised him she wouldn't look at another boy while Hodge was off at war. And sure enough, she was waiting for him when he came home. But returning to sleepy Opelousas had proved dangerous for a young unemployed black man with a chip on his shoulder and a jones for the hooch he'd smoked in Nam. That was asking for trouble in a small southern town full of white cops. So they got married in her daddy's church and moved to the Big Easy and tried to make a go of it. They lived in a divided shotgun near the Magnolia Housing Project and Rochelle went to work as a nanny for a wealthy white family in the Garden District. For awhile Hodge installed AC window units with two hippie Vietnam vets who ran their own business. When the owner was killed in a car wreck, it all fell apart and he ended up finding a steady job at a refinery in that little company town halfway up the river to Baton Rouge. That's what you did when you were a man and you had mouths to feed. You knuckled down and punched a time clock, if nothing better came along. You didn't run away and leave your woman and children stranded in a hurricane.

Duval sat on the boat's gunnel and swatted at mosquitoes feasting on his face. The alarms had died out but the frogs were still croaking all around them in the secret shallows of the flood. The clouds had moved off and the night was surprisingly clear, the Big

Dipper commanding the sky like he'd seen it on crisp winter nights after a blue norther had blown through. He plugged the earpiece back in and listened to WWL, the only radio station on the air. The man was saying that part of the roof had caved in at the Superdome and people were wet and hungry and tromping around in their own waste. He was saying that looters had cleaned out Wal-Mart and had broken into the clothing stores on Canal Street. Things were bad everywhere and nobody seemed to be in charge.

"These fucking skeetuhs eating me alive," Duval said. "Time to boogie on."

Hodge raised his chin and looked at him. "If anything happens to me," he said in a distant voice, "you make damn sure you take Dee and the kids back to Opelousas. You copy that?"

The old man was beginning to spook him. "Why you talking like that?"

"Take them back to my farm, Duval. That's the mission."

On the far side of the bridge they splashed the johnboat back into the floodwater and found themselves fighting an even stronger current at their tail. Another piece of the levee had collapsed only a block away, on the east side of the canal, and the torrent was propelling them into dark Gentilly Terrace as if they were riding whitewater rapids in a mountain river. Hodge struggled to use his paddle as a rudder, his muscles straining to keep the plywood craft upright in the driving stream.

"We headed in the right direction?" he yelled at Duval.

"Word!" Duval yelled back, dipping his paddle, stroking. He recognized where they were.

Within minutes, the sky was streaked with light and Hodge could hear a Coast Guard Jayhawk fluttering over the rooftops ahead. The bird was searching the neighborhood house by house, looking for marooned survivors, and Hodge wondered if these puddle jumpers could help them find Dee's place. He sensed her house was near and they weaved their way through murky streets, paddling with a newfound urgency. They were crossing Elysian Fields not far from the Catholic high school when they saw the chopper's searchlight jigging in the night sky two blocks away.

"Come on, man, let's fly!" Duval shouted. "They at Dee's street!"

They knifed the water, stroke after quick stroke, and moved down-current with greater speed than at any time since the old Merc had died. Hodge was breathing hard with his mouth open, sucking wind as he tried to match Duval's frantic pace. All at once they were heading on a crash course toward a street sign and Hodge scrambled to avoid hitting the pole, back-paddling and ruddering with all his strength. They ducked and scraped underneath the dangling limbs of a massive oak tree and were delivered into the hazy white globe of the helicopter's searchlight illuminating an entire block. Two people were being hoisted up into the bay doors of the HH-60, a helmet-wearing Coastie and a woman he was hugging in his harness.

Duval shouted at the helicopter, waving his paddle, trying to capture their attention, but the rotor noise was so loud his voice was lost even to Hodge sitting behind him. They watched the bird lift higher in the whirling turbulence and veer southward over the swaying trees, shutting off its bright searchlight as it ferried away.

Was that Dee being hauled into the chopper? Hodge felt the life go out of him. They had come so far and worked so hard. How were they going to find them now?

Darkness swept over the johnboat like a peaceful wave. Duval could hear the frogs again and mosquitoes buzzing around his head. In the slow and defeated slap of paddles, with the bungeed flashlight guiding their course, they soon reached the submerged house where the woman had been rescued. Floodwater had risen as high as the rain gutters, and the raised porch and front door were underwater.

"Gotta be their house," Duval declared glumly. "Give me your flashlight. I'ma go up on this roof and see what it be like."

They steadied the boat alongside the gutter and Duval tied the rope to a rainspout. He took the flashlight from a silent Hodge and climbed onto the roof. The helicopter had washed the surface clear of leaves and he had no trouble negotiating the incline. Blankets and the contents of a gym bag had been scattered all around the roof. Among the T-shirts and other clothing he found a woman's wet bathing suit, ripped at the crotch, and a pair of torn shorts. Jesus, what had happened here?

He strode up to the peak of the house and strafed the other side with his flashlight beam. A small dog was lying on its side and it looked dead from where he was standing. At first he thought the little thing had drowned. Then his light revealed a long trail of blood on the shingles. He walked down for a closer look and saw the bloody, matted hair and nasty gash in the dog's belly. Flies were buzzing all around her beautiful golden coat. Had she been cut by flying glass during the storm? He recognized the little collie now. The children talked about her all the time. She belonged to the old Creole lady who lived next door.

A voice said, "Hey, bruh!" and it startled him. He turned full circle, pointing the light in every direction.

"Over here by the backyard," the voice said.

Duval aimed the light into the treetops. A homeboy wearing a black do-rag was clinging like a treed cat to the branches high up in one of the oaks.

"You looking for that lady and her two kids?" he said, his voice carrying strong in the heavy wet air. "The copter took them off."

Duval drove the light directly into his face. "What you doing out there, niggah?" he said.

"Just trying to hold on, bruh. You got a boat? The lady said her daddy was coming in a boat."

"You talked to her?" Duval held the light steady on him until homeboy raised a hand in front of his face.

"Lady said y'all would give me a lift out of this jam."

Duval knew what Hodge would say about that. Can't trust nobody. Might try to snag their boat. "You know where they taking them?" he asked the man.

"Prob'ly the Superdome. Where everybody at."

Duval walked back up the pitched roof to its peak. "Hey, Hodge, this bruhthuh say they taking them to the Superdome," he said, shining the light down into the johnboat.

Hodge had collapsed onto the duffel bag and was grabbing his chest. The pain had returned, like a fist to the solar plexus, only this time he couldn't find the medicine kit. It was too dark, and Duval had taken the flashlight. His left arm was numb and it felt as if someone had reached into his ribcage and squeezed his heart like a soft ripe fruit until the juice was running down his belly.

"Hodge!" Duval shouted, making small quick steps down the roof. He hopped into the boat and seized the old man by the shoulders. "What I do, man?" he said, shaking him. "Tell me what I do!"

Hodge tried to tell Duval about the nitro tablets in his medicine kit but the pain was so intense he couldn't form the words. The pain was worse than he'd ever felt it. Worse than the attack that had sent him to the ER.

"Where your meds?" Duval asked, trying to raise him up on the bench. It only made the fist squeeze harder. "Come on, man, talk to me!"

He ripped into the duffel bag, searching for those pills he'd seen Hodge slip under his tongue. He found the medicine kit and unzipped it with trembling fingers. "We gonna find you a hospital, ah-ight? They'll fix you up, man." He fumbled with the cap of the plastic bottle. "Just don't fucking die on me, Hodge. Ya heard me? Don't leave me out here in the dark to paddle this fucking boat all by myself."

He placed the flashlight on the duffel bag so he could see what he was doing and dumped tiny pills into his hand and tried to feed one into Hodge's slack mouth. But the old man was unconscious now and drooling down his chin. He didn't seem to be breathing anymore.

# 21

When the Coast Guard pilot brought the helicopter down on the wide plaza of the Superdome, he announced to his crew that central command was grounding all flights until further notice because of reports that choppers were being fired upon by snipers. "Who the hell is shooting at our birds?" asked one of the men in neon orange. Dee and her children were the lucky ones rescued on the final mission of the night. Thousands would remain stranded in sweltering attics and on dark rooftops and interstate overpasses.

They weren't the only civilians aboard the Jayhawk. The crew had pulled three people off a roof below Gentilly Boulevard, on Lavender Street—a woman and her teenaged son and the woman's disabled mother. EMTs were waiting for them on the ground with a wheelchair. Dee and the children thanked and hugged their rescuers, and in a fog of diesel fumes they followed the wheelchair toward the rear entrance of the Dome.

Three National Guardsmen were stationed at the handicap ramp. "Do you or your children need medical attention?" asked a tall black guardsman with a rifle slung over his shoulder. He was wearing camo fatigues and a military fatigue cap, and he stood in a pool of light from a butane gas lantern.

"No," Dee said, aware too late it was the wrong answer. "But we're hungry and thirsty and we've been stuck on a roof for four hours." The Coast Guard crewmen had given them bottled water but had nothing to eat.

"I'm sorry, ma'am," he said, "this is the entrance for people with special needs—if you're hurt or need meds."

Dee watched an EMT roll the old lady in the wheelchair up the ramp and through a dark entranceway, her daughter and grandson at her side. "Then how do we get in?" she asked, glancing up at the lurking dark silhouette of the Dome.

In the lantern light she could see that the guardsman looked exhausted himself. "You don't really want to go inside this place, ma'am," he said. "It's a zoo in there. The toilets are broken and people are walking around in their own filth. Fights are breaking out. Females assaulted. I advise you to wait until more help shows up and we get control of the situation."

Dee didn't know whether to be touched by his sincerity or outraged at the hopelessness of what he was saying. "Where the hell are we supposed to wait until Jesus shows up?" she asked him, sounding more angry than she intended. "Back out there in eight feet of water?" She wondered if they would've been better off staying on their roof until her Daddy arrived.

The guardsman shook his head and gazed off toward another Coast Guard chopper landing on the heliport, where a second team of EMTs was waiting with a gurney. "I wish I knew what to tell you, ma'am," he said, raising his voice to be heard above the whistling rotor. "All I know is what I've seen inside this place since last night, and it's dangerous. Word is they found a little girl with her throat slit in one of the bathrooms." He was looking at Ashley with concern. "It's nowhere to take your children."

"I know this much," Dee said, cocking her hip. "If it was all rich uptown white folk stranded in this Dome, George Bush would've already sent limousines and a cruise ship to pick everybody up."

The three guardsmen exchanged glances and chuckled. "You got *that* right," one of them said.

"Ma'am, please go around to the front of the Dome and wait for the buses," said the tall one, who seemed to be in charge. "We're told they're on their way."

As they set off into darkness, LaMarcus pulled the flashlight from his backpack and pointed its beam at the gigantic curved structure. In Dee's mind she pictured a huge dark suffocating human warehouse with roving gangs like the ones she'd encountered out on the interstate. The guardsman was right. It was not where she wanted to stay overnight with two small children. But where else could they go? At least this elevated plaza was high above the flooding. And with the National Guard nearby, she felt safer than she did on an isolated rooftop with a rapist roaming in the shadows.

They wandered past rows of rain-washed vehicles with City of New Orleans insignias, their windshields blown in by Katrina's winds. Dee took the flashlight from her son and shined it around the cars, exposing a gleaming frost of glass.

"I'm tired, Momma," Ashley complained, slapping her feet on the concrete as if she was wearing oversized clown shoes. "When are we gonna stop somewhere and sleep?"

"We're all tired, baby," Dee said. She could hear her mother's voice in the back of her head telling her to keep moving, no matter what. "We've got a ways to go, so keep it together, child. No whining."

She shined the light on her son's face and he winced, ducking his head. "How about you, Mr. Wizard?" she asked him. "How you holding up?"

LaMarcus walked along in silence, staring up at the colossal convex outline of the Dome looming in the night. "Momma, did you know that the Superdome is six hundred and eighty feet in diameter and holds seventy thousand seats?"

She smiled at him. One of a million trivial facts he'd stored in his beautiful noggin. "My brainiac," she said, squeezing the back of his neck. She admired anyone who could be consoled by mathematics at a time like this.

They walked on until they came upon a squadron of National Guardsmen huddled in a halo of emergency lights from the upscale shopping mall near the plaza. Ashley tugged at her mother's T-shirt, saying, "Who are all these people, Momma?"

Refugees were straggling across the plaza from the flooded regions of the city. They'd been wading for hours through the deep waters that had swallowed their homes, and they were wet and exhausted and dragging black leaf bags stuffed with all that remained of their possessions. By the time Dee and her children had reached the group of guardsmen, a dozen arguments had already broken out between the men in uniform and the growing crowd.

"I'm sorry, people, but we're not admitting anybody else into the Superdome tonight," announced a stocky white guardsman with sergeant stripes on his camo sleeve. "There are twenty thousand people in there right now and they've run out of food and water. Conditions have deteriorated," he said, holding up his hands to quiet the chatter. "It's nearly dark inside and the roof has collapsed in one area and violence has broken out. We can't ensure your safety if you go in there. So please cooperate with us. We're trying to make other arrangements for you. The mayor is talking about opening up the convention center. But right now we don't have anything to offer."

There was a collective groan. "Tell me what I'm s'posed to do for my baby girl!" shouted a large young woman with an infant in her arms. Although the night was warm, she'd wrapped the baby in a cotton blanket and bounced it against her breasts. "She have a fever and I got no medicine to give her! What you gone do 'bout my baby girl?"

Others began shouting at the guardsmen. Outnumbered, they quickly formed a protective circle, sliding their rifles off their shoulders and bracing them across their chests. The sergeant attempted to answer questions, raising his hands again and saying, "One at a time, please." But the insults were being hurled at him like bricks, a hostile barrage of cursing and pleading and hysterical tears.

"You not doing your job, soldier boy!" shouted a toothless old man wearing a long stained shirt and white baseball cap. "Making us stand around out here and wait for some thugs to whip up on us and take all we got left!"

The sergeant stood his ground as the crowd surrounded him and his platoon. "Buses are coming," he assured them. "They'll take every one of you to a safer shelter!"

Dee glanced around the impatient crowd. Some of them wanted to believe the sergeant and sat down on the plaza to rest their weary legs.

"What about that mall over there?" shouted a feisty older woman with multicolored bits of cloth tied to her dreadlocks. Her long African robe was spattered with mud. "Why don't you put us up in there till the buses come?"

"I'm sorry, ma'am, but that's a private shopping mall and it's off limits," said the sergeant, glancing over at the glass entrance. "They've shut it down tight."

"Then go kick them doors down, baby," she said with a hip-swaggering laugh. "Come on, now, we'll help you. Me and my grandsons here." Three surly teenage boys all wearing basketball jerseys that reached their knees. "You the law out here now, baby. You got the guns. Who's gonna get up in your face? Go 'head and make the call."

A cry of approval went up. The crowd cheered her on.

"Their security guards won't let anybody inside, ma'am," said the sergeant. "They're concerned about looting."

"You're too hung up on *don't* and *won't*," the woman said. "Times like this, everybody's got to be flexible. There's plenty room inside that mall for every living soul out here! I'm not gonna try on their Guccis. I just want a soft patch of carpet under my derrière till our coach arrives."

Dee looked over at the mall's domed entrance and saw a lone figure stationed behind the glass doors. "Come on, y'all," she said, taking her children by the hand. "Let's go see if we can talk our way in. Do your best to look pitiful, okay?"

"That won't be hard for Ashley," LaMarcus said.

"I'll slap your face, boy," his sister said. She was so sleepy she could hardly keep her eyes open.

"Okay, you two, *focus!*" Dee said, giving their hands an admonishing squeeze.

They crossed the concrete walkway that bridged the plaza and the mall. Standing in a portico of light at the mall's elegant entrance was a middle-aged black man wearing a dark blue security guard uniform. There was a set of heavy glass doors between him and the outside world. Dee stood so close her breath was fogging the glass.

"Can we please rest in there for a little while, mister, until the buses come?" she said in a loud voice. She peered down at her children, who stood silently on each side of her, holding her hands and looking frightened and on the verge of tears. "Please, sir, we won't bother anything. Just let us sleep on the floor somewhere. It might start raining out here again."

"I'm sorry, ma'am, I cain't do that." His voice was muffled by the doors between them. "Orders from management. I cain't let nobody in."

Dee heard a ruckus and turned to see the large woman in the African robe marching across the walkway with her grandsons and a score of others. When she turned back around, the security guard had trotted off to retrieve two other guards stationed farther back in the dim-lit lobby. Sensing a confrontation, the three guards rushed toward the glass doors with hands on their holsters.

"Let's get out of here," Dee said to the children, leading them quickly away. The guards were armed and she didn't want to get caught up in the explosive intensity of the moment.

"Momma, can we help crazy ribbon lady break into this place?" LaMarcus asked, tugging at her hand.

Dee glanced back at the National Guardsmen circled together on the plaza. They saw what was happening but made no effort to move from their position.

"No, honey," she said. "This could get real ugly."

As she hurried them away, the children kept turning to watch the confrontation. The hostile crowd was pounding on the glass doors, their numbers growing and threatening bloodshed. Dee urged them along until they'd reached the outer darkness of the plaza, where the mall's backup generator lights had no effect and nighttime surrounded them. They found themselves standing alone near the safety wall, staring out into a shadow world of tall buildings rising in the moonlight. New Orleans was dead. She had never seen the city like this before.

LaMarcus directed his flashlight at the street twenty feet below the plaza. "Hey, Momma," he said, "it doesn't look like there's any water down there."

Dee followed the flashlight beam as LaMarcus moved it slowly across a wide track of shattered plate glass that had fallen from nearby hotel windows. Her son was right. The streets were not flooded in this part of the city. "Amazing," she said, wondering if the grassy levees along the Mississippi River had held strong against Katrina.

Ashley was the first to hear the sobbing. "Somebody's crying, Momma," she said, turning a half circle to look around in the darkness.

Dee heard the sound now, too, and took the flashlight from LaMarcus and pointed it to where the sobs were coming from. The light caught the faint trace of a figure standing near the edge of the plaza.

"Stay close behind me," Dee whispered to the children.

She felt their small hands gripping the hip pockets of her shorts as she slowly approached the crying woman. "Hello there," Dee said in a brave voice. "Is everything all right?"

Closer now, she saw it was the heavy young woman with the blanket-draped baby. She was holding the bundle against her breasts and swaying back and forth, tears glistening on her soft cheeks in the directed light. Dee stopped a few feet away and studied her. She wasn't much older than a teenager, with thick bare legs and a loose white T-shirt covering her bulging upper body. She rocked the baby as she stared back at Dee, unable to speak through the tears.

"Everything's gonna be okay, darling," Dee told her, offering her hand. "The buses will be here soon and we'll all get some food and water. Your baby will be just fine. "

There was a deep and inconsolable pain in the mother's wet eyes. She backed away from Dee and stepped up onto the safety wall. It was a long deadly drop to the street below.

"How is your baby feeling?" The young mother mentioned a fever. "Is it all right if I hold her?" Dee asked with a forced smile, desperate to say something—anything—that would comfort her. "Tell me her name."

The young woman began to cry even harder. "Her name Laquita," she said, rocking the baby against her chest.

"Why don't you let my daughter and me hold Laquita?" Dee said. Ashley was still clinging to Dee's hip pocket but peeking around her mother, watching the woman on the wall. "We both love babies. Is it okay if we hold her?"

Dee steadied the flashlight on the woman and they stared at each other in some primal, unspoken understanding between mothers. *We hold each other's babies. When things are bad, we help each other out.* Dee was smiling calmly at her and struggling to connect in any way possible. She feared what was going to happen if she couldn't talk this poor distraught girl down from the wall. But just when Dee thought all was lost, the young woman sniffed and managed to speak. "You have two beautiful chil'ren," she said in the sweetest voice. "God has been good to you."

"Thank you, darling," Dee said, handing the flashlight to Ashley and stepping closer. "He's been good to you, too. Children are a blessing."

The woman wiped the tears from her face. "My baby was born early and small-like," she said. "She haven't took to my milk."

Dee remembered how awkward it had been with LaMarcus until the two of them got better at it. "My oldest was the same way," she said. "It takes practice, doesn't it?"

"I didn't know what to do when the water come up so fast," the young woman said. "I started walking from the Lower Nine with my baby in this blanket. A nice man and his boy caught us up in they boat, brought us over thisaway. Said everything would be all right in the Dome."

They stood within arm's reach of each other, the young woman only a step away from backing up into oblivion. "The buses will get here soon and everything will be just fine, darling," Dee assured her, reaching out for the bundle. "Let me hold Laquita while you catch your breath."

There was a tense moment when the woman drew back, holding the baby tighter to her chest. But then something released inside her and she took a deep shuddering breath, closing her eyes and blinking away the tears flowing down her cheeks. When she opened her eyes again, she looked down at Dee with a haunting desolation and held out the bundled baby for her to take. Dee smiled and received the baby in her arms, but instantly she knew something was wrong. The small body inside the blanket was limp and lifeless, and when Dee touched the child's tiny gaunt face, her skin was cold and there was no sign of a pulse.

"Oh my God, I'm so sorry," Dee said, filled with grief herself as she glanced up at the young woman and noticed that her T-shirt was yellowed by milk that had gone sour.

The woman took another trembling breath, smiled sadly at Ashley, and turned to face the darkness. Then she stepped over the ledge and dropped into the deep pocket of night.

# 22

Hodge woke to find himself floating through a dark wood. He wasn't certain he was still alive until he heard the feathery sound of his own shallow breathing. He realized he'd pissed himself and was slumped against the duffel bag in a slop of floodwater and urine, bringing back memory fears of lying facedown in the patrol boat while tracers fired over his head. He tucked in his chin and tried to collect his thoughts. The fist had let go of his heart, giving him breath again, but he sensed that spasms of pain were only a few ragged beats away.

A dark figure was paddling the johnboat through the grim flooded streets, and when the man turned to gaze down at Hodge, his eyes burned like the eyes of all the dead men he'd known in that war long ago. Unless this was a dream, they had taken on another passenger. His head was wrapped in a shiny black do-rag and he sat on the front bench, stroking the water with long muscular arms. Where was he taking him? Not that it mattered anymore. Dee and the children were gone now and he would never find them in all this darkness and ruin.

They passed a huge white house where candles were burning in every window and overfed cats perched on sills and on top of a tall chifferobe, dozens of them watching the boat go by. "Where we at?" he heard himself ask, the words echoing underneath this heavy canopy of silence.

The dark stranger turned and stared down at him again. "You told me he was dead," he said, his eyes like white-hot coals.

"Hodge, you ah-ight, man? I thought you winked out on us."

Duval was sitting on the back bench in the steering position, which meant they would never find their way out of this dark wilderness.

"Water," Hodge said.

Duval reached down for one of the bottles rolling underfoot and twisted off the cap for him. "We taking you to a hospital," he said. "Bound to be one still open. You gotta get checked out, ya heard me?"

Hodge held the bottle in a shaky hand and drank, his dry throat choking on the lukewarm water. He tried to sit up but couldn't find the strength. His left arm was numb and his ankle stung where the Honda's window glass had cut him. He felt feverish and wondered if all this dirty floodwater had caused an infection. On his second attempt, he managed to raise his head high enough to make out shapes in the foggy glow of the flashlight bungeed to the prow. The bloated body of a Rottweiler was floating past them in a nest of tangled sticks. He thought he could hear other dogs howling deep beneath the water itself, and then he realized they were human voices calling from somewhere back in the dark neighborhood, stranded people begging for help.

Up ahead, a pile of debris was drifting toward them with a man standing on top, outlined in the burning light from a tiki torch. He thrust his wreckage along using a long bamboo cane pole, and when he drew closer, Hodge saw it was a makeshift raft fashioned from a stack of plywood and aluminum siding roped down on bobbing beer kegs. He was a large, heavyset white man wearing what looked like an old railway porter's cap and a grimy white uniform shirt with a patch on one sleeve. Buttons were missing on the shirt, and his gray chest hair and beard were smeared with soot.

"I'm here to pick them up," he said, poling slowly in their direction.

A long silence passed. Duval said, "Better get yourself to someplace dry, mistah. That pile of junk you riding on is gonna come all to pieces pretty soon."

It was a miracle that the raft was still afloat, its rickety deck sinking and rising, muddy water washing across the man's heavy boots as his pole plunged deep into the mire. "I never seen nothing like this," he announced, grunting with every pole thrust. "Betsy. Camille. I been through 'em all. Nowdays I go where the Lord sends me. And he sent me here to save whoever I can."

He reminded Duval of some homeless old coot begging for spare change with a cardboard sign. "Put some thought into saving yourself, my man," he said.

The boatman was wheezing through his open mouth, his hairy chest heaving. "Come with me," he said. "The Lord needs your boat tonight."

"The Lord's gonna have to find his own boat," Duval said. "Got a sick man over here. Nearly died on us. We gotta find a hospital."

The two vessels pulled alongside each other and the old boatman raised the burning tiki torch to get a better look at Hodge hunched against the duffel bag. "The hospitals are under siege," the man said. "Junkies breaking in, stealing drugs. You'll never get past them. They'll kill you for this boat."

He rubbed his dirty beard and looked doubtfully at Hodge. "Godspeed, brother," he said. "I'll be seeing you again, by and by."

Duval watched the man pole his mangled raft into deepening darkness. "How you s'pose that thing hang together in one piece like that?" he asked no one in particular.

"Let's get the fuck on away from here," the stranger said, dipping his paddle.

There was light ahead, and when they emerged from the residential trees into wide Gentilly Boulevard, they came upon two buildings burning down to the waterline, a Tower record store on one side of the street and a Walgreen's on the other. Flames were rising from their rooftops and sparks swarmed like fiery insects over the waterway that was once a street.

"Keep her steady down the middle of the road, Duval, and we'll slide right on through," Hodge said, struggling to pull himself onto the middle bench.

The two men paddled hard and Duval did his best to steer the boat straight, relying on submerged street signs as their guideposts. No Left Turn. Speed Limit 30. Caught in the blazing crosswind, they could feel the intense heat now, the smoke dark and oily and billowing out of the shattered glass walls of the record store, rolling across the water like a dense black fog. Hodge began to cough and choke. "Paddle like you got a pair!" he shouted in a hoarse voice.

Glowing ash floated all around them and burning cinders rained down into the boat. The stranger brushed them off himself, yelling, "We gonna burn up, niggah!"

"Keep paddling, son," Hodge said, coughing from the smoke sucked into his lungs. He leaned over the gunnel and dipped his cap in floodwater, dousing the red embers searing into the plywood. "Too late to turn back now."

In another forty yards they'd escaped the worst of the smoke and heat and falling ash. They rested their paddles in their laps and let the boat drift into the darkness near Dillard University. The stranger removed his smoking shirt and shook it out. Hodge noticed scratch marks on his arms and a nasty bite on the side of his face. It looked as if he'd been in a fight with a vicious animal.

"We get anywhere near dry land," the stranger said to Duval, "I'm bailing out of this crate. You can find a fucking hospital for the old man your own self."

Duval poured bottled water over the burn holes in his hoodie sleeves. He was still breathing heavy. "Yo, bruh, it's solid, you helping us out here," he said contritely. "We couldn'ta made it this far without another pair of arms."

"I'm just sayin'—"

"Give me your paddle," Hodge said in a weak voice. He was slumped over on the middle bench, head down, elbows branched across his knees. He looked like he didn't have the strength to swat a fly.

"Chill, Hodge," Duval said. "We got this."

“I’m good,” Hodge said, raising his chin. “I can paddle.”

“Just chill, ah-ight? I’m not gonna let you die on me, man. I’m already in deep enough shit with Dee.”

The johnboat had drifted near the iron fence surrounding the Dillard campus grounds. Duval pointed the flashlight beam through the fence at the sunken arcade of oak trees that stretched toward the tall white columns of the university’s main hall. He had once worked there as a custodian and had swept and mopped those dorm rooms more times than he cared to remember. This was where he’d met Dee that day in the library, when she mistook him for a student. He didn’t exactly lie to her, but he didn’t tell her the truth. She was an innocent nineteen-year-old girl from the sticks, a little on the heavy side, with beautiful eyes and a radiant smile. He’d never been with a college girl before and he wanted to see what it was like. They made love in her dorm room whenever they could get away with it, and she opened a new world to him. He had always liked to read books and she gave him more books, different music to listen to, another way of looking at things. He’d never met a girl as smart as Dee Grant. Which was why he was afraid to show her how he lived when they weren’t together. The ghetto life in the St. Bernard Housing Project only a few blocks from her dorm. Bros and hoes and getting crunk every night. Rolling with rappers, cutting tapes till all hours. Crack cocaine.

That’s how it went during their four years together. Not exactly a lie, not exactly the truth. In and out of her bed, breaking promises, slamming doors, begging for forgiveness. She wanted the kind of marriage her parents had. He was too busy living that other life. Even when she cried and said she loved him. Even when she carried his babies.

Most mornings he couldn’t look himself in the mirror for the way he did that girl. The mother of his children. Every time he tried to man up, be the father he never had, something came along and turned his head.

"Listen to me, son." Hodge's voice had deepened into a smoky whisper. "We gotta go to Plan B. Which means we get on down to the Dome. That's most likely where they've taken them."

Duval shined the flashlight on him. He looked like a man spitting blood between his knees. How many ticks were left in his busted old ticker? If they didn't find him a doctor soon, he was going to be just one more floating corpse tied to a tree.

"You don't seem to understand the situation here," Duval said. "We cain't go looking for Dee with you blacking out all the time. You gotta see a doctor, first things first."

"I can make it to the Dome," Hodge said, his words slow and groggy. "We'll find them. Take them back to the truck in Metairie and go home."

The stranger turned on his bench to regard Hodge, then Duval. His face was somber and his eyes were still burning. He held the paddle in his hands like a club. "I don't give a fuck about your plan or what you niggahs do when you hook up with somebody," he said. "I just want out of this fucking storm water fast as I can. Stop chirpin' and let's bounce."

He faced forward again and started paddling, and Duval plugged the earpiece into his ear and took up his paddle as well. WWL was still on the air, broadcasting news reports nonstop. The New Orleans police chief was saying there was rampant looting and raping and rioting all over the city. Snipers were shooting at cops and rescue workers. The Lower Ninth Ward had been completely destroyed by levee breaches along the Industrial Canal. Senior citizen homes in St. Bernard Parish were demolished by the tidal flood and everybody had drowned. Streams of people had made their way to the Superdome all day long, as many as ten thousand wading from the flooded neighborhoods and brought in by boat. The Dome was unable to take any more, so the mayor was sending city workers to open up the convention center. And then Duval heard something he really didn't want to hear. The hospitals had lost power and backup generators were beginning to fail. Patients were dying from the heat and lack of drinking water and depleted oxygen supplies and shut-down life-support systems. *Where was the Red Cross?* the reporter asked, his voice cracking in an emotional plea. *Why so few National Guard? Were most of them in Iraq? Had anybody seen a New Orleans cop on the job? Where were the buses that FEMA had promised? Why wasn't somebody doing something?*

They searched for open water routes that would lead them south toward downtown and the hospital district. The street signs meant nothing to them. They passed the old French mansions engulfed along Esplanade and discovered scrapped grocery carts and submerged automobiles underneath the elevated interstate. Duval kept an eye on the old man. He was sitting upright, more or less, and staring out at the shabby houses and corner storefronts boarded up along Claiborne Avenue.

"I can hear them now, too," Hodge said finally, his words breaking the long silence. "They're all around us."

"Say what?" Duval asked, removing the earpiece.

"I used to hear them in the Delta sometimes," Hodge said. "The voices of the dead. Thought I was through with all that."

Duval listened hard for several hushed moments. Frogs were croaking and a slight wind rustled the leaves high in the standing trees. The stranger said, "This dude buggin' like that crazy old fool on the trash pile."

Dark silhouettes were moving through the floodwater ahead. They had appeared out of nowhere in the swamped streets. "They's people out there, Hodge," he said. "You hearing people, man. That's all."

The water was shallower in this part of the city, only crotch deep, and he could see them wading through the tunnel darkness underneath the I-10 overpass.

*"Hey, y'all got room in that boat for me and my girls?"*

A woman was staring into their flashlight beam.

*"You got clean water to drink?"* The burning tip of a cigarette was

coming toward them from another direction. "*We dyin' from thirst, dawg.*"

Hodge thought it best to distance themselves from these roving bands. "Keep paddling, boys," he said. "Don't slow down."

Suddenly they were under attack. Shadow figures were grabbing the gunnels and rocking them from side to side. Too many of them to handle. A deep male voice said, "*Let me in that boat, bruh. I been wading in this shit all day long and I cain't wade no more.*"

Somebody was pulling on Duval's sleeve, his hood. He shrugged him off, saying, "Let go, ya heard me! We cain't help you right now. We gotta get this man to a hospital."

A teenager wearing a backwards cap and long white T-shirt bellied onto a gunnel and tried to wiggle his way into the boat. The stranger smashed him in the head with his paddle and the boy cried out and flopped back into the water. "Don't come up in here, niggah," the stranger said. "I will take you out."

Hands were reaching across the dead outboard motor, tearing at Duval's baby dreads, and he swiveled around and swung his paddle, cracking skull. In the wobbling flashlight beam he could see it was a young girl not much older than Ashley. The blow had knocked her away and she was wailing in pain.

"*Oughta be ashamed of yo'self,*" somebody said, "*hitting a little girl like that.*"

Duval was horrified by what he'd done. He tried to apologize to the girl but her mother wrenched the paddle out of his hands and jabbed him in the chest with the butt end. Others were gripping his arms and hood, trying to drag him into the water.

In the violent rocking motion of the boat, Hodge pitched over backwards onto the duffel bag and went digging for the old Colt handgun, having no choice but to scare these frantic people away. He was groping through the bag, searching for the pistol, when he saw the stranger pull a knife from his waistband and slash at a raggedy man climbing aboard. The man howled from the gash across his shoulder and wrestled with the stranger, and a flurry of punches flew from out of the darkness. A woman screamed, "*You do us that way, motherfucker!*" Waders were fighting to haul the stranger overboard and the boat listed badly, taking on water. Hodge was tossed from one side to the other and lost his grip on the duffel bag. With the strength of numbers, the waders rocked and dipped the gunnels until the starboard sank underwater. Hodge tried to hang onto a bench but the johnboat flipped up and over, capsizing quickly, and he found himself trapped underneath.

He'd swallowed a mouthful of water and could taste gasoline leaking from the outboard engine. He gagged and sputtered and tried to find an air pocket under the boat, straining to lift the shell that encased him. In his panic he banged his head against a bench and everything went into woozy slow motion, and at that moment he thought he would surely drown. He made one last desperate lunge toward the side of the johnboat and felt a hand grab his arm and pull hard, helping him scuttle his way out. Duval had managed to raise the boat high enough to set him free.

When Hodge stood up in the water, gasping for air, his legs went rubbery on him and he collapsed against Duval for support. They stood holding each other, soaked to the bone, Hodge's beloved johnboat upside down, the duffel bag nowhere in sight. People were shouting at each other in the dark. A fight had broken out and Hodge could see the stranger slashing at shadows with his knife. There was a strong reek of gasoline all around them.

"Let's get the fuck out of here," Duval said.

"My boat!" Hodge said, clutching Duval's arm. The boat he'd sawed and glued and sanded to perfection. It was like another child to him.

"Let it go, man," Duval said. "Let 'em have it. We cain't fight the whole world."

"My boat," Hodge said again, only this time with the full weight of loss in his voice.

It was a struggle to lead the tall lanky old man away from the crowd and the capsized johnboat. Duval set his shoulder up under

Hodge's armpit, slung an arm around him, and forced him onward into the darkness. Hodge kept turning to look back at his boat. They could hear them fighting over it. A cigarette tip glowed bright red, someone taking the last deep drag before flicking it into the air. There was a quick whump as it touched off the floating gasoline. Fire raced across the bobbing hull and shadow figures scattered away from the flames, voices screaming in anger and panic. Hodge and Duval stood silently in water crotch deep, watching the old johnboat burn.

# 23

Dee took the dead baby to the group of National Guardsmen huddled on the plaza and told them what had happened. Their squad leader dispatched four men to go look for the young woman's body on the street below. He didn't know what to do with the small bundle and appeared reluctant to accept the baby or to touch it in any way.

"Her name is Laquita," Dee said, trembling as she spoke. Her children stood beside her, silent and shaken. "Please take her. File a report, or whatever you're supposed to do. I can't hold her anymore."

The squad leader ordered one of his female troops to receive the baby. "We may need to speak to you again as an eyewitness," he said to Dee.

"Fine," she said, "but I may not be around when you come looking for me. Since y'all can't provide anything for us, I've got to go find my children a safe place to spend the night."

Dee wandered away from the guardsmen in a tearful daze, the children taking her by the hands as if guiding a shell-shocked survivor of a bomb blast.

"How did the baby die, Momma?" Ashley asked in a tiny voice.

"I don't really know," Dee said. "Her mother was having a hard time feeding her. I imagine there was something wrong with the poor thing and her mother didn't know how to deal with it. She wasn't much more than a child herself."

Dee didn't know where they were going. She had no plan, no destination. They walked along in a tense silence toward the outer darkness. She felt so tired and burdened by this day that she stopped and sat down on the concrete and gathered LaMarcus and Ashley to her side. She was going to hold her children for as long as it took them to believe they would survive this awful day.

"Momma, you would never do that, would you?" LaMarcus asked, his face buried against her damp arm.

"Do what, honey?"

"Leave us like that."

"No, hon, I'm never gonna leave you," she said, patting the side of his face. "Not now, not even when you're forty years old. I'll be living with you and your wife and children, making sure you brush your teeth every morning before you go off to teach calculus."

His giggle was sweet and warm. It made her smile.

"What about me, Momma?" Ashley asked with a petulant shake of her mother's other arm.

"You're gonna be a movie star, babe. Remember?"

"*Boo*-ya," Ashley said to her brother. "I won't need my Momma telling me when to brush my teeth."

The three of them sat together in an exhausted doze, propping up one another like the slanted poles of a teepee, the concrete hard and unyielding underneath them. A helicopter was landing somewhere in the distance.

"How is Pawpaw going to find us now?" Ashley asked.

Dee had been worried about that herself. "Maybe the phones will be back in service tomorrow," she said. She'd stored her cell phone in Ashley's backpack. "We'll call Pawpaw and tell him where we are, and he'll come get us." Even as she said this, she knew it wouldn't happen that way.

"What if the phones don't work tomorrow?" Ashley said.

"Daddy will find us," LaMarcus said confidently, resting his back against his mother.

"Daddy doesn't come see us even when he knows where we live," Ashley said. "He won't come looking for us now."

"You don't know squat about Daddy," LaMarcus said. "So why don't you shut your big fat pie hole?"

"Momma!"

"Give it a rest, now, both of you," Dee said. "We're in public, for God's sake."

She looked around the dark plaza and laughed at herself for sounding exactly like her mother. Hundreds of displaced people were camped all around them. Some kind of *public*.

In a short while, a handful of guardsmen began circulating through the camps, distributing MREs. Meals Ready to Eat. A flashlight shone in her face. "Hey there, ma'am," said the guardsman who knelt down to hand them pouches of food. It was the same tall black man who'd refused to let them enter the Dome with the medical cases. "How are you and your children holding up?"

"Oh, we're having the sleepover of our lives," Dee said.

Her sarcasm dampened his good cheer. He smiled shyly. "I'm sorry it's this way, ma'am," he said. "I wish there was something I could do."

"You can start by not calling me ma'am. I'm not your grandmother."

In this fragile light she could see he was a handsome man, even though his face sagged from fatigue and he needed a shave.

"What do you go by, then?" he asked her.

She considered whether or not to tell him. "Deidre Grant," she said finally. "Everyone calls me Dee."

"And what about these fine young children?"

She told him their names. LaMarcus was tearing open the food pouch with his teeth and said, "How do you eat this stuff?"

"With a spoon, my man," the guardsman said, finding it for him in the pouch. "Let me see which one you've got. Okay, spaghetti and meat sauce. Applesauce. Some crackers and spread. Pound cake. Mmm, you hit the jackpot, LaMarcus."

LaMarcus giggled because the man had actually listened to his name. He spooned into the applesauce and made a dramatic moment of smacking his lips. "Not exactly Chili's," he said, his idea of fine dining.

The guardsman swatted LaMarcus affectionately on the shoulder and stood up. "You take care of yourself and these beautiful children, Miz Grant," he said.

She tried to return his smile, but she felt dirty and ugly and ten pounds overweight. "What's *your* name?" she asked him, squinting to see if he was wearing a ring.

"Robert Guyton," he said, spelling his last name. "I'm from Ville Platte. You know where that is?"

She nodded. "My Daddy lives in Opelousas," she said. "Just down the road."

"Soon as we all get out of this Katrina mess, Miz Grant, I'll treat you and the kids and your daddy to supper in Opelousas." He smiled down at Ashley. "How's that suit you, young lady?"

Ashley dug her spoon into the spaghetti packet. "That'll work," she said.

"Maybe so, Robert Guyton," Dee said. "If I can get a shower first."

The guardsman walked away to hand out more MREs, and the three of them finished their meals in silence, ravenous and too tired to speak. Dee knew there were soldiers in Iraq who were eating out of these pouches at this very moment, halfway across the world. She felt like she was fighting her own war tonight.

Ashley cuddled with her stuffed wiener dog named Otis and soon fell asleep against her mother's shoulder, drooling a little down her arm, and LaMarcus played quietly on the small lighted square of his Game Boy until Dee said in a soft voice, "Sweetheart, you should probably put that in your backpack. Somebody's liable to come by and try to take it from you."

LaMarcus quickly hid the Game Boy in the pack at his side and then slumped over without a word and laid his head on his mother's thigh, curling up against her and closing his eyes with a drowsy yawn. Dee's eyes grew heavy, but she was too vigilant and wary of their surroundings to give in to the warm seduction of sleep. She kept herself awake by forcing her mind to consider all the possibilities of where they might find shelter. She could no longer rely on her Daddy or the buses to arrive and take them to some faraway happy place. Whatever happened next was in her hands, and she would have to make every small decision count.

God, she wished her brother was here right now. PJ would know what to do. She wondered where he was at this hour. Was he living in the city anymore? He'd called about three months ago to ask how the children were doing. *You made two beautiful children, Dee. Momma was proud of those grandchildren.* That was the last she'd heard from him. An old high school friend had told her that PJ had gone to Detroit. Her father had heard a rumor that he was back in jail. It grieved her to think he was in trouble all the time, because she knew that deep down inside, her brother was a decent man. He'd always been her protector. She remembered the time she was being harassed every day at school by a gang of trashy girls—the kind of girls who hated anyone who made good grades, answered questions in class, and got along with their teachers. They'd cornered her one day at her locker and were pushing her around, calling her names and knocking her books to the floor. PJ showed up in that uncanny way he had of always knowing when his little sister needed him. He was big and tough and fearless, and he had no qualms about slamming one of the girls against the lockers. He told them if they ever threatened his sister again, or even spoke to her, he would come looking for them. And he told them to tell their boyfriends and brothers and the old bastards who'd raised them that if they had a problem with that, to meet him behind the football stands after school. He'd waited there for an hour, but no one showed up. And no one ever bothered Dee again.

She spent her teenage years worrying about her brother's temper and recklessness and his run-ins with the local cops. He'd hurt her feelings when he left home the first time and didn't tell her where he was going. She thought they were closer than that. When her Pops went driving to New Orleans every evening, searching for him, she begged to ride along and help him look. Her parents said no, she had homework to do. She was the good child who was going to be the first in their family to attend college.

She didn't visit PJ when he was in Dixon. Ashley was a baby and it was a two-hour drive. And to be honest, Dee didn't want to see her proud brother wearing prison grays.

The first time she'd ever seen him cry was at their mother's funeral. He told her to keep a close eye on LaMarcus and make sure he didn't grow up in the thug life. PJ promised he would stay in touch. True to his word, he phoned her every couple of months from a pay phone. He wouldn't tell her where he was living or how to contact him. *I'm here and gone, Dee,* he always said. *It's better if I call you.*

Bright lights and a roaring motor jolted her wide awake. Her first alert thought was that the buses had finally arrived. She heard someone nearby declare the same thing: "*The buses are here!*" An old man shouting again, "*The buses are here, y'all! Thank you, Jesus!*"

She rubbed her face and stared into the headlights of a monstrous vehicle rolling slowly across the plaza. LaMarcus sat up, yawning. "What is it, Momma?" he mumbled.

"The buses, baby," Dee said, hugging him. "Everything's gonna be all right now."

The vehicle stopped, its headlights flooding the darkness. Doors opened and men emerged in a tangle of equipment—cables and long boom microphones—and Dee realized it wasn't a bus but a large van with the CNN logo on its side and a satellite dish overhead. A tall thin white man wearing a navy blue windbreaker hopped out of the vehicle and made his way to the cluster of guardsmen and shook their squad leader's hand.

"It's not a bus, Momma," LaMarcus said. "It's the news."

One moment hope, the next moment despair. Dee watched the crew set up a stand of field lights, creating a circle of intense daylight that stretched far beyond their truck. The media had arrived.

Outsiders, professional analysts. Reporters and commentators whose lives would not be altered forever by this calamity.

"That's a nice roomy van you get to sleep in, baby," shouted the large woman dressed in an African robe who had led the unsuccessful march on the shopping mall. She'd risen from her campsite and was speaking in a grand voice as she sauntered toward the silver-haired young newsman in the blue windbreaker.

"I bet there's a hot meal waiting for you back in Baton Rouge when your program is over. And clean sheets in a swanky hotel with room service."

When he finally noticed her, the newsman unfolded his arms and stepped away from the National Guard unit to listen to what she was saying to him.

"But what's gonna happen to all these folk sleeping out here on this hard see-ment? And every miserable soul inside the Dome. When do we get a hot meal and a clean place to sleep? Tell me this, Mistah C-N-N. What's gonna happen to my people after y'all pack up your TV cameras and go on back home?"

The woman had cornered Anderson Cooper and she wasn't going to let him get away without a lecture and a series of demands. He seemed to be listening carefully, and at one point he motioned for the cameraman and the guy assembling the sound boom to get this on tape. She played to the camera with a sassy attitude, wagging her finger at the National Guardsmen nearby. People sleeping on the plaza were waking up now and cheering on the crazy lady with the colorful bits of cloth in her dreads.

The noise and lights had finally stirred Ashley and she pulled on her mother's arm, whining, "My butt hurts, Momma. When are we gonna find a real place to sleep?"

The woman threw up her arms in a grand theatrical manner and turned on her heels, storming away from the camera crew. Anderson Cooper looked surprised, and Dee was left with the impression that she'd terminated the interview midsentence. Her grandsons loped after her, trying to keep stride with the old lady whose muddy robe dragged along the plaza as she marched from camp to camp, entreating everyone to wake up.

"Come on, y'all, we're passing down to the convention center!" she intoned. "Don't worry, it ain't far. Mistah C-N-N says they're s'posed to have cots and food and clean water down there. Come on, now, we're not tolerating this kind of treatment another damn minute. They give us a pouch of dry food to keep our mouths shut and don't ax questions. Buy us off. That ain't working for me, y'all. Fussing with these weekend soldier boys is like fussing with Pharaoh's army. So get up on your feet and come with Sistah M and my boys. We're leaving out of this bitter place!"

She stalked through the plaza like some ancient priestess, imploring everyone to follow her down into the dark empty streets of the business district. When she reached Dee and the children, the old lady stopped and gazed down at Ashley. "I love those beads, *ma mignon*," she said, admiring the beadwork in Ashley's braided hair. "You're my kind of girl. How you getting along? My name is Miriam, but everybody calls me Sistah M," she said, extending her hand. Ashley reached up and took the woman's wet fleshy hand and let her pull her to her feet.

"Tell your momma to get up off that hard see-ment and come on with me and my tribe." She had a voice as deep as a man's and she was smiling a grandmotherly smile at them. "It cain't be any worse down there."

The people camped on the plaza had begun to rise and gather around with their carrying things. They looked dispirited and beaten down and exhausted beyond measure, but they were ready to follow her anywhere.

"Let's go with them, Momma," Ashley said, tugging on her mother's hand.

Dee watched four guardsmen appear out of the darkness, transporting a heavy black body bag between them. They had found the sad young mother who had jumped.

She glanced over at the news reporter and the platoon of

National Guardsmen staring at them like a bewildered army waiting for their marching orders on the shores of an invaded land. She knew the buses were never coming. These people didn't matter to anyone except each other. Their backs were against the sea. Like the dead girl, they were looking for a tatter of something to believe in. Their choice was to despair out here among the lies and deceptions, or to turn and follow the only voice offering them a promise and a prayer.

# 24

Light burned through his eyelids and woke him. He raised a hand to block the piercing ray. At first he thought that Jasmine or Edgar had taken the flashlight. "Where you going?" he said. "Put that light out."

"Who the fuck you talking to, niggah?" A dark presence was lurking behind the light. "What you doing in my bitch's bed?"

PJ sat up, still shielding his eyes. He had a feeling he knew who this was. "Your name Maceo?" he asked the man.

"You got that right. You owe Maceo some money, playuh? Where my bitch at?"

His light ranged across the sleeping children and settled on the girl named Jasmine. Her eyes opened slowly, blinking, distant. Baby Darius was lying on her chest.

The mattress was like a sponge now, waterlogged and useless, the flood only inches from washing across their bodies. PJ picked up the flashlight wedged against the sleeping Edgar and shined it in the man's face. Maceo winced and turned his head. "Take that light out my eyes 'fo I cap your ass," he said.

Edgar rolled over and mumbled something in his sleep. He was wearing the Saints cap and it had slipped over his eyes and nose. "Why don't we go talk in the kitchen?" PJ said. He didn't want the children to hear what had happened their mother.

"Tell me, do I *know* you, playuh?" Maceo said. "Hurricane or not, why you think you can walk into Maceo turf without paying him proper respeck?"

PJ swung his legs off the bed and dipped them into the lukewarm water. He ran the light up and down Maceo's slender frame. Baggy jeans, long white T-shirt to his knees, snap-brim golfer's cap on backwards. Gold bling around his neck, on his fingers, gold grille, getting his shine on. Niggah pimp written all over him. He was as tall as PJ, well over six feet, but looked fifty pounds lighter. The only advantage he had was the pistol bulging underneath his wet T-shirt.

"Your woman's in the bathroom," PJ said, rising from the bed. "Condition she was in when I got here."

Maceo waded into the dark bathroom, his flashlight beam jiggering in the cramped space. PJ stood in the doorway and watched him search around, then slide back the mildewed shower curtain. Floodwater was leaking over the ledge and into the tub like rainwater dripping from a clogged roof gutter. Maceo's light found the dead woman's gaunt face. He studied her in silence, his light lingering almost affectionately on her hard features. "You do this to her?" he asked in a solemn voice.

"No, dude. You did. You the one keeping her on the pipe."

The silence grew longer, Maceo gazing into the tub. "You come here looking for some pussy, playuh?" he asked, finally.

"I saw a light. I come here looking for food and a dry spot to crash. This is what it is."

He stepped out of Maceo's way as the man sloshed back into the bedroom and began tossing the mess on the dead woman's dresser, rummaging through her flung-open drawers. He was looking for what PJ had looked for. Cash.

"It ain't nothing there. Why don't we go discuss this in the kitchen?" PJ said for the second time.

"Nothing to discuss," Maceo said, flinging clothes out of the drawers.

"These children," PJ said. "Somebody needs to take them out of here before the water gets too much deeper. Who they daddy?"

Maceo laughed. "Got no clue, dawg. Sheree couldn't say, neither, far as I know."

PJ stared at the small fragile figures sleeping on the bed. "You need to take these children someplace dry," he said. "Least you can do for they momma."

Maceo straightened his shoulders and stared into the mirror above the dresser, his reflection weak and ghostly in the grim light. He exhaled impatiently, then turned and shined the flashlight on the bed. Jasmine closed her eyes, pretending to sleep, holding the diapered baby against her chest. Maceo waded closer to the bed, splashing a brown wave onto the mattress.

"Maceo taking this little bitch here," he said, his beam running up the baby's naked back and settling on Jasmine's face. "You can keep the other two."

Her eyes opened again and she sat up quickly. The baby stirred, whimpering in his sleep. "I ain't going nowhere without my brothers," she said, her voice groggy but defiant. "And I ain't going nowhere wichew."

Maceo laughed at the girl's boldness. "Yo, this li'l hot wing got flavor. She gonna make a tasty treat for my clientele," he said. "Get up off that bed, girl, and come on with Maceo. We gotta bounce 'fo Katrina rise up any worse in this house."

"I ain't going wichew," Jasmine said. "I know how you did my momma."

"Your momma need to make groceries, sweet thang, just like everybody else. She had to work for it. Like you gonna do."

Their voices had awakened Baby Darius and he was crying now. Jasmine rocked him in her arms and scooted against Edgar's small coiled body. She searched for PJ in the pale light, and he could see tears streaming down her cheeks.

Maceo reached down and snapped the tiny silver chain off her ankle and stuffed it into his pocket. "Come on, girl, don't be making Maceo *drag* your skinny ass outside in all this water," he said, grabbing her by the leg. "Leave that baby here. We gotta flow."

"Maceo," PJ said in a calm voice.

When the pimp squared around with an annoyed expression, PJ

hit him hard in the ribs just below his heart and felt something crack like a rotten fencepost. Maceo groaned and fell back against the dresser, gasping for air, reaching for the gun underneath his long tangled T-shirt. PJ raised back and smashed his flashlight across the pimp's forehead, scattering batteries and plastic, knocking off the golf hat. The man sank into a sitting position in two feet of water, and PJ stuck his hands underwater and removed the gun, which felt like a heavy .44 magnum, the kind Dirty Harry used. He set the huge pistol on the dresser and looked down at Maceo. He was immersed to his armpits in water, holding himself and panting, his flashlight glowing under the surface like a chunk of phosphorus.

"You busted something," Maceo managed to say through wheezing breaths.

PJ guessed he'd fractured a rib. He knew he'd hit this skinny fucker real hard, and it wasn't just Maceo he'd hit but U-Rite and the CO who'd shot him in the chest and the boatload of deputies who'd beaten up old Crocodile and the off-duty cop who'd killed D'Wayne and everybody whose face he'd wanted to smash since he was a snot-nosed boy Edgar's age.

"You try and get up," he told the pimp, reaching underwater for the flashlight, "it's gonna get a lot worse."

Maceo coughed and spit blood, and PJ wondered if the broken rib had punctured a lung.

"Why you come hard at Maceo, bruh?" he whined, his gold grille stained juicy red. "You wanna turn her out, go ahead, man. Take her. No use hating on ourselves over one li'l bitch."

"You talking about a little girl," PJ said. "I don't play that, pimp."

"I watched her taking a baff the other day. She ain't a little girl no more."

Jasmine covered her face with her hands, embarrassed by such talk.

"You know if your momma got any duct tape in a drawer somewhere?" PJ asked her.

She slid her hands away and looked at him through teary eyes. "What that?" she asked.

"Go find me some heavy tape," he said. "You got lamps in this house? Pull the plugs out of the wall sockets and yank the cords loose and bring them to me."

She was reluctant to leave the squalling baby on the bed, but PJ told her it would be okay and handed her Maceo's flashlight. She rose and waded off into the kitchen, moving with the slow fearful caution of a child who has wandered too near a dark swamp.

"Something wrong here, bruh," Maceo said, a voice in the darkness. It was pitch black now in the bedroom and PJ held onto the .44 magnum for safekeeping. "I cain't catch my breff. How come you hit Maceo so hard, man? Hit me like Mike Tyson. Maceo need a doctor, yo. You gonna let me sit here and croak in this fucking water?"

"Chill, balluh. You gonna live. Just don't be moving around too much."

Jasmine returned with the light beam roving ahead of her, filling the room with grainy shadows. She hadn't found any tape, but she'd ripped loose two long lamp cords and held the flashlight while PJ pulled the ailing Maceo to his feet. When the man tried to straighten up, he cried out in pain. PJ took the flashlight and said to Jasmine, "Stay here with your brothers. Be back in a minute to get you."

He clutched the doubled-over Maceo by the arm and led him into the kitchen, where he tied him to a chair with the lamp cords, wrapping and cinching him securely and tying the knots behind his back. The water was rising in the old house but it was too dark outside, the middle of the night, for anyone to leave now.

"Sit your ass quiet till the sun comes up," PJ said. "Don't make me hit you again."

Maceo was wheezing hard, like somebody having an asthma attack. He'd spit up more blood onto his white T-shirt. "You gotta get me to a doctor, bruh. Maceo ain't gonna make it till daylight."

"S'matter, pussy pimp daddy? You like to slap women around but cain't take a punch your own self?"

Maceo raised his bloody chin, his eyes blinking, struggling to focus. "You gonna keep me here like this, dawg?" he said. "Tied to this chair till the water come up over my head?"

"I'm thinking about it," PJ said, wading back toward the bedroom. "Better hope I don't leave it up to the girl."

When PJ entered the room and trained the light on the bed, he saw that Edgar was awake now and peering out from under the Saints cap. "Hello, Mistah Man," the boy said. "It wet every place."

"True that, little man. Come on, y'all," he said, slipping the .44 magnum into his waistband, "let's go to the kitchen. The water's gonna be over that bed pretty soon."

He picked up Edgar and carried him into the kitchen with Jasmine and the baby trailing close behind. He set the boy on the countertop and shoved dirty dishes into the sink to make room for all of them.

"Yo, hero," Maceo wheezed. He was sitting knee deep in water, bound to the chair. "Whatchew gone do when all this water rise up to your own chin?"

PJ thought about slapping the pimp upside his head. He didn't want Jasmine and Edgar to worry any more than they had already. "Best keep your mouth shut till I say you can talk," he said.

He truly didn't know what he was going to do. The water was rising inch by steady inch and the Orleans Parish deputies were out there looking for him. Things would be a lot easier on his own. He hadn't figured on traveling through deep water with a bunch of rug rats in tow.

Did this old house have an attic? He shined the flashlight on the kitchen ceiling, searching for a hatch. Maybe he could put these kids up in the attic and tell somebody where to find them. Could they survive up there in all that summer heat? D'Wayne's Grammy's attic felt like a burning furnace. No air or water, it might fry the little baby's brain.

Jasmine sat on the other side of the sink with Darius, her back braced against a cabinet door. PJ settled himself on the counter and placed the pistol beside him, dangling his shoes in the water. Edgar wiggled into his lap, fidgeting with the Saints cap, peeking out from under the wide bill. "What we doing up here, Mistah Man?" he asked.

Maceo laughed, a hoarse raspy sound. "Answer the boy," he said, laboring to make himself heard. "Whatchew gone do 'bout this, hero?"

"Shut the fuck up," PJ said, kicking water at him.

He turned off the flashlight to conserve the batteries. The house was as dark as a cave and smelled like a muddy drainage pipe. PJ sat in the darkness with Edgar in his lap, considering how to ditch these kids and the pimp and slide on down the road. In a short while Baby Darius began to cry again and PJ told the girl to do whatever she had to do to make him hush. Edgar squirmed for the longest time, playing with the Saints cap, shifting his small body this way and that, and then he finally grew calm, drifting into sleep again, and peed warmly in PJ's lap.

# 25

When they reached the dark flooded streets of the hospital district, they saw emergency lights blinking in the lobby of one of the medical buildings ahead. Duval urged Hodge on, his own legs beginning to wobble and strain under the freight of a much larger man. As they waded closer to the building, gunfire erupted in the darkness, muzzle flashes that stopped them dead still in the middle of the street. A gang of looters was breaking through the lobby's glass doors, some on foot, others in a canoe. One of the looters was shouting through the doors at a loyal security guard intent on doing his job.

*"This is our house now, motherfucker! You better step off, fool."*

Duval knew what they were after. Pharmaceuticals. Bins and bins of drugs, anything you wanted just sitting there on the long shelves of the hospital pharmacy. Pills and powders, clean syringes.

"Trippin'," he said, wanting no part of this scene. "We best bump on out of here."

But the looters had already spotted them out in the street, a couple of wet civilians in the wrong place at the wrong time.

"*Yo, man, hold up!*" A banger was yelling at them from the canoe. *"Hey, where you going, niggah? Stay where you standing."*

"Got a old man here need medical attention," Duval shouted back, leading Hodge away from the violence. "Looking for a hospital, is all."

There were two young looters in the canoe and they paddled quickly, overtaking Hodge and Duval after a dozen gliding strokes. "What you niggahs holding?" asked the paddler in the rear. He was a lean shirtless teenager wearing a headband of Rasta colors and a string of shell beads around his neck. In the blinking light from the hospital lobby, Hodge could make out the CP3 tattoo on his forearm and a puckered scar stitched into the taut flesh of his belly. He'd seen enough bullet wounds in his day to know when a man had been gut shot.

"Empty them pockets out and show us what you got," the Rastaman said, his gold incisors visible in the dark.

Hodge studied the canoers. The one up front appeared to be a few years older and a few pounds heavier than his Rasta friend. A red kerchief do-rag covered his head with an Aunt Jemima twist tie, and his cutoff black T-shirt said WE BOUT DAT. The word DEFENSE was inked into his bicep below the tattoo of an AK-47, and the fat grip of a real .357 magnum was sticking out of his waistband. Of the two, he was the enforcer—the one to worry about.

Duval held up his hands as if they'd already pulled the piece on him. "We don't have nothing, bruh," he said. "Lost it all when our boat tumped over. Billfolds, everything."

"My dawg B Shocker is gonna merk your sorry ass if you don't empty them pockets out and throw what you got in the boat."

Duval stuck his hands underwater into the pockets of his long baggy shorts and pulled them out like wet wadded rags, showing them he had nothing on him.

"What about you, old man?" the Rastaman said. "How many pockets you got in them soldier pants?"

Duval expected Hodge to cooperate so they could get this over with and move on. Instead, the old man lurched forward and grabbed the side of the canoe, saving himself from sinking down into the water. "Help me," he said, clutching his chest. "Help me, please. My heart."

"Hodge!" Duval said, seizing the back of his T-shirt, trying to hold him up. "Take it slow and easy now. We gonna get you to a hospital."

"This old fool gonna croak on us?" the Rastaman asked.

"Got a weak heart," Duval said. "That's why he need a doctor."

It looked as if Hodge was trying to pull himself aboard. The canoe listed badly, and the two occupants shifted their weight and cursed him. "What you doing, crazy old fool?" said the Rastaman, jabbing Hodge with his paddle. "Get on away from this boat 'fo B Shocker bust a magnum in your bumpy old head."

"Please help me," Hodge said, hoisting himself halfway into the canoe. "I cain't walk no fu'ther, son. Please take me to the ER."

Duval was afraid they were going to hurt Hodge. They'd probably been smoking crack all day and didn't give a fuck about a messed-up old geezer with a bad heart. "Come back down off there," he said, tugging on Hodge's fatigues.

Hodge was struggling to pull his legs out of the water, and the canoe rocked wildly back and forth. "What we gonna do 'bout this niggah?" said B Shocker, the large one with the gun.

The Rastaman jabbed Hodge in the shoulder again with his paddle. "Yo, get that watch off his wrist," he said. "Then pitch his old bones back in the water."

B Shocker leaned over and started yanking on the band of Hodge's wristwatch.

"He's out of his head," Duval pleaded. "He don't know what he's doing."

Hodge had managed to drag his legs into the swaying canoe and was clinging to B Shocker. "Please take me to the ER," he cried. "I'm not gonna make it without my meds. I got grandchildren out here somewhere."

In their wrestling embrace, B Shocker's kerchief do-rag had come untied. He shoved and elbowed Hodge, saying, "Let go of me, motherfucker," fighting to untangle himself from the moaning old man. When Hodge wouldn't let up, B Shocker punched him in the temple.

"Don't fuck him up!" Duval said.

"He don't get out this boat," the Rastaman said, reaching over to grab Hodge by the wet T-shirt, "B Shocker gonna cap *him* and *you boaf* and feed you to the catfish."

"I don't think so," Hodge said.

Suddenly he wasn't moaning anymore and his voice had become calm and deeply resonant. There was a metallic click and everything went silent for what felt like the slow turning of night into day. It was the wicked sound of the .357 magnum's hammer cocking back, ready to snap the firing pin. Hodge pressed the nose of the pistol against the ribs of the careless young man called B Shocker.

"Next punch you throw, son, will be your last," Hodge said.

Duval exhaled a long weary breath. *That crazy old fox.* The two paddlers sat silently in the canoe. They could all hear looters shouting and glass shattering at the hospital lobby a half block away.

"I want you both in the water and heading the other way," Hodge said. He was curled on his side, gazing up into the stunned face of the young banger kneeling over him. "You first, Bob Marley," he said to the Rastaman. "Leave your paddle and climb on out of here."

The Rastaman hesitated. "You some kind of soul-ja," he said to his partner. "Fucking let a old man take your leng off you."

"This is fucked up, man," B Shocker said, humiliated. "How I know he was doing some dirt?"

"Get out of the canoe, son," Hodge said to the Rastaman. "I've shot better men in the jungle and I will shoot you both. Don't fuck with me."

The Rastaman stared at him for several tense seconds, then threw his paddle down and crawled overboard with a splash.

"Give me my watch back," Hodge said, nudging B Shocker with the gun barrel. When the young man handed over the watch, Hodge said, "Now drop your big ass down in this water, boy. You've lost your boating privileges."

It was an awkward exchange, B Shocker plopping into the floodwater, Duval climbing aboard, the canoe shifting back and forth. The two looters backed away with their arms raised, cursing him, threatening to hunt them down. But by the time they'd waded back to alert their buddies, Hodge and Duval were paddling swiftly away, finding the rhythm they'd learned together in the johnboat, the sleek canoe carving through the dark water faster than that heavy old handmade tub.

"*Fade them motherfuckers!*" They could hear the Rastaman shouting to his buddies. "*They got our boat!*"

There was a barrage of gunfire, more muzzle flashes in the darkness. Hodge said, "Head down, son! Lay flat." It was a father's instinct, this need to protect the young. Even when the bullets were meant for you.

The shots echoed through the canyon of tall medical buildings rising out of the flood. Hodge lowered his shoulders and kept paddling while Duval hunkered down with his hood pulled up, as if that would stop a hot chunk of lead. Soon they were out of firing range and out of earshot of the threats being hurled at them from the looters.

"That was some mad crazy shit you pulled back there," Duval said, cautiously raising his head and gazing into the darkness behind them. "They teach you that in Nam?"

Hodge chuckled. "Saw it in a movie show."

"Sweeet," Duval said, grinning now, grabbing his paddle. "How you hanging, man? I been worried about you. Seem like you got a second wind."

"Need my meds," Hodge said, feeling like a man kneeling over a toilet bowl. He knew something was coming and there was no way to stop it. "I had some nitro tablets, we could head on to the Dome and find Dee and the kids."

"Right up here is a hospital. They bound to have your meds."

Soon they had reached a wide palm-lined plaza leading up to the hospital's entrance. In the moonlight they could see the tall trees bent by Katrina and the majestic steps mostly underwater now. The building was dark except for roving lights on the upper floors.

"Somebody up there moving around," Duval said. "Got to be the hospital crew."

"I know this place," Hodge said. It was the hospital where Rochelle had lost her battle with cancer.

Duval knew the hospital, too. It had always been good to black folk. He vaguely remembered the time his aunts had rushed him here when he was a child and had stirred up a nest of yellow jackets. His eyes had swollen shut from a dozen stings and he would have died—or so his aunts had always told him—if the ER doctors hadn't performed a miracle.

When they paddled around the building to its backside, looking for the emergency entrance, they discovered more looters breaking into submerged vehicles in the hospital parking lot. The cars belonged to medical personnel who'd stayed behind. Gangs of teenagers were shattering glass, searching glove compartments. Somebody was trying to jimmy open the rear doors of an EMS truck.

Hodge glanced at the .357 magnum lying on the floor of the canoe. "Let's get inside before I decide to use this thing on these jackasses," he said.

They paddled up to the ambulance ramp, which slanted out of the water at a sharp angle, and dragged the canoe onto a stretch of grease-stained concrete. A faint light glowed behind the sliding glass doors to the emergency entrance at the top of the ramp. Hodge slid the pistol into the waistband of his fatigues. "Quick in and out," he said to Duval. "I'll score enough meds to last me till we get back to Opelousas."

Soaked to the bone, they slopped up the ramp, Hodge feeling the lightheaded, almost hallucinatory sensation of something not right, the hand closing slowly around his heart. The automatic doors to the ER waiting room were jammed open and broken glass crunched underfoot as they entered a poorly lighted sitting area immersed in six inches of brown water.

"Nobody home," Duval said, surprised that the place was empty.

The rows of plastic bucket chairs were all vacant in the quiet gloom. "Where they at?" he asked, kicking an empty liter of Diet Pepsi bobbing like a fishing float.

"Upstairs somewhere," Hodge said, sloshing toward the double doors that led into a warren of small outpatient rooms where minor emergencies were addressed. "Let's find a way up."

It was darker down this corridor. They'd gone no more than a few splashing steps when a man stepped out of a doorway and shone a light on them. "Down on your dicks!" he shouted, pointing an assault rifle at them. He was a white man wearing a flak jacket over a crisp uniform shirt. Not a New Orleans patrol cop, maybe SWAT. A miner's light was attached to the side of his riot helmet.

"Whoa, mister, we come here looking for medical attention," Hodge said, raising his hands cooperatively. "My heart is giving me trouble."

"Take that weapon out of your pants and set it down nice and easy," the man said. His light had homed in on the butt of the .357 magnum. "Do it now and grab some tile—both of you."

Hodge removed the gun by the grip and placed it in the shallow water out in front of him. Duval had already knelt down. "Don't do us this way," he said. "We ain't looters. This man need a doctor for real. We been in the water all day long and he blacked out awhile back."

They didn't see where the second man came from but suddenly he was there, standing beside the combat trooper. He was a hospital security guard, a barrel-chested black man wearing a baseball cap, with a flashlight in one hand and a service revolver in the other. "You ain't looters," he said, "why you come in a hospital strapped like that?"

"I took that gun off a bad citizen," Hodge said. "They tried to rob us. Figured I might need it if there was more bad citizens between me and a doctor."

Hodge could read the word on the white trooper's sleeve patch.

*VIProtex*. He'd heard of them. High-priced bodyguards in Iraq and other foreign places where rich executives needed muscle. What was he doing here in this worthless old town?

"Hug the floor," the trooper said. "We need to see some ID."

Duval stretched out, as if doing a pushup, trying to keep his face above the shallow pool of water. "This is seriously harsh," he said. "This man need to see a doctor."

Hodge dropped to his knees with an exhausted splash, like a weary penitent kneeling to pray. "Listen to me, gentlemen. We lost everything we had when our boat turned over," he said. "I don't have an ID anymore. My driver's license is somewhere out in Lakeview and my meds are underneath a burning johnboat."

He told them his name was Hodges Grant and that he was from Opelousas and he'd come looking for his daughter and her children. The hospital security guard studied him carefully, as if deciding whether to believe his story. Then he sighed and holstered his weapon. "Okay, I got this one," he said to the VIProtex trooper. "Y'all step over here and let me pat you down. I'll take you up to see a nurse."

With the assault rifle trained on them, the security guard frisked Hodge and Duval and then turned to the man aiming the rifle. "It's okay, hoss. They're clean."

"Leave your piece in the water," the trooper said. "And don't count on getting it back."

They followed the security guard and his flashlight down the corridor toward an illuminated exit sign. When he shoved open the door to a stairwell, hot trapped air boiled out, reeking of human waste.

"Sorry for the formalities, fellas," the guard said, his light dancing over a pile of stinking biohazard bags dumped at the foot of the stairs. Duval gagged as they stepped around the bags, cupping a hand over his mouth. The heat and the smell were overwhelming.

"We got a problem with people breaking in and stealing drugs," the security guard said. "The home office in Baton Rouge sent down these dick-swinging cowboys from some private security outfit." He shook his head. "I got my whole crew working the building—didn't none of them cut and run—but some doctor gets shit in his neck, thinking us local boys can't handle a few looters, and the next thing you know, Baton Rouge is sending in Rambo to sling his AK around. You ax me, they gonna kill some poor old lady looking for a bed pan. And then the lawyers'll be ten years sorting it all out."

On the second-floor landing, his flashlight revealed a woman squatting over a bucket. "You mind not shining that light on me while I'm taking a crap," she said. She was a nurse, the pants of her faded green scrubs pulled down to her knees.

"Sorry, ma'am," the guard said, diverting his beam.

When they reached the next landing, he turned to Hodge and Duval in a low voice. "It's bad up in here, gents. The basement flooded and took out the emergency generator. We got no power or running water and the toilets are backing up, so the staff's doing their business on the stairs. They wanna keep the smell and disease off the floors where the patients stay. What they do, they tie it all up in bio bags and drop 'em straight down to the bottom floor. No telling when they gonna clean that mess up. After everybody is evacuated, I reckon."

The climb up three flights had drained Hodge even more, and the heat and stench had curdled his stomach. But nothing had prepared him for what they found on the next landing. Three body bags stacked one on top of the other. He hadn't seen this kind of thing since the war.

"We already lost a few and don't know where to put 'em. The morgue's down in the basement, full of water," the guard said, his light tracing the contours of the black bags. "Couldn't save these folk here. All the equipment's dead. Ventilators, monitors, you name it. Gonna get worse up on the twelfth floor, where they keep the hospice cases. You don't wanna go up there."

Hodge knew about the twelfth floor. That's were Rochelle had lived out her final days.

"They tell us the Chinooks are on their way to evacuate everybody. But don't sweat it, my man. We gonna get you checked out first. You say it's your heart? My sister-in-law, she had a triple bypass and lived another seven years."

He offered his hand to Hodge. "Name's Tucker, by the way," he said. They gave each other a power shake—all three moves—and laughed at how old and familiar it felt. "Wearing them fatigues, I figure you were there."

"Patrol boat, Mekong," Hodge said. "You?"

"LRRP in Quang Ngai, bro'."

Hodge knew who they were. Long Range Reconnaissance Patrol. Spooky bastards. Ear collectors.

"Quang Ngai was crawling with Charlie. My brothers in LRRP, we was one with the night."

Hodge had met LRRPs in country and it was hard to imagine this kind older man creeping through the nighttime jungle with burnt cork rubbed all over his face. Tucker's belly was soft now and his face was soft and creased and there was a hitch in his step, like a man with back trouble.

On the next landing, he opened an exit door that issued them into a dark hospital wing. The air was still and thick and unbearably hot. A nauseating odor, more chemical than human, permeated the place. Tucker walked ahead with his flashlight bouncing along the bleak corridor. They were careful not to step on the nurses curled up on floor mats, taking their sleep shifts. Several patients occupied gurneys, their family members holding their hands and offering quiet consolation.

"It's safer out here in the hallway. Most of these rooms got bad wind damage," Tucker explained. He shined his light into one of the patient rooms. The windows were shattered, their broken glass swept into piles. Twenty hours after the hurricane had passed through, rainwater still pooled on the tile floor.

Farther down the corridor they came upon a tall, solid-built nurse showing a young woman how to manually operate a jerry-rigged ventilator to help her mother breathe through a bag valve mask. "Nurse Shannon," Tucker said, "can you see this man when you get a spare minute?"

Nurse Shannon was a white woman in her midforties, with loose shoulder-length blonde hair streaked silver. She appeared haggard but intensely focused. "Let's get your blood pressure," she said to Hodge after he'd described his medical history and what had happened to him today.

She escorted him into one of the empty rooms and he sat on a bed stripped of linens while she administered the cuff to his arm, pumping it tight with air. Tucker directed the flashlight beam so she could see the gauge. She didn't seem to trust the first reading and pumped him up again. A breeze as warm and moist as human breath wafted through the broken windows and Duval stepped over to watch a helicopter's red taillights descend onto the Superdome plaza a few blocks away.

"Hmm, it was right the first time. One seventy-nine over ninety, Mr. Grant," the nurse said, ripping the Velcro cuff off his bicep.

"Climbing up all those stairs," Hodge said.

She took his pulse, then shook her head. "Lie back and rest a minute, please," she said, lowering his shoulders onto the bare mattress. "You need an EKG and a chest X–ray, sir, but the power's dead and none of that's gonna happen tonight."

"Can you give me a shot of B twelve or something?" Hodge said. "A little rest, I'll be good to go. We need to get on back out there and find my daughter and grandchildren."

"You're not going anywhere right now, Mr. Grant," she said in a firm professional voice. "Stay right here and relax, okay? I'm going to find a doctor."

# 26

In her mud-spattered robe, with wide-swinging hips, Sistah M led them down the long ramp to the dark streets below. Two hours ago, these streets had been bone dry, but now they were steeped in a foot of brown lake water. Their somber parade picked up fifteen or twenty others trying futilely to talk their way into the Hyatt, most of them Vietnamese families rescued by Wildlife and Fisheries boats out at a Catholic church in New Orleans East. Sistah M knew this business district and quickly found dark Poydras Street, which angled down to the river. The blue BellSouth sign high atop one skyscraper emitted the only light in the narrow valley of office buildings. Hurricane winds had blown their windows onto the streets below, and when Dee felt broken slabs of plate glass shifting under her sneakers, she bent down and let Ashley climb onto her back and carried her like a pack animal. One of Sistah M's strapping grandsons offered to carry LaMarcus, and he rode astride the young man's shoulders, shining his flashlight into the darkness ahead.

The march down Poydras was solemn and quiet, a band of strangers who didn't entirely trust one another, splashing along in their own separate cocoons of silence. Even Sistah M's cheerful humming, and her occasional eruptions into gospel hymns, couldn't soothe Dee's apprehensions. She felt alone and vulnerable to the lawlessness that had ripped through the city, and she wasn't terribly comfortable around these young gangsta grandsons. She was still shaken by what had happened to her on the roof of her home.

"Anybody need a drink of water?" asked Sistah M, pulling two bottles from the mysterious folds of her robe. "I liberated these from those soldier boys. Everybody take a swallow. Stay hydrated."

As the bottles were passed from hand to hand, Dee heard a voice say, "You have beautiful children." It was a Vietnamese man, gray-haired and fit, perhaps her father's age. He walked holding hands with his two daughters, lovely teenage girls with long straight black hair and faces as delicate as orchids.

"Thank you, sir," Dee said. "Your daughters are so pretty."

The father introduced himself as Charles Tran and told her he owned a small grocery market in the little Saigon neighborhood of Village de l'Est, New Orleans East. The neighborhood had been destroyed by the overtopped levees of the Industrial Canal and the Intracoastal Waterway. His daughters were named Dao and Trinh, and they giggled shyly when they shook Dee's hand. Their entire family, including his wife's eighty-year-old mother, had been rescued from their church's choir loft, where they had fled from the floodwater. With a thick shock of white hair and her back bowed by age, the old woman sloshed along with the others, a stick-thin arm interlocked with Mrs. Tran's. She spoke in Vietnamese and her family laughed.

"What did she say?" Dee asked.

Charles Tran smiled. "She says this not so bad as working in the rice fields all day."

Farther down Poydras, the water receded to ankle deep and then gradually went dry, as if they'd waded out of a shallow pond. An NOPD cruiser appeared from the darkness, its overhead lights flashing colors. The driver hit the siren, whoop whoop whoop, three sharp bursts as the vehicle's brakes squealed to a halt, cutting off the group's passage. Two uniformed officers occupied the car, a black female driver and a white male sitting in the passenger seat, a shotgun braced between them. The white cop rolled down his window and spoke to them without getting out of the cruiser. "Where y'all think you going?" he asked. "You out here looking for another flat-screen TV? The Wal-Mart's done been cleaned out."

Sistah M stepped forward. "We're on our way to the convention center, officer," she said with equal measure of politeness and authority. Dee could hear in her voice the desire to avoid conflict. "They won't let anybody else in the Superdome tonight, so we're headed where they have more room. We got little ones to look after," she said, turning to search for LaMarcus and Ashley and the half-dozen Vietnamese children clinging to their parents. She wanted the policemen to understand they weren't looters.

The cop exchanged a few quiet words with his partner and they both laughed. Then he leaned his head out the window. "We catch any y'all looting or carrying a weapon," he said, "we'll take you down."

He looked them over from the safe enclosure of his vehicle.

"You don't want that to happen," the cop said. "Central lockup is underwater. You'll end up in a wire dog cage down at the train station or cuffed on a bridge somewhere. And no telling what work farm they gonna send you to upstate. So keep your nose clean, people."

He slapped the door of the cruiser and the driver pulled away, their carousel of lights soon disappearing back into the darkness. The grandsons hooted after them, using street language Dee didn't want her children to hear, bumping chests and high-fiving as if they'd chased the police away. Sistah M scolded them. "Hush, now, boys," she said. "Don't be talking trash. We got a long way ahead of us and we cain't be asking for trouble from the laws."

The group trudged farther down Poydras toward the riverfront, at least forty strong by now, passing near dark cheerless Harrah's Casino and soon making their way onto the dry wide boulevard that ran from the aquarium and Riverside shopping mall to the convention center. It was nearly three a.m., according to LaMarcus's wristwatch, but the streets were not deserted. Dee could hear voices calling to one another and realized they were not the first travelers to reach this destination.

As they approached the leaning palm trees and shattered glass doors at the main entrance of the convention center, they encountered a handful of city employees who had been sent by the mayor to examine the facility. "I wouldn't go in there," one of them said. He and his crew wore uniform jumpsuits and carried flashlights, toolboxes. "Some thugs have busted in and are running wild. We're getting the hell out of here until the National Guard shows up."

Sistah M said, "We were told y'all had food and clean water and a place to sleep."

The workmen laughed. "Who told you that, awnty? Ain't nothing in there but broken pipes and bad news," another crewman said. "Me, I'd find myself someplace else to roost, I was y'all. Kind of people roaming around in there right now . . . Mmm-mmh."

Sistah M turned to her followers standing under the A-framed portico. "Stay cool and hang together. We don't need any more grief tonight," she said, her words aimed primarily at her grandsons. "Oughta be plenty room for everybody inside this big old building."

"Some homeboy bump my shit," one of the young men said, "I'ma flip the script."

"Now that's what I'm talking about, Desmond," she scolded him. "You're gonna stick by my side and chill. Y'understand me, child?"

The entrance doors had been smashed by cinder blocks, and broken glass was scattered everywhere. Charles Tran and another Vietnamese gentleman used their flashlights to lead the group cautiously into the atrium. The steamy hot air smelled of mold and damp carpet and spoiled milk and something earthy, like wet potting soil. They all clung to one another in a protective clan as they ventured slowly into a vacant exhibit hall. The flashlights ranged all around, exploring their surroundings. Dark figures were roaming through the cavernous space like dazed cave dwellers shying away from the light. Dee could hear faint screams echoing somewhere in the distance and held her children close.

They moved as one toward the center of the hall, not a word exchanged among them, even Sistah M momentarily speechless by the strangeness of this place. Suddenly a motorized cart was bearing down on them, like the kind in airports, flashing its headlights and beeping its horn, the electric motor whining at full throttle. Dee could see young men piled on top of each other and hanging off the sides, whooping and hollering and pumping their fists. The cart plowed through their group, scattering them in all directions. Dee yanked her children out of the way and wrestled them to the carpet. The old Vietnamese grandmother stumbled and collapsed in a heap of sharp bones. One of the riders grabbed at the girl named Trinh and nearly tore her blouse off as he tried to drag her onto the cart. Dee looked up and saw Sistah M standing like a solid oak in the headlights zooming toward her, hands defiantly on her hips. But the cart failed to slow down or swerve, and in the next instant her large body lay sprawled on the carpet in a tangle of orange and blue robe.

# 27

The doctor looked concerned. He was a bespectacled middle-aged white man with graying hair and the early stubble of a beard. He read Nurse Shannon's chart by penlight and ordered her to take blood and administer nitroglycerine, heparin to prevent clotting, and a beta blocker to reduce Hodge's blood pressure. He called for an IV drip to restore his fluids.

"I'm sorry, Mr. Grant, but we don't have a cardiologist in the building," he told Hodge. "I understand there's one at the hospital across the street and I'll do my best to contact her. You need to be in a fully operational facility, sir. We'll do everything we can to get you out of here as soon as possible. We've radioed Baton Rouge for medevac helicopters, but so far I haven't seen any. There are a few people ahead of you on the triage list, but we'll put you in a bird as fast as we can."

Hodge gripped the doctor's wrist. "I cain't go to Baton Rouge, Doctor," he said. "I drove here from Opelousas to find my daughter and her children, and I cain't leave without them."

The doctor patted his hand patiently. "Mr. Grant, you're in no condition to be wading around out there," he said, nodding toward the broken windows and the dark night. "All the indications show you're in unstable condition and need the immediate care of a cardio unit."

Hodge stared at the man. He felt trapped and his mind began to devise ways to escape this place.

"Look, Mr. Grant, even if you find your daughter and grandchildren, they're going to end up taking care of you. And if they're like everybody else in this city right now, they don't need the extra burden. Do you follow me? The shape you're in, you'd be an anchor around their necks. The best thing you can do for your loved ones is to stabilize and get well."

Hodge released his grip and sank back against the mattress. He'd told Dee not to worry, he was coming to get her. He'd never in his life let his daughter down. Never. He couldn't let her down now.

"Duval, where you at?" he said, searching for him in the dark room. "We've got to do something."

"I'm right here, man," Duval said, standing at the foot of the bed.

The doctor squeezed Hodge's shoulder. "Try to rest, Mr. Grant," he said. "You can't help anyone until you get some help yourself."

The doctor took Nurse Shannon aside and spoke to her in a cautious whisper. In a short while she returned with a burly male nurse pushing a gurney. With Duval's help, they slid Hodge onto the gurney and rolled him out into the dark corridor with the other patients. The two nurses removed Hodge's wet boots and rolled up his fatigues, and by flashlight they cleaned and dressed the slash above his ankle.

"Let's keep an eye on this," Nurse Shannon said to the other nurse. "We'll start him on an antibiotic if it begins to look infected. In the meantime, let's get that IV going."

Desperate for sleep, Duval sat on the damp tile floor with his lower back braced against a gurney wheel. The IV dripped slowly into Hodge's arm and he rested quietly in the sweltering heat. *What the fuck were they going to do now?* Duval wondered as he drifted in and out, listening to the sounds of misery all around him. Someone crying in despair, someone whispering desperately to a coma patient strapped to the next gurney. Farther down the corridor, a team of nurses was wrestling with an old man having convulsions. It was like a lunatic asylum in here, broken people babbling and begging for mercy. There was not enough food and water, not enough medication to kill the pain, not enough hope to fill a rinse cup. Duval pressed his hands against his ears and tried to shut it all out, but the sounds were in his head now and the smell of death was on him. He wouldn't let himself fall asleep for fear they'd mistake his body for a corpse and drag him out to the landing in a black bag.

*"Duval."*

Hodge was calling his name. *"Duval, you there?"*

"Down here, Hodge."

"Come talk to me, son."

Duval rose to his feet and stood next to the IV pole. Flashlights were moving up and down the corridor, nurses busy at work, and in the passing light he could see Hodge's face awash in sweat.

"We're in a jam here, Duval. Looks like I might be holed up in this place a spell. No telling how long." His speech was slurred from fatigue and the drugs they'd pumped into him. "Dee and the kids are out there somewhere. That means you got to do this thing, Duval. Y'understand? It's on you now. You got to go find your children."

Duval was afraid Hodge was going to tell him something like that. But as much as he resented the old man, he didn't know how he could do this without him. It was dark out there and waist deep in water and everybody on the street was thugging and looting and running up on you every whichway you turned. It was like some zombie fucking horror show.

"I don't know, man," he said, scratching his arm through the burn holes in his hoodie sleeve. His skin had been itching for an hour, like a rash. "Tell you the honest truth, I don't know where to start."

A nurse dashed past them, sprinting down the corridor toward the medics struggling to save the convulsing man. A woman was crying and shaking the poor man, his wife or daughter, and they had to drag her away.

"Go to the Dome," Hodge said, his voice calm despite the chaos. "Lots of people in there, son, but do what you can. Look around. They brought them in by chopper a few hours ago. A woman and two little children. Maybe somebody logged them in."

He unbuttoned the side pocket on his camo fatigues and fished for what sounded like jingling keys. "That girl I pulled out of the car," he said. "Her folk live in a mansion on St. Charles and they didn't evacuate. She said if we run into trouble, they'll take us in."

Duval almost laughed. "Let me get this down on paper. I'ma walk up St. Charles Avenue and ring a doorbell and ax some rich white people if I can stay in they big fancy house?"

Hodge told him that the house stood at the corner of St. Charles and Arabella Street. That's what the young woman had said. A large white mansion with white columns and a wrought iron fence at Arabella and St. Charles.

"Find Dee and the children and take them to that house, and when I get out of this damn place, I'll meet you there."

Duval shook his head. "When you gonna be there, Hodge? Tomorrow? The next day?" he said. "You heard what the man say. You ain't fit to be wading around in storm water. They gonna pack your ass up and fly you off to Baton Rouge."

Hodge handed him a mess of worn keys he'd pulled from his pocket. "Listen to me, son. It may be today, it may be tomorrow—I'll get there quick as I can. I'm not going to Baton Rouge in a fucking medevac chopper. You can bet the farm on that. I been in a medevac chopper one too many times."

Duval stared at the ring of keys cupped in the palm of his hand. It was all here—Hodge's house and truck and tool sheds and probably a safe deposit box buried somewhere in a credit union and who knows whatall. "If you gonna meet us on St. Charles," he said, feeling the weight in his hand, "why you giving me your keys?"

Hodge was slow to respond. The drugs were tucking him under their dark wing, slowing his thoughts. "In case you have to drive the truck on out of here without me," he said, finally.

The idea silenced Duval. He closed his eyes and realized that the convulsing man at the end of the corridor had gone quiet. The nurses were trying to console the woman at his side.

After a long duration, Hodge said, "You still here?"

"I'm still here, man."

"Don't get cozy, son. Take that canoe downstairs and paddle on over to the Dome. Hell, it's so close you can backstroke from here."

Duval didn't trust himself in the dark night. He couldn't swim, and he couldn't paddle worth a damn by himself.

"Are you a little scared, Duval?"

"Maybe I am. I'm not proud of it."

"What scares you the most, son? Drownding—or taking care of two children for the rest of your life?"

Duval scratched his arm again. The old man could cut you to the bone.

"If you're man enough to make a baby," Hodge said, "you ought to be man enough to take care of it." He worked himself up on his elbows so he could have a closer look at Duval's face. "You and Dee, you're finished. You both know that. But you got kids to raise up in this world. You got a job to do together. That boy, LaMarcus, he needs a father to show him how to be a man. And Ashley deserves to see how a woman should be treated by a good husband. You hear me talking to you?"

Duval nodded. "Yes, sir, I do." Even from his sick bed, this man could put the fear of God in you.

Hodge dropped flat on his back with a tired sigh. "Then go do your job, son," he said, panting from the effort. "Go find your children and take care of them till they're old enough to be on their own. That's what a man does, Duval. It ain't changed in ten thousand years."

Speechless and uncertain, afraid of what lay ahead, Duval stood looking down at the dark figure on the gurney. He wondered who would be with this man when he breathed his last breath.

"And Duval," Hodge said before giving in to sleep. "Don't lose my keys."

Duval waited until he was sure that Hodge was unconscious. He pressed his thumb into the man's leathery old neck and felt a pulse. "Fuck me," he said to himself, scratching his wrist. Did he have it in him to do this by himself?

With his arms outstretched in front of him like a sleepwalker, Duval made his way down the dark corridor past the line of gurneys and the sleeping mats occupied by nurses and weary children. Out in the stairwell he could smell the bodies ripening on the landing where the orderlies had piled them. He felt his way along the handrails, descending floor by floor, and he knew he was close to ground level once he'd caught wind of those stinking biohazard bags the nurses were dropping from the upper floors. At the bottom of the stairs, stumbling along without a flashlight, he stepped on one of the bags and it exploded underfoot like a land mine. Human shit spewed all over his legs and he gagged, trying to catch his breath. When he forced his way through the door leading back into the ER, he discovered that the water was deeper now in the hallway between outpatient cubicles. He stopped to grip his shorts and dry heave several times, still trying to pull himself together.

"S'matter, dude?" said the man who stepped out of a cubicle with an AK pointed at him. "Hospital food don't agree with you?"

It was the uniformed white rent-a-cop from that outfit in Baton Rouge. The fucker who'd made them kneel down in the water.

"Empty that clip in me, Matrix man," Duval managed to say, "or shove it up your ass."

The security guard sniggered. "How's that old guy with the bad heart?" he asked. "He gonna make it?"

Duval straightened up and waded toward the swinging doors of the waiting room. "Like you give a shit," he said. He thought he could feel the light from the guard's helmet lasering into the back of his head.

"You leaving the building?" the guard asked.

"'Fraid so. Do I need a hall pass to get back in?"

The guard lowered his weapon. "Some serious shit going down out there," he said. "You be careful, amigo."

Duval crossed the empty ER waiting room and wandered through the jammed-open doors at the ambulance entrance, gazing down the slanted driveway ramp, expecting to find the canoe where they'd left it. But the canoe was gone. His heart sank. In the moonlight he could see that floodwater had crawled higher up the ramp and he didn't know if the canoe had floated away or if someone had taken it. What the fuck was he going to do now?

"Looking for something, homeboy?"

A voice emerged out of dark shadows. It was the skinny Rastaman, with B Shocker at his side.

"Don't even think about running, motherfucker," the Rastaman said.

# 28

Dee was still trembling when she grabbed LaMarcus's flashlight, rose from the carpet, and hurried over to the fallen woman. The cart had sideswiped Sistah M and she'd twisted a knee in the fall. Her grandsons were stooped over her, trying to help the woman to sit up.

"Where's *ma petit pois?*" she asked with a maternal cluck, looking for Ashley among the crisscrossing flashlights. "Come here, pretty girl, and give Sistah M a hug. Looks like I'm gonna have to camp a spell."

Ashley raced over to hug the old woman's neck.

"You stay close and take care of your momma, now, sugar. Lot of mischief going on in this place. Looks like we reached the Land of Canaan," Sistah M said, magically retrieving another bottle of water from her robe and taking a long drink. "Here, you need some water, child?"

The runaway cart had shattered the group's fragile unity. Frightened and angry, they tended to one another in small scattered clusters of family. Charles Tran was incensed by the assault on his daughter and spoke in livid, rapid-fire Vietnamese as he comforted the girl and helped his wife revive her mother. Dee didn't know what to do. Things were falling apart, and it appeared that nothing could stop the worst from happening. She thought about hustling LaMarcus and Ashley back outside and returning to the Superdome plaza, but she was too terrified to make that long dark journey alone with two small children.

Charles Tran had organized the families from his church in a protective circle. The women and children sat inside the circle, huddling close to one another while Tran and a half dozen Vietnamese fathers positioned themselves as sentries around the group. "Miss Dee," he said, shining his flashlight on her. "Please," he said, gesturing like a theater usher, "you come with your children. We keep you safe."

Dee looked at Sistah M and her grandsons. She didn't want to walk away from her own people. The old lady seemed to understand her hesitation. "You go ahead, now," she said to Dee. "They're good folk. They'll make sure no harm comes to you."

Dee and her children camped on the carpet in the center of the circle. Everyone had turned off their flashlights to conserve batteries—and for fear of giving away their location. Within the circle there was a collective odor of stale sweat and sour clothing, like the smell of wet towels after a week in a clothes hamper. The ponytailed Mrs. Tran and her mother were praying softly in Vietnamese. The two teenaged sisters, Dao and Trinh, sat back to back, dozing and sometimes whispering to each other. Gunshots echoed somewhere in the distant halls.

Dao said to Dee, "Don't worry, ma'am. My father and these men, they survived a war. They know how to protect what is theirs."

Dee was touched by this. The chivalry of aging soldiers who thought they could defeat armed thugs with their bare hands. "My father was wounded in that war," she said. "When I was little, he used to show me his medals. He kept them in a shoe box."

Charles Tran overheard her. "We fought hard for the Americans," he said. "Afterwards, we came to this country. Thirty years now. Life has been good to us. But this . . ." He hesitated, grasping for words. "We have lost everything, Miss Dee. And you?"

"Yes," she said. "Everything."

They fell silent again, each one measuring the weight of this tragedy on their own shoulders. Dee wanted to sleep but she was too aware of ghostly figures passing in the darkness, wandering souls searching for a patch of carpet to claim until this long night was over. As time went by, more and more of them appeared, at first a smatter of voices, but in another hour the random voices had become an echoing hum. Camps had cropped up all around their circle, the newcomers confused and afraid and sometimes angry, sometimes in despair. Those distant gunshots struck fear in them all. Tension was mounting and there was a sense that something dangerous was building and might explode at any moment.

Dee felt her strength flowing out of her, and she fought the drowsiness that was pulling her down. She was lost in some faraway dream when Ashley raised her head from her lap and whispered, "Momma, I've got to pee. *Bad!*"

"Oh Jesus," Dee mumbled. "Oh honey. Really? Do you think you can hold it a little while longer?"

"Maah-muhh," Ashley said, grouchy and impatient, wiggling her legs. "I've been holding it a long time and I'm gonna pee in my pants."

"Okay, sweetie, okay," Dee said. She needed a moment to gather herself and remember where the bathrooms were. She had been in this building before.

"Miss Dee." It was the girl named Trinh. "I need to go, too. Do you want me to take her?"

Charles Tran roused from his sleepy silence. "You must not go alone," he said, clicking on his flashlight. "You come with me. We will find it together."

Dee retrieved her son's flashlight and stood up unsteadily, with the breathless sensation of floating in deep space. Mr. Tran said something in a low voice to the men sitting around the circle, then pointed his flashlight beam into the darkness as the four of them set out to find the facilities. Dee held one of Ashley's hands and Trinh held the other, and Charles Tran walked ahead of them like a nervous scout searching for the quickest passage through an ambush. They wandered past camp after camp, hundreds of them now, more than Dee had imagined. Babies were crying. An emaciated elderly woman slumped in a wheelchair. Project boys roamed the darkness in packs. One surly old man said, "Git that fucking light out of my face," batting at the air as if the light beam was intruding smoke. Someone else said, "Y'all ain't got no food for us, git the hell on away from here."

The bathrooms were located in a small recessed alcove at the rear of the exhibit hall. Dee shined her light on a door marked WOMEN. They could smell the sewage from twenty feet away. She wouldn't let her daughter sit on a shit-smeared seat. "Let me take the girls inside," she said to Charles Tran. "You wait for us right here."

When she pushed open the bathroom door, the smell hit them full force. Raw human waste. But the floor was dry and there were no signs of overflowing toilets. All they needed was one clean seat. "Come on," she said. She could feel Ashley tugging the back of her T-shirt as they inched slowly into the facility, with Trinh at the rear. They had advanced only as far as the sinks when Dee heard grunts and rutting sounds coming from somewhere ahead in the darkness.

"Stop," she said, holding up a hand. "Stay here."

She pulled herself away from Ashley's hold, but her daughter said, "No, Momma, I'm coming with you."

"Stay with Trinh," Dee insisted, giving the girl a slight shove backwards. "Don't move from this spot. Do you hear me? I'll be right back."

Pointing the flashlight like a handgun, Dee walked quietly past a row of stalls and discovered a right-angle turn into a larger area with even more stalls. The floor back here was littered with used toilet paper. A teenaged girl was kneeling on all fours near the paper towel dispensers, an older man mounted behind her, grunting, his thighs slapping her flesh in a crude rhythm. Horrified, Dee recoiled a step, her lungs burning in the putrid air. What had happened on the roof came rushing back, the way he'd ripped her pants off and thrust his finger into her. She took a deep breath, stepped forward, and directed the light into the man's eyes. Tattoos stained his bare arms and a bath towel was wrapped around his head like a turban.

"*You bastard,*" she said, her voice dropping into a low seething rage. He blinked his eyes and turned his head aside, blinded by the light. "Let go that girl," Dee said, going street on him, her skin prickling with sweat, "or I'll bring my boys in here to *handle* yo' ass, fo' sho'."

The man stared into the light, speechless, his squinting eyes glassy and stoned. The girl raised her head and said, "Get the fuck on away from here, bitch, 'fo I come up there and slap you down. This my man and you cain't have him. He taking care of me, girl."

Heat surged into Dee's face. "Oh," she said. She felt like a fool. "Oh Jesus, my bad," she said. It was the only thing she could think to say.

She backed around the corner and shined the light on the girls standing petrified near the sinks. Trinh had covered Ashley's ears so she couldn't hear what was being said.

"We have to find another place," Dee said, walking back toward them.

Ashley freed herself from Trinh. "Momma, I have to pee so bad."

"Come on," Dee said, taking her daughter's hand. "We can't be in here."

In the alcove outside the bathroom, Dee leaned close to the waiting Charles Tran and explained quietly why the girls didn't use the facilities. He looked shocked. "You want me to go in and chase them out?" he asked.

Dee shook her head. She didn't want the older man to get into a fight.

"Miss Dee, your daughter is going," Trinh said.

"What? Where did she go?"

In a panic, Dee stepped out into the exhibit hall and called Ashley's name, swinging the flashlight in every direction.

"No," Trinh said, gently touching her shoulder. "She's going over there."

Ashley had squatted down near the water fountains and was urinating on the carpet. Her mother's daughter, Dee thought, walking toward her with a smile. She remembered all the times her parents had stopped the car on a woodsy backroad because Dee couldn't hold it a minute longer.

"Papa, please turn off your light," Trinh said with a giggle. "I'm going to join her."

Dee and Charles Tran stood shoulder to shoulder in the darkness, listening to the sound of two girls peeing. "We are living like animals," he said in a quiet, melancholy voice. "This is not why we came to this country."

Dee wished there was something she could say to this kind gentleman to comfort him in such a terrible hour. *You are blessed with beautiful daughters and a loving wife, Mr. Tran. You are surrounded by friends who will stick with you through the worst. You have your faith in a caring God. Don't be discouraged by this storm. We will get through this, my friend. You will find relief. You will build again. Someone will help you. Someone will help us all. Our neighbors will come to our aid. Everyone loves this city. No one will forget us. It's the greatest country in the world. Help is surely at our doorstep.*

# 29

They'd beaten the hell out of him and might have beaten him to death if that old hospital security guard named Tucker hadn't appeared in the ER doorway with his service revolver. He fired a couple of rounds over their heads and chased them down the ambulance ramp to where they'd stashed their canoe. "Better come on back upstairs and let a nurse take a look," the old man said as he holstered his weapon and bent down to examine Duval's bloody face. "Might need some stitches in that lip."

Duval had been knocked down and stomped on, but he was sitting upright now and clutching his knees in the oil-stained loading zone. His lip was split open, one eye was closing quickly, and several teeth felt loose in his mouth. He'd always told Dee he was a lover, not a fighter, and this beating had been the awful proof. He might've held his own against that beanpole Rastaman, but the thug they called B Shocker knew how to bust a head.

"I cain't go back up there," he said, rubbing the side of his swollen face. "Your Nam buddy—I cain't let him down."

"You don't get that lip took care of, it's gonna leave a bad scar."

Duval worked his tongue around the skin shredded inside his mouth. "I'll be ah-ight," he said, spitting blood. "Just need some bench time and I'll be good to go."

Tucker straightened up, shifting his weight from foot to foot as if he'd lost circulation in his legs. He shined his flashlight down the ramp. "Where you think you going in this flood?" he asked, letting his light veer out into the submerged parking lot. "It's pitch dark out there, son. Ain't nothing but heartache everywhere you turn."

Duval scooted on his ass and braced his back against the brick wall of the hospital. He was hurting all over and feeling dizzy, the old guard and the loading dock and the starry night spinning in his head. The wall kept him anchored to something reliable and sturdy.

"Do me a solid, chief," he said. "Don't tell the old man you seen me like this. We straight? He's got enough on his mind already."

Long after Tucker had gone, Duval sat listening to phantom voices in the darkness. An hour passed, maybe two. He had lost all measure of time. Shadows drifted past the hospital, lost souls astray on the waters. He could hear them arguing with one another. He could hear them bawling like children. He didn't know if he had the strength to stand up and follow them to the Superdome, that lurking dark presence he could see from here, a black hole in the nighttime sky. The water was deep and the night was dark and he was afraid he might not make it, the shape he was in.

He must have fallen asleep because the woman's voice startled him. He almost swung a fist. "Easy, now," she said, kneeling in front of him. "Tucker told me you were down here. Hold this on your eye. It'll stop the swelling."

It was the tall white nurse who'd taken care of Hodge. She placed a hand behind his neck and pressed an ice pack to his eye. "Come back upstairs," she said in a firm voice. "We'll look at your lip."

He shook his head. "Let me rest," he said, the ice sending a cold shiver straight through his eye and into his brain. "I'm gonna bounce out of this place soon as I can."

The next time he woke, someone was trying to steal the Nikes off his feet. He kicked wildly and found solid bone and heard the thief skid across the dry concrete. When he opened his good eye, he saw it was a boy no older than LaMarcus. His younger brother was trying to help him up and they were laughing at the beat-up man.

"Why you do my boy like that?" yelled a woman from somewhere down the ramp.

Duval pulled his knees to his chest. The ice pack was resting in his lap, more water than ice. "What kind of mother tell her boys to go steal a man's shoes?" he barked at her. His lips and teeth were crusted with dried blood and it hurt him to speak.

"We thought you was dead," said one of the boys.

"Get the fuck on away from me 'fo I kick your skinny ass again."

Pointing and laughing at him, the boys scampered off to their mother. She cursed Duval before the three of them retreated down the ambulance ramp and back into the water. He realized now why he could see them clearly, and why he could see others wading through the flooded parking lot. Daylight was breaking across the city.

Gunfire kept Dee awake. It sounded like cracks of lightning somewhere off in the cavernous gloom. With every report, Ashley jumped in her sleep and burrowed deeper into her mother's side. The hotwired cart returned several times, young thugs terrorizing the dark exhibit halls. Sistah M and her grandsons were outnumbered and powerless to do anything. When they saw the vehicle approaching, Charles Tran and the other Vietnamese men would rise from their slumber and stand with outstretched arms, making a fence, trying to divert the marauders away from the circle of women and children. The thug driver delighted in speeding toward them and hitting his brakes at the last moment, then backing up and zooming at them again and again, stopping just short of running over Mr. Tran. Dee was moved by his courage. He held his ground and never flinched. These fathers were willing to throw themselves under the tires to save their loved ones from harm.

On the third or fourth assault—she'd lost count by now—Dee had had enough. She got to her feet and slipped between those outstretched arms, leaving the circle and venturing out toward the headlights blazing in her face. "*Leave us alone!*" she shouted, shaking from fatigue and anger. She knew they had weapons, but she didn't care anymore. "You ought to be ashamed of yourselves! We don't have anything you want. There are children and old people here," she said, widening her arms to show them. "Go hate on somebody else."

There was a momentary silence behind the bright headlights. And then the catcalls began.

"Yo, I gotta hit dat."

"Me and you be kickin' it, girl. Doin' the nasty."

"Come on over to my crib in the baffroom."

Charles Tran was quick to grab Dee by the arm and lead her back to the circle. "Please, Miss Dee," he said. "They can't be reasoned with."

Soon after the incident, people camped in the surrounding darkness made their way over to the Vietnamese group to share bottled water and juice boxes and food scavenged from their pantries before leaving home. An older bearded man named Malik said, "Y'all be careful, now. Stick with your people. They found a nekkid li'l girl with her throat slit in one of the bathrooms."

Dee had heard the same thing at the Superdome. Another rumor making the rounds.

"They say they stacking bodies in a walk-in meat locker back in yonder," someone added, and soon the talk turned to the many horror stories people had heard. Little babies being raped at the Superdome. Mercy killings by the cops. Snipers on the overpasses. Old people found tied together by a rope in a retirement home. Ten thousand drowned in their attics. Wild dogs eating the lame and the dead.

"For Gawd sake, where is the NOPD and the National Guard?" complained one of the ladies who'd brought over cans of Vienna sausage and Beanee Weenees to share with everyone.

"You know what NOPD stands for, don't you?" Malik said. "Not Our Problem, Dude."

LaMarcus laughed his silly yucking laugh, and Dee kissed him on the forehead. It was good to hear laughter again.

In time the visitors returned to their own camps and everyone settled into vigilant silence. Dee dozed off with her children draped around her, but before long she was jolted awake by loud cheering.

She rubbed her eyes and saw a dozen flashlights carving through the darkness near the atrium. A platoon of National Guardsmen had entered the convention center. Dark figures were rushing toward them now, praising Jesus and clapping their hands and crying in jubilation. *Thank Gawd y'all have come!* The guardsmen tightened their ranks into a defensive formation and resisted engagement. But people were desperate and pressed themselves upon the uniformed men, unleashing all their fears and frustrations, begging for help, throwing themselves at their feet.

Unable to cope with the chaos—overwhelmed by the squalor they were witnessing all around them—the guard unit marched off toward some dark destination in the distant corners of the building. To Dee, it looked less like a practiced drill than a quick retreat. She would later be told they were an engineering unit trained for surveying and clearing debris, not law enforcement, and they barricaded themselves in an exhibit hall at the rear of the facility and refused to come out for fear of being attacked.

In all the noise and confusion, Dee noticed something else. Daylight was peeping through the high atrium skylights near the front entrance. The long night was over.

"Wake up, kids," she said, shaking LaMarcus and Ashley. "It's morning outside. Let's get the hell out of this horrible place."

Duval dragged himself to his feet and put full weight on his legs, testing their ability to bear him. In the morning light he could see roofs emerging out of the floodwater and the grim gray high rise of the interstate appearing silent and abandoned except for a few pitiful faces peering down from the guardrails. He waved at them. He didn't know why. Maybe because they'd fled up there overnight and were in the same sad fucked-up shape he was in and had lived to see a new day.

He shoved off from the wall and walked down the ramp to the water's edge. His legs were weak and his head felt like it had been packed with razorblades. Parts of his face didn't fit. An eye swollen in its socket, a piece of lip split off from his mouth, his front teeth bloody and loose when he probed them with his fingers. This face had made two boys point and laugh. He wondered what LaMarcus and Ashley would think if they saw him like this.

People were wading toward the round gray Dome a short distance away. They looked as if they'd been fighting the floodwater all night long. He stood on the small dry jetty of ambulance ramp and watched the parade. A tall young man showing off his build in a wife-beater T-shirt came sloshing by with a baby in one arm as he pulled along an inflated child's wading pool with two small kids riding in it. Their mother floated beside them in an inner tube, holding onto the plastic pool and talking the gentle way mothers talk to their children when they're afraid. The father glanced in Duval's direction and nodded at him, as if to say, *Everything's cool, we're gonna make it.* But Duval wasn't so sure. How deep was the water between here and the Dome? What was this dude going to do with those babies if the ground slipped away underneath him and water gurgled over his head?

When he gazed toward the interstate again, he saw that crazy old coot boatman cane-poling toward him on the trash heap that passed for a raft. The contraption appeared even more ridiculous in the light of day. Duval laughed out loud. Why hadn't that thing fallen apart by now? The old coot paid no attention to his earthly surroundings as he poled between submerged automobiles. He seemed to be staring toward the hulking structure of the Superdome.

"*Yo, mistah boat man, can I catch a ride?*" Duval yelled at him.

The man looked older and more ravaged in the clear morning light. He turned his head slowly and stared at Duval as if he was just another piece of driftwood. The tiki torch had finally burned out and was leaning badly, ready to drop into the water. A lumpy blue tarp was spread at the boatman's feet like a collapsed tent.

Duval knew it was now or never. He stepped down into brown floodwater warmed by the summer heat and waded out toward the raft. He was never going to get used to this nasty shit. The water deepened as he splashed ahead, churning his legs underwater, and when the raft neared, he made one final lunge, reaching for the wicked edge of a sawed plank. He caught hold and pulled himself over the beer kegs and onto the flat sheets of aluminum siding that formed the raft's deck. Panting like a wet dog, he crawled over the lumpy tarp and collapsed facedown onto a surprisingly soft surface. It was the only thing on the raft that didn't have jagged edges and rusty nails and long jutting splinters. He lay still for a long while, enjoying the quilt-like comfort, but when he glanced up at the pilot, the old man was peering down at him with an openmouthed look of disgust.

"Traveler," he said in a deep voice, "you are desecrating the dead."

Duval sat up quickly and noticed a blue hand protruding from under the tarp. Then a hairless leg. There was more than one body. "Jesus," he said, scooting off the mound of corpses. He smelled them now and it made his stomach turn.

"Lower your head, boy, and say a prayer for their souls, and the souls of all the faithful departed," said the old boatman, thrusting the bamboo pole into the water. "There's a lot more where they came from."

# 30

PJ woke to the sounds of a man drowning. In his struggle to untie the lamp cords, Maceo had tipped over sideways with a loud splash, still bound securely, and now thrashed about under three feet of water, choking and fighting to raise his head above the surface. PJ thought about letting him drown. One less hassle to deal with. He thought about it for several seconds while Maceo bubbled underwater. After careful deliberation, he pulled the sleeping Edgar onto his shoulder, slid off the kitchen counter, and waded over to drag Maceo upright. Vertical again, the pimp gagged and spit rust-colored water and labored to catch his breath. The cords had come loose across his chest and PJ figured the odds were fifty-fifty he would've worked his hands free before he drowned.

"Going for a swim, Maceo?"

He could understand why the man had tried to break loose. The floodwater had risen nearly to his shoulders. "Bust a cap in my head and get it over with," Maceo said, water dripping from his nose and chin.

PJ turned and looked for the .44 magnum. It was still resting on the counter next to the sink full of dirty dishes.

"I'm hungry, Mistah Man," Edgar said with his face nuzzled against PJ's neck.

Baby Darius had begun to cry. Jasmine was awake now, too, rocking the child to shush him. She stared at PJ through dark eyes hooded with sleep.

"They all hungry," Maceo said, chuckling and shaking his head. "What you gone do now, hero? Take us all to IHOP for pancakes?"

With Edgar's skinny arms clinging to his neck, PJ waded over to the sink and stared out the grimy window. The first signs of morning light had appeared at last, and he could see that the flood had deepened in the backyard. There was movement to the water, a slow toiling current, more river than lake. Garbage cans were floating among the broken tree limbs and sections of fence and clumps of debris. Was that a dead body out near the fence line?

"What you go by?" Jasmine asked him. She was rocking Baby Darius and staring out the kitchen window at all the water.

PJ hesitated. "Mistah Man," he said.

Edgar giggled. "He name Mistah Man," he said.

"All right, Mistah Man," Jasmine said without a trace of humor, "what you planning to do?" She sounded like a grown woman again, demanding and impatient, her attitude masking fear. He knew what she was thinking. Now that it's a new day, what's going to happen to me and my little brothers?

"That's what I'm talking about," Maceo said with a brutal laugh. "You got something in mind, hero? 'Cause my side feels like I got shanked where you hit me and I'd like to get the fuck on out of here while I can still walk."

PJ knew there was only one smart thing to do now that it was daylight. He should leave all this behind before the hacks came hunting for him again in their motorboat. If he could keep his head above water, he would make his way on down to his old girlfriend's neighborhood below the Garden District, in what they called the Irish Channel, and hotwire a ride somebody had left in their driveway. That ride was going to be his ticket out of this fucking town.

"I'm hungry, Mistah Man," Edgar said for maybe the fifth time since he'd opened his eyes. Darius was still squalling, despite his sister's attention, and she kept one eye on PJ, expecting an answer. But he didn't have an answer. He didn't know what to do with these little shit turds. Leave them up on the roof and hope a helicopter would spot them?

He imagined that his sister had evacuated with her two children and they were all sleeping safely under dry sheets this morning at Pops's farm outside Opelousas. She'd always been the responsible one, too sharp to get caught up in a nightmare like this. He wondered what Dee would do if she was standing in his shoes right now, gazing out a window at the flood rising up over everything he could see. He watched a broken section of white fence bobbing in the slow current. If he had a working phone, he'd call her up and ask what to do with three little kids and a pimp tied to a chair.

"Where my boat, Mistah Man?" Edgar asked him, looking around the kitchen. "You see my boat?"

"Fuck it, no, Edgar, I don't see your boat," PJ said, setting the boy and his pee-soaked shorts on the counter. "Sit right here, ya heard me? Don't fall off in the water."

PJ tucked the .44 magnum in the waistband of his blue warm-ups and waded to the back door.

"Where you going?" Jasmine called after him. "Please don't go! I'll do whatever you want!" Sunlight was shining through the kitchen window onto her sagging updo and tender face. "For real, Mistah Man. I don't care what it is. Just don't leave us up in here with Maceo."

Eleven years old and she was offering herself to a grown man.

"See, now that's what Maceo been telling you. This li'l bitch ready to be turned out." He cackled at the look of disgust on PJ's face. "Go ahead, home slice. Take her back in yonder and do her, fair and square. I won't say a word to nobody. And it won't cost you a dime."

PJ wanted to punch this son of a bitch in the ribs again. "Shut the fuck up, talking like that," he said, "or I'll drowned your pimp ass with my bare hands."

Maceo tried to suppress his laughter. "I'm just saying, man."

When PJ pried the door open, a wave rolled across the kitchen. "Yo, man, you cain't walk out and leave Maceo like this," the pimp said, spitting water that had splashed in his face.

"My boat out there, Mistah Man?" Edgar was smiling that handsome little smile and kicking his legs in the brown water that had nearly reached the countertop. "Can you bring me my boat back?"

PJ stepped down onto the submerged top step and started wading out into the flooded backyard. He heard Maceo shouting, "Yo, man, untie me! You cain't leave a man to drowned! Untie me!"

Outside in the early light, the water was deeper than he'd counted on. Steam was rising off the warm, slow-moving surface, and the air was low and heavy like the swamp air on Pops's fishing trips in his johnboat, a taste of green in the mouth. Could he make it all the way to the Irish Channel fighting this much water? God, he wished he had that old johnboat right now.

PJ stood still in the middle of the sunken yard, his arms floating beside him, and listened for a boat motor in the quiet morning. Were those deputies still out here looking for him? He reached underwater, slipped the big Dirty Harry .44 out of his waistband, and threw the pistol toward a neighbor's sagging fence. He couldn't risk having a piece on him if Five-O ran him down.

With his hands resting on his head, he slogged toward the alley, weaving around floating patches of garbage and scum. What he thought was a dead body turned out to be a spread of children's clothing from somebody's trunk or chest-of-drawers. He looked back at the house and saw Edgar standing in the kitchen window, smiling at him and waving sweetly, moving his lips, calling out something that PJ couldn't hear. That boy was a heartbreaker.

He waded over to a split-off section of fence bobbing loose on the water. The wood slats were six inches wide, with half as much space between them, the entire piece five or six feet long. When he pushed down on the slats, trying to sink them, the wood popped back up with reliable buoyancy. He grabbed the splintered end-slat and dragged the fence behind him, towing it back toward the house. When he sloshed up the steps and into the kitchen, he discovered that Maceo had freed himself from the chair but was bent over, wincing in pain and straining to untie his hands. He glanced up, surprised to see PJ again.

Jasmine had slid off the counter into the water and had backed into a corner near the refrigerator. She held Baby Darius across her bony shoulder and a crusty butcher knife in her free hand. "He come at me," she said to PJ, "I'ma cut him bad."

"Be cool now, girl," PJ said, raising his hands to calm her. "We're leaving out of this place."

He helped Maceo untie the lamp cord cinched around his wrists. "Come on with me, dawg," he said, taking him by the arm and leading him toward the door like a nurse walking a senile invalid. The man's movements were slow and awkward, the broken rib stabbing him with every step.

Out in daylight, struggling to keep his balance in deep water, Maceo looked weak and drawn, the blood drained from his face. PJ wondered how far the pimp could go in his condition.

"Hold onto this fence," he said. "You have to keep up your end."

"Maceo need a doctor, bruh," he said, bracing his forearms on the floating fence.

"Doctor don't make house calls, balluh. Hold onto this thing. It's our ride."

PJ waded back into the kitchen and picked up Edgar from the counter. The boy latched onto him, his strong little arms strangling PJ's neck. The jubilant smile had disappeared and he was on the verge of tears.

"You okay, Edgar?" he asked him. "Where my happy little stinker?"

"Where you go, Mistah Man?"

"To find us a boat bigger than the one you been pushing around the house. You ready for a sea cruise?"

PJ steadied one side of the fence section, Maceo the other, and Jasmine sat on the wood slats like Cleopatra riding high on her barge, with Baby Darius in her arms and Edgar slouched against her shoulder. They set out across the backyard, testing the craft's stability. Water sloshed up between the slats but the fence stayed afloat even with the children on it. As long as the water didn't get much deeper, PJ figured they would head south toward the Garden District and Irish Channel. He had no reason to believe things would be better down there. Or the water less deep. But he was familiar with the 'hood where his old girlfriend lived and it was farther away from those deputies and the Orleans Parish Prison and he needed to find hope in something.

"Don't know how far Maceo can make it," Maceo said, already winded and struggling to keep his side of the fence from dipping underwater and spilling the children into the flood.

"We're gonna get you some help, man," PJ said. "Hang with us a little while longer, ya heard me?"

"Might have to let go pretty soon. My side is killing me."

"You let go, Maceo, I'm coming around after you. You won't make it out of this yard."

With the sun in their faces, the two men guided the wobbly raft between houses and forded slowly toward the open street. The city was a brown lake as far as they could see in every direction. PJ could feel the return of summer. The air was warm and blue jays were screeching in what was left of the trees. He listened for the motorboat and the deputies' voices but heard no other sounds in the distance. Had they given up on him? He turned their raft southward and the children hung on, Edgar happy and giggling at the strangeness of this game they were playing.

"Where we going, Mistah Man?" he asked.

"To find dry land, Edgar. Like Columbus and them explorers long ago. We're looking for someplace solid to plant our flag." Someplace where he could dump these kids and get on about his business.

They moved steadily through deep water, the long row of flooded houses dark and silent on both sides of the street. It was morning, the second day. A horrible stench wafted across the floodwater. PJ could smell the dead.

# 31

Charles Tran was sitting in a straight-backed lotus position, asleep, when she touched his shoulder and told him they were leaving. He roused himself, stood up, and tried to talk her out of it. "You're safer here with us," he said. "It's dangerous out there, Miss Dee. I worry for your children."

"We'll be fine, Mr. Tran," she said, hugging him. The others in the circle were fast asleep in a web of limbs, except for Trinh, who gave Dee and the children a warm hug and said to Ashley, "Come back if it's too freaky out there, girlfriend. We'll pee on the floor again, no problem."

Dee couldn't imagine coming back. The stray bullets, the thugs and sleazy sex, the overpowering smell of human bodies stewing in an oppressive heat. Anywhere but here.

The children put on their backpacks and Ashley said, "Let's say goodbye to Sistah M." But Dee didn't want to look for the old woman among the chaos of campsites that had cropped up everywhere. She grasped the children's sweaty hands and walked them out through the sleeping bodies and into the blessed light of the atrium. Even at this early hour, dozens of displaced people were streaming through the entrance, defeated and desperate, toting their belongings in paper bags and picnic coolers, many of them old and feeble and staggering on brittle legs. *This is a hell hole,* she wanted to shout at them. *There is nobody in charge and nobody to help you out. You're better off on the streets.* But after wading for hours through dangerous storm waters, they all looked relieved to have found this shelter, any shelter. Three church ladies were holding hands and singing gospel songs together. A toothless old man was clapping and shuffling his feet in a soft shoe dance. Dee couldn't bring herself to tell them there was no happiness or salvation here.

Standing in stark sunlight on the sidewalk outside the convention center, she was surprised to find the boulevard completely dry, with no trace of flooding. Was it coming their way on a slow relentless tide? She closed her eyes and squeezed her children's hands and breathed in the soothing smells of a warm summer morning in the drowsy old town. With her eyes shut and her face to the sun, she could almost believe this was any humid New Orleans morning after an overnight rain.

"What're you thinking, Momma?" Ashley asked, tugging on her hand.

"I'm just glad to be out here in the fresh air again," Dee said, opening her eyes and hugging them to her side. Sweat was drying on her neck and breasts. She could smell the funk all over her body and the children's, too. "How are you guys holding up?"

LaMarcus said he was hungry. Ashley wished she could take a bath. Dee wasn't paying close attention to what they were saying. She'd noticed two NOPD cruisers parked across the street, the cops leaning against their doors.

"Hey, what y'all doing over there?" she shouted at them. "Hey, they need some police officers inside this building!"

Four cops were lounging back with their arms folded, talking quietly with one another, watching people straggle into the convention center. They gave her a quick glance and then ignored her.

Dee grabbed the children's hands and marched across the median toward the patrol cars. "They need some law enforcement real bad in there," she said as she approached them, her voice rising in anger. "Thugs have taken over. They've got guns and they're scaring everybody. Why are y'all standing around out here?"

The cops stared at her, their faces hard as stone. She recognized two of them—the white cop and his black female partner who'd stopped their group on Poydras Street. They'd probably been up all night patrolling a lawless city. They looked as tired and frayed as she was, and they made it clear they had no patience for her scolding.

"We go in there, lady," said the white cop, "it's gonna turn into a war zone. They're gonna shoot at any uniform they see, and we'll shoot back, and innocent bystanders gonna get hurt. And then the whole place is gonna panic and stampede for the exit and people gonna die. We can't play it like that."

Dee couldn't believe what she was hearing. They were willing to let the thugs and bullies have their way. "So you're saying if the situation is dangerous, the police won't deal with it because it's dangerous?" she said.

The cops shifted their stances, adjusted their gun belts, leather holsters creaking. They wanted her to go away and stop bothering them. "The National Guard went in there a little while ago, lady," said another cop, looking over her head as he spoke, not meeting her eye. "It's on them to get it under control."

LaMarcus let go of his mother's hand. "You know what NOPD stands for?" he said in a defiant voice. "Not Our Problem, Dude."

Dee clasped her hand over his mouth. "I'm sorry, officers," she said, glancing apologetically at the policemen. "He heard that inside."

The white cop said, "Why don't you and your smart-mouthed boy take a hike, lady? You're not making any friends here."

Blood surged into her face. Her body was suddenly hot all over, sweat nettling the back of her neck. "Come on, kids," she said, turning and leading her children away. But outrage was welling inside her, clouding her better judgment, and after a few swift paces she turned back around. *"Hey, Barney Fife,"* she said to the cop who'd made the remark. *"Do your fucking job, okay? This is what we pay you for,"* she said, slinging her head toward the convention center.

Ashley jerked on her hand. "Mahh-muh," she whispered, mortified by her mother's language.

Dee dragged the children with her as she stormed off down the sidewalk. She didn't know where she was going. Her anger wouldn't let her think straight. She glanced toward the center again and noticed a sheet-covered body sprawled by the curb. People were walking past the dead man as if he were trash left out for the city garbage trucks. Dee shuddered and thought about her father. What had happened to him and Duval? She stopped and fished her cell phone out of Ashley's backpack. The phone still held a charge but couldn't find a signal. Everything was down. "Damn it," she said, shoving the phone back in the bag.

"Who you calling, girlfriend? George Bush?" someone said with a booming laugh. "He too busy clearing brush on the back forty."

It was the man named Malik who'd brought them water and juice boxes last night. He was crossing the street with three other men. "Y'all hungry, chirren?" he said to LaMarcus and Ashley. "Come on with us, you want breakfast. We fixin' to go rustle up some eggs and bacon over by the hotel I cook at."

He was a large man with a wide friendly smile behind a graying beard. His belly sagged underneath a Neville Brothers T-shirt, and his long gray dreadlocks looked dusty and neglected, like a shaggy headdress too complicated to clean. He struck Dee as an eccentric crossover between a Muslim and a Rastafarian. She had liked him instantly when he came to their camp bearing gifts. She trusted his smile. He reminded her of the Marine buddies who dropped by to visit her Daddy when she was growing up in Convent.

"What's on the menu this morning, Mr. Malik?" she asked with a tired grin. "A champagne brunch with flowers and piano music?"

"I'm 'on cook up all the food in the walk-in cooler 'fore it goes bad. Yeah, might even crack open a bottle or two of Korbel Brut. You in or out, young lady? I'll whip up some pancakes for them good-lookin' chirren of yours."

LaMarcus smiled and his eyes grew large. "Can you make pancakes kind of runny in the middle?" he asked. "That's how I like them."

The hotel was only a few blocks away, near Harrah's Casino. There had been no flooding in this part of town yet, the lower warehouse district near Canal Street. Malik had a key to the kitchen entrance at the back of the hotel. He and the other men went in first, to make sure there were no looters or broken glass or live wires hanging loose. He returned to the outside door and beckoned Dee and the children to come in. "Welcome to *chez moi,* y'all," he said with widespread arms and a jolly laugh. "How you take your eggs, girlfriend?"

The men raided the walk-in cooler, bringing out armloads of food. "Still pretty cool in there," Malik said, igniting the gas grill with a Bic lighter, "but it won't keep for long. Not in this heat."

He and his three compadres had grown up together in the Desire Housing Project. They set about scrambling eggs, frying bacon and sausage, whipping pancake batter. Dee and the children ate every scrap put in front of them. They drank milk and orange juice from proper glasses. LaMarcus got his pancakes exactly as he liked them.

"You ready for that complimentary glass of Korbel, young lady?" Malik asked Dee.

She shook her head with a grateful smile. She couldn't imagine enjoying the lightheaded euphoria of champagne at a time like this. "I'll raise a glass with you when it's finally over, Mr. Malik," she said.

After they'd eaten, she and the children joined the production line, turning bacon on the grill and flipping pancakes. Malik's friends were like doting grandfathers. They showed the children how to shape pancake batter into animal figures.

"Which one of you smart chirren is gonna be president of the United States someday?" asked one of the men.

LaMarcus and Ashley laughed and shrugged their shoulders.

"Let me ax you this. How many black presidents we had so far?" the man persisted, pouring more batter onto the grill.

"That's easy," LaMarcus said. "Zip."

"How you know that?"

LaMarcus shrugged again. "Haven't you seen the money?"

The men howled with laughter. "You was president," Malik said, "we'd have some help down here by now. Ain't that right, commander in chief?"

Dee was enjoying their company. It was the first time she'd felt safe in days.

"What are we gonna do with all this food?" Ashley asked as she piled grease-dripping bacon onto paper towels.

Malik stepped away from the sizzling grill with a spatula in his hand and wiped his sweating forehead with the apron he was wearing. "Well, Miss Ash, we gonna—"

Before he could finish his sentence, they heard a key turn the lock on the door that led into the hotel dining room. Everyone fell silent and stared. Suddenly the door banged open and a uniformed security guard stepped into the kitchen with his revolver pointed at them. "Don't move!" he shouted. "Hands in the air, all of you!"

Malik glanced at the other men and they all raised their hands slowly and reluctantly. "Jimmy," he said, "put that damn gun down before you hurt somebody. Cain't you see there's chirren in the room?"

"Malik?" the guard said, still pointing his revolver. "What the hell you doing back here? I thought you dudes were looters."

"You hungry, Jimmy? Put that gun away and come eat some breakfast with us."

"Damn straight I'm hungry," the guard said, holstering his weapon. He was a middle-aged white man with the ruddy features of an Irish cop. "Haven't eaten since Sunday night. I could smell the bacon from the lobby."

"Help yourself, my man. We got plenty."

Malik and the security guard were fellow employees of the hotel. The man ate his fill of bacon and sausage and eggs, washing it all down with juice and piling his plate with pancakes for dessert. He told them stories about riding out the hurricane in the tall swaying hotel, trying to keep the guests safe from gale-shattered windows in the upper floors. They'd camped on mattresses in the hallways, a group of conventioneers from Kansas and some foreign tourists pooling their money to hire a private bus from Baton Rouge to come and rescue them. They'd been waiting for more than twelve hours, but the bus hadn't arrived yet.

"You ax me," the guard said with a mouthful of food, "that bus ain't never gonna show up. Somebody took it over. National Guard or the cops or maybe some local homeboys, I don't know. Soon as it hit the city limits, somebody snagged it and said, 'You're *my* ride now, podnah.'"

LaMarcus wandered over to the dining room door and peered in. He saw them sitting silently at tables, older white people with sad faces, many of them his Pawpaw's age, their suitcases stacked around them as if they were waiting for a taxi. A nice lady with yellow hair smiled at him. She wore glasses and her cheeks sagged like that cartoon dog Droopy's. "Good morning, young man," she said in a teacher's voice. "Looks like you made it through the storm all right."

"Our house is under water," LaMarcus said, straightening his shoulders as if he was standing beside his school desk, answering a math question. "We had to go up on the roof. A helicopter rescued us in a basket."

"Oh my goodness, you poor child," the lady said, her forehead wrinkling.

Her round-faced old husband stood up and limped over and knelt down on one stiff knee, giving LaMarcus a grandfather hug. "I'm glad you're okay, son," he said.

Dee stepped into the dining room and smiled at the old man. She placed her hands on her son's shoulders and looked over the exhausted occupants of the dining tables. Thirty or forty of them who'd gone through more than they'd bargained for on a vacation trip to the grand old garden city. At least they hadn't been stranded on a roof or forced to wade through deep floodwater, like most of the people crowding into the convention center. These folk had nice suitcases and their clothes weren't glued to their bodies with dried sweat.

"Welcome to the Big Easy," Dee said with a mischievous laugh.

They all laughed, too.

"Y'all hungry?" she asked.

Everyone spoke at once.

"Tell you what we'll do," she said. "We'll trade you a good breakfast for a ride on that bus you paid for. My two children and me. We don't care where you're going, as long as it's out of this town."

Someone questioned whether there was enough room on the bus for everyone from the hotel.

"We'll make room for you and your children, honey," said the woman with the yellow hair and glasses. "I promise you that."

When Dee and LaMarcus walked back into the kitchen, Malik and the security guard were having an animated disagreement over the food. "Technically speaking," the guard was saying, "this food belongs to the hotel, Malik, and those people are paying guests. Breakfast included. It's *their* food, man."

Malik was waving his spatula. "Technically speaking, Jimmy, it's my kitchen and we just cooked a shitload of breakfast for my people over at the convention center. And that's where we gonna take it."

"I don't know if I can let you do that," said the guard, setting aside his empty plate and hooking his thumbs in his gun belt.

He was the only person in the kitchen with a gun. Malik's friends moved slowly away from the grill and spread out, each with something in his hands. An egg whisker, a chopping knife. Dee didn't like what was happening here.

"Malik," she said, "we're gonna feed those people in the dining room. There's enough for them and a whole lot more. We'll take as much as we can over to the convention center."

The guard scratched at his fleshy Irish face. "Better listen to this lady, Malik," he said. "She's got it right."

Malik stared at her solemnly. He seemed disappointed that she would take the security guard's side.

"Go in there and look those people in the eye," she said to him, nodding toward the dining room. "Then tell me if you can let them go hungry."

Malik glanced toward the door, then back at Dee. His face burst into a generous smile. "Okay, homegirl, we'll do it your way," he said. "Only you're gonna have to marry me when this is all over with."

An hour later, she and the children were walking with Malik and his friends down the wide boulevard toward the convention center, carrying jugs of milk and orange juice and aluminum pans full of scrambled eggs and bacon. She watched a truck pull up in front of the center. A platoon of National Guardsmen jumped out of the canvas-covered bed in the rear. Rifles slung over their shoulders, they huddled on the sidewalk near that shrouded corpse. Someone had placed an orange traffic cone next to the body to direct people around it. And now there was a second body—an ancient woman slumped over in a wheelchair, her head draped with winter blankets and her feet curled inside soiled house slippers.

"Those people, Momma," Ashley said. "Are they dead?"

"Yes, sugar, they are. You don't have to look at them. Turn your head."

"How did they die?" LaMarcus asked.

"They were old and probably sick, hon. This was too much for them."

"I hope Tante Belle is safe," Ashley said. "Do you think she'll be home when we get back to our house?"

"It's going to take awhile for us to get back there," Dee said. She didn't have the strength to tell them they may have lost their house forever.

"We'll have to tell her about Tempo," Ashley said with a glum face. "That's going to make her cry."

The guardsmen were keeping their distance from the abandoned bodies. Two of them split off from the group and marched across the street to talk to the NOPD officers stationed at their patrol units.

There were scores of disoriented people milling about the sidewalk and spilling out into the street. They seemed unwilling to enter the convention center itself. Word had spread that conditions were deplorable inside, the carpet slick with sewage from overflowing toilets and predators roaming wild. They chose to remain out in the sunshine where they could breathe clean air and see trouble coming. When Dee and the others approached with their pans full of steaming food, Malik held out his arm, slowing them down. "Let me handle this," he said.

They were quickly surrounded by hungry people reaching and shoving and groping for the food they could smell. Malik and the three men demanded order. "Make a line, y'all!" he yelled like a high school gym coach. "We ain't serving nobody that cain't behave themselves!"

People pushed and jostled and, to Dee's surprise, eventually arranged themselves into something resembling a line. There were trash talkers. Disgruntled folk complaining about the way they were being treated. Lunatics raving nonsense. Hysterics shrieking about what had happened to them before they were rescued. One man with crazy eyes and a scraggly goatee kept shouting, "Where the buses at, Ray Nagin? Where the fucking buses at?" Dee tried to ignore him and the other complainers. She and Malik's men had quickly set up their sidewalk buffet operation on stacks of ice chests, and they spooned eggs and two strips of bacon and a pancake on each hotel plate and handed them out as fast as they could. LaMarcus was in charge of giving out forks, and Ashley poured milk and juice into plastic cups.

The National Guardsmen wandered over to see what all the noise was about. Malik grinned at them. "Better get in line 'fore it's all gone, gents," he said. "This beats eating out of a tin can, don't it?"

A police squad car rolled slowly down the boulevard, crawling past the entrance to the convention center. People in line began to yell at the vehicle. *Do something, yo! Get us out of here!* Someone threw a water bottle that thudded against the windshield. Dee saw the Man with Crazy Eyes stumble into the street and throw himself in front of the police car, bumping against it with his thighs and slamming his palms on the hood, as if trying to stop them. "*You got to do something 'bout all this, man!*" he shouted at the two officers in the car. He sounded drunk. They turned on their overhead lights and whooped the siren. He stepped back a few paces, slightly dazed, then charged again, slamming his fists on the hood and cursing them.

"*Get the fuck out this car and do something, you chickenshits!*"

They edged their vehicle against him and he flopped onto the hood, clowning like he was hurt. Then he rolled off the hood and pulled what looked like a box cutter out of his pants pocket and waved it in the air. The cops opened their doors and got out, withdrawing their revolvers. "*Put down the weapon!*" the driver commanded. But the Man with Crazy Eyes refused to obey. He kicked their headlight and slashed the air with the box cutter. "*I said put down that weapon!*" the cop barked, training his revolver on him. The man waved the box cutter and threatened to cut off the cop's balls. People on the sidewalk were laughing at the crazy fool, egging him on.

*Cut they pants loose, Zorro! Stick 'em good!*

Dee was sure he was just some deranged old drunk playing around, performing for a captive audience. She didn't believe he intended to harm anybody.

A gunshot boomed. One of the cops had fired his weapon. Then a second loud report. Malik and the people in the food line dropped to the sidewalk, covering their heads. As Dee reached for LaMarcus and Ashley, someone tackled her from behind, taking all three of them to the pavement with long arms wrapped around them like protective wings. When she managed to lift her chin, she saw the crazy man sprawled on the street in front of the cop car, blood pooling around his body. The two police officers were standing over him, pointing their guns. One of them kicked away the box cutter lying nearby. The man wasn't moving. They had shot him dead.

"It's over," said the figure who was spread-eagle across Dee's back, shielding her and the children, his long fingers resting on the nape of Ashley's neck.

Dee rolled over to face him. It was the guardsman named Robert Guyton. He pulled himself off her and stood up, reaching out his hand, helping her to her feet. "You all right, Miss Grant?" he asked, bending down to check on LaMarcus. "Anybody hit?"

The crowd was stirring, hundreds of shocked witnesses. Malik and his buddies were on their feet now, yelling at the cops. Women were screaming. *You killed that man! You killed that man!* Someone hurled a hotel plate at the patrol car. People surged out into the street, shaking their fists at the two cops, quickly surrounding them. The scene was getting ugly. The officers stationed across the boulevard were advancing with shotguns they'd removed from their units.

"Come on, let's get y'all out of here," Robert Guyton said, "before this whole place goes Rambo."

# 32

There it was, the *thut thut thut* of chopper blades coming for him. He was dreaming he was in the jungle again. They'd docked their PBR in a mangrove swamp and waded neck deep onto marshy land, an armed patrol searching for the snipers who'd been shooting at them for days. Ernie Garza was walking point when he stepped on the Claymore. Bloody pieces of flesh and bone were scattered all over the dense green foliage. Hodge had been trailing him by thirty feet and took some frag in his leg and hip. A brother named Louis Ford tied the tourniquet just below his knee, and Hodge writhed on his back in the mud, absorbing the pain, waiting for the dust-off to find them in the patch of jungle his buddies had cleared with machetes.

And here it was, finally, the *thut thut thut* of the air ambulance reaching their coordinates. Only it wasn't Ernie Garza they were scraping into a poncho. It was Rochelle. She'd flatlined while he was holding her hand in the terminal care unit. One final deep breath and then the silence of eternity. He tried not to let go of her hand, but they were cinching up the poncho. *Don't leave me out here like this,* she said, opening her eyes. *Not like this.*

He was awake now, lying in a ring of sweat on a gurney with an IV needle in his arm. The chopper noise was real. Had they flown him to that little provincial hospital in Long Xuyen? There was motion in the dim corridor all around him, squeaking shoes, a young woman panting hard and pinching her breath, someone urging her to *push.* Daylight was slanting through a doorway just beyond his feet. His mind was clearing slowly and he remembered where he was. The chopper was coming to transport him to Baton Rouge. He had to get up and find his way out of here before they wheeled him into that medevac.

Hodge ripped the tape off the syringe and removed the needle implanted in his vein, then replaced the tape over the small hole to stop the trickle of blood. When he sat up, he felt normal. No dizziness, no tightness in his chest. The good sleep and the meds had done their job. He swung his legs off the gurney and located his wet fatigues and boots tucked underneath the cart. No one seemed to notice. The nurses were occupied with the young woman giving birth down the corridor. *You're doing fine, doll,* they kept saying to her. *Keep pushing, you're almost there.*

He dressed quickly in the gray light and slipped into the room where they had examined him last night. The chopper noise was louder here and he stepped over a swept-up pile of glass and stood at the open window, a humid breeze blowing in his face as he gazed around for the bird. Down at street level, daylight made the flood look much worse. Four feet deep, maybe deeper, debris floating everywhere. The people wading around in it were waving desperately at the helicopter angling toward the hospital roof across the street.

Despite the chopper racket, he thought he heard a backfire or a gunshot. Then another one. The waders were scattering in slow motion, searching for cover out in the open water. Was there a shooter out there?

He walked back to the doorway and stood watching the nurses deliver the baby in a haze of sweltering heat and poor lighting. *You're almost there, sweetheart. Keep pushing. I can see the crown.* No one stopped him as he ambled down the dusky corridor to the exit door. I'll just fade on out of here, he told himself, make my way down to the street. Nobody will know I'm gone.

When he opened the heavy door and shuffled out into the dark landing, groping for the handrail, he smelled the bodies decomposing on the stairwell. The odor was ripe and churned his empty stomach.

A sudden beam of light burst into his eyes. "Say, m'man, what you doing out here?" The security guard named Tucker was coming up the stairs with a flashlight. He was wearing a painter's mask over his mouth and nose. "You s'posed to be resting back in yonder with an IV in your arm."

Hodge raised a hand to shield his eyes. "Everything's cool, brother," he said. "Just needed some fluids and a blow. They checked me out and I'm ready to rumble."

Tucker lowered the flashlight. "Cain't hardly beat down an old devil dog for long," he said with a chuckle. "Where you going now?"

"Down to the beach. Like I said, my daughter and her kids are waiting for me out there."

"That young dude was with you. Baby daddy. Last I checked, some thugs was stomping a mud hole in him. Took y'all's canoe."

Duval was supposed to be way ahead of him by now—at the Superdome, hunting for Dee.

"Where's he at?"

"No idea. Nurse Shannon tried to help him out. He was sitting on the ramp for a long time, pretty messed up. Now he's gone."

Tucker raised the light and Hodge saw he was wearing a flak jacket, with a hunting rifle strapped to his shoulder. "You best not go outside right now," he said. "There's a sniper out there, shooting at civilians. Two of our docs were taking a boatload of patients over to the hospital across the street and somebody drew down on 'em. We don't know where he's shooting from. I gotta go up on the roof and see if I can spot that motherfucker. I do, I'm taking him out."

"I thought I heard something myself. Couple of gunshots."

"I could use some backup, soldier," Tucker said. "From somebody's been there."

Hodge scratched his neck. He needed to put some distance between himself and that medevac team. "I don't know, man," he said. "Been a long time since I shot at somebody."

"You mize well come with me. 'Cause if this fucker is for real, he'll shoot your ass soon as you walk out the building." Tucker adjusted the rifle on his shoulder. "A bullet in your gizzard ain't gonna help you find your daughter."

They walked up six flights of stairs, and the climb caused pressure in his chest. He wasn't as strong as he'd thought. The problem hadn't gone away, only crawled up underneath the chemicals for a spell, until he'd stirred everything up again. When they banged through the metal door and strode out into bright morning light on the hospital roof, Hodge did his best to control his deep ragged breathing and not give himself away. He knew now he should have stayed on that gurney for a while longer.

The retaining wall at the edge of the roof was only waist high. Tucker set the scoped rifle against it and stood peering out into the sultry air with his binoculars. The chopper had landed on the roof across the street, its rotors still echoing through the wide chasm between buildings. "That hospital over there, they got deep pockets," he said, adjusting his sights on the upper floors of the parking garage. "They hired some private fly boys out of Shreveport to come and get them. Us, we're stuck waiting on the seventh cavalry to show up over here. They keep saying, 'the cavalry's coming, the cavalry's coming.' I'll believe it when I see it, bro'. Too many poor black folk in this old bone shop underneath us. We'll be the last in line."

It was the first time Hodge had seen Tucker in clear light. He was a stout man with thick arms and thighs bulging through his uniform and a three-day beard that looked like grains of rice sprinkled on his jowled cheeks. There was merriment in his eyes and a world-weary grin on his face, and Hodge felt he'd known this man all his life.

"Here, give it a look," Tucker said, handing the binoculars to Hodge. "If our bad boy is out there somewhere, I cain't find him."

Hodge raised the binoculars to his eyes and fingered the knob, bringing into sharp focus the upper floors of the university hospital and the parking garage next to it. The windows were blown out over there, as well. He steadied his hands and peered into the lenses, moving slowly from level to level, up and down the open ramps of the garage. It was the perfect nest for a sniper. But he detected no movement, no glinting metal, only a handful of vehicles parked in shadow.

"You come back to the N. O. after your tour?" Hodge asked him, slowly scanning across rooftops until he found the upper deck of the interstate.

"Bounced around at first. Detroit, Chicago. Nothing but hard times up there. Came on back home about thirty years ago, been here ever since. Raised three kids in this town. Good kids, never been in trouble. When the news said Katrina was coming, I sent my wife and gran'chirren to her kinfolk in Rayne."

Hodge could see hundreds of people stranded on the interstate overpass. Clusters of white T-shirts, teenagers looking down from the guardrail at the floodwater below. Could that sniper be shooting from the interstate?

He lowered the binoculars and looked at Tucker. "What's gonna happen to this old town?" he asked.

Tucker chucked the bill of his cap and scratched his forehead with a blunt thumbnail. "Cecile and me, we live over by the Ninth Ward," he said. "Won't be nothing much left to go back to. I don't know what we'll do. Get through it, I s'pose. Take it little by little."

They stood gazing down at the desperate people wading through the flooded streets thirteen stories below. Tucker retrieved the binoculars and began searching the rooftops again. "Maybe our boy is taking a coffee break," he said, "firing up some reefer. I don't see hide nor hair of him."

"You sure it was a sniper?"

"What them two doctors said. They turned their boat around when they heard gunfire."

"It's one of those times when everybody's hearing things. Seeing things," Hodge said. "You never know."

Tucker walked south along the retaining wall and took up another position to search the surrounding buildings with his binoculars. He was covering different territory now, another angle of the landscape. Hodge brought the rifle and waited next to him, feeling the smooth curved stock just behind the trigger guard, a memory sensation as intimate as the curve of his wife's breast. It had been a long time since he'd held a rifle, but he remembered how it worked. Three of your fingers cupped the polished grain, your trigger finger resting steady against the curl of cold metal. He lofted the rifle to his shoulder and squinted through the scope, fixing the Superdome in the crosshairs. Magnified, the massive dome felt close enough to hit with a rock. Where you at, Dee? he wondered. And you, Duval. Are you following the plan, young fool?

He lowered the rifle and closed his eyes to the warm summer breeze gusting against his tired body. He could hear chopper blades again, louder this time, and he realized it wasn't the same chopper from the hospital roof across the street. There was another one airborne somewhere, and he opened his eyes to look for it.

"Do me a favor, Tucker," he said, thinking about his wife and that dust-off coming for what was left of Ernie Garza. "When the time comes, don't let me rot in the stairway with rats chewing on my nuts. Wrap a poncho 'round these old bones and tell my grandchildren I died like a soldier."

Tucker lowered the binoculars and stared at him. "You're talking some shit, now, Opelousas," he said, narrowing his eyes with an uneasy smile. "Ain't nothing like that gonna happen to you. You feeling awright?"

The Chinook appeared out of nowhere, its long misshapen body rising up through the clustered buildings of the medical complex until it was hovering above the hospital rooftop where the two men stood washed in its downdraft.

*"Here comes your seventh cavalry!"* Hodge shouted at Tucker.

It was time to get on out of here before the staff tried to put him on that transport.

*"I don't think that's the medevac!"* Tucker shouted back. He waved his cap at the chopper, the windstorm blowing his uniform wildly.

The bay door of the Chinook opened up and there was a moment when all Hodge could see was a black hole in its side and shadowy movement deep in the bowels of the machine.

"Lay that rifle down!" Tucker yelled at him, still waving his cap. "Do it quick! They might think we're the bad guys!"

Hodge knelt down and placed the rifle carefully on the stained concrete. When he looked up again, things were raining down on them from that dark bay door.

# 33

Maceo held up his side of the raft in an obliging silence for block after block. They encountered few people moving on the water. An ancient stoop-backed preacher rescued from his flooded church by parishioners in a canoe. Grimfaced project teenagers sloshing along, hanging onto a buoyant swim-lane line they'd found who knows where. The water's depth was slowly dropping as they moved farther south away from the lake and the broken levees. It was only waist deep on PJ when an older white lady slogged up out of a side street with a rope slung across her shoulder, dragging a door behind her like a mule sled. She had bungeed her husband's blanket-wrapped corpse to the floating door.

"It's Harold," she announced as she waded toward them. "Insulin shock, I figger. We been married forty years. I didn't want to leave him behind in the house. Y'all heading to St. Charles? Radio says it's dry on St. Charles and from there all the way down to the river. For the time being, they say."

She was a large woman with flabby arms and a head full of tangled gray hair, and she wore drugstore sunglasses that had slid down her nose. Not one of those fussy uptown ladies but a woman who'd worked all her life behind a meat counter or in a muddy kitchen shucking oysters.

Edgar was sitting up straight as a little prince, his head smothered under PJ's Saints cap. "Miss white lady, who that tied to yo' door?" he asked the woman.

"Hush, now," Jasmine said to her little brother.

"That's my husband, dawlin'," the woman said. "He died on me, poor dear."

PJ said, "I'm sorry for your loss, ma'am." It was the way his mother had taught him to speak to people, no matter black or white. A lesson he usually ignored.

"You mind if I tag along with your party?" Her large droopy breasts were bulging through her wet T-shirt, and PJ tried not to stare. "It gets much deeper, y'all might have to pile me on top of Harold and tie us up to a stop sign."

Their tattered little fleet ventured steadily down the flooded avenue with little energy for words. When they neared the Magnolia Housing Project, condemned by the city and closed down long before the storm, Edgar noticed something on the water and pointed. "What that is, Mistah Man?" he asked.

They had waded into a colony of fire ants that encircled them like a winding red-brown trail of topsoil floating on the water. "Yo, Maceo, we got a situation," PJ said, splashing at a patch of seething ants. His Pops had once run over a nest as big as a medicine ball out on Bayou Teche, and it was hell keeping them out of the johnboat. They would eat these children alive.

"They *fire* ants!" Maceo yelled, slapping at the water and wiping his arms. "They sting Maceo, my throat close up! Almost killed me one time when I was a shorty!"

"Be cool, Maceo! I'm sliding thisaway," PJ said, moving to the rear of the raft. "Watch out, ma'am!" he cautioned the white lady. "Get behind me and follow close. You, too, Maceo."

PJ pushed the raft from the rear, plowing through the teeming navy of ants with enough speed to carve an open channel. Jasmine grabbed her brothers and held on, and Maceo and the white lady followed in the raft's wake, dragging her dead husband tied to the door.

"That's all Harold needs—fire ants crawling up his legs," she said, huffing to keep up. "He never could abide these mean little bastards."

Once PJ was certain they'd gained enough distance from the ants, he began splashing water across the slats, washing away the crawlers that still clung to the wood. Jasmine brushed ants from her bare legs, and Edgar made a game of pounding them with a doubled fist. "They coming back again," he said, making that familiar blubbering sound with his lips.

"The ants are gone, little man," PJ said. "They're not coming back."

Edgar shook his head, saying, "The boat by our house."

PJ heard the motor now, the only sound besides birdsong in the peaceful morning air. Was it those parish deputies out looking for him? He turned to search for the sound and spotted a flat-bottom fan boat roaring in their direction. The hulking topside engine sounded more like a tractor than a motorboat. As it drew closer, he saw that the pilot was a white woman sitting in a chair with the stick throttle in her hand. She was surrounded by grubby wet evacuees she'd hauled up out of the water.

"Y'all need a lift?" she shouted at them. "We can make room."

Maceo was the first to speak. "Yes, ma'am, Maceo fo' sho' could use a ride out of this swamp," he said, wading over to the idling boat. "I'm busted up pretty bad and need me some medical attention 'fo I pass out."

This was what PJ had been waiting for—a chance to unload these children where they would be safe, then get on down the road.

"Welcome aboard," the pilot said. She was a small muscular woman wearing blue jeans and a shapely tank top, with tendrils of blonde hair escaping under an Evinrude cap. "We're the Cajun Navy," she said, bringing laughter from a couple of ruddy, hard-bitten construction workers sitting at her feet. White boys from hick towns in Acadia and Jeff Davis parishes. One of them was holding a sawed-off shotgun. "We convoyed in last night from Jennings," the pilot said. "Eighteen boats and a division of redneck Cajuns. Heard y'all had some good fishing down here."

Clutching his ribs and grimacing, Maceo was pulled aboard by one of the Cajuns. PJ handed Baby Darius to the man with the shotgun and helped Jasmine and little Edgar crawl off the raft and into the boat. Then he turned to lend a hand to the white lady with her bungeed husband.

"I'm sorry, ma'am," the pilot said, "we can't bring that body on board. Police orders. They said we've got to leave the dead alone. Too many health risks. Might expose everybody on this boat."

The white lady looked stunned. Her mouth hung loose as she tried to cope with this news. "What am I going to do with Harold?" she asked, removing her sunglasses to wipe her eyes with the sleeve of her baggy T-shirt. "We been married forty years. I couldn't leave him in the attic. I just couldn't."

The pilot wasn't much older than PJ, with a kind face and a girlish spray of freckles across her nose. She had sweated through her tank top. "I'm sorry, ma'am," she said. "I wish I could do something for you."

PJ scratched his jaw and neck. "Cain't you tie this door up to the back of the boat and tow it?" he asked the pilot. "Won't be no dead man in the boat with the rest."

After huddled deliberation with her traveling companions, the pilot agreed it would be okay. PJ helped the white lady secure the rope to a cleat on the stern of the fan boat, then held his breath and ducked underwater and seized the heavy lady up under her wide bottom and hoisted her onboard like a three-hundred-pound cotton bale soaked to the core.

"Looks like we've got company," the pilot said.

PJ was wiping water out of his eyes when he saw the Orleans Parish motorboat speeding toward them with that hard-ass sergeant at the wheel and four uniformed men seated behind him with shotguns. His throat went dry. He had no choice but to climb aboard the fan boat and crawl up next to Jasmine. He slipped the Saints cap off Edgar's head and put it on his own, gathering the children closer to him.

The pilot waved at the deputies with a pretty smile and the sergeant raised his chin in response and maneuvered his boat alongside hers. He was wearing sunglasses and his countenance was somber and businesslike as he shouted, "Morning, skipper. I see you got quite a load there. Where'd you get this boat?"

"Belongs to me," she said, sitting erect in the pilot's chair like a sales manager sitting at her office desk. "We came in from Jennings and Crowley last night." She glanced at the sunburned Cajun kneeling beside her with a sawed-off shotgun resting on a shoulder. "We've been working with the NOPD. They know we're here. You guys with the Orleans Parish Sheriff's Department?"

"Roger that. We're looking for escapees from the parish prison. You run across anybody wearing orange?"

"Just these people here," she said. "We're delivering them to the staging areas."

The sergeant stared at the man with the sawed-off shotgun. "You got a reason to be carrying that thing, pal?" he asked him.

The Cajun smiled darkly. He was a man of few words. The woman did all the talking for them. "Just a precaution," she said. "We've heard the stories. NOPD said we'd be wise to arm ourselves."

The sergeant studied the passengers jammed together on the deck of the fan boat. A moment passed. A long tense moment when voices fell silent and the two boat motors idled in a steady groan. And then the sergeant spoke: "Yo, man. You under the Saints cap—Look at me!"

PJ pretended to speak softly into Edgar's ear. He turned and muttered nonsense to Jasmine. Anything to avoid the sergeant's gaze.

"I'm talking to you, Coolio," the sergeant said. "Lemme see your face. Ain't you the dude we talked to yesterday up by the Calliope projects?"

The pantomime was over. "You talking to me, officer?" he asked with an innocent shrug.

One of the deputies in the boat rose to his feet with a firm grip on his shotgun. "Thass gotta be him, sarge," he said. "Thass Coolio, straight up. One that like to take a baff in shitwater."

The sergeant showed the faintest smile. "Up on your feet, Coolio," he said. "Let's take a look at you."

PJ glanced up at the pilot. She looked concerned. "What's this all about, officer?" she asked the sergeant.

"Police business, skipper," he said dismissively. "We have reason to believe this man may be one of our runners."

PJ held Edgar against his chest like a shield. "You must be mistaken, officer," he said. "I ain't been in jail. I been taking care of my three kids in this hurricane."

"Get up nice and slow, Coolio. We found your orange Sunday suit."

PJ glanced at Maceo. The pimp was resting against the gunnel, holding his ribs, staring back at him with a focused hostility. He was the one man on this boat who could tell the deputies that PJ wasn't the father of these children, just some drifter who'd broken into their house last night.

"Make it easy on yourself, Coolio," the sergeant said, motioning to his men. Two deputies stood up and pointed their shotguns at him. "Come on out of there. We don't want nobody to get hurt."

Maceo pulled himself upright, wincing in pain. PJ could see that the pimp intended to tell the sergeant something and there was no way to stop him.

"Nobody taking my Daddy away from me and my brothers."

Jasmine was rocking Baby Darius like the perfect dutiful daughter. When she hooked an arm around PJ's arm, there was pride and devotion in the expression on her face.

"I don't know what you talking 'bout—been in some kind of prison—'cause my Daddy be with us ever since I'm alive and he be with us the whole time the hurricane blowing outside. If it wadn't for him, we woulda drownded up in our house, me and my two li'l brothers here. Why you wanna be taking my Daddy away from us, Mistah Po-lice Man? Our Momma gone to Jesus already. Who gonna feed us and put us to sleep at night, like he do every night, twenty-four seven? What we gonna do, my brothers and me, you take him off somewhere? Baby Darius not even a year old," she said, rocking the boy. "Who gonna be his Daddy now?"

The sergeant stared at Jasmine. He was clearly unprepared to hear this. He turned to his men. There was confusion among them as they exchanged whispers.

"This fella's not a jailbird," said the white lady. "He's a decent man who helped me out with my Harold," she said, gesturing over her shoulder at the door floating behind the boat. "Y'all go on about your business and let us get on with ours."

The sergeant and his men were straining to see the blanket-draped body bungeed to the door.

"Like my daughter said, officer, our house is gone and everything we own. I need to get these children someplace safe," PJ said, glancing over at Maceo again. The pimp was braced against the gunnel in obvious pain, trying to say something out loud.

"These children lost their momma to the crack pipe some lowlife pimp pushed on her," PJ said, fixing his eyes firmly on Maceo, delivering his message. *You bust me, I'll bust you for pimping and dealing crack.* "I'm all they got left in this world," he said. "I cain't leave them now."

The sergeant folded his arms and stared at PJ. He wanted this bust so bad.

"Sounds like you've got the wrong guy, officer," said the pilot, revving the engine with her stick throttle. "I've gotta transport all these people to dry land. Some of them are banged up and need medical attention," she said, nodding at Maceo and a few others with bandages and open wounds. "Good luck finding your man!"

She engaged the gears and edged away from the sheriff's boat without waiting for the sergeant's response, the fan boat trudging ahead like a barge loaded with heavy oil drums. When PJ glanced back, he saw the motorboat idling where they'd left it, rocking in the fan boat's wake, one of the deputies following their progress with binoculars. He expected the sergeant to come after them, but to his surprise, the motorboat remained where it was. He looked at Jasmine with a grateful smile, but her tender face had hardened and she'd let go of his arm and was staring at him with unexpected anger. She'd saved him from the cops, but she didn't look happy about it.

They passed a flooded cemetery, whitewashed tombs engulfed in the brown marsh, and in time they reached Dryades Street and PJ could see clear pavement a short distance away, almost like a mirage. It was where the water thinned out and then stopped, like the shore of a lake. He could see the streetcar tracks on St. Charles Avenue cluttered with downed oak branches, but there were no pools of water anywhere around them. They had found solid ground.

"It's too shallow to go any fu'ther," the pilot announced to her passengers. "Anybody wants off at St. Charles, I'm gonna have to drop you now. The rest of y'all stay on board and I'll take you to the Superdome. The buses should be coming today to evacuate everybody."

When they slid off the boat into the water, it was only knee deep on Jasmine. PJ handed the baby to her and settled Edgar in his arms, thanking the pilot and wishing the white lady good luck with her husband. She shook his hand like a man and leaned overboard to press those large breasts against Jasmine and Baby Darius in a grandmotherly hug, saying, "God go with you, dawl. Take care of yourself, awright?"

Maceo was still sitting against the gunnel, holding his ribs. "Maceo get patched up, he come looking for you, playuh," he said to PJ with a cruel smile. "You and that tasty li'l hot wing." He raised his hand and dangled the delicate silver bracelet he'd snapped off Jasmine's ankle.

Jasmine stood patting and rubbing Baby Darius on the back. "You come looking for me," she said with that sullen expression, "I put a butcher knife in your belly for what you did to my Momma."

PJ took her firmly by the shoulder and led her toward St. Charles Avenue. It was an easy wade, no more than a block, and he kept glancing back to see if those deputies were following them in their boat.

Soon they were walking on dry land past a small elegant hotel whose circle drive had been crushed under heavy oak limbs. A yellow school bus was parked in a cleared space near the entrance, and he wondered what it was doing there. On St. Charles, the streetcar tracks were buried in mud and wet green foliage. They fought their way through the jungle of branches on the neutral ground, and when they reached the other side of the stately old avenue, the brooding Jasmine stopped and grabbed PJ's arm.

"You owe me," she said, a skinny eleven-year-old girl talking to a grown man that way.

He nodded. "You right. I owe you, girlfriend."

"Don't you be thinking 'bout leaving us somewhere."

She was reading his mind.

"Where you taking us? We all hungry and Darius need diapers and Edgar could use a baff."

They were standing at the edge of the wealthy Garden District. "My girlfriend lives down there," he said, pointing south down the leaf-strewn sidewalk. He wasn't going to say ex-girlfriend to an angry child. "She'll take us in."

He was hoping Charlene hadn't evacuated. She hated his guts now, but she'd always had a soft spot for children.

Jasmine looked impatient. Her updo had wilted flat in the damp weather. "Another thing," she said. "Don't be talking 'bout my Momma. Calling her a coke 'ho in front of people. I don't want these babies to hear they Momma called a bad name."

PJ admired her attitude. "You something else, Jasmine," he said with a smile. "But you right. They shouldn't hear that. I won't do it again."

He set Edgar down on the sidewalk and said, "You ready to do some walking, little man? I'll pick you up when you get tired."

"Ready," the boy said with a giggle, latching onto PJ's hand. "You still my daddy, Mistah Man?"

PJ sighed wearily and looked back to see if anyone was following them. Not another soul on the street and no sign of the deputies anywhere. He mumbled something to himself and they started walking into the windblown neighborhood. All the beautiful flowers were uprooted and the graceful homes were shuttered and quiet in the morning light. It looked too easy to break into these places and snag some valuables lying around, enough to trade for pocket change out of town. He knew he could get away with it—find an easy window to bust or a back door to kick open—if only these kids weren't hanging on his arms. If only for these goddamned kids.

When they reached the wrought iron archway of the old Lafayette cemetery and Commander's Palace boarded shut across the street, PJ could smell burning wood and noticed dark smoke rising through the tall oak trees ahead. One of the majestic mansions of the Garden District was on fire. A block farther on, they were nearly run down by teenagers dashing past them with armloads of loot from the burning house. A police siren was approaching the neighborhood, growing louder, closer. PJ lifted Edgar into his arms and hustled Jasmine and the baby across the street, fleeing south toward the Irish Channel. Five-O was all over it now and there was no way in hell he was going to spread his legs for another man's crime.

# 34

A crowd had gathered around the dead man sprawled on the street in front of the convention center. Malik and several others were shouting at the armed policemen who were ordering them back to the curb. Robert Guyton took Dee's arm and said, "I know a place where you'll be safe."

He broke rank with his guard unit and escorted Dee and the children down the sidewalk toward the touristy shopping mall called Riverwalk Marketplace. At a loading dock between the convention center and the mall, a rusted metal staircase led upward above the dumpsters to a concrete walkway built across the backside of the building. The four of them climbed the stairs and stood gazing out at the rippling muddy waters of the Mississippi River. The current was running high and strong, engorged by Katrina's rain, and waves splashed against the old pilings below them. Dee had never seen the river so empty of traffic. The sightseer paddle-wheelers and the usual cargo ships and tugboats and industrial barges had all disappeared, safely anchored out of harm's way or washed ashore somewhere. Sunlight gleamed off the towering spans of the Crescent City Connection, the twin bridge over the Mississippi that linked New Orleans to the sleepy towns of Gretna and Algiers on the west bank. She cupped her eyes and looked for traffic movement on the bridge, some sign of buses or ambulances or transport trucks driving across, anything that would signal rescue. She wished she and her children were high up on that bridge right now, heading out of town in a Greyhound bus, taking old Highway 90 down through the marshlands to Houma and on up through Cajun country to Opelousas. But the traffic lanes were all empty this morning, an eerie spectacle for a major bridge into a major American city. No one was entering or leaving this place.

"The buses aren't coming," Robert Guyton said, studying the bridge as well. "They're all sitting in bus yards, up to their doors in floodwater. And that's not the worst of it. There aren't enough licensed drivers in town to drive them out of here."

Dee had told Mr. Tran not to become discouraged, but she didn't know how much longer she could hold out herself. She was beginning to lose hope.

"What's going to happen to us?" she asked him, holding LaMarcus and Ashley to her side.

"For right now," Guyton said, "I'm going to get you settled someplace safer than that circus you were in. Before the day's over, the convention center's going to turn into a cesspool. The whole thing is out of control."

Dee looked up into his handsome unshaven face, his eyes almost hidden under the bill of his cap. "Why are you doing this, Robert Guyton?" she asked him. What did he expect in return?

He smiled at Ashley. "I have a daughter your age, young lady," he said, resting a hand on her braids. "She lives with her mother in Lafayette. I get her every other weekend. I wish I had more time with her." He turned to Dee. "If it was the other way around, I'd want somebody to make sure my daughter was safe."

He seemed like a good man. But Dee didn't know how much to trust him. "So what's your plan?" she asked.

Guyton adjusted the rifle strapped to his shoulder and motioned for them to follow him down the walkway. "When I was a student at Southern," he said, "I had a job in this mall. Wore one of those striped referee shirts and sold shoes at Foot Locker. I know this building pretty well."

The half mile of shops and restaurants in the narrow Riverwalk Marketplace were enclosed under a single long roof. As they passed a milky skylight, Dee peered down into a chic women's boutique whose party dresses hung undisturbed in pale rays of sunlight. She knew it was only a matter of time before looters discovered a way in.

Robert Guyton found a maintenance entrance and tried the handle on the glass door. When it proved to be locked, he slung the M-16 off his shoulder and bashed in the glass with the rifle butt. Dee was startled by the noise, the bold decision. She grabbed her children and backed away. "What the hell are you doing?" she cried.

"Watch your step," he said, knocking out more glass with the rifle butt. "It'll be okay once we get inside."

LaMarcus pulled away from his mother. "Momma, are we doing what I think we're doing?" he asked, incredulous and excited all at once.

Guyton was standing on a bed of glass on the other side of the doorway, smiling at them. "We're just going to borrow this building for awhile, young man," he said. "We'll give it back when it's over."

They trailed down the dark service stairs to an emergency exit door that opened onto the ground level of stores. They didn't need to use their flashlights. The mall's long center lane was suffused in natural lighting from a bank of skylights that ran the length of the mall. After a few quiet steps toward a kiosk advertising sunglasses, Guyton stopped and held a finger to his lips, listening for sounds. Nothing. Dead silence. A shopping mall without a trace of commerce or commotion.

"Hard to believe, but we're probably the first ones in," he said in a hushed voice. "Let's get you guys settled. I've got to get back to my unit before they count me AWOL."

The mall catered primarily to tourists visiting the nearby aquarium and casino, and people wandering over to take photos of the river. Dee walked down the center lane with Guyton and the children, looking at all the upscale stores she couldn't afford to shop in. Elegant jewelry, fashionable sun wear, bath and beauty products, naughty lace. What good were these things now? She would have killed for a hot shower at a YWCA gym and clean underwear and a T-shirt that didn't smell rank.

Guyton said, "Here ya go," and marched over to a shop known for fine linens and bedding. He swung the rifle off his shoulder again and smashed the door, and Dee once again shuddered at the sound of crashing glass. She turned a half circle, looking around to see if anybody was watching their break-in. Was it okay to do this? She was reluctant to follow him into the store, but her children showed no hesitation.

"Awesome," LaMarcus said, trotting after the guardsman.

"Woo-hoo. Wait for me," Ashley said, releasing her mother's hand and dashing after them.

The children raced past Robert Guyton and deeper into the store. He turned and smiled at Dee. "You coming?" he said, beckoning her with a wave. "They've even got a couple of demo beds back there. Y'all can get comfortable here until a better offer comes along."

She stepped through the broken door and walked slowly toward him, watching LaMarcus and Ashley laugh and shove each other playfully as they disappeared somewhere back in the bedding section.

"What else do you need?" he asked her. "Food? Something to wear? I'll go open up a couple more stores. If the power's out for a week, all this stuff will go to waste. You and your kids should use up as much as you can."

She gazed around the store at the stylish displays of towels, scented bed sheets, ritzy window dressing, all of it for people whose homes she would never enter, except maybe to do a little cleaning.

"I'll be back to check on you when I can. I've got to stick with my unit until we get the job done."

"And then what?"

He looked puzzled by her question.

"What do you think I'm going to do for you, Robert?" she said, growing serious. "You think I'm going to fuck you back there in the pillow section? 'Cause if you're thinking like that, don't bother to come back, y'understand? It ain't gonna happen. I've already had to fight off one motherfucker on my roof and I'll fight you, too, if you play out something in front of my children. I don't care how big that rifle is. You'll have to kill me first."

Her anger had caught her off guard and she was suddenly ashamed of what she'd said to him. And then she found herself crying uncontrollably, her shoulders shaking, her entire body. He set his rifle aside and embraced her. She resisted at first, her arms crossed tightly against her breasts, but he held on, letting her sob and shake and stain his uniform with tears. It was the kind of embrace someone would offer to a friend who had just lost a loved one.

"Were you hurt, Miss Grant?" he asked her in a tone that sounded like official interrogation. "Is that how your knees got all scratched up?"

She nodded, her face still buried in his chest. "He put a knife to my throat," she mumbled, raising back to show him the dried scab.

He gently examined her throat. "Do you want to file a report?" he asked.

She shook her head. "Maybe later," she said.

He held her shoulders. "I think you and the kids are going to be okay in here," he said, looking around. "I'll go open up that café across the way. The food should still be good in their walk-in. There's a Gap next door and I'll open that up, too. When you get hungry or want to put on some clean clothes, they'll be available. I'll come back whenever I can and check on you guys. If things get strange down here, go back outside and look for me."

"What kind of strange?"

"Looters," he said. "The bad kind. They're gonna bust in this place sooner or later. Be careful around them."

It was an unsettling thought and she turned to locate her children. She could hear them laughing somewhere near the bathroom accessories. It was the first time she'd heard them having fun since the hurricane had struck.

"Keep a low profile down here, okay? I'll come get you if any buses show up."

He retrieved his rifle and walked toward the store's entrance, glancing back over his shoulder. "We're still going to have supper in Opelousas when this is all over with," he said.

She watched him venture out into the quiet mall and wondered if she would ever see him again. And then she set off in search of Ashley and LaMarcus. "Kids!" she yelled. "Where are you?"

She could hear them giggling somewhere. She could hear Robert Guyton bashing glass doors out in the central lane.

"LaMarcus! Ashley! Tell me where you are!"

Silence. Whispering. "Come and find us, Momma! We're hiding."

"No!" she yelled. "No hiding. We can't play games right now. We have to stick together."

Silence again. More whispering. "You'll never guess what Ashley's doing!" LaMarcus said, his voice far away in the maze of nooks and corners.

"Where are you guys?"

"She's taking a bath, Momma!"

Lost in some distant fantasy world, her daughter was laughing like a madwoman. When Dee finally found them, their backpacks tossed aside in a model bathroom display, Ashley had shed her clothes and was sitting in a marble bathtub, oiling her chunky seven-year-old body with fragrant lotions and creams. The modest LaMarcus refused to watch his naked sister frolic about and had wandered away to inspect a shelf of exotic shampoos.

"What are you doing, girl?" Dee said. She didn't know whether to laugh or to scold her daughter for being so reckless at a time like this.

Ashley offered her slender wrist like a gift box. "Smell this, Momma. It's called p-a-s-s-i-o-n fruit." She spelled the first word, not knowing what it meant. "Want to put some on? It'll make you smell pretty."

Dee wondered if she would ever smell pretty again. She found a display of towels labeled as *super pile luxury towels handcrafted in Portugal and woven from 100% Egyptian cotton.* "Come on up out of there," she said, spreading a towel in her hands. "Let's wipe that stuff off you. What if somebody else was wandering around in this store, Ashley Grant?"

"She is so totally gross," LaMarcus said, giggling, his back still turned, refusing to be a part of this scene.

Ashley ignored them both. "I don't see anybody else," she said, lying flat in the tub and rubbing her arms with scented oil. "You want to join me, Momma? It helps to get the stink off."

# 35

It was raining food from the military Chinook. Cases of bottled water, canned vegetables, boxes of uncooked ravioli and sacks of rice. The chopper was hovering forty feet above the hospital and many of the containers exploded on impact across the concrete rooftop.

"You crazy fuckers!" Tucker was yelling up at them, waving his cap, his words swallowed by the rotor noise. "You're too high up there!" He motioned for them to come down lower. "You're wasting this shit!"

A dented can was rolling toward Hodge's boots. He bent down and picked it up. Cat food. *Are they trying to feed us cat food?*

Tucker dug his hands into a split-open bag of raw beans. "What's wrong with you fools?" he screamed up at the chopper, throwing beans at them. "We got no way to cook this stuff down here!" He turned to Hodge and shouted, "Don't these dog-face fucks know we got no electricity?"

He started barking into the walkie-talkie he'd pulled from his police belt. "Edwards, where you at? Hill, come in!" he shouted, tracking down his security team roaming somewhere in the dark building. "I need you up here on the roof! We got some vitals to distribute!"

Hodge found a plastic-wrapped pack of bottled water that had landed on a pile of burlap rice sacks. Standing underneath the chopper's downdraft, his T-shirt and fatigues whipping his skin, he drank an entire bottle in a single long breath. He felt a little dizzy, his temples throbbing. Probably all the meds in him, he thought. Got to piss them out. When he lowered his chin and dropped the empty bottle, wiping an arm across his mouth, Tucker was staring at him with a knowing expression on his face.

"My boys are looking for you," he said, wagging the walkie-talkie to show Hodge how he knew. "The nurses want to talk to you, man. Everybody's worried you went over the wire. You shoulda been straight with me, Opelousas. They say you're not gonna make it if you don't get your butt back down there on a cot and let them watch after you till medevac gets here."

Hodge shook his head. "Cain't do that, my man. You know how it is," he said, the faces of Dee and her children floating through his mind. "Cain't leave our people behind."

"A dead man's no good to them, brother."

Hodge knew he meant well. "Semper fi," he said with a tired smile. "You know what a brother does for a brother."

Tucker tried to return the smile, but there was too much sadness in him. He glanced at the concrete bunker that housed the exit door to the stairwell. "They're coming for you, man," he said. "They want me to detain you so they can talk some sense into that stubborn head."

Hodge peered up at the soldiers hurling supplies from the Chinook's bay door. "You got a whole lot of work here—getting all this good stuff down to the people hurting for it," he said, surveying the mound of boxes and bags stacking up in the drop zone. "T-C-O-B, man. Forget you ever saw me."

He walked toward the exit door, the downdraft chasing whirlwinds of dust all around him. Just before he reached the door, he turned and gave Tucker a grateful salute.

The security guard was standing near the retaining wall, staring at Hodge with the scoped rifle in his hands, and for an instant he wondered if Tucker was going to use it on him. "You hit the water, keep your head low!" Tucker shouted, jerking his chin toward the flooded street below. "That sniper might be for real."

The stairwell was as dark as a mine shaft and Hodge groped his way down the stairs, following the pipe railing, one cautious step at a time. In a short while he heard voices approaching from below, at least three people, and one of them was female. Someone said Tucker's name. Security guards, he figured, with a nurse. The woman said *enough cc's to take the edge off.* His heart was racing. He'd reached a landing and could see a strip of daylight under the door leading into one of the hospital floors. Flashlight beams were bouncing up the stairs just below him. He found the door handle and discovered it was unlocked. Seconds after he slipped out of the stairwell, voices swept past the door, a shuffle of quick footsteps and nervous laughter, the team headed upstairs to confront their patient on the roof.

After some time, Hodge realized his forehead was still pressed against the warm metal door. He struggled to catch his breath and calm down. When he finally turned around, he saw an old white woman watching him in the foggy light of the corridor. With her long white gown and bony feet, she looked like a starving bird stuffed into a sack, her gray hair loose and frazzled around her face and neck. She stared at him in a haunting silence. He didn't know if she was capable of speech. Where were all the patients? he wondered. Why was this floor so deserted?

"I've been waiting for you," the woman said in a dry brittle voice that sounded like a pencil scratching words on sandpaper. "It's time for my enema, young man."

He knew where he was now. It was different from the other wings of the hospital. He walked toward the old woman, passing an open doorway where a patient was lying on a bed in his own filth, a dead oxygen mask strapped across his mouth and nose. Hodge recognized the cheerful colors and homey furnishings in that room, the unusual fabric walls and family seating area. He'd been on this floor before. It was the terminal care unit managed by some private health care company. The ward where Rochelle had spent her final days.

A nurse stepped out of a room down the hall and said, "Here you are, Mrs. Benjamin. Come on, dear, let's get you back to your bed. I have something to help you rest."

The nurse was an imposing dark-haired white woman with a

muscular build and thick legs. She took the old lady by the arm and led her into a beam of daylight slanting through a doorway. For an instant the two women glowed like holy angels in their white clothing and pale skin. When the nurse noticed Hodge standing in the corridor, she seemed alarmed by his presence. "What are you doing here, sir?" she asked him in a stern voice. "You're not supposed to be on this floor."

Hodge felt confused, his temples still throbbing. He didn't know what to say. "My wife used to be here," was the best he could do.

The nurse held the old woman's frail hand. They looked as if they were floating in that ray of light. "No one is allowed on this floor," she said, her long dark hair drifting off her shoulders in the bright flowing sunlight. "Please leave or I'll call security."

Duval wandered through the campsites spread out across the Superdome plaza, searching for Dee and his children. One eye was swollen shut and his teeth were crusted with dry blood and every inch of him hurt from the beating he'd taken. He knew his appearance was messed up because of the way people looked at him. Somebody said, "Niggah, they got medics around here somewhere. Go get yourself cleaned up."

The pain and the morning heat sent sweat down his forehead and he felt like this wasn't real, like he was somebody else walking in these wet shoes. He roamed through the camps looking for the little boy and girl he'd held in his arms when they were first born, and after awhile he grew desperate and began calling their names. *LaMarcus! Ashley! Dee, girl, are y'all here?*

Somebody told him to be cool, people were still trying to sleep. But he kept calling their names, his tongue a little thick and the skin torn and tender inside his mouth. He had to find them and take them to that house on St. Charles Avenue. Wait for Hodge to meet them there. That was the plan, and that was all he could figure on right now.

He stopped to rest his legs and looked down at three teenage homeboys, maybe brothers, stretched out on the concrete like somebody's crew crashing 'round the bong. Watching them shade their eyes, too wasted to give him shit, the strangest revelation went through his mind. He remembered that book he'd read in the Dillard library on his lunch breaks, the one about slaves kidnapped from their villages and brought to trading posts on the shores of Africa, where they waited in shackles for the ships that would carry them across the ocean. He wondered if this was so different—these boys, this scattering of poor raggedy-ass niggahs flushed out of the projects and waiting for the Man to pick them up and take them to God knows where.

He raised his eyes and said aloud, "Shit, man, how far we gotta go?" And some church woman told him to watch his language, he was standing among Christian families.

He approached a group of National Guardsmen smoking cigarettes near the locked doors at the entrance to the Dome. He asked one of them, a black soldier, how he could find out if his wife and kids were inside the building or out here on the plaza.

"Depends on when they came in," the guardsman said, staring at Duval's ruined face. The brother was a dark-skinned man with a slight accent from the islands or some such place, sporting the trimmed mustache of a momma's boy who'd gone to college and now worked in a nice soft office. "We locked it down about ten o'clock last night," the guardsman said. "When did they get here?"

Duval tried to think. He had no idea what time they'd seen Dee being hoisted up into the Coast Guard chopper. "I don't fucking know, man," he said, rubbing his good eye. "But I got to find them. Where do I start?"

The guardsman nodded toward the crowd gathered on the plaza. "You looked around?" he asked.

"I been walking around for an hour, bruh. Back and forth, in and out. I don't see nobody I know, and nobody seen me."

"Some people headed off to the convention center early this

morning," the guardsman said. "The mayor opened it up to handle the overflow. They might be down there."

Duval looked southward across the plaza. "The convention center?" he said.

The guardsman was staring at his face again. "First thing, my friend, you need to get yourself looked at," he said. "Let me take you to the nurses' station."

Duval shook his head. "I'm ah-ight," he said. "Them people that left for the convention center—they have a little boy and girl with 'em?"

He described LaMarcus and Ashley the best he could. He thought the guardsman might remember Ashley's beaded hair.

"Man, it's all a blur right now," the guardsman said. "I've been up for thirty-six hours straight and I've seen too many people come and go. Braids, weaves, cornrows, updos, naturals—you name it, I've seen it. I can't tell you who was in that group. Some old Voodoo lady was leading the parade."

Duval made his way through the campsites one last time, calling their names again until he found himself standing at the south edge of the plaza, near the safety wall, gazing down Poydras Street toward the river. A long trail of people splashed through shallow pools, leaving the Dome area for the convention center and whatever lay ahead.

He sat down on the hard concrete and rested his back against the wall, closing his good eye. He needed to sort this shit out. Twenty-four hours ago he was smoking reefer with his dawgs in a nice dry motel room fifty miles away, watching Katrina blow in on the television screen, getting his dick sucked. Today he was soaking wet and tore up and knee-deep in the middle of this bitch. That wasn't right. That wasn't even close to right, and it didn't look like right was going to show up anytime soon.

"Yo, bro', I know you, man."

Duval opened his eye. A doper white guy was wandering by with two chicks who looked like needle skeezers searching for their next spoonful. One sweating dark-skinned girl, one sickly pale white girl with a map of delicate blue veins on her arms and thin neck.

"We did a session together at the studio awhile back. I can't remember if it was Li'l Wayne or C Murder or who it was, man." He had long stringy brown hair and full-sleeve tattoos that looked like the Bible story of creation all down his arms, and he was missing a front tooth. "What happened, man? Somebody handle you?"

Duval recognized him now. He wasn't a rapper or producer or technician but some fly-on-the-wall dealer who brought killer weed to one of the sessions Duval had made a hundred bucks at, singing an old Curtis Mayfield loop with a couple of horn players from Tremé.

"This dude's got a sweet voice," the white guy said to his two companions. "Motown and shit. Old school sweet."

The frail white girl said "Awesome" with dead eyes and a lifeless expression.

The white guy looked around at the crowd camped on the plaza. "This whole scene is getting too heavy, man. We gotta bolt. You wanna come with us to the Quarter? They're saying it's high and dry and the bars are open twenty-four seven."

Duval shook his head. He still tasted blood in his mouth. "I got obligations," he said.

The dark-skinned woman squatted down in her stained summer dress to examine his face. She was either black or Latin, or a little of both, he couldn't tell. She pressed her thumb against his chin, opening his jaw to study his teeth. She touched his split lip and then probed at the tender swelling around his eye.

"You thinking about buying me, girlfriend?" he asked her.

Her hair was dark and thick and coarse, and her eyebrows were coarse, too, like a woman's from some chicken scratch village south of the border. Her face had once been pretty, four or five years ago, before she started living the life. Sweat trickled down her neck and onto her liquid smooth chest and he could see brown nipples behind the fluff of her dress. He could look down past her spread knees to the sweat beaded on the silky brown skin of her inner thighs.

"I can take care of your *obligations,*" she whispered to him, softly touching the swollen side of his face. "You have a credit card, baby? We can all go have some fun in the Quarter."

It hurt when he laughed. "I had a credit card, girl, I'd be in Chicago by now."

She stood up and backed away, and the white guy extended a hand. "Come on with us, bro'," he said, offering to help Duval up off the hard concrete. "We don't find the party, we'll make our own."

"Will he sing for us?" said the white girl with dead blue eyes. "Rolly, I want to hear him sing."

"Sure, baby, he'll sing if you treat him nice."

# 36

Charlene lived on one side of a shotgun double on Annunciation Street, not far from the warehouses along the river. The Irish Channel's wooden row houses had held up against the battering rain and wind, but now the steamy streets were caked with mud and tree limbs were down and roof shingles littered the yards and the cyclone fences were bulging and twisted. With Jasmine close by his side, the baby in her arms, PJ held Edgar's hand and knocked on Charlene's door. The last time he'd stood on this porch, she'd shown him a restraining order behind five inches of chain-latched door space and told him to go away or she'd call the police. He was counting on the children to soften her attitude. She wouldn't turn them away, no matter what she thought of him. She'd wanted kids as long as he'd known her—and now here they were.

When she didn't answer the door, he knocked harder, the sound echoing through the empty neighborhood like hammer blows on a metal roof. "Nobody home, Mistah Man," Edgar said. She'd probably evacuated, he thought, like every sensible soul in this town. He let go of the boy's sweaty hand and stepped over to the window, cupping his eyes and peering into the shuttered front room. The furniture sat undisturbed in golden strips of sunlight streaming through the blinds. Like his mother, she was a tidy woman who appreciated the finer things of life. Nice furnishings and climbing plants and pictures on the walls. What a fool he'd been. He should have given her the children she wanted. He should not have stolen her jewelry when they broke up.

"She gone away," Jasmine said, carrying a wide-eyed and naked

Darius on her hip. When he'd filled his final diaper with runny, mustard-colored shit, they'd tossed it behind a neatly manicured hedge in the Garden District. "What we gonna do now? We need to find this boy some diapers."

PJ stepped over to the front door and thumbed the handle. Locked. He backed away and looked down the sidewalk, one way then the other. The street was dead silent except for a mangy brown mutt lapping at a muddy rain puddle.

"Let's find us something to eat," he said, kicking the door with the sole of his shoe. The sturdy wood didn't give. He stepped back and kicked again, putting more body into it, and this time he felt the wood crack near the deadbolt. He was fixing to kick the door a third time when he heard a voice say, "Get on away from here, son. Don't make me use this thing on you."

An old man had slipped quietly out of the other half of the shotgun and stood on the porch in fuzzy slippers with an ancient Louisville Slugger baseball bat in his hands. He'd set his feet in a batting stance and looked like he knew how to step into a pitch and swing for the fence.

"Yo, be cool now, Barry Bonds," PJ said, raising his hands as if the man held a gun on him. "Cain't you see I got children with me?"

The old geezer was somewhere north of seventy, with a sagging face and the wet yellowed eyes of a drinking man. The bat wobbled in his unsteady hands. Even though it was a hot summer morning, he wore a cardigan sweater over a button-down shirt with a frayed collar, and his gray moth-eaten work khakis had seen better days. He studied PJ with both fear and the mistaken confidence of someone who thought he might get in one good whack.

"I believe it's that boyfriend of Charlene's." He heard her voice before he saw the woman. "The one that's not supposed to pass here anymore."

The old man's wife was standing behind him in their doorway. She was diminished by age, and it was difficult to get a clear glimpse of her.

"You the one always coming 'round here to fuss and fight with Miss Charlene?" asked the man. The raised bat was beginning to weigh heavy in his hands.

"I got these children with me," he said, nodding at Jasmine. Edgar was hanging on his leg, wiping his nose on PJ's warm-up pants. "They're hungry and the baby needs diapers and milk. Can you help us out? We come looking for Charlene, but she's gone."

"Don't be trying to break into her house," the man said. "She got a peace bond swore out against you."

"I won't bust her door down if you can help a brother out."

PJ wasn't sure if that was true or not. He might still break in and go through her underwear drawer where she sometimes hid her cash.

"Can you do me a solid and put down that bat, my man?" he said. "You're scaring the baby."

As if on cue, Baby Darius began to cry. The old woman stepped out of the doorway and stood beside her husband, her hand clinging to the sleeve of his sweater. She was heavy and waddled in her loose sack dress, and her hair was wavy and light-colored like a white woman's. "Who do these children belong to?" she asked in a scolding voice. "Are they yours?"

"I found them left by themselves in a house full of water. Their momma passed," PJ said, looking at the sad expression on Jasmine's face. "They need somebody to take care of them."

The old woman studied the children. "Is that right, child?" she asked Jasmine.

The girl nodded, dropping her eyes.

"Mistah Man my daddy now," Edgar said, wrapping his strong skinny arms around PJ's thigh.

"Lord God Jesus," the woman said, her hand flying quickly to her mouth. Tears sparkled in her eyes. "Put down that baseball bat, Alton," she said. "These children need to come on inside and eat something, bless their little hearts."

PJ smiled down at Edgar. He'd found what he'd been looking for. Somebody to take these kids off his hands. It's all but cut loose now, little man, he thought, rubbing Edgar's buzz-cut stubble. This cinder block tied around my neck.

Piling up duvets and frilly throw pillows that looked like they belonged in a Cape Cod cottage, Dee built a walled fortress between two luxurious beds in the bedroom décor section of the store. "Let's not hang around out in the open," she told the children. "We'll stay right here in our little cubbyhole until Robert Guyton comes back for us."

"Is he your new boyfriend, Momma?" Ashley asked with a mischievous smile.

"Don't be silly, girl. I just met the man. He's trying to help us, is all."

"He wants to take us out to eat in some other town."

Dee stretched out on a plush comforter she'd arranged on the hardwood floor and propped a pillow under her head. "That'll never happen," she said.

"Why not?"

"It's just something somebody tells you when they're trying to make you feel better. He feels sorry for us because of the hurricane."

Ashley lay down beside her mother on the comforter. "Is it like when Daddy says he's coming over and he doesn't really mean it?" she asked.

"Daddy's coming to get us. Him and Pawpaw," LaMarcus said firmly, showing his annoyance. He was sitting on top of a lacquered walnut dressing bureau, looking down at his mother and sister hiding behind the wall of pillows. "So stop hating on him like that."

Ashley challenged him. "How will he know we're in this mall?"

"Because he'll smell your nasty dog breath a mile away."

"Momma!"

"Hush, now, LaMarcus," Dee said, closing her eyes. She hadn't had a moment of real sleep in three days. And she wouldn't sleep now. Not with crazy people on the prowl all over town. "Come on down here with us," she said. "You need to get out of sight."

When she opened her eyes again, she knew something was wrong. She could hear voices echoing through the store. Running feet. Teenagers talking trash, ribbing one other. She sat up, rubbing her eyes. She wasn't sure how much time had passed. Ten minutes, twenty. Maybe longer. She reached over and felt Ashley's sleeping body coiled against a duvet. But where was LaMarcus? She rolled to her knees and checked the beds beside their fort. Empty. His backpack lay at the foot of the pallet, next to Ashley's.

"LaMarcus!" she called out, rising to her feet. She was fully exposed now. Anyone could see her. "LaMarcus, where are you, son?"

Two project boys were chasing each other down the aisle near their hideout. Caps on backwards, long NBA jerseys flapping against their knees. "Marcus, yo momma callin' you, bwah!" they laughed as they ran. "Better come get you some milk titty!"

She didn't see her son anywhere. She crawled across a bed and stood in the aisle where she could look in both directions. People were roaming everywhere. One loud party was moving through the kitchenware department, laughing and knocking things off the shelves.

"LaMarcus!" she shouted again, turning in a slow circle, searching for him with panic bubbling up inside her. "Come back here right now!"

He didn't answer. There were looters all over the mall now and she didn't know where her son was.

The old man said his name was Alton and his wife's name was Olive and their last name was Lee. Alton and Olive Lee. They led PJ and the children back through their narrow shotgun home, one dusky room leading to the next, the sealed air smelling of cigarettes and mildew and the sour odor of old people who'd simmered too long inside their own unwashed skin. A radio was reporting the news in the kitchen at the rear of the house, where the Lees had gathered themselves around a red Formica kitchen table stacked with their few remaining canned goods and empty beer bottles and paper plates stained with food and twisted cigarette butts. PJ noticed an army of pill containers stationed on the counter near the sink. A lazy overfed cat was sleeping by the rear door.

"We don't have much left, but y'all are welcome to it," Olive said, searching for the can opener in the mess on the table. "When was the last time you had a proper meal, child?" she asked Jasmine.

"Some crackers last night," the girl said, gazing fondly at a large opened bag of potato chips.

The old woman served the last of their stockpile, pork 'n' beans and canned ham with white bread and chips. Edgar spilled warm soda all over his SpongeBob T-shirt and shared an orange with his sister.

"There's a grocery store up by Magazine Street," the old man said. He fished beer from the melted ice in a blue cooler and watched PJ suspiciously, the baseball bat never far from his reach. "I been pondering whether to go up there and see if I can get in. This goes on much longer, we're all gonna go hungry."

Olive held Baby Darius and fed him apple sauce she scraped from the bottom of a jar. She'd fashioned a diaper out of a cup towel and fastened it with safety pins. "We've got four grandbabies of our own," she said, smiling at the child in her lap. "Our son lives in Dallas and our daughter in Charlotte, and they don't get back home enough to suit me."

"Young people got to go where the money is," Alton said, lighting a cigarette with an antique Zippo lighter.

They listened to the radio as the children finished their orange slices and Alton enjoyed his cigarette. Station WWL, a white reporter who used to be on the television news. He said National Guard reinforcements had still not shown up in the city. Frustrated NOPD officers were walking off the job, leaving town in brand-new Cadillacs they'd stolen from a dealership.

"We saw them this morning here in the neighborhood," Olive said with a disapproving cluck. "Catting around in a yellow school bus, taking what they wanted. NOPD, mind you. Going into houses and walking out with television sets, hi-fi's, what have you."

"A school bus?" PJ said. He remembered the yellow bus he'd seen parked in front of that hotel on St. Charles Avenue.

"More room to load up what they take," Alton said. "Who's gonna stop 'em? They're the laws."

Olive looked upset in the telling of it. "Alton walked out to the sidewalk—to see what was going on—and they hollered at him to mind his own business and get back inside," she said.

"They try to break in this house," he said, nodding at the baseball bat on the floor near his feet, "I'm gonna go down swinging."

They all fell into a drained silence and listened to the radio. The reporter said that no one knew what had happened to the buses sent from other cities to help evacuate New Orleans. FEMA promised they were sending a fleet of their own buses, but no one had seen them. Shelters were full all over the state. Baton Rouge, Lafayette, New Iberia, Opelousas, Alexandria, Lake Charles. They couldn't take any more evacuees. Houston was now the nearest place to find refuge. *If you're lucky enough to get out of the city,* the reporter was telling his listeners, *go to Houston. The mayor is opening up the Astrodome for you. My friends, go to Houston if you can.*

"What happened to your ear?" Olive asked PJ. She was bouncing Baby Darius on her knee.

"Wade around in deep water long enough," he said, "something's gonna pop you, sooner or later."

The old woman handed the baby to Jasmine and left the kitchen to find a bottle of hydrogen peroxide and a tube of antibiotic cream. She made PJ remove his cap and sat beside him, cleaning around the crusty scab with cotton balls and applying cream. "I ought to dress this thing with a bandage," she said. "It's looking pretty bad."

She reminded him of his mother. She was a good woman and she wouldn't let anything bad happen to these children.

They listened to the radio for a while longer and then PJ stood up from the table. He glanced over their meager supplies and knew the Lees didn't have enough to feed themselves for another meal, much less three hungry children. It was a good excuse to make his play.

"I'll slide on up by Magazine Street and see what I can find," he said to the old couple. "Watch after these kids. I'll be back with some food and diapers."

Alton Lee sipped his beer and studied PJ through moist yellow eyes. PJ could tell the old man didn't believe him. He knew a lie when he heard one. And yet as they exchanged this secret knowledge, PJ saw that Alton didn't have the heart to call him out in front of his dear trusting wife and these helpless children. It would have caused them too much hurt. The old man was going to give him a pass. Even though it meant untold misery ahead for him and his wife and these kids that weren't their own.

Jasmine followed PJ down the narrow hallway to the front porch. "Hey," she kept saying, "Hey, Mistah Man, you gotta talk to me."

When he opened the screen door and turned around, he saw that the entire household was following after him. Edgar pulling on his sister's shorts, Olive holding Baby Darius, the doubting Alton shuffling in the rear in those fuzzy slippers.

"I'm coming wiff you," Jasmine said with a fierce determination.

"You gotta stay here with your brothers, girl."

"How I know you coming back?" There were tears in her eyes. "You better promise me you coming back."

"Keep an eye on the boys, ah-ight?" he said, patting the top of her fallen updo. "Stick with these good people. They'll take care of you."

"I'm coming wiff you, too," Edgar squealed, laughing and running toward PJ.

He picked up the boy and hugged him, rubbing his back, then set that warm squirming body back down next to his sister.

He walked down the steps and out onto the muddy sidewalk,

turning to wave at everyone for the last time. Tears were running down Jasmine's face. The Lees looked concerned. But it was Edgar's adoring smile, more than anything else, that PJ would remember for the rest of his life.

# 37

The only time LaMarcus had seen anything like this was when he'd gone to watch Spider-Man with his mother and sister. When the doors opened, a horde of teenagers waiting in the long line had rushed into the movie theater, running up and down the aisles, fighting over the best seats. And now a gang of teenagers was dashing past him the same way, laughing and screeching and shoving one another as they raced down the open lane between stores. They'd found their way into the mall somehow, maybe through the same door the guardsman had bashed with his rifle, and they were acting crazy over all the choices.

*Looky here. They got ice cream!*

*Niggah, check this out. Boo-coo Game Boy shit all up in here.*

He wasn't afraid. He felt invisible. They didn't care about a nine-year-old boy wandering alone in the mall. They were too busy kicking at metal grates and busting into display windows.

He figured he had some time before his mother and Ashley woke up and discovered he was gone. He was tired of being cooped up in that fake bedroom place and angry at his stupid sister for always hating on their Daddy and he needed to get away from them for awhile because that girl was getting on his nerves.

He stopped to watch looters hustle through the shattered storefront window of a place called EB Games. His PlayStation 2 was underwater at home, ruined forever, and he thought maybe he could pick up a new one. Could he carry the box around with him until they got back home again? Would his mother let him keep it or would she make him take it back and apologize, like she'd done the time he'd stuffed his pants with toys at that old Eckerd's Pharmacy when he was little? He'd made it all the way to the car seat before she discovered what he'd stuck in his pockets and down the legs of his jeans.

He was thinking maybe he'd go inside the store and look around at all the video games on shelves and spinner racks and stacked up behind the counter. Just hold them, see if he could read the descriptions in the weak light, look at the pictures. Games he'd read about in his magazines but hadn't played yet. *Katamari Damacy, Burnout 3, Tony Hawk's Underground 2.* The ones he wanted to save up his money for when this was all over and he could earn his allowance again.

"I know what you're thinking." A grown man was standing behind him now, watching the looters pour into the store. "Should I hop on in there with the rest of 'em?"

He was a big gangsta-looking man who reminded LaMarcus of his uncle PJ. He was wearing a football jersey with number 13 on the chest and there was a spider web tattoo on his neck and Chinese letters on his forearms. He smiled at LaMarcus with a mouthful of gold teeth.

"I feel ya, my man. It's a hard call. Worse part is," he said, "you hustle up some good shit in there and then one of these bigger boys come along and take it away from you. Maybe fuck you up over it."

He was carrying a black plastic garbage bag slung over his shoulder like a gangsta Santa Claus. No telling what was inside that bag. Maybe some clothes. Maybe loot he'd picked up from the stores.

"It always go down like this. You want something, you gotta take it from somebody else. It's cold, I know. But the sooner you learn that, young blood, the better off you be."

His mother had told LaMarcus and Ashley never to talk to strangers. And to damn sure never get in their car.

"How you like to make twenty bucks, my man?"

A warning light went off in LaMarcus's head. He thought about tearing out of here and running back to his Momma asleep in the bedroom display.

The man must have read the fear in his eyes. "Chill, young blood. I'm not gonna suck your dick. It ain't like that," he said. "You see that store over there?" He nodded toward a place called the Luggage Depot across the lane from the game store. "I need a better grip to carry my shit in." He slid the garbage bag off his shoulder and showed LaMarcus how flimsy and cumbersome it was. "You watch my back while I'm in there, I'll give you twenty bucks for your trouble, straight up."

LaMarcus found his voice. "All I have to do is be a lookout?"

"Yeah, you right. Hollah if somebody come snooping around while I'm doing my bidness."

"Do I have to stop them?"

The man laughed at the worry in LaMarcus's voice. "You don't have to stop nobody. Let me know they coming, I'll do all the stopping they can handle."

LaMarcus stared at the display behind the wide glass window. Suitcases, handbags, backpacks, luggage of every description. "You going to break that glass?" he asked.

The man smiled at him and dragged his garbage bag over to a thin-leaf tree growing out of a large concrete cylinder. Several chalky white rocks were embedded in the potted soil around the slender tree trunk. He worked a rock the size of a softball out of the dirt and weighed it in his hand. "Po' man's door key," he said with a laugh. He marched toward the display window and threw the rock. The glass exploded into jagged knives, a noise echoing through the long narrow mall.

The man turned to LaMarcus and waved a twenty-dollar bill. "They open for bidness now," he said. "You coming, bwah?"

The Luggage Depot smelled like a baseball glove that had been left in a dewy yard overnight. A little like a wet animal. LaMarcus crouched behind a cashier's counter, watching looters roam past the broken display window with little interest in what was inside this store. Who needed fancy leather bags at a time like this?

LaMarcus didn't know what he was supposed to do if looters decided to step through the broken window and come into the store to snoop around. He didn't know exactly where the man had gone. Somewhere in the back, behind the maze of tall display shelves. A few minutes ago, he could hear him moving stuff around. But now everything was quiet. What was he doing back there? He wondered how long he would have to stay here to earn that twenty dollars.

As time went by, he began to feel a little scared hiding behind the counter. He missed his mother and wondered if she and Ashley had woke up yet and freaked out because he wasn't there.

More time passed, a longer silence. He was certain now that the man had played a trick on him. He didn't want to stay here anymore, twenty dollars or not. He stood up from his hiding place and walked toward the shattered display window. But then his curiosity got the best of him and he turned and started walking down an aisle deeper into the store. The light grew faint and the place was spooky quiet, so he picked up his pace, trotting past long zippered clothes bags hanging like dead bodies and those leather satchels that lawyers carried on TV programs. He dashed around a corner past a display of suitcases on wheels and found the man sitting on the carpet, counting paper money as he transferred it from the black trash bag into a brand new backpack. A pistol was lying on the floor next to him and he reached for it, quickly pointing it at LaMarcus.

"Damn, bwah, you coulda got your dome capped, sneaking up on me like that," he said, still pointing the gun at him. "Whatchew doing back here? You s'posed to be up front, watching my back like a spy boy."

The gun looked bigger and scarier than the one Ashley had fired at that stranger on the roof. His mother had always told him to run home if he ever saw somebody with one of these things. "I thought you left," he said in a small nervous voice.

The man set the pistol on the carpet next to his thick thigh. "You know how to count money, my man? Make a grip?"

LaMarcus wasn't sure what a *grip* was.

"Sit your skinny ass down here and he'p me count this money so we can get the fuck out of here."

LaMarcus was afraid of this man and did what he was told. He sat down next to the trash bag and started counting money. His body felt paralyzed by fear, but his mind was working mad fast. Numbers, figures. Always numbers. "If you look beside the number twenty," he said, his hand shaking as he held up a twenty dollar bill, "it says 'United States of America Twenty Dollars USA' in tiny letters you can't see without a magnifying glass."

The man studied him. His eyes narrowed. "How come you wandering around owchere all by yourself, Perfessor Short Britches? You lost or something?"

He didn't know why he was going to say what he was going to say. He thought maybe the man would understand. "You ever get mad at your momma?" he asked him.

The man laughed, a loud and menacing sound that came from deep down behind those gold slugs in his mouth. "What you mad at your momma 'bout?"

"She never says anything good about my Daddy," he said with a shrug. "She lets my sister talk trash about him all the time."

The man nodded with a knowing smile. "How old you are, bwah?"

"Nine."

He laughed again, only this time in a quieter way. "Word up, son—it only get worse between you and your momma. The way it is. The way it always gonna be. Young boy trying to get out from under her skirt and be a man, like his daddy, the bitch holding on to him, 'fraid he end up thuggin'. When I was coming up, my momma took me to church all the time, tried to do me right, find me a job at this and that." He rolled a stack of bills into a tight grip, wagging it at LaMarcus. "I found out I could stand on a street corner and make more jack in a day than the wodies frying chicken at Popeye's in a whole month. Ya heard me? You listen to your momma, you gonna end up licking chicken grease off your fingers the rest of your life."

LaMarcus didn't know what to think about that. He had always listened to his mother.

"Where your daddy at?"

"Him and my Pawpaw came looking for us in a boat. We don't know where they are."

"What he do, your daddy?"

LaMarcus shrugged. "He wants to be a rapper," he said.

The man laughed that deep down laugh again. "That how it is in the N. O.," he said, making another thick roll of twenty dollar bills. "Every niggah be a playuh, every bitch tie him down."

LaMarcus was afraid to ask him where he got all this money. He sat counting the bills, smoothing out the wrinkled ones, arranging them in piles of Hamiltons and Jacksons so the man could ball them into a spool that fit perfectly in his huge palm.

"Grip," the man said, showing the money roll to LaMarcus. "You doing bidness on the street, you gotta pass it off quick. Lemme see you do it."

LaMarcus folded a stack of tens, squeezed the bundle in his hand, and smiled.

The man ripped a twenty dollar bill from his grip and handed it to him. "Put that in your pocket, Perfessor," he said. "You roll with me, everything be ah-ight. I take care of my boys. You won't need a daddy or momma, one."

# 38

Hodge knew that the chapel was down this corridor somewhere because he'd prayed for Rochelle many times in that quiet little space when her life was slipping away. The chapel had been a cool dark refuge where he could collect his thoughts and ask the Lord for mercy. Now it seemed like a good place to hide out until everything calmed down and he could leave the building without being hunted like a fugitive on the run.

He found the door—a small chrome cross, a panel of rose-colored glass—and stepped into the soft violet radiance from a stained glass window behind the altar. It looked as if a service had just ended. The altar was draped by a white tasseled cloth, with tall candles arranged beside an open Bible resting on a stand. But instead of the comforting scent of incense and candle wax, something was fouling the air. His instinct was to back away, but then he saw the bodies lying on the carpet in front of the altar. They were shrouded in white sheets and baby blue blankets. He pulled his T-shirt up over his mouth and nose and ventured down the aisle between pews until he was standing only a few feet from them. Someone had placed the three corpses side by side in an orderly row. An old white man's limbs and lower face were concealed by a sheet, but his long thick white hair was spread across a pillow as if a loving granddaughter had brushed it out for him. A black woman's splayed legs were exposed, as though she'd kicked them free of the sheet in a final desperate spasm of life. The third body was tightly wrapped like a mummy except for an uncovered hand, its wrist ringed by a plastic ID band. He supposed this was better than stacking them in the stairwell. At least they were in repose in a house of worship.

Hodge was kneeling down and praying for their souls, feeling the heavy weight of death all around him, when the door banged open and two nurses entered the chapel pushing a gurney. Hodge stood up awkwardly on unsteady legs and stepped aside near the pulpit. They were bringing another sheet-wrapped body to place next to the others.

"Is that you, Tucker?" It was the Dark Nurse—the one he'd seen in the corridor. When she realized Hodge wasn't a security guard, she said, "What are you doing in here?"

He didn't know what to say. "Y'all need some help with that?" he offered.

"No, sir, we do not," the nurse said. She was wearing a surgical mask and latex gloves, and so was the smaller nurse pushing the gurney. "You're not authorized to be on this floor. You need to leave immediately."

"God bless you," Hodge said, staring at the body strapped to the gurney. A pink blanket—like something from a child's cedar chest—was hiding the face. "I know this cain't be easy."

Out in the corridor, searching for the exit to the stairwell, he felt the full tug of his own mortality dragging at his slow legs and weary body. Was he going to end up like these sick old people, netted up in a trap of sheets and laid out on the floor like an ancient leathery terrapin fetched up on a fishing pier? Then what would happen to Dee and his grandchildren? Who would take them back to Opelousas? Duval didn't have the smarts or the intestinal fortitude.

He passed door after door, room after room, a long procession of silent bedridden patients too near death to notice him. But then he heard someone crying for help in a room farther down the corridor. It was an old woman, and he stopped at her door and listened to the mournful sounds coming from her small shriveled mouth. Seeing her stirred painful memories of Rochelle. The woman was crying for the nurses and pushing the dead call button. The dark monitors and empty IV stand were little more than clutter around her bed. He could smell the overflowing bedpan in the stuffy heat of the room.

Her sheets and hospital gown were soaked in urine.

She opened her wet eyes and stared at him. He saw now that she was a woman of mixed race, a Creole of color, her skin lighter than a paper bag. What the old crackers used to call a *high yella.* You came across more of her people in New Orleans than in his part of the state. He'd always felt there was something delicate about them, even the men. Well-educated, white-collar folk unaccustomed to working with their hands, lawyers and mayors and schoolteachers.

"For God's sake, please help me," she muttered. "Can't you see I'm hurting? Give me something for the pain." Despite the crack and strain of her voice, her mind seemed to be working. "Why have y'all left me here to suffer like this?"

"Ma'am, I'm not a doctor or a nurse. I'm sorry. I don't know what they can do for you right now."

She turned her head on the pillow to draw him into sharper focus. Her thin gray hair was curled with sweat. "Are you here to clean me up?" she asked.

"I'm here to find my people," he said, walking slowly into the room. He grabbed a handful of sheet and dabbed away the sweat rolling down her forehead and into her eyes.

"Is it bad outside?"

"Real bad, ma'am. The city's full up with water. I came here in a boat."

"Then I'm going to call you Noah," she said. Her body was radiating a high fever. "One of my husbands was named Noah, the dear man."

She smiled, taking pleasure in the soft soothing touch of the bed sheet against her burning forehead. He'd done this for Rochelle when she was in this ward. Toweled her dry whenever she'd sweated through her gown.

"I was born and raised up in this city," the woman said with her eyes closed. "Had five children with three different husbands—one of them a Frenchman from Paris. The men have all passed and my children are grown. My youngest girl, Cecile—she told me I'd be safe up here when the storm came. I don't know where that girl got off to."

Hodge found a paper cup of tepid water on a tray next to the bed and brought it to her sticky mouth. She raised her head slightly and drank it down.

"You ever eat at Zallie's Jazz Kitchen?" she asked, licking her lips. "That was my place. Seventh Ward. People came from all over the world to eat my food and listen to the music. Louie Armstrong himself walked in one night that time he was King of Zulu. Said it was the best soft shell crab he'd ever tasted."

He knew the restaurant by reputation, but he'd never eaten there.

"What's going to happen to me?" Her long thin fingers clutched at his arm. "Are they going to leave me here to rot away like a dried up old crab?"

He patted her hand. "They're gonna take you out of here in a helicopter," he said. "They'll fly you to another hospital and everything's gonna be all right."

She opened her eyes and showed him the sly flirting smile she must have used to her advantage in her younger days. "Will you stay with me, Noah?" she said. "Soon as I get my strength back, I'll make you a happy man."

Her face and neck and bare arms were beaded with sweat. He daubed her skin with the sheet. Suddenly her eyes darkened and she dug her brittle nails into his wrist. "They're coming around door to door, you know. Giving all the feeble ones a shot. You understand what I'm saying, Noah? A shot to put us out of our misery." She had worried herself into a state of panic. "They know we can't survive like this and they're putting us old ones down. Did you see what they did to Miz Benjamin?"

He wondered if there was any truth to what she was saying. It's what they'd done in the Nam. Put down the ones who weren't going to make it.

"My name is Zallie Lalande. Find something and write it on my arm, Noah. Just put Zallie—everyone will know who that is." Her lungs were laboring now, struggling to channel air. "When they dump my body out in the sewer with all the rest, I want my children to know which one I am."

"Rest now, Missus Lalande," he said, tenderly squeezing her hand. "Everything's gonna be fine. Get some rest until the nurses come."

Tears were flowing down her cheeks. She slid his hand under the bed sheet and pressed it to a sagging breast. "Take me out of this place, Noah," she said, clutching his fingers against her damp skin. "Take me home and we'll go back to the way it was and I promise to make you laugh again."

She closed her eyes and dozed off, her breath slowing, slowing. He removed his hand and stood looking down at her, wondering whether to go find the Dark Nurse. He didn't know if he could trust that stern woman.

Before lapsing into a deep sleep, Zallie groped for his arm and said, "Don't leave me, Noah. Promise you won't leave until Jesus comes."

He sat on a chair next to the bed, feeling helpless and sad for her family. He didn't know this woman, and yet he felt he should stay by her side until her final moment came, like he'd stayed by Rochelle and what was left of Ernie Garza while their spirits were lifting upward into that last good light.

He must have nodded off in the chair. What jarred him awake was the rattle of the bed railing. The Dark Nurse was standing over Zallie with the other nurse he'd seen in the chapel. The Dark Nurse said, "I don't understand why you keep turning up. Are you a family member?"

He sat up and rubbed his face. "She asked me to stay with her," he said. He wasn't feeling well himself. A dull pain was throbbing in his neck and down his left arm, as if he'd slept crooked. A thousand needles were pricking his skin.

"You've got to leave now," the Dark Nurse said. "We have to examine Mrs. Lalande."

"She's afraid you're going to shoot her up with something."

He stood up on legs made heavy by sleep and gazed at the old woman. Her mouth was parted slightly and he wasn't sure if she was still breathing.

"We're going to help her rest more comfortably," said the other nurse. She looked Asian, her dark brown hair pulled off her shoulders and pinned up like an unruly horse tail. A stethoscope was looped around her slender neck.

Hodge knew what they intended to do. He'd seen it too many times. A spike of morphine in the thigh of the poor bastard whose guts were oozing onto the muddy ground. *You're gonna be all right, bro'. Hang tight. Huey will be here before you know it.*

A syringe appeared in the smaller nurse's hand. The long needle looked like a sinister weapon. Like an instrument of death.

"What are you gonna give this woman?" he asked them.

The Dark Nurse walked around the bed and took his arm. "You'll have to step outside while we examine Mrs. Lalande," she said.

She was tall and strong, and her gym-hardened biceps flexed as he ripped his arm away from her. She frowned at him as though at a disobedient child. He knew if they got into a tussle he'd have to hurt her because she wouldn't give up until he did.

"Please leave before I call security," she said.

He glanced at the old woman in the bed. Maybe she was already dead. He touched her forehead. Her skin was still afire but she seemed to be at peace.

"I know what you're doing," he said to the Dark Nurse. "You don't have the right to make that call." He stared into her cold dark eyes and felt a shiver pass through him. "God is calling her," he said. "He doesn't need your help. Let her be and get the hell out of here."

"Sir—"

He grabbed the IV stand and lofted it in the air like a spear. His arms were weak and shaking but he meant business. "I said *get the hell out of here!*" he shouted at them.

The two nurses retreated quickly to the door. "I don't know what you think you're doing," said the Dark Nurse. "I'm calling security. You'd better leave this ward right now."

He advanced toward them with the IV stand raised menacingly over his shoulder. They backed out into the corridor and he used his foot to slam the door in their faces.

He set the IV stand down and stood at Zallie's bedside, gripping the safety rail to steady himself and feeling as old and frail as she looked. He could smell her unclean body and he wondered what shape he would be in when his time finally came. Would they wrap him in a pink blanket and dump him on a pile of corpses? He remembered the Bible story of the women going to the tomb of Jesus with spices and oils to anoint his body, according to the custom of the Israelites. It made sense, cleansing off the filth and preparing the dead for the next world, a final act of decency and love. And so he lowered the railing and undid the three buttons of her wet gown and worked it off her shoulders and down her skeletal ribcage and hips until he could pull it free of her long matchstick legs. She was naked now, and he was shocked to see her body reduced to bare bones, like someone in a death camp. Disease had left only the faint soft traces of her womanhood. She looked more like a stringy old man.

He went to the small closet and found a towel and another gown, a frilly lavender thing that her family must have bought for her, and he began wiping her body gently with the towel, rubbing away the stinking sweat that oozed from every pore. He was patting dry the gaunt hollows of her face when she opened her eyes and smiled at him with a strange peaceful smile, as if she was sunning herself in some sweet consoling dream. "There's an angel standing beside you, dear man," she said in a voice so weak he could hardly understand the words. "Don't be afraid to go with her. She knows your name."

Her alertness lasted only a moment and soon she was unconscious again. It wasn't easy dressing her in the new gown because her body had turned lifeless and brittle. As he worked the gown over her head and shoulders, he asked the angel standing beside him to give him more time. He wasn't ready yet to take that long journey.

He searched through her handbag in the closet and found an ink pen. He wrote the name ZALLIE in large block letters on her arm. His own skin was too dark to clearly show his name and social security number. The writing would probably wash off under his heavy sweat. But he wrote his name anyway, and those nine random numbers he'd memorized as a young soldier long ago. He hoped it would help Dee to identify him among all the others.

Hodge was sitting in the bedside chair, holding the dead woman's hand, when the door opened. A sizeable crowd had come for him. Tucker and two of his security guards. The two nurses standing in the hallway directly behind them. And someone else, as well. He could feel her presence in the room. Someone familiar and comforting.

Tucker looked perplexed, yet resigned to what he'd been called on to do. "Here you are," he said. "It sounded like you. What kind of grief you talked yourself into, brother?"

Her hand had lost its warmth. "She's ready for you now," Hodge said.

Tucker glanced at the name written on the dead woman's arm, then at Hodge. "You don't look too good yourself, chief," he said, motioning to the nurses. "Help me get this man up out of the chair."

Hodge didn't fight them. He was at peace now, too. There was a bright glowing presence in the room, standing among them, and she knew his name.

# 39

He wandered through the deserted Irish Channel, street after street, looking for a car to hotwire. He'd picked the wrong neighborhood. There were no cars, no people outside, only roaming packs of dogs and the occasional junker up on cinder blocks, its rims rusting in the weather. What was he going to do if he couldn't gank a car?

It wasn't long before he came upon the yellow school bus. Uniformed cops were loading it with loot from the houses they'd broken into. The homes of working people, double shotguns and small bungalows, a few of them fixed up nice by white folk with a little money. PJ knew that these dirty cops didn't dare cross Magazine Street and kick in the doors of Garden District mansions, because rich people had security systems and pit bull lawyers and you didn't fuck with their belongings.

He stepped back behind a shaggy, low-limbed magnolia tree to watch them. They worked quickly, like Third Ward homeboys, in and out in three minutes. Televisions, computers, DVD players. One of them was rolling a barrel barbecue pit out of somebody's garage. He looked down the street to where PJ thought he was concealed behind the magnolia branches.

"Yo, nosy motherfucker behind that tree!" the cop shouted at him. "Better move on, 'less you want my foot up your crap hole!"

PJ retreated quickly around the side of the house and started running in long loping strides toward Magazine Street. He was an eyewitness to their evil shit and they would split open his head if they caught up with him. Or drop his big ass in the river with a chain wrapped around his hands and feet.

Magazine Street was still dry. The flood had yet to reach this stretch of boarded-up shops. He saw a man wheeling a full grocery cart out of a corner market, and then a scrawny old white woman wobbling out behind him with six-packs of sodas and chip bags stuffed into a green plastic hand basket she could hardly carry. When PJ arrived at the store, the shattered entrance doors were braced open with trash cans and voices were echoing inside. He thought about Jasmine and her little brothers and how hungry they would be when the Lees ran out of food and all the stores were shut down for days, their groceries rotting in the late summer heat.

He strode across broken glass into the store and stopped near a checkout counter. Daylight washed through the large plate-glass windows marked with sale prices. He took his time, feeling out the action. There were looters roaming around in here and he didn't want to spook some shaky crackhead with a gat.

A young ward boy barely old enough to shave wandered out past the candy shelves with an armful of wine bottles. "Better go make groceries, mistah, while they's still something on a shelf," he said, grabbing a box of chocolates on his way out of the store.

PJ thought maybe he should stock up on some grind, and maybe a bottle or two of muscatel like the young brother, and hide it close by until he found a car to stash it in. It was going to be a long road trip out of this messed-up state and he didn't know how he would buy food or gas. He didn't like the idea, but he knew he might be thugging here and yonder to make it all add up.

An empty grocery cart was parked near an aluminum ice-bag freezer that was oozing water onto the tile floor. He pushed the cart down an aisle lined with frozen food lockers, their glass doors dripping condensation as if they'd been sprayed with a hose. Two little girls no older than Jasmine were laughing and drinking soupy ice cream out of gallon cartons, and they grew quiet as he passed by with his cart.

"Smell it 'fore you eat it, girls," he said to them. "You gonna make yourself sick. Where's your momma at?"

One of the girls said, "She home feeling bad. Send us out to get some food and Tie-yenol."

"Then take care of bidness and get on back home, now. Ya heard me? Y'all shouldn't be out here all by yourself."

He was grabbing items off the shelves like one of those game contestants given ten minutes to snatch everything he could, quickly filling up his cart with stuff that wouldn't spoil—crackers and chips and bread and peanut butter and beer and canned fruit and containers of pre-cooked meat—when he turned the corner and ran up on three teenagers hassling an old man pushing a cart. PJ wasn't sure it was him until he saw the man yank his Louisville Slugger out of the basket like a long loaf of French bread and threaten them with it. "Get on away from me," he was saying, "or I'll wrap this thing upside your heads."

The boys would dash past his cart and snag something, then duck away fast when he swung the bat at them. It was a game they were playing, like Steal the Flag, to impress the pretty girl with cornrows who was leaning against a shelf and giggling at their clowning.

"Yo," PJ said, pushing his cart slowly toward them. "Maybe you comics want something out of my basket."

The boys fell silent when they saw him coming. His size, his streets. "I'm talking to you, wodie." What you called a ward boy from the projects. "You wanna play, come play with me."

"Naw, bruh, this old dude be grittin' on us," one of them said, "bumpin' our shit. We didn't start this confrontation."

The old man was set in a batter's stance, the way he'd faced PJ on the porch of his shotgun home. "Didn't expect to ever see you again," he said, glancing sidelong at PJ.

"We mindin' our own bidness, keepin' it true, keepin' it lit, and this old niggah jump our shit, tellin' us we cain't take this, we cain't take that. I ax him if he the sto' manager and he diss us some mo'. He lucky I don't shove that bat up his old prune ass."

This boy had his shine on, flashing his grille and repping to make the girl laugh. He was all mouth, a sawed-off little porch boy with his white drawers showing.

"Step off, killah," PJ said to him. "Let it go. Ya heard me? Else we gonna have a serious situation."

The teenagers backed away, the girl giggling and latching onto the arm of the other boy, who was laughing and holding up a peace sign. The sawed-off porch boy gave PJ the finger. "I'ma come back with my toaster and fade you niggahs!" he said as they disappeared around the corner.

PJ and Alton Lee stood looking at each other across their grocery carts like neighbors greeting at the corner mart. "I see you're still making friends with that bat," PJ said.

The old man shook his head. He looked worn down, as if he needed a nap or a stiff drink to settle himself. "Figured you'd be long gone by now," he said with an edge to his words.

"Look, man, they ain't my kids. Find a good home for 'em."

"The little girl says you promised to look after them," Alton said. "You told her you was coming back."

"I gotta get out of this town. Some people are looking for me, y'understand? You got any idea where I can find some wheels?"

"If I knew that, we'd done been gone ourselves."

PJ studied the old man's slack face and yellow eyes. He was a hard drinker, for sure, but there was kindness in his heart. "Be good to them kids, Mr. Lee," he said, gripping the red handle of his cart. "Turn 'em over to your church or something. They're better off now than with their momma."

PJ tried to push away but the carts had locked together somehow, the wire baskets caught against each other, and he had to jerk and lift and work his cart before it came free. The old man was smiling at him. He hadn't lifted a finger to help.

"Sometimes, when you're all hung up in a world full of wreck and ruin," Alton said with a wise smile, "the man that comes out ahead is the man that stands real still and waits for his move."

"I'll write that down in my diary when I have a spare minute," PJ said.

The old man laughed. "Wait for your move, son. It'll come. There's something good inside you or you wouldn'ta brought them kids this far," he said. "Wait for your move and do what Gawd intends for you in this life."

Suddenly there were rowdy voices at the front of the store. It sounded like a fight had broken out. PJ drove his cart to the end of the aisle and stopped to watch a half dozen uniformed cops fanning out past the checkout counters. They were laughing and barking orders at the looters scattering like mice throughout the store.

*"Attention, looters! We have a bargain on aisle seven. Come out, come out, wherever you are,"* shouted one of the cops.

Another cop hollered, *"Y'all better not took all the big canned hams!"*

Through the store's plate-glass window PJ could see a yellow school bus parked out at the curb. It was that platoon of dirty cops who'd been doing their own looting in the neighborhood. He turned and flicked the back of his hand at Alton Lee, shooing him away. He knew that the old man had some history with these cops and he didn't want him swinging that baseball bat at them.

"What we got here, Shugah Bear?"

When he turned back around, two cops were standing in front of his cart, examining the contents of his basket. The black cop said, "Shugah Bear got some crackers and potted meat. Un-hunh, and some peanut butter and bread. 'Nuf for a little picnic."

The white cop pulled a six-pack of Miller Lite out of the basket and said, "Gonna live the high life."

The black cop was middle-aged and out of shape, his gut bulging the buttons of his navy blue uniform shirt. "Don't I know you?" he said, staring hard at PJ, trying to place him.

"No, sir," PJ said politely.

"You ever been a guest of the state, Shugah Bear? I ever run you?"

PJ shook his head. "You got me mixed up with some other brother," he said. "I'm just making groceries for my kids. Diapers for the baby."

"I know where we seen this dude," said the white cop. He talked country and was built like a big white high school tackle who'd let himself go. "You the one peeping behind a tree."

It was that bastard who'd rolled a barbecue pit out of somebody's garage. "I'm out here trying to bounce back, officer, like everybody else," PJ said. "Pick up some things for my family."

"Our computers were up, I'd run your ID, Shugah Bear. Then what would I find?" said the black cop.

"He's my boy, gentlemen." Alton Lee was guiding his cart toward them. PJ wanted to smack him upside the head for not heeding his warning. "He ain't never been in trouble with the laws. Not long as his momma and me have drawed breath. Like he said, we come up here 'cause we got three little ones at home. No telling how long the grocery stores gonna be shut down."

The two cops exchanged glances. The black cop took a king-sized Butterfinger out of PJ's basket and peeled back the wrapper, studying it before biting off a chunk. "Awright, Sanford and son," he said, chewing. "Take what you got and get the fuck on out of here. I don't wanna catch your looting asses around here again."

"Hold up a minute," said the white cop, digging down into PJ's basket. "Let's make sure ol' Shugah Bear ain't taking the last canned ham."

PJ and Alton Lee drove their carts side by side over the broken glass at the store's entrance and rolled outside into the strong mid-day sunlight. Two cops were smoking cigarettes next to the yellow school bus. PJ could see stolen goods propped against the mud-streaked windows where the faces of schoolchildren normally smiled out at you. A tall lamp, the top of a huge Panasonic TV, a gray file cabinet. The passenger door was folded open and he could see a boom box and what looked like a pile of women's clothing stashed next to the driver's seat. And he saw something else, too. Wires were hanging loose underneath the steering column, the ones to spark-flash the yellow monster and start it up.

"Keep moving," said one of the cops, flicking ash at them. "Ain't nothing here to look at."

Three blocks below Magazine Street, when they felt they were far enough from the police, they stopped and faced each other across their carts. "What kind of trouble you in, son?" Alton asked him.

PJ wasn't going to talk about it. "Here," he said, transferring cans of peaches and tuna fish and an extra loaf of bread into the old man's basket. "The kids'll eat this."

"What you want me to tell that little girl and her brother? You gave them your word you was coming back."

PJ stared at the packages of disposable diapers in Alton's cart. "Find a good family they can live with," he said. "That little Edgar is sweet as they come."

Alton gave him the same look his Pops had always given him when he was disappointed in him. "You saw what I saw back there," the old man said with a sling of the head.

PJ wasn't sure what he was talking about. He dragged a warm six-pack of Miller Lite out of his basket. "This is for your ice cooler," he said. He was saving the other six-pack for himself. "Don't drink it all in one night, unk. Pace yourself."

The old man pulled a warm beer from its ring and cracked it open. He wasn't waiting for ice. "Gawd has a plan for us all, son," he said, sipping the beer and then glancing at the can, as if reading the label. "You got any idea what I did for thirty-five years before I retired?"

PJ shrugged. "No clue, Kojak."

"I was a bus driver," the old man said. "Thirty-five years with the New Orleans school district. You hear what I'm saying?"

He was smiling at PJ with an unsettling smile. There was something crafty behind those yellow eyes. PJ twisted a beer free of the ring and popped the tab, saluting Alton before he drank. It was like drinking bathwater but he didn't mind. It had been far too long since he'd tasted alcohol.

"You saw them wires hanging loose," Alton said. "They got it hotwired—you don't need a key. I'll be at home waiting for you, son. Four in the morning, it don't matter. Me and the wife, we'll get everybody together."

"You talking shit now, Mistah Lee."

"Wait in the tall grass till it gets dark and the time is right. They're gonna drink up what they looted and party all night long." Alton tipped his can at him as if offering a toast. "Wait for your move, son. You'll know it when you feel it."

"It ain't gonna happen, man."

"You in trouble with the laws, son. You can wander around town till they pick you up, or you can bring me that school bus," Alton said. "This is what Gawd put you on this earth to do. Bring me that school bus and I'll drive us all to Houston."

A fucking school bus. "I don't know the first damn thing about driving a bus," PJ said.

"You'll figure it out," Alton said. "I got faith in you."

He wheeled the grocery cart off down the street, tilting back his head and drinking beer as he rambled in an old man's pace toward his home and wife and the children he intended to save.

# 40

Dee searched the store they'd camped in, her son's backpack slung across her shoulder and Ashley walking close by her side, pale and half asleep and worried into silence that her brother might be lost forever. They covered every department, the elaborate bathroom displays and floor-to-ceiling aisles of bedding and linens and the faraway corners, Dee calling his name as the panic grew inside her. Packs of teenagers were roving through the store like unruly schoolchildren on a museum field trip, examining mysterious objects from some exotic culture. She stopped them all, but no one had seen a nine-year-old boy wandering around by himself.

At one point Dee and Ashley came upon two older ladies in kitchenware, looking at an assortment of tea kettles as if they were shopping for Christmas gifts. "So many chirrens roaming loose right now," said a large copper-skinned woman with unusual green eyes and short hair dyed blonde. "What he look like?"

When Dee attempted to describe her son, she realized he looked like a million other kids his age. Her words caught in her throat and she brought a hand to her mouth.

"It gone be all right, baby," said the second woman, a bony little grandma with sharp cheekbones and the worst wig Dee had ever seen on a human head. She took Dee by the wrist and gently shook her arm. "He gone turn up safe. You'll see."

"You say he go by *Marcus?*" said the larger woman.

"La-Marcus," Ashley said quickly, giving her mother time to catch her breath. "He's a math genius. He knows how far it is to every planet."

"Then we best get busy finding that smart boy," said the grandma with a sweet consoling smile. "Ain't enough of 'em we can afford to waste one."

They joined Dee and Ashley in their search, recruiting others to help them as they marched through the store and out into the pedestrian area with its benches and potted trees and information kiosks.

*"We got a boy missing, y'all!"* announced the larger woman. Her name was Joy and she had the deep-throated voice of an aging gospel singer. *"Y'all seen a little nine-year-old wandering around by hisself?"*

A small crowd gathered, looters wearing unlaced Adidas and Nikes right out of the box and eating food they'd found in a café storeroom.

*"Come on, now, I know somebody seen this boy!"*

Dee was surprised by how serious the crowd had become, even the noisy teenagers. The mood had turned instantly into an Amber Alert, and all she could think about was that story of the little child they'd found naked in a shopping mall bathroom with his head shaved and the Sign of Satan painted on his chest.

Dee stepped up onto a bench so everyone could see and hear her. "His name is LaMarcus," she told the crowd. "He's about this tall and he's wearing an Audubon Zoo T-shirt with animals on it."

"Oh, man, I seen that little shorty!" said a teenager wearing a baseball cap with the long bill turned at a slight angle. "I seen his T-shirt. He was walking rightchere with some big dude seem like his daddy."

Dee felt as if her heart would explode. Her son had been lured away by a child molester. How many times had she told him not to talk to strangers?

"Dude busted a rock into one of them spots down there," said the teenager, pointing.

He wasn't sure which store he'd seen the man throw a rock at, so the crowd split up and ventured into a half dozen stores with broken display windows on that side of the mall. A chorus of voices began calling his name. *LaMarcus! LaMarrrrcus!*

Dee hurried along with Ashley in tow, trying not to hyperventilate. Ashley said, "Look, Momma, what about that one?"

Dee couldn't imagine why anyone would want to break into a luggage store, but it was the only place nobody had chosen yet.

*"LaMarcus!"* she cried out as they stepped over broken glass and into the shop. *"LaMarcus, are you in here?"*

She thought she heard a small voice at the back of the building. *"LaMarcus, is that you?"* she called again. *"Where are you, baby?"*

Squeezing Ashley's hand, she stopped to listen for the sound again. The store was dead silent. She waited longer, calling his name once more, and this time she was certain she heard voices.

She headed off down an aisle with Ashley clinging to her hand, trying to keep up. The row of leather merchandise took on a menacing presence in the faint light, like strange creatures watching them from the low branches of a tree. She rounded the corner by a display of luggage on wheels and suddenly he was there, running toward her in a full sprint.

"Momma, he's got a gun!" her son cried, racing into her arms.

The man was standing halfway down the aisle, zipping up a backpack, looping it around his muscled shoulders. He was wearing a football jersey and jogging pants, his neck tattooed with a sinister spider web. He dipped a knee and picked up a pistol resting on the carpet.

*"What did you do to my son?"* Dee screamed at him, clutching LaMarcus to her chest. She didn't know how, but she would find a way to kill this man if he'd harmed her son in any way.

"It ain't like that," said the man, smiling at her through a gold shine. "He just he'ped me do some numbers, is all."

LaMarcus said, "He paid me to count money."

"Hey, Perfessor, don't give no secrets away, ya heard me?"

He walked toward them in a slow hip-rocking gait, the gun dangling loose in his hand. "You didn't tell me you had such a fine-looking momma," he said, studying Dee. "Why don't you and your sister run off for a little while, Perfessor, and find you something to do till your momma and me are through working this thing out."

With Ashley latched to her hip pocket and LaMarcus buried against her chest, Dee backed away slowly, as if backing away from a mad dog.

"You don't have nothing to be scared of, pretty momma. I got resources at my disposal. I'll take good care of you and your kids. Y'understand what I'm saying? Hang with U-Rite and we'll find ourselves a nice dry crib till everything get back up straight."

Dee stared at the gun in his hand. "We . . . have family," she managed to say, still backing away in an awkward tangle of limbs. "We have our own people."

He laughed at her. "Don't be lying to me, girl. I know you ain't got no man to look after you and them children. The boy told me how it is," he said. "Let 'em run play, now. You and me, we'll work this arrangement out."

"No . . . we," Dee stammered.

He was only a few feet away when he stopped and raised the gun, aiming it at her. "What the fuck y'all want?" he said in a gruff voice, and Dee realized he wasn't pointing the gun at her but at something behind them. She turned to see the woman named Joy and the grandma with the bad wig and a dozen teenagers coming up the aisle.

"You found your boy, baby?" cried the grandma. "Praise Jesus, he awright?"

"Who that niggah pointing a nine?" said the teenage boy with the long-billed cap. "Hey, man, you mess with that little boy?"

The man thumbed back the hammer with a threatening click-click. "Step the fuck off or I'll take every one of y'all out, bitch by bitch," he said.

Dee kept backing away, dragging the children with her, until they were standing shoulder to shoulder with Joy and the grandma and the surrounding teenagers. Summoning all her courage, Dee glared at the man and said, "Please just leave us alone and go."

The man's aim was steady and unyielding, and Dee knew he was capable of shooting them all. As the silence grew more tense, Joy raised her voice and spoke with commanding authority. "You heard the lady," she said. "Let it go, man. Walk on!"

He thumb-released the hammer and raised the gun near his ear, like a professional killer in a movie, and continued walking toward them. A couple of teenagers turned and ran; the others backed against the merchandise shelves. Joy and the grandma threw their arms around Dee and the children. There was no time to retreat.

The man stopped at arm's length and reached toward them with his free hand. Dee shuddered, thinking he was going to touch her. Instead, he chucked her son's chin. "You old enough to get out from underneath all this skirt, son, and be a man." LaMarcus was hiding in his mother's embrace. "Stand up tall, ya heard me? Don't let these bitches put a dress on you."

He tucked the gun in the waistband of his jogging pants and laughed at the timid huddle of bodies, his eyes dark and fierce. He was still laughing when he brushed past them and walked toward the entrance, the backpack secure against his huge shoulders as teenagers parted out of his way.

# 41

An Indian with grackle black hair flowing down his back offered to sew up his lip if they could find a needle and thread. "I was a medic in Iraq, the first year on the ground," he told Duval from the bar stool where he sat nursing a tall can of malt liquor in the flickering candlelight. "You wouldn't believe the shit I had to clean up, brah. But Iraq was no worse than what's going down out there," he said, nodding toward the door. The heat was thick and oily inside this bar, and sweat ran down the wolf's head tattooed on the Indian's bicep. "Some white dude caught a looter in his house in Bywater and turned him over to NOPD. They cuffed the brother and let the dude put a cap in his head. It's payback time for whitey, brah. Better watch your back."

Duval had smoked a blunt on deserted Royal Street with his traveling posse—Jolly Rolly, Gypsy, and the Girl with Dead Eyes—and they'd stumbled into this dark bar a couple of blocks behind the cathedral. The bartender was a tall crater-faced white guy with a gray ponytail and he gave them the first Budweiser on the house, dripping cold from an ice chest behind the bar, and then traded two more rounds for half of Rolly's lid and a tongue kiss from the Girl with Dead Eyes.

Around the L-shaped bar, ghostlike silhouettes shifted in the candlelight, shadowy figures swapping tales of their survival. They all knew one another, barfly regulars who lived in the Quarter and made their daily rounds from tavern to tavern. They were proud of themselves for staying behind and toughing it out, and they talked fondly about the roaring winds and the copper roof flashing blown around the streets like flying razor blades and ancient chimneys collapsing onto cars parked on the street. An old man with a long yellowing beard sat on a stool in the corner and told them he'd heard about a shoot-out on a bridge in New Orleans East between the cops and four black men with automatic rifles. Somebody else had heard that snipers were shooting at rescue helicopters. Women were getting raped in the Superdome and riots had broken out at the convention center. It was open season on white people and there was no bag limit.

"Homeboys will be homeboys," said a woman with a whiskey voice and a cigarette smoldering between her fingers. "It's N'awlins, dawl. Does any of this surprise you?"

Duval was trying to get his freak on and forget everything that had happened to him over the past thirty-six hours, and these uptight fucking paranoids had killed his buzz. His beer can was empty and he needed another toke of Jolly Rolly's weed and he leaned against the bar and looked for him in the dark smoky reaches of the room. Somebody was sleeping on a mattress thrown on top of the pool table. A couple of firemen were drinking quietly near the door. The Girl with Dead Eyes was sitting on Rolly's lap at a corner table, making out with him, and the dark-skinned woman named Gypsy danced in slow sensuous circles to music nobody else could hear.

"It comes down to it, we gotta take care of our own," said a young shirtless white guy wearing bathing trunks and a camo baseball cap.

A red-headed man with a chest-length red goatee tied with twine like a kite tail pulled a Glock 9 from his carrying bag and set it on the bar. "No offense, my man," he said to Duval, "but if your people come looking for shit in the Quarter, they're gonna get all they can handle."

Duval gazed around in the dim lighting. No one had to tell him he was the only black person in this bar. "Take a look at this pretty face, *my man*," he said, staring at the gun on the bar top. "I been lit up twice 'cause everybody want the boat I had. White boys, black boys both. Everybody taken they shot at this face. You want your turn, Ginger, go ahead and pull the trigger," he said, sliding the gun toward the red-headed man's forearms resting on the bar. "Otherwise, run that color bullshit on somebody else and leave my ass out of it."

The old white-bearded man at the end of the bar laughed jovially and applauded Duval. "Bravo, Mercutio, bravo!" he called out. "Well done, lad."

"Put that fucking gun away, Nigel," said the bartender, walking out of the darkness of the storeroom. "And don't bring it in my bar anymore."

The woman named Gypsy suddenly appeared at Duval's side. "You getting into more trouble, baby?" she said, resting her slender arm on his shoulder. She handed him the joint she was smoking. Sweat glistened on her neck in the amber glow of candlelight. "Rolly says it's time to split for the next party," she said, her stale breath hot against his ear. "Come on with us, sugar. Let's get better acquainted."

There was only an inch of rainwater in the pitch dark streets of the French Quarter and they splashed along Orleans Street until they reached the wrought iron gates of a courtyard where a party was under way in the primitive light of a hundred candles. The man sitting in a lawn chair by the gate held a shotgun across his lap and swatted at the mosquitoes buzzing around his face.

"'Sup?" Rolly said to him. "John the Blade told us to drop by."

The gatekeeper looked like a biker or professional wrestler, a burly giant with long hair and a pierced nose. "What's the password?" he asked.

Jolly Rolly handed him a blunt and lit it for him with a Bic lighter. "John the Blade didn't say."

The gatekeeper pinched smoke in his lungs, saying, "That's good, man, 'cause there ain't no password." When he noticed Duval in their company, he said, "He with you?"

"He's cool," said Jolly Rolly.

"He's a recording star," said the Girl with Dead Eyes.

The gatekeeper eyed Duval. "Go on in," he said. "John's back there somewheres."

The courtyard was surrounded by what appeared to be old wooden barracks two stories high. They may have been slave quarters in the far-off days, but now they were divided into apartments. Duval could smell meat cooking on a grill and he realized how hungry he was. All he'd eaten in two days was a couple of power bars.

A dozen white people were lounging around a leaf-covered swimming pool in the middle of the courtyard. They had raked aside the debris of branches and palm fronds to clear a space for their party. One foreign dude was playing a guitar and singing old hippie songs in his foreign accent, and a couple was swaying arm-in-arm to his music.

John the Blade carried a long hunting knife sheathed at his side. A cigarette dangled from the corner of his mouth as he stood watch over the hamburgers smoking on a grill. "Hey, you rascal!" He greeted Jolly Rolly with a sloppy hug. "Glad you could make it, bro'. Y'all are just in time for the discount buffet. Need a drink? Hey, Amy, get our guests something to drink."

A pretty blonde woman wearing a skimpy bikini rose from her lounge chair and dove into the pool, opening a hole in the floating carpet of leaves. She resurfaced with a six-pack of Heinekens. "Only way to keep 'em cool," said John the Blade. "Y'all help yourselves. There's plenty more on the bottom."

Duval drank beer and smoked the reefer being passed around and ate a hamburger on a plain bun, but it didn't satisfy his hunger so he grazed the patio tables gorged with bags of cheese puffs and smoked oysters and gooey slices of Spam. More white people arrived and he drank more beer fetched from the bottom of the swimming pool and tried to dance with Gypsy to one of those folksongs but his heart wasn't in it. He left her and went looking for more food and stumbled on a stash of random items dumped on a card table.

"We liberated that stuff," explained a very drunk woman. "Go ahead and take what you need."

He sifted through the collection of toothpaste and tampons and shampoo and tourist postcards from Mardi Gras. There were bottles of sherry and vermouth and sweet liqueurs that nobody in their right mind would steal. He laughed and said, "White folk liberate, black folk loot. That how they tell it?"

He was thoroughly wasted by now and feeling a little unsteady on his feet, and he wandered over to a vacant lounge chair at poolside and made himself comfortable nursing a bottle of dark ale imported from a country he couldn't spell. Mosquitoes buzzed around his ears, the little bastards. He thought he heard a gunshot in the distance. Suddenly a loud whirring noise drowned out everything around him and a wind kicked up, blowing leaves across the pool. He thought maybe the patio was caving in from all this fun with white people. A helicopter appeared overhead, hovering in the dark sky and shining its spotlight on the courtyard and the partygoers drinking and eating and dancing to the guitar player's drunken songs. Everyone stopped to wave and cheer, and the helicopter quickly roared away, as if disappointed with what it had found.

He didn't know how long he'd been sitting in that lounge chair when he realized the candles were burning out and the party was winding down. Couples were straggling off to dark corners of the courtyard. Others were swimming naked among the leaves. He closed his eyes, slapping at the mosquitoes biting his face, drifting into sleep. Something sharp was jabbing his thigh, something like a knife point in his baggy shorts. He slid a hand into his pocket and discovered it was the keys that Hodge had entrusted to him.

He was dozing off again when he felt a woman's body nuzzle against him in the long narrow chair. He thought it would be Gypsy but it was the Girl with Dead Eyes. She curled against his arm and shoulder, resting her warm hand on his chest. "Will you sing for me?" she asked in a sweet fragile voice.

"I ain't in no shape to sing right now, girlfriend. Whatchew doing close up against me like that? Where your man?"

"Gypsy wants to suck your dick," she said.

Duval stared out into the dying candlelight. Everything was moving in a slow dizzy dance. Gypsy and Jolly Rolly were sharing a joint with John the Blade, the last ones standing. They all seemed to be looking at him. What the fuck was he doing here with these people?

"Gypsy's a tranny," she said. "A dude from the waist down. I thought you should know that, in case you hadn't figured it out."

Duval suddenly felt sick to his stomach. "Get the fuck off me," he said, brushing her hand off his chest. Trashy fucking white stoners, man. You couldn't trust them. They would burn you every time. "Go on, girl. Get away from me. And tell that bitch if he comes anywhere close to my dick, I'ma drown his faggot ass in this here pool."

The Girl with Dead Eyes started to cry. "You don't have to be so mean," she said.

"Go on," he said, shrugging her off his arm. "Go find you some other niggah to niggah around with. I got serious obligations."

She sat up in the lounge chair, her golden hair hanging loose in her sad eyes. She was as wasted as he was. "What kind of obligations?" she asked him, wiping slobber from her mouth.

"A momma and two children. An old man half dead in the hospital. They all depending on me to get them out of this shit. Girl, I don't even know where my own momma at." She'd phoned him on Saturday to say she and his two aunts were leaving town on their church bus. She didn't know where they were taking them, maybe to Florida. "It's real out there, yo. People dying and high water everywhere. Y'all in here having a party. Drinking shit from Amsterdam."

He glanced at the bottle in his hand and then flung it into the swimming pool.

"What makes you think you're better than the rest of us?" She said this with childlike innocence, a younger sister fighting back. "I don't see you helping anybody right now."

He felt like slapping her pretty little face. Instead, he pulled himself up off the reclining chair and tried to stand. The light had almost vanished in the courtyard and the damp night air exerted a peculiar force around him, like the gentle pressure of waves against his legs. He could feel their tug on the swaying rhythm of his body. He didn't know if he could put one foot in front of the other.

"Why don't you sit back down before you fall over?" said the Girl with Dead Eyes. She was hanging onto the lounge chair as if it was a lifeboat in rough water. Mosquitoes dotted her tender white face like specks of dirt, but she didn't seem to notice.

"Like I told you, girlfriend. I got obligations," he said, taking his first unsure steps toward the patio tables, using them as safe ports as he staggered off in search of the wrought iron gate.

Somewhere in the whirl of dark empty space he heard Gypsy's voice say, "Where you going, baby?"

"Stay away from me, faggot," he said, his words slurring now.

The biker-looking gatekeeper was still sitting on a lawn chair with the shotgun in his lap, but he'd fallen asleep and was snoring. Duval thought about grabbing that shotgun and firing a couple of rounds in the air, ghetto-style on New Year's Eve. Shake these happy white people up. Fuck 'em all, he thought. Fuck 'em and their smoked oysters and long-legged blonde women swimming naked and all the sick motherfuckers pretending to be something they were not.

He wandered down the sidewalk in the silent darkness of the French Quarter, scraping his hand along the brick walls to keep from falling down. He'd made it a block, maybe two, when he stumbled to his knees and puked against a huge metal dumpster set back in an alcove. He crawled on his hands and knees, trying to get free of his vomit, and found himself trapped somewhere behind the dumpster, overwhelmed by rotting garbage and the sour mess on his hoodie and what smelled like a dead animal back here. He puked again and again, losing everything he'd eaten tonight. His sides were aching and he could hardly catch his breath and he passed out facedown in a pool of his own filth.

# 42

When it turned dark, PJ stole through the forest of downed oak limbs covering the streetcar tracks on St. Charles Avenue and found a hiding place behind a thick green hedge that bordered the hotel's circle drive. The yellow school bus was parked in front, where he'd first seen it. He knelt on the damp grass and peered through a breach in the wall of bushes, watching the cops unload the bus while he ate two packages of cheese crackers from the grocery store. They were laughing and drinking beer in a swirl of flashlight beams as they hauled their takings into the dark hotel. Mostly electronics, from what PJ could see—flat screen televisions and laptops and DVD players—but also a bulky chair that took two men to handle and even a glass chandelier that sparkled like a thousand tiny mirrors in the crisscrossing lights.

"Yo, Bobby, that chandelier's gonna look good in your momma's whorehouse," one of the cops said.

"Yeah, you can come over and watch your sister blow me under it."

What had he gotten himself into? If there was any other way out, he would have jumped on it. He'd thought about breaking into garages to see if he could find a car left behind. He'd thought about thugging people driving down the street, but he hadn't seen a car all afternoon. He'd thought about walking to the city limits and sticking his thumb out, taking his chances, but it was a long hike to the nearest bridge and he knew that the first car to stop would be a black and white. Hard as it was to believe, his best shot was an old drunk named Alton Lee who said he could drive them to Houston in a fucking school bus.

He heard something stirring through the hedge, a cat or some other creature prowling in the darkness, slowly making its way toward him in the undergrowth of wet leaves.

A cop said, "Hey, you hear that?"

His buddies froze, listening.

"Where, man?"

"Over there," the cop said, pointing his flashlight at the hedge and slowly dragging the beam from one end of the long boxed row to the other. The light filtered through the thick wall of greenery and PJ could see a fat possum crackling along over the leaves not ten yards away.

"You hear what I'm hearing?"

*"Hey, cocksucker,"* shouted another cop, *"if you're on two legs, you better come out and show us your hands!"*

They waited in suspended motion, their arms filled with stolen goods as they watched the flashlight beam search the long hedge.

"One way to find out," said the country-talking cop PJ recognized from the grocery store. He set down a pair of speaker boxes and withdrew his sidearm. "Give me some more light, boys."

Half a dozen flashlight rays pierced the hedge and the cop began firing his gun. PJ rolled over on his side, protecting his head with his arms. Bullets ripped through the foliage all around him. He curled into a ball, waiting for the piece of lead that would shatter his body. When he peeked between his arms, he saw the possum scramble out from the hedge and scamper toward the hotel in clear sight. Someone hollered "*Light that fat fucker up!*" and the men pulled their weapons and took target practice on the panicked creature, laughing wildly at the splatter of hair, gristle, and bone.

"How we know it's dead?" asked one of the cops after the firing had ceased. "It might be playing possum."

They laughed and shot several more rounds into the dead possum, then holstered their weapons and resumed their work unloading the bus.

PJ lay coiled like a snake, not daring to move. He held his breath until his lungs burned, afraid they would hear him breathing. Eventually he sat up and hugged his knees and waited in his hiding place behind the hedge while the cops laughed and joked and transported stolen property into the hotel. They loaded smaller things into an idling squad car and a couple of brand new Cadillacs parked nearby. Soon they'd cleared everything out and the cars drove off and the men disappeared into the hotel for another round of drinking. Alton Lee had been right about them. They were going to party late into the night while the city fell deeper and deeper into chaos.

Darkness settled around him like a black tarp and time slowed down until he had no sure sense of how long he'd been sitting there. After awhile his ass was wet and numb and he couldn't hear them celebrating anymore. It had been the hardest two days of his life and he could barely keep his eyes open. He thought about eating the last three Slim Jims he'd stuffed into the pockets of his jogging pants, but he'd lost his appetite. He tried to picture himself crawling behind the wheel of that yellow school bus parked in the circle drive. There was a stone cold cell waiting for him in Angola penitentiary with his name carved on the wall, but if he could spark the wires dangling underneath the steering column of that bus, he was never coming back to Louisiana. Never.

The night was warm and crickets sang all around him in the heavy garden air. He hadn't seen any cops in hours. He rubbed his face and knees and remembered what Alton had told him. *Wait for your move, son. You'll know it when you feel it.* He crouched against the hedge and spread the tight branches, taking one last look. The bus sat under a dome of dark oak trees in the quiet moonlight, the old engine no longer ticking. There was nobody out there, as far as he could tell. He was starting to feel it. His pulse pounded in his ears. If he was going to do this thing, the time was now.

He forced his way through the hedge like a man bending into a driving windstorm, and once he was free he broke hard in a dead run toward the circle drive. Keeping his head low, he quickly reached the yellow bus and pressed his back against the mud-caked side below the long row of windows. He fought to slow his breath, listening for human sounds, footsteps, voices, a door opening at the lobby. Nothing except the screaming crickets.

He discovered that the folding door was shut tight, but he dug his fingers under the rubber-seal flap and opened it with a squeak. He snuck up the steps to the driver's seat and sank onto the leather cushion, which released air like a punctured balloon. It was pitch black inside the bus and his hands fumbled underneath the instrument panel, searching for those wires. And then suddenly a glaring white radiance flooded the glass windows, filling the bus's long dark enclosure with light. He slid off the seat and crawled down the aisle as fast as he could, hunting for a place to hide his large body in these seats built for schoolchildren. What he realized now was that two cars had swerved off St. Charles into the hotel's driveway and had stopped alongside the bus, their engines idling and doors opening, loud voices invading the silence.

"They clear everything out?"

"Let's take a look. Don't want none of that shit left hanging around."

PJ crawled into the tight leg space of a seat halfway toward the rear. He remembered hiding down behind a seat like this on a school field trip with a boy named Cedric Augustine because they didn't want to go on a tour of the local rendering plant. But now he was twice that size and he struggled to squeeze his arms and legs into the space, burying his face against the leather seat.

He heard them climb the steps into the bus, one cop after the other. A flashlight beam jerked all around the dark interior like a playful puppy yanking on a leash. "Looks like they got it all," said the lead cop. He was moving slowly down the aisle, inspecting each seat with his light. Somebody was laughing outside the bus.

"What's he saying?" he asked the cop behind him. They were only two seats from PJ's hiding place, hosing everything with a spray of light.

"Something's dead on the ground out there."

"Another stiff?"

A third cop was rapping on a window. "Hey, y'all come check this out," he said. "There's a possum shot to shit over here. Least I think it's a possum."

Boots shuffled on the gritty bus floor. The light faded back toward the door.

"Sounds like supper," said one of the retreating cops. "Bag it up, cuño, and let's smoke the bastard on that grill Kenny snagged."

"You Cajuns are sick motherfuckers," the other cop said. "Eating swamp rat and possums and shit."

"Before this rodeo is over, *cooyon*, you might be begging for a bite of possum."

PJ's face was buried in leather that smelled like lunch meat and pee. He could hear them laughing and talking about the dead possum. When he was certain they'd gone inside the hotel to join the others, he pulled himself out of his hiding place and crawled back up the aisle to the driver's seat. He sat for several moments in complete darkness, peering out the windshield, the side glass, listening for voices, looking for shadows with a human shape. He'd never driven a bus before, but he knew how to use a clutch and could probably find first gear. He'd drive this clumsy fucker in one gear all the way to Mexico if he had to.

Taking a deep breath, he reached under the steering column and found the two wires. When he touched them together, there was a spark and a smell of burnt coil and then another spark, and the old engine roared to life. He engaged the clutch and jiggled the stick shift, searching for a gear that worked, and soon he was under way with the lights off, lurching ahead out of the circle drive toward the street. He expected the hotel doors to bang open, cops chasing after him, shooting at his tires like they'd shot at that poor possum. But when he looked in his side mirror, the hotel remained as dark and quiet as a crypt.

He steered the rattling beast across the cluttered streetcar tracks on St. Charles Avenue, roaring south toward the river. When he was two blocks away, he found the switch on the dash panel that flipped on the headlights. Tree branches and flowery foliage choked the streets of the Garden District. Heavy oak limbs were heaped around the white mansions as if they'd been piled up for a bonfire. Driving was slow, and he kept looking in the side mirror to see if anyone was coming after him. Could he really pull this mad shit off? Slapping the steering wheel and shaking his head, he started laughing and laughed until tears rolled down his cheeks. He had wheels!

In the blaze of headlights he could see a lean figure ahead, hurrying down the sidewalk past a long row of wrought iron fences. The dude glanced over his shoulder at the approaching bus lights and picked up his step. Was he breaking into these places? PJ could tell he was a white boy by the bird-legged way he carried himself. A tall thin young dude wearing a baseball cap and side-striped jogging pants and a red San Francisco 49ers jersey that said *A. Smith* over number 11.

He gunned the bus in the only gear he trusted and soon caught up with the boy, trying to get a better look at him through the glass panels in the folding door. The boy hunched his shoulders and moved faster now, pretending there wasn't a huge fucking bus cruising alongside him in a dark deserted city after a hurricane. He paced the boy for half a block, sure it was him, not sure it was him. There was only one way to find out. He yanked on the lever and the bus door opened with a squeal.

"Yo, Tulane," he called out. "Is that you, man? Come on and get in."

The boy kept walking. Staring straight ahead.

"Hey, man, they got Crocodile. And they almost got me," PJ said. "I'm glad you made it out."

The boy refused to acknowledge the bus and the driver and maybe even this whole crazy nightmare they'd been swept up in.

"I know it's you, Tulane. We shop at the same store. Nobody wants a Forty-Niner jersey, bruh. I got stuck with the fucking Houston Texans."

The boy stopped. PJ hit the brakes, skidding the old bus across a slick bed of live oak leaves. He thought the kid might change direction and run for it, but he didn't. He walked slowly toward the open passenger door and stood watching PJ from under the bill of the baseball cap, his face obscured in darkness.

"Come on, climb in, dawg. I know an old man says he can drive this thing in more than one gear and get us the fuck out of Dodge."

The boy kept looking at him from the darkness. "I saw them take Crocodile," he said in a voice carved to a sharp edge.

The stick shift groaned as PJ tried to find first gear again. "They'll drag our sorry asses back to O-P-P, too, niggah," he said, "if you don't get your bad wall-pissing self in this bus."

Because Robert Guyton did not return, as he'd promised, and there was no sign of his National Guard unit anywhere, Dee decided that she and the children would spend their night outside on the elevated walkway that hugged the mall. She wouldn't feel so trapped out there, where she could see the flashing lights of police cruisers and the crowd milling about in front of the convention center but remain twenty feet above the turmoil.

LaMarcus and Ashley helped her drag a queen-sized mattress, sheets, and pillows from the linen store up the rear emergency stairs and out onto the landing. To her surprise, a white family had already made camp there in the glow of lantern light. A couple sat on stylish canvas lawn chairs at a small glass table, gazing out at the dark choppy river like tourists at a sidewalk café. They said they were from Connecticut. Their son was sleeping on a duvet at their feet.

"Cheers," said the husband, raising a bottle of Gatorade the color of mouthwash. He told Dee they'd brought their son down to check into his Tulane dorm room over the weekend and were stranded by the storm. This was their first experience with Louisiana.

"You folks hungry? You're welcome to join us," he said. "We found some snacks in the mall. Try these pralines." He pronounced it *prawleens*. "We're taking a whole suitcase full to our friends back home."

The table came courtesy of a store named Kitchens, he said, and the chairs were from Dollar Days and the duvet and bedding were from the same place Dee and the children had stayed.

"We shopped early to avoid the crowds," said the wife with a laugh that darkened quickly into worry lines at the corners of her mouth.

Dee and the kids pitched their mattress next to the Friedman family and sat up watching a steady stream of unhappy evacuees from the convention center climb the stairway and claim ground space on the long narrow ledge.

"Y'all got the right idea. We better off up in here," said a young man with a baby in his arms and a wife by his side. "I heard they beating old people to death inside that place," he said, glancing back toward the dark building. "Y'all don't mind, we'll pull up some rug righchere and chill for the night."

"Welcome aboard," said David Friedman, waving his hand over the scattering of food on their table. "You're just in time for dessert."

Soon there were a hundred people nesting on the walkway. Her children huddled against Dee on the mattress with their backs to the concrete wall, listening to the turbulent tide splash against the pilings below. Mosquitoes were swarming in the breeze off the river. Dee and the kids tried to hide under sheets, but it was too hot and airless to remain under covers for very long. Draping herself like a Muslim woman in a burka, with only her face showing, she peered out into the starry darkness toward the twin spans of the Crescent City Connection. No bridge lights tonight, no headlights entering the city. The buses weren't coming. They had been abandoned in this harsh place, left here to survive like stray dogs nosing through a garbage dump.

"Momma, did you know that mosquitoes can buzz around for four hours without stopping?" said LaMarcus. "They can fly almost ten miles a night."

"You'd think they'd be tired from all that flying around," said Dee, "and leave us alone."

"Mosquitoes have been around for thirty million years." Gandhi Friedman was a handsome college boy with curly black hair piled high like an old-fashioned 'fro. He was lying on the duvet with his hands behind his head, staring up at the stars. "The Japanese used to think they were hungry ghosts. Reincarnations of the dead."

The two boys talked about strange random things until the night weighed down on everyone with its cries and distant gunshots and smoke drifting in from something burning somewhere. A sleepy silence settled over the dark walkway, an occasional cough, the rustling of bodies seeking comfort on the hard concrete. A bent old man braced himself against the safety railing, staring out at the dark waters. "Radio said it's dry across the river in Gretna and Algiers," he said with a toothless drawl, as if he'd been holding onto this shred of information for hours and had just now thought to mention it. "Said they didn't take near as much damage and there's transportation sitting around over there—buses and such—waiting for folk to cross over and drive 'em off."

Her children were curled up on the mattress, asleep now. Dee fetched the flashlight out of LaMarcus's backpack and climbed to her feet with the sheet still wrapped around her. She stepped over sleeping bodies and stood next to the old man at the rail, shining the light out into the fearsome blackness. The old muddy river was running fast and chunked with storm debris. She leveled the beam to see how far it would project across the wide water. There were no lights on the far bank at Algiers Point or anywhere else, and she imagined this was what it was like two hundred years ago, when nothing but swampland and wilderness lay on the other side.

"How do we get over there?" she asked him.

"Way God intended," he said. "One foot in front of the other."

"Unless you can walk on water like Jesus," she said to the old man, wiggling the light over the river like a classroom pointer, "how you gonna do that?"

He straightened up and lit a cigarette, his match flaring in the darkness. "That big bridge up yonder," he said, a puff of white smoke pluming all around him. "We walk over the bridge. Simple as that."

Dee trained her flashlight on the spans of the Crescent City Connection, dark arches in the nighttime sky. Her heart was beating quicker now, as if a ghostly hand had stroked her sweating back. It was the first time in two days that her spirits had lifted. The old man was right. "We can do that," she said, more to herself than to anyone listening. "We can walk our way out of here."

# 43

Alton Lee peeped above the sagging door chain with a flashlight in one hand and the Louisville Slugger in the other. When he recognized PJ, he unlatched the chain and stepped out onto the porch, staring at the yellow school bus humming in the dark street. "I'll be damn," he said with a sleepy smile. "I didn't think you'd really do it, son."

"Shake your old lady and wake up them kids," PJ said. "We gotta bump. The heat's probably out looking for this rig right about now."

Alton shined his flashlight on the panels of dark glass. "That somebody looking out the window?" he asked.

Tulane sat in one of the bus seats like a lonely third-grader. When the light hit him, he raised a hand to shield his eyes.

"White dude I know. Needs a ride out of this bitch, like everybody else," PJ said. "Come on, gramps, we kicking it Old School Bus."

The children were sleeping together in a spare room that must have been the Lee children's bedroom long ago. The room was hot and stuffy, even with the window open, and moonlight bathed the three small figures lying on top of the covers. When PJ's eyes adjusted to the darkness, he could see that Baby Darius's head rested on Jasmine's chest and Edgar was curled against her arm.

"Hey, girl," he said, wiggling Jasmine's ankle. "Time to wake up. We're leaving out of this place."

Olive appeared in the doorway behind him, carrying two grocery bags stuffed with the food and bottled water and diapers that Alton had taken from the store. She looked more alert than her husband, as if she'd been waiting for hours with those bags in her arms. "Praise the Good Lord," she said. "I didn't think we'd ever see you again."

Edgar was sitting up in bed now, rubbing his eyes. "Mistah Man back," he said, shaking his sister. "Wake up, Jazzy. Mistah Man back."

He crawled across the covers and threw himself into PJ's arms. He smelled like that school bus seat—potato chips and pee and little boy funk.

Jasmine moaned and pushed the baby aside, rising up on her elbows. "You came back," she said in a groggy voice.

"Get your hustle on, girlfriend," PJ said. "We gotta load up. Y'all ever been to Houston?"

Tulane climbed out of the bus to help them transport bags and blankets from the house. Alton slid behind the wheel and adjusted mirrors and the cushion underneath him, flipping on switches and checking gauges. Olive spread a blanket and pillows across the seat directly behind him, making a soft nest for her and Jasmine and Baby Darius. PJ sat across the aisle with Edgar on his lap, and Tulane stretched out on the seat behind them, digging into packages of cookies and chips in one of the grocery bags. He'd been hiding out in St. Louis Cemetery for two days, he'd told PJ, and he hadn't eaten a bite of food.

"We don't have enough gas to make it to Texas," Alton announced, pointing at the gauge.

"We'll worry about that on down the road," PJ said. "First thing, cap'n, scratch some rubber between this damn town and dry land."

Alton shifted the bus into gear and they pulled slowly away from the somber shotgun house, heading toward the river in a low shuddering roar that echoed through the silent neighborhood. When they reached Tchoupitoulas Street and the railroad tracks running alongside the long row of warehouses, the old man made a wide turn and steered the yellow bus toward downtown. Beyond the grainy headlights, the darkness was absolute. PJ stared out the window into shadow and emptiness and couldn't believe they were on their way. Soon they would climb the on-ramp to the Crescent City Connection and rise up high over the dark muddy river, fleeing this doomed city forever. He glanced at the young man slouched in the seat behind him, munching on something that smelled like pretzels. He and this poor scared white boy had escaped the Orleans Parish Prison by the seat of their jumpsuits, and it looked like they were going to dance on out of this wet fucking sump hole without getting killed or caught.

"Listen up, Tulane," he said, lowering his voice so the Lees couldn't hear him. "We get to Houston, you call your people and tell 'em to send you money. Get on a plane for wherever you come from and don't ever come back to Louisiana. Ya heard me? They'll be looking for you, sooner or later. Buy yourself a high-price lawyer, whatever it takes. But don't ever come back down here again. You don't want to know what'll happen if you do."

Tulane leaned closer. He seemed like a good kid, raised up right. His people hadn't heard from him in days and they were probably burning up the phone lines looking for him. "What are you going to do?" he asked PJ.

PJ rocked Edgar on his knee and the little boy giggled, wide awake now. "Don't worry 'bout me, bruh. I know how to flip the trip. You just take care of yourself, ya heard me? Get on back to some home cooking and start yourself a new life. Forget you ever thought about schooling down here."

An uneasy silence settled between them in the dark enclosure. Edgar wriggled in PJ's lap, singing a little nonsense song about living in a pineapple under the sea. The bus bounced across deep potholes that shook the chassis like bomb craters. When Alton missed the on-ramp, rumbling past it and downshifting underneath the towering spans of the bridge, PJ thought maybe the old man had simply made a mistake.

"Say, unk," he said, his voice deep and resonant in the tunnel-like space of the empty bus, "Wadn't that our turn, my man?"

Alton stared through the streaked windshield at the abandoned streets and stark crumbling warehouses ahead. "We're gonna make a stop first," he said.

PJ didn't like the way that sounded. "What kind of stop you talking 'bout?"

"Convention center," the old man said. "Straight up here a couple more blocks."

"You yanking my crank, Alton?"

"This bus holds fifty people, son. Radio says there's thousands stuck in the center. No food and water, no meds for the old folk. We cain't drive to Texas in an empty bus. That just ain't right."

"They're our people, child," said Olive in a quiet voice. She was holding Baby Darius now while Jasmine rested her head against the old woman's soft fleshy shoulder. "They need a lift out of all this misery."

PJ slid Edgar onto the seat beside him and swiveled his legs into the aisle, crouching forward to leer at them. "You outcherfuckinmind, niggah!" he said to the old man. "You stop a bus anywhere near that place, they'll tear the door off to get inside. Baghdad fixing to break out all over us, man. Who's gonna handle all them thugs wanna take this big-ass whip for their own selves?"

"Like I told you—I have faith in you, son," Alton said, his hands firmly on the wheel. "You'll figger something out."

In the bus lights they could see a throng of people ahead, a thousand sleeping bodies wallowing in their own trash for an entire city block. They were piled against one another like corpses in a mass grave.

"*Turn this fucking bus around and get the fuck on out of here!*" PJ yelled at the old driver.

His angry voice scared Edgar and the boy began to cry. Alton downshifted again and toed the brakes, slowing the heavy wheels to avoid the random stragglers wandering across the street in a daze. Three police units were parked on the outskirts of the crowd. When PJ saw the armed cops leaning against their doors, jungled together for their own protection, his bowels turned to water. Wouldn't they have heard about this stolen bus by now? He should've known this whole fucking plan had been too good to be true. Just like D'Wayne's brilliant plan to rob that last liquor store.

Tulane was sitting on the edge of his seat. "Hey, man, what're we gonna do?" he whispered. He had seen the cops, too.

"I'm thinking 'bout pitching this old fool out in the street," PJ said. "You know how to drive a bus?"

Tulane shook his head. "We are seriously hosed," he said.

When they saw the headlights approaching, haggard people rose from their sidewalk camps and crowded out into the street, forcing Alton to stop the vehicle. Hands pounded on the door, the windows, voices crying out to let them in. Edgar stood up on the seat and pressed his face against the glass. "My momma out there?" he asked in a sweet teary voice. PJ saw four cops leave their cruisers and march toward the bus. Did they know what their buddies had been up to at the hotel? Maybe they were all part of the same dirty gang.

The cops were shoving people aside, parting the crowd as they moved toward the center of attention. It was too late to escape. PJ realized there was only one way to play this now. "Shit, man. Okay, open that door," he said to Alton. "Let these people in."

The old man gave him a narrow look, then glanced back at his wife for reassurance. "Go ahead, Alton," she said. "Let's take as many as we can."

"Amen, Sistah Olive," PJ said with a resigned sigh, pulling Edgar into his lap as if to brace for a wreck. "Bring it on."

Alton switched on the interior lights, swiveled the chrome hand crank, and the door folded open. There was commotion outside, loud voices, chaos. The first ones to mount the steps were a waddling, immovable mother as wide as the door itself and her three small children tagging along after her. Behind them the pushing and shoving had begun in earnest. PJ could hear the cops barking orders as they tried to manage the unruly crowd. One of the cops was tapping on the driver's window with a nightstick.

"Open up your window and talk to me, podnuh!" he shouted at Alton. "Who y'all with?"

PJ handed Edgar to Tulane and stepped out into the aisle. "Come on in," he said, taking an old man's bony arm and helping him up the steps. "We got plenty of room, but hustle up. It's a long drive to Texas."

It was the only way he was going to save his hide. Pack the bus with desperate people who were hungry and thirsty and suffering every imaginable horror. People who had lost everything they owned and were sleeping on the street. If the police tried to pry them out of this bus, they would have a riot on their hands.

"What the hell we got going on here?" the cop was demanding at the driver's window. "Where'd you get this bus, podnuh? Show me some ID!"

Alton slid the glass open and said, "We're from the New Kingdom Tabernacle of Our Lord and Savior Jesus Christ. This is our parish bus, officer. The Good Lord has called us to take these folk to Houston."

The cop stepped back and looked at the side of the bus. "It don't say Tabernacle nowhere on this rig. Jesus give you a license to drive this thing?"

PJ stood at the top of the steps, extending his hand, dragging people inside and directing them to find seats in the rear. He watched two policemen position themselves by the door like nightclub bouncers, eyeing the rowdy people fighting to get in.

"*Settle down, y'all!*" one of the cops kept shouting with his hands raised. "*Settle down and form a line! Wait your turn!*"

Many of the boarders were toting bags. One man carried an ancient brown suitcase tied shut with rope. When two crying old ladies made their way to the top of the steps, they hugged PJ and kissed his cheek. "*Thank you, Lord Jesus! Thank you, dear God! Bless you, young brother, bless you!*" PJ smiled his best Sunday service smile at everyone who passed. Now that these people were embedded in the bus, claiming seats, the cops couldn't flush them out with an Alabama fire hose.

"They don't have nothing but the shirt on their back," Alton was saying to the police officer at the window. "But the Good Lord has spared me and my wife and these grandchirren. We been praying on it, my wife and me, and we figger God wants us to drive his people out of all this calamity."

The old dog was good, PJ thought. Denzel couldn't have played the part any better.

"Hey, man, check this out." Tulane was pulling on the back of PJ's jersey. "Take a look out there. You see who I see?"

PJ squatted down to peer out the window.

"Cutting in line, man." Edgar was bouncing happily on Tulane's knee, looking out the window as well. "The dude with the back-pack."

PJ saw him now in the cone of pale light from the bus windows. A thick-set bruiser forearming people aside, claiming ground closer and closer to the door. PJ recognized the Arizona Cardinals jersey and the number 13 on his chest. He recognized the spider web tat-too. U-Rite had traded in the black trash bag for a nice new back-pack that was holding a whole lot of loose cheddar and a 9mm Ruger he'd used to put that crusty scab on PJ's ear. The head buster thought he was going to slide on up into this bus and make his getaway with another man's money. Leave the N. O. just like that and settle down someplace cozy and start living the life again. Niggah chillin', dopin'. Courvoisier and filet mignon. Blow and bitches doing the nasty. Freestyle, like it used to be.

There was only one thing standing in the man's way. Only one thing that could stop him from getting away clean. "Well, now," PJ said. He moved to the landing between the driver's seat and the steps, letting eager boarders stream past him. U-Rite had worked his way to the front of the line and was only four or five people away from board-ing. He didn't notice PJ. But he did notice the two cops stationed by the door and he pulled the cap low over his eyes, fronting as just another distressed citizen catching a bus ride out of town.

PJ gazed down the aisle, where people were cramming them-selves and their meager belongings into every spare inch of space. The bus was full now, overflowing. "Ah-ight, y'all!" he bellowed. "Find a spot and chill! We're fixing to take off!"

A cheer rose up, random claps and hooting. Several *Amens* and *Praise Jesus! Praise his holy name!* PJ leaned over to breathe in Tulane's face. “Be cool and keep your head down. Make sure this boy’s okay,” he said, knuckling Edgar’s soft chin. The boy tried to crawl into PJ’s arms but he said, “Stay by Uncle Tulane a little while longer, Edgar. I’ll catch you back in a minute.”

He stepped over and rested his hand on Alton’s shoulder, then crouched down to address the face in the window. The cop was demanding to see a commercial driver’s license and Alton was searching through his tattered billfold. “Yo, officer,” PJ interrupted him, “I seen a man over here put a gun in his backpack. We don’t want nobody carrying a weapon on this bus.”

The cop stopped chattering at Alton and looked up at PJ. “What’d you say ’bout a gun, podnuh?” he asked him.

“Man over here in line with a spider web inked on his neck,” PJ said, nodding toward the bus door. “Carrying a piece in his backpack. I seen him slip it in there. Looked like a big nine em to me. You don’t believe me, tell your boys to search his pack. We don’t tolerate no weapons on this bus.”

The cop moved to the side and tried to peer over the hood of the bus, then stepped back and said to Alton, “I’m not through with you yet. Don’t go nowhere.”

The crowd surrounding the bus had grown larger and more hostile. Scuffles had broken out. PJ watched the cop march around through the headlight beams and elbow his way into the ruckus with his nightstick drawn.

“Get ready to whip on out of here, Alton,” he said to the driver.

“The man told me to set right here till he gets back.”

“Do what I say, Alton. He might not be coming back. I say roll, you roll, ya heard me? I say roll, you put the pedal to the metal and head for the bridge.”

“What’s going on here, son?”

“Do what I tell you, Alton, and nobody gets hurt.”

“You better tell me what’s going on.”

PJ bent down close so Olive and Jasmine wouldn’t hear. “Thug out there with a gun. Him and me, we got some history between us,” he said in a scratchy whisper. "He comes on board, we're gonna bump each other's shit. Ya feel me?"

Alton's double chin sagged and his mouth dropped open, as if he wasn't getting enough air. A yellow wad of sleep had collected in the corner of one eye, and he looked too old and spent to deal with any of this. "We got chirren on board," he said, trying to peer around PJ's wide body to see who he was talking about.

"Stay frosty, Alton," PJ said, patting the old man's shoulder. "I say roll, you hit the gas."

PJ set his feet at the top of the steps. He saw that U-Rite was next in line after a teenager helping his grandmother negotiate her walker up the narrow entrance. PJ looked for the cop with the nightstick, but the man hadn't made it through the tight crowd yet. He'd counted on Five-O taking the head buster down before he reached the bus door, but it looked like that wasn't going to happen. U-Rite kept inching forward with the backpack strapped across one shoulder, a calm, sturdy boat in a sea of heated voices and banging bodies.

The cops stationed near the door were handling two guys who'd exchanged punches. One cop was shouting, "*Settle down! Be cool or we'll take your ass out!*"

Somebody in the crowd yelled, "They ain't no room for all of us, man! Take my awnty first! She need medical attention!"

Another voice shouted, "When the other buses coming? When they coming, officer? You answer me that!"

U-Rite had arrived at the door—looming large, ready to board, his gold slugs flashing a satisfied smile as he took the first step up into the bus. PJ looked again for the cop with the nightstick, but he was still lost in the crowd. He knew he had to do this himself. When U-Rite took the next step, PJ said, "Hey, motherfucker, you need a ticket to ride my bus."

U-Rite glanced up at him. Something flared behind his eyes, a split second of recognition, and he swung his backpack around to get to the gun. But the sole of PJ's huge running shoe was already shooting toward the man's chest and it kicked him full force in the exact place where PJ had been hit by the beanbag bullet. The blow knocked U-Rite backwards off the steps and he landed on the pavement between the two cops who were struggling to control the crowd.

PJ pointed a stiff finger at him. *"That man got a gun in his pack!"* he yelled at the cops. *"He's trying to jack this bus!"*

The other cop had finally broken through the crowd, brandishing his nightstick. "Let me see what's in your backpack, podnuh," he said to the man sprawled on his back.

U-Rite was staring up at PJ with rage in his eyes. He dragged himself slowly to his feet and slung the backpack across his shoulder. He wasn't going to give up all that money without a fight.

The cop said, "Put the bag down, hoss. Put it down now!"

The crowd went quiet, people backed away, clearing street space.

U-Rite stared at PJ and said, "You a dead man."

Two of the cops had pulled their service revolvers and were crouched in a defensive position, aiming at U-Rite's chest. *"On the ground, motherfucker!"* one of them shouted. U-Rite hesitated, as if he was considering whether to obey that order or flee.

PJ reached over and cranked the lever and the bus door closed with a bang. *"Roll!"* he said, turning toward the driver.

Alton was slow to respond. He seemed paralyzed by the drama unfolding outside the door.

"I said *roll*, goddammit. Take us the fuck out of here!" PJ said, seizing Alton's shoulder. "Don't make me drive this fucking bus myself."

"Okay, son, okay," Alton said, slipping the stick shift into gear and pulling slowly away. When PJ looked again, he saw U-Rite kneeling on the street with his hands on his head. Guns were pointed at him, more cops now. The crowd had cleared back even farther, retreating into darkness again. One of the cops was unzipping the backpack. He was in for quite a surprise. All that money D'Wayne had squirreled away. Three, four thousand dollars. All those jobs until the last one.

PJ clung to the safety pole by the door and watched out the glass as the strobe of long police flashlights grew fainter and finally receded into the black night. He knew how this would go down. The money would end up in some precinct locker and disappear little by little. U-Rite would go upstate in leg irons to wherever they were sending inmates from the flooded Orleans Parish Prison. It was going to be a long time before everyone in this dirty business could wash their hands clean.

Alton had no trouble locating the on-ramp to the bridge. He drove the busload of sixty-odd grateful sobbing cheerful souls upward into the curving concrete architecture overhead, the headlights finding only darkness and wide empty expressway high above the city. They passed a car abandoned in the breakdown lane, its windows blown out, and then another one farther along. PJ was feeling triumphant and free. He and Tulane sat side by side with Edgar standing up on the seat between them, staring back at all the people who were singing gospel songs and praising the Lord. The bus was crossing the river now, its dark lurking presence far below them like some ancient fearsome reptile hiding under your house.

Olive reached across the aisle and touched PJ's arm. "These folk must be hungry," she said. "We ought to share what we brought."

PJ wiped his sweaty face with his jersey and scratched at his week-long stubble. "True that, Sistah Olive," he said. He felt like he'd been through a twelve round bare-knuckle fistfight with Mike Tyson and he didn't want to fight anymore.

"Jasmine, girl, you wanna help me out with this?" he asked.

Passengers were packed shoulder to shoulder into the seats and aisle. He and the girl stumbled one behind the other through the rank squalor, passing out bottled water and shaking chips and nuts and Goldfish into cupped hands like deacons delivering communion. "How y'all doing?" he asked, feeling hands grab him in the darkness, some for food, others in gratitude. "Everybody be cool, ah-ight? We're gonna take this one mile at a time. Won't be long till we find a better place to stay."

Jasmine discovered two girls her age and stopped to share a bag of cookies with them. It was the first time PJ had heard her speak more than a few words and it made him smile. She was going to be all right. The boys, too. They would find a good foster home for them in Houston. He would stick around to make sure that happened before he moved on.

When the bus began its gradual descent toward the West Bank, on the other side of the river, the headlights illuminated a metallic green sign that said WELCOME TO GRETNA and the passengers began to cheer. He was running short of chips and had turned back to get more food when he felt the hydraulic whoosh of the brakes and the bus slowing down. Police lights were whirling at the base of the bridge, casting wild colors against the bus's windshield. PJ crouched down to see what was going on. Tulane had left his seat and was retreating toward him, stepping around people in the aisle.

"Hey, man. Trouble," he said.

They had crossed the Mississippi River and had reached the dark, storm-battered town of Gretna. But there was a police roadblock in their way. Two armed officers with flashlights were signaling for them to stop. PJ didn't like the looks of this. Had those New Orleans cops radioed ahead to cut them off?

"Grab some floor and chill," he said to Tulane, and they both squeezed down between bodies.

PJ counted two cop cars and a pickup truck blocking the outbound lanes to the expressway that would take them southwest toward Houma and Morgan City. A couple of white men in civilian clothes were sitting like duck hunters in lawn chairs in the bed of the pickup with shotguns resting on their shoulders. "Must be the Gretna welcome wagon," he said.

A police officer was tapping on the bus door with his flashlight. Alton swiveled open the door and said, "Is there a problem, officer?"

The officer stepped up into the bus and slowly scanned his light across the somber passengers. He was a tall white man wearing rimless glasses and a thick mustache, and the gold trim on his epaulets glowed in the dark. "Y'all can't come over here," he said to Alton as he aimed his flashlight into the raw red eyes staring back at him. "We've already taken in as many bridge walkers as we can. Our power is dead, like y'alls. We don't have any food or clean water and our medical facilities are all shut down. You're gonna have to turn this rig around and head on back. Our mayor's issued an order—no more people from New Orleans."

A groan went up from the passengers. Alton said, "We're just passing through, officer. We're not stopping. Gonna swing on out the expressway to Highway Ninety, heading for Texas."

The officer lowered the flashlight against his pants leg, making a bright pool around one of his boots. "You're gonna have to find another way out, my friend. Mayor's orders. No more refugees from the other side of the river. No passage through," he said. "Officer Thompson and I will direct you to turn this vehicle around."

The exhausted passengers raised their voices, shouting at him, cursing. An old woman cried, "*We cain't go back to that awful place, officer. Lawd, we cain't go back.*"

The cop trained his light on the angry dark faces and said, "This is why you people can't come over here. We don't want a fucking Superdome on our hands."

When the cop stepped down out of the bus, PJ rose from his knees and climbed over hunched bodies until he reached Alton sitting like a bruised child behind the steering wheel. "Ain't no better way out of town," the old man grumbled. "Huey P. Long Bridge, maybe, if we can even get there. Radio says forget about I-Ten. It's under water. Where else we gonna go?"

The two Gretna cops were standing fifteen yards in front of the bus now, both of them motioning with their flashlights, signaling them to turn around. The vigilantes had crawled out of the truck bed and were stationed with their shotguns a short distance behind the policemen. PJ studied the three vehicles stretched across four traffic lanes in a cascade of flashing lights.

"Ain't enough room to squeeze a bus on through," he said to Alton.

The old man gave him a look of horror. "We try something foolish, they'll shoot our tires out," he said, slowly shaking his head. "Hurt some of these chirren."

"The expressway is right straight ahead, Brother Alton. You get by these Mayberry fuckers, everybody can sing 'Free at last, free at last'."

The old man stared out the windshield at the signaling cops. "We're not gonna get past these men, son. You see those peckerwoods with twelve-gauge shotguns? They want to shoot a New Orleans nigger so bad they can taste blood."

PJ turned around and looked at the poor wretched passengers jumbled one on top of the other in this rickety yellow school bus, the elderly ladies with swollen ankles and the scared children and tough street teens cut loose on their own, strangers to one another, homeless now, with no future to count on and no ride out of this town either before or after the hurricane laid their lives to waste. He couldn't abide the idea they had to return to the hard sidewalks and dark shit-stinking holding pens they'd been herded into for nearly three days. He watched Jasmine stepping over people, returning with an empty cookie bag, and he thought about that nice Christian family in Houston that would take her and the boys in, give them the decent life they deserved after all they'd been through. He couldn't live with himself if it ended up some other way, if she and her little brothers had to turn back now and wound up in a cattle pen somewhere, hungry and wallowing in filth for days until they were finally rescued. It was wrong to make it this far, right up to the edge of freedom, and be denied.

PJ stared out the windshield. The only thing standing between this bus and Texas were two police cruisers and a white pickup truck. Four men with guns.

In the seat behind the driver, Olive was watching PJ with Baby

Darius asleep in her arms and Edgar nestled against her soft belly, humming to himself in a sweltering half-dream. PJ smiled at her. "You get to Houston, Miz Olive," he said, "you make sure these children find a good Christian home."

The old woman was concealing her alarm. "I know what you're thinking, child," she said, and he had no doubt she could read his mind. She was so much like his mother in that way. "Please," she said. "I don't want to see you get hurt."

He remembered what his Momma had always told him. Stand up, son. Stand up no matter what it costs you. It had gotten him in trouble more times than not—standing up when he should have shut up. But sometimes you had to stand up even when it was better to stay in your corner. Sometimes you had to stand up and step out into the ring so you could feel better about who you were when you woke up every morning for the rest of your life.

PJ knelt down beside Alton and locked his arm around the driver's bent shoulders. "You remember what you told me after the grocery store?" he said. "You told me to wait for my move."

"Mm-hmh," Alton mumbled.

PJ could feel a nervous tremor in the old man's body. He'd been studying the two cops out in the road. One of them had lost his patience and stepped closer to the bus, shouting something, waving his flashlight. The two vigilantes spread out from their pickup truck as if to flank the action. PJ smiled at this. Leaving their truck unguarded was the biggest mistake they would make tonight.

"Now listen to me real good, Alton. This is how it's going down," PJ said in a quiet voice that did little to soothe the old man's fear. "I'ma go out there and move that pickup out of the way. When I do, it's your move, Alton. Y'understand what I'm saying? You gotta shoot the gap and keep on going. No matter what happens, you gotta head on out the expressway till you're free of this fucking Mayberry town."

Alton turned his entire body to stare at PJ in disbelief.

"Stay focused, Alton. Last time we did this, you were way slow on the pedal, my man. You gotta be quicker. You see the truck move out of its spot, you stomp that fucking pedal and shoot the gap. Are we clear?"

The old man's mouth had gone dry. He worked his fleshy lips. "They liable to kill you," he finally managed to say.

"Liable to," PJ agreed, watching the two vigilantes roam toward the bus with their shotguns.

"There's four of 'em, son."

PJ smiled a wicked smile. "It don't hardly seem fair," he said. "Only four of 'em."

There was a slight quaver in Alton's voice. "Don't do this, son. We can turn around."

"We're not turning around, Alton. We're through with turning around," PJ said. "Now take a deep breath. In and out real slow. You got a job to do. Maybe it's a calling, like you told me. I don't know. But you cain't let all these people down."

The old man was trembling. PJ held onto him until he felt Alton breathing normal again, his shoulders beginning to relax. "I wish I had a beer," Alton said.

"Drink one for me when you get to Houston."

When PJ stood up, someone gripped his arm. It was Tulane. "They'll take you out," the young man said. He'd listened to every word of the conversation. "If they don't kill you, they'll drag you back to the yard."

He gave Tulane a friendly wagging shake of the neck. "Look after these folk," he said with a grin. "And stay out of trouble, bruh. Don't go pissing on no more walls."

He reached into the pockets of his jogging pants and pulled out three Slim Jims and a handful of cheap jewelry he'd stolen from the dead mother's bureau. He handed the Slim Jims to Tulane and the jewelry to Jasmine.

"Hey, girlfriend, this belonged to your momma. Only thing left out of that house you was raised up in. Keep it to remember her by. She did the best she could in this life."

Holding the jewelry in her cupped hands, Jasmine stared at him with confusion in her deep brown eyes. "What you doing, Mistah Man?" she asked.

He touched her soft cheek. "Take care of your brothers. Do good in school, ya heard me? Get yourself an education, girl. Stay off the street."

He patted Alton's arm and said, "You ready steady, my man? Be quick. And don't look back. Keep driving, no matter what. I'll occupy these Gomer Pyle assholes long as I can."

Olive was saying something to him but he'd shut out all the voices now. He rolled and limbered his shoulders like a boxer, inhaling a sharp yoga breath he'd learned from a con up in Dixon. And then he thundered down the steps and out into the humid darkness in a dead heat, breathing in the dank fishy river air, the wind yanking the Saints cap off his head. He raced past the signaling cops and the vigilantes slow to swing their shotguns and reached the pickup truck before their shouted threats caught up with him. He threw open the truck door, slid behind the wheel, and discovered they'd left the key in the ignition, just as he'd figured. All four men were rushing toward the truck now, their guns pointed at him, but he'd already cranked the engine and hit the gas. In the space of a second or two he rammed into the nearest police car with such impact, engine to engine, that his face would have smashed through the windshield if the airbag hadn't exploded against his chest. A vigilante was pulling on the door handle, ordering him out of the cab, but he threw the truck in reverse and shook the man loose, zooming backwards in a dizzy stream of red and blue cruiser lights, slamming into the other cop car like this was a demolition derby, crushing the driver's door where it said Gretna Police Department. Hunks of fender and grille were clanging to the pavement and two car alarms were screeching at once. He stomped the gas pedal again and sideswiped the first car, sheering off its side mirror, but the shooting had begun and glass shattered all over the back of his head. He collapsed sideways onto the seat with a thousand stinging cuts in his scalp, his neck, his shoulders, slivers as sharp as an ice pick. He lay on the seat bleeding and trying to suck air into his lungs, and when he opened his eyes there was a pistol in his face and a shotgun hovering above him at the other door, their voices growling they were going to kill him. He started laughing at them. Their three rides weren't going anywhere, the mess they were in. When he pulled himself upright, coughing from the airbag fumes and spitting blood, the men backed away from the cab a step or two, still aiming their weapons at him and screaming orders. Chunks of glass were all over him and blood was running into his eyes, but he looked out the blown-up rear window and saw that the yellow school bus was gone. It was gone. Wiping away blood and tears with his jersey sleeve, he could see red taillights disappearing south down the expressway. He couldn't stop laughing. He couldn't stop crying. That old drunk Alton Lee had found his calling and the bus was on its way to Texas.

# 44

The weeping woke her. In the damp gray haze of first light, Dee could see that nice Yankee gentleman, Mr. Friedman, holding his wife near the safety rail, trying to console her. "We're going to get killed down here," she kept crying. "Look at them! We're going to get killed with all the rest."

Dee freed herself from the sheet-tangled limbs of her children sleeping on the mattress and stumbled over to see what the couple was staring at on the loading docks below. Teenagers were lifting a dead woman from a wheelchair and laying her on the stained concrete next to three other bodies covered by blankets.

"They're killing the weak ones first!" Jill Friedman cried.

Her husband caressed her in his sturdy arms, saying in a soft voice, "No, darling, that's not what's happening. Those boys are removing the dead people from the general population."

"How do you know that? How do you fucking know that?"

"I've been awake most of the night, love. I've watched them come and go. They're doing everyone a mitzvah."

Dee touched the woman's shoulder. "We're walking out of here, Mrs. Friedman," she said. "Come on, let's wake up our kids. We're walking over the bridge." She could see its twin spans taking shape in the morning mist as thunder rumbled across the heavy sky. "There's help over there—in Gretna and Algiers."

She roused LaMarcus and Ashley and the people sleeping around them on the walkway, and in a short while their troops were following one another in a silent procession down the stairs to the loading zone and out into the boulevard, where thousands were stranded on the trash-heaped sidewalks in front of the convention center.

"Where are we going, Momma?" Ashley asked, gripping her mother's hand and dragging her feet in an exhausted shuffle.

"Out of all this misery," Dee said, squeezing her daughter to her side. "Can you handle that, babe?"

"Hey, look, Momma, there's that white lady from the hotel," said LaMarcus, pointing. "And that man who was nice to us."

A large crowd of white people, out-of-town tourists by the look of their clothing, was trudging up the boulevard from downtown, the elderly couple among them, weary and weighed down by the same kind of expensive luggage the Friedman family was carrying. There were at least two hundred in their group and they banded close together, like a battalion expecting attack, as they made their way toward the sprawling squalor of the convention center.

Ashley shouted hello and waved at the sweet lady with yellow hair walking with her hobbled husband. "Remember us?" she yelled. "We're supposed to ride on that bus y'all are buying."

The old woman stopped and squinted at Ashley through thick oval glasses, slow recognition collecting into a kind smile. "Come here, young lady, and give us a hug," she said. "It's so good to see you're flourishing!"

Her husband dropped their bags in the dusty street and placed his hands on the small of his back, stretching himself. He looked as if he wouldn't bear up for much longer. "As you can see, sweetheart," he said with a grimace that morphed into a toothy grin, "the bus never arrived. So we've hit the bricks."

They were the Dannemillers from Topeka, Kansas, and everyone gathered around as Mrs. Dannemiller explained that the hotels had finally turned them out this morning and locked their doors because of unsanitary conditions and safety concerns. Hundreds of stranded hotel guests from Canal Street and the French Quarter had wandered over to the police command center at Harrah's Casino, a few blocks from here, but the police had told them they had no food or water to spare and they wouldn't allow anyone to camp in front of the casino.

"We made enough of a fuss," she said, "and a police commander came out and told us there were buses waiting for us on the other side of the river. All we have to do is walk over that bridge up there and they'll put us on buses and take us to Baton Rouge."

"Yes, but I demand once again, why should we believe them?" asked an agitated young man with a foreign accent. He was small and refined and sported a dapper goatee, more bohemian than typical tourist, and he lugged a complicated North Face backpack over his shoulders like a seasoned hiker. "They have lied to us at every turn. Why should we believe there are auto-booses on the other bank?"

Mr. Dannemiller rocked his hips in a circular motion, trying to limber his stiff back muscles. "Take a look at that sea of humanity, Lars," he said, nodding toward the crowds ahead. People camped on the sidewalks were beginning to wake and move about. Babies were crying. "We can hang around with all those sad sacks, hoping the buses will show up before we die of dehydration, or we can walk up to that bridge and take our chances on the other side of the river. Me and the missus here, we'd rather try the bridge."

Other voices spoke up, the agreement to cross the bridge nearly unanimous, two hundred strong. They set off following the boulevard toward the expressway ramp. Dee and their group blended in. When they reached the crowds stirring underneath the storm-bent palm trees in front of the center, someone shouted, "Hey, young lady, you ready for that glass of champagne yet?"

It was Malik with his shaggy Rasta dreads and bearded smile. "Mr. President, where you going with your momma so early this morning?" he asked LaMarcus.

"Over the Crescent City Connection," the boy said. "We'll be walking approximately one hundred and seventy feet above the river."

Malik laughed and studied the group marching with their luggage in tow. "West Bank?" he asked, looking up toward the elevated expressway.

"The police told us there are buses waiting for us over there," volunteered Mrs. Dannemiller.

"Zat so?"

"Come join us, Mr. Malik," Dee said, showing him the closest thing she could summon to a hopeful smile. "When we get where we're going, somebody's got to cook up some breakfast for all these good people."

She searched the crowds for signs of the National Guard. What had happened to Robert Guyton? Why hadn't he returned to them, as he'd promised?

The shabby campsites seemed to spread out forever under the gloomy gray sky. The sidewalk was a wreck of shopping carts and office chairs on wheels and tall cafeteria tray carts. Overturned tables, trash everywhere. Ashley spotted Sistah M's colorful robe. She was sitting like a tribal matriarch on a folding chair, surrounded by her grandsons, with her leg propped up on a cardboard box.

"Give Sistah M some sugar, *ma petit pois,*" she cried, offering her outstretched arms to Ashley running toward her. "Mercy Jesus. Thank you, Yahweh. I see y'all have survived Pharaoh's army one more day."

Dee noticed the camo uniforms now, a small cluster of guardsmen near the front entrance of the building. They appeared to be interrogating someone.

"Can you come with us?" Ashley asked, collapsing into Sistah M's soft enveloping bosom. "We're walking over the bridge to where everything is better."

"My oh my, the Promised Land. I wish I could get there with you, *ma jolie,*" the old woman clucked, waving at Dee and LaMarcus. "My old knee is busted up pretty good and I'll have to sit this one out. But I'll pray for your safe journey, child. Y'all find some milk and honey on the other side, send a truckload back thisaway."

The word had spread quickly that buses were waiting on the West Bank. Many people stranded on the sidewalks gathered their belongings and joined the march. The numbers had doubled in a matter of minutes, and the procession continued in its slow insistent pace like a New Orleans second-line funeral.

"Miss Dee, Miss Dee!"

The girls Dao and Trinh had merged into the crowd, as well, with the weary entourage from Village de l'Est tagging along behind them. Dee and the children hugged the girls and their mother and shook hands with the beaming Charles Tran. As Dee embraced the limping old grandmother, she gazed over the woman's narrow shoulders and noticed a tall National Guardsman writing something on a notepad while he listened to a distressed young woman who was flinging her arms and storming around him in circles. It was Robert Guyton. He looked up and noticed Dee at the same time and stopped writing. They stared at each other across the distance. He seemed relieved to see her. She was surprised by the sudden flutter in her chest and the heat in her cheeks.

It wasn't right to be angry with him for not returning for them. He had hysterical people hollering at him nonstop and a mounting score of the dead and dying all around. It was an impossible job. She offered him a forgiving smile, but small hands were grabbing her wrist, pulling her on, and she realized that the children were trying to get her attention because she'd stopped in the street while everyone walked around her. Dee dropped her eyes and accepted her children's hands and turned toward the lofty columns of the elevated expressway ahead. Thunder rumbled across the sky. She caught her breath and put one foot in front of the other, sadness weighing on her heart as they shambled toward the ramp in the light spattering rain that had begun to fall.

She thought she heard him call her name, but she didn't stop or turn around. The cold rain had hunched her shoulders. "Dee, wait a minute!" This time she knew for certain. And then his hand was touching her arm.

"I'm sorry I didn't make it back," he said, walking in stride with them now. "All hell broke loose in there last night and my unit needed me."

"It's okay, Robert. We did just fine," she said, staring into the distance. "We have a plan now. We're walking over the bridge."

The rain was coming down harder. The guardsman kept pace with the three of them moving along arm in arm. "We don't have confirmation that there are buses on the West Bank," he said. "It might be just another wild rumor floating around. There's a new one every hour."

"My children and I are very grateful to you, Robert. When we get out of this mess, if you'd like me to write a letter of recommendation, or whatever it's called, to your commanding officer . . ."

He took her arm and turned her firmly so she had no choice but to stop and face him. "Dee, I don't need a letter or a pat on the back. I'm a middle school science teacher in Ville Platte with a daughter I get to see only twice a month, and I do this on weekends because it makes me feel like I'm helping people."

She almost smiled. "I'm glad you were here to help us," she said.

He looked back over his shoulder. Four rifle-bearing guardsmen were waiting for him in front of the convention center with serious expressions on their faces. "Listen, I'm sorry, but I've gotta go. I just wanted to say hello again." Rain was dripping off the bill of his camo cap. "You kids mind your mother, okay? Everything's gonna work out. This is not the last time you'll see this face."

Dee watched him march back toward his unit, confident in his long stride, the rain dancing off his cap and shoulders. They were a grimfaced squad, nervous, all business, their eyes darting about warily at the people demanding their attention.

"Momma, I think he really likes us," Ashley said.

"He's a science teacher," LaMarcus said. "I wonder if he knows that thing about pi and the pyramids of Egypt?"

They caught up with the crowd and walked holding hands in the slow soaking rain. Before long, Dee's T-shirt was clinging to her skin and the children felt glued to her hips as if she were a tent that would keep them dry.

"Only shower I've had in days," laughed Malik, throwing back his head to wet his beard and tongue.

They were approaching the on-ramp with jubilation and hope, four hundred people taking matters into their own hands, leaving all this suffering behind. In a short while they began trudging up the steep curving incline to the expressway, many of them struggling to negotiate the slick wet climb, the people on crutches and everyone with a grocery cart or baby stroller and a shirtless man slipping and straining to steer his old neighbor in a wheelchair. Those with free hands pitched in to help the strugglers, and in time they reached the level surface of the overpass high above the old cotton warehouses and a cheer went up like a victory cry at the end of a muddy ball game.

Exposed to the rain and elements a hundred feet above the city, they set off walking along the empty traffic lanes toward the bridge. Ominous gray clouds were drifting overhead, but patches of morning sunlight shone through, burnishing the glass walls of the tall office buildings they could see in the central business district. Dee and her children had worked their way near the front of the crowd when she noticed dark-clad figures getting out of two cars parked on the bridge a short distance away.

"Who is that?" she asked, a question for anyone near her.

A half dozen men in dark uniforms spread out the width of the bridge with what appeared to be shotguns in their hands.

"What they think they gonna do?" asked Malik, splashing along in the rain with his old buddies from the Desire Housing Project.

Before the crowd had reached talking distance, the men raised their shotguns and began firing over their heads. People panicked and fled screaming back toward the ramp. Dee grabbed her children and sat down on the wet pavement, smothering them with her body, protecting them from the stampede. She couldn't believe this was happening.

Ashley's face was buried against her mother's breast. "Why are they shooting at us, Momma?"

"I don't know why, baby! Must be some mistake!"

When she looked up, taking measure of the situation, she discovered that dozens of walkers had defiantly stood their ground. Malik and his buddies, the Friedmans, Charles Tran and his followers, Mrs. Dannemiller and her feeble husband, the foreign tourist with a mountaineer backpack. In spite of the gunfire, they weren't retreating.

Malik stepped forward and faced the line of cops with his hands on his hips. They were no more than forty yards away. "Can you believe this nonsense?" he said. "Trying to keep us off the bridge." Then he shouted at them, "*Hey, what the hell y'all doing, man, shooting at women and chirren? This ain't your bridge!*"

"They can't do this to us," said Jill Friedman, wedged between her husband and son. "We're American citizens, goddammit."

"*Sorry-ass Rambo motherkillers!*" Malik was shouting at them with his arms stretched wide. "*You gonna shoot me, dawg, shoot me!*"

He began advancing toward the armed policemen but his buddies seized him and wrestled him back into the small huddle of people. "Lemme go," he said, fighting to free his arms. "I'm gonna plant a size twelve huarache up they ass."

"*No,*" Dee said emphatically. She had had enough of being bullied around. She crawled to her feet and asked Dao and Trinh to look after LaMarcus and Ashley. "Let me go talk to them," she said. "You stay here, Malik. They won't appreciate your dreadlocks."

Malik took a deep breath, blew it out. Tried to calm down.

"Momma, don't leave us here!" Ashley cried, latching onto her mother's leg.

"Be strong, now, Ash," Dee said, bending down to kiss her daughter's wet beaded braids. "I'll be back in a minute, okay? LaMarcus, watch your sister."

The cops were standing silently in the rain without slickers, the shoulder grips of their shotguns resting against their hips. They did not look happy to be out of their patrol cars in this kind of weather. Dee had no idea what she was going to say to them, or how she would persuade them to step aside and let all these folk pass over the bridge. She heard footsteps slopping through the rain puddles and glanced over her shoulder. A handful of people was following close, Mrs. Dannemiller with dripping yellow hair and the foreign guy with the backpack and Charles Tran and a ponytailed male nurse from San Francisco in town for a medical convention. David Friedman tromped along as well, waving a white handkerchief over his head to signal they were approaching in peace.

"I'm a labor lawyer," he said in his strong Yankee accent. "I've negotiated with goons before."

Dee was afraid of what might happen if the cops felt threatened or insulted. She raised her chin at Friedman and the others and said, "Okay, be cool. Let me do the talking." Her father had always told her she had the silver-tongued gift of gab. *Gab, don't fail me now,* she thought as she approached the stoic policemen staring at them through sunglasses in spite of the gray overcast sky.

"*We're under strict orders not to let anybody cross over the bridge!*" shouted a stocky white cop with a two-day beard. Raindrops were plopping off the stubble on his melon-shaped head. "*Y'all need to turn yourselves around and head on back where you came from!*"

Dee stopped a short distance from the barricade of armed men. The others remained a few steps behind her. "NOPD told this lady here that buses are waiting for us over on the West Bank," she said, gesturing toward the older woman. "We just want to walk over there and get on a bus and leave this place, officer. We've got children and old people to take care of."

"There ain't no buses on the West Bank, lady." Their sleeve patches said *Gretna Police Department.* "We've taken in all the people we can take. Our chief and the mayor say nobody else is coming over the bridge into our community. End of story."

"The police commander promised us," said Mrs. Dannemiller.

"Trying to get y'all out of his butt crack," volunteered another cop. His buddies chuckled at the remark.

"Go on back and tell them other people standing around over there to get off the expressway. It's not a safe place to be," said the first cop. "Television trucks are running up and down all through here, eighty miles an hour."

Dee turned and looked back to where her children were standing with the Vietnamese girls. No sign of traffic coming from that direction. She looked past the two police cars parked on the bridge and saw no one coming from the West Bank, either. She noticed that a gray-haired cop was resting an arm on the open door of one of the parked cruisers, talking into a CB radio and gazing up at the dense sky.

"Go on back," said the stocky cop, shifting his shotgun to the other hip. "The West Bank ain't gonna become another New Orleans. Looting and burning and all that shit."

Dee knew exactly what he was saying. "What you mean is you don't want poor black folk crossing over into your nice little white town," she said, unable to control her tongue.

"Call it whatever you want. I don't give a good shit," said the cop. "Now turn your asses around and head on back down to street level so we can all get the fuck out of this rain."

Everyone started talking at once. David Friedman citing law and Mrs. Dannemiller challenging the claim about the buses and the foreign guy mixing up his English and Charles Tran saying something unclear about the final evacuation of Saigon. One of the cops fired his shotgun in the air. The loud boom shook Dee, so deafening and close, the report echoing across the warehouse rooftops just below the overpass.

"*Get the fuck on out of here and take those people with you!*" yelled the stocky cop. "*You people stay on your side of the river and we'll stay on ours!*"

Their truce party straggled back to the larger group and they all huddled in the rain, exchanging a flurry of strategies. David Friedman wanted them to camp right there on the expressway lanes, where they had a better chance of capturing the attention of the media. "They won't talk so tough if CNN shows up," he said. "And they damn sure won't be firing those shotguns." Malik was convinced they could wait out the cops until nighttime and cross the bridge in the dark. "They gonna get hungry and tired, sooner or later," he said, "and head on back to they pork 'n' beans."

But Dee was discouraged. The rain was pouring down on them and the shotguns frightened her and she felt a sharp unspoken fear that there were no buses on the West Bank or anywhere else within a hundred miles of this city. She watched others begin to trail off and disappear down the ramp. She understood why they were giving up. Her children were wet and hungry. Ashley's nose was running, and LaMarcus was holding himself and shivering. Dee was afraid they would all come down with something terrible if they didn't find cover soon.

"I'm sorry, y'all," she said to Malik and the Friedmans and the Vietnamese families circled around her. "I can't keep these children up here like this."

The foreign guy with the backpack barked something sudden and forceful, and at first Dee thought he was protesting her defection. And then she heard the rackety motor noise and everyone looked up toward the heavy gray clouds. The foreign guy blurted another string of words in his own language and they all saw what had captured his attention. A helicopter was angling low over the bridge, flying toward them from the West Bank. David Friedman thought it was a news chopper and started waving his arms and wailing, *"Here we are! Here we are!"*

But Charles Tran said no, shaking his head, no. He was pointing down the expressway at the gray-haired cop talking on the CB radio. The man stepped away from his cruiser and signaled to the chopper. *"He's calling them in!"* Tran yelled. *"He's calling them down on us!"*

Dee didn't understand what he meant until Malik shouted, "Police bird! Po-*leese* bird!"

And suddenly the helicopter was upon them, hovering twenty feet overhead, bringing neither rescue nor news coverage but furious rain and wind blasting the huddled group like a typhoon tearing through an island village. Malik was shaking his fist at the chopper and cursing, his clothes blowing wildly all about him.

*"They trying to chase us off!"* he kept howling. *"They trying to chase us off!"*

The wet whirling downdraft knocked LaMarcus and Ashley to the pavement and Dee clutched their backpacks, pulled them to their feet, and led them stumbling toward the ramp in the blinding storm. Women were screaming, voices cursing the helicopter. She fought to stay on her feet, dragging her children along, hoping to find the guardrail or something sturdy to hold onto. It was impossible to see anything, the water stinging her eyes, lashing her skin. The children were crying that she was hurting their wrists but she wouldn't let go and she wouldn't stop moving. And then suddenly she slammed into a wall of bodies, an old man calling for his wife, Dao and Trinh crying for each other, and she found herself pushing against them, at the mercy of her own blind instincts, pumping her legs and shouldering into soft flesh until the bodies gave way, collapsing underfoot. Dee lost her balance and hit the pavement, scraping her scabbed knees, losing her grip on the children. *"Ashley!"* she cried. *"LaMarcus, where are you?"* But everyone was calling names now, searching for their loved ones. They were crawling on hands and knees, battered by the downdraft, trying to retreat back down that long curving ramp.

*"I've got your boy!"* It was the Friedman's son, the college kid.

*"Where? Where?"*

*"Keep moving, people! Don't stop! Where's the ramp?"*

*"LaMarcus, where are you? Ashley!"*

*"I've got her!"* Trinh or Dao. Words in Vietnamese. *"I've got her!"*

Dee struggled to her feet, the downdraft still blinding her, the chopper noise unbearable. She was being shoved down the ramp by the people behind her. *"Who has my children?"* she screamed. It was like that nightmare she'd dreamed over and over when they were babies. She was wandering through a dark house with many rooms and she could hear them crying but she couldn't find their cribs.

*"Does anybody have my children?"*

She felt a breathless moment of panic when she imagined them knocked over the guardrail, falling fifty feet to the hard street below. She rubbed water out of her eyes and saw LaMarcus halfway down the ramp, free of the violent turmoil, standing alongside the drenched Friedman boy, both of them panting and waving at her. And she heard Ashley calling "*Momma!*" and turned to find her weaving down the ramp through the wet stumbling bodies, Dao and Trinh following close behind.

A few minutes later the helicopter had vanished and they were all hugging one another in sopping wet clothes at the bottom of the ramp. Dee glanced back to see Malik and his buddies carrying a body down out of the blowing mist. It was that nice old white man, Mr. Dannemiller. His wife was at his side, holding his head up, talking to him in a quiet voice or perhaps praying. Dee could see his eyes rolling back in his head and his mouth gaped open, his body hanging limp in the men's grip.

"Is he dead, Momma?" Ashley whispered.

"God, I hope not, honey. Let's say a prayer for him, okay?"

He wasn't dead, only unconscious. He had fallen and hit his head on the pavement and had been trampled in the escape. There would certainly be broken bones, Dee thought, maybe a skull fracture.

"We gotta get him on back to the center and see what kind of medics they got provided there," said Malik.

The solemn procession back to the convention center was like a death march in a drizzling tropical rain. When they rounded a street corner by an old soot-black warehouse, the bent palm trees and sprawling, restless crowds came into view again, and Dee didn't know if she could survive another day of this. What were she and the children going to do now? Sit on a curb in the raw weather for God knows how long without food or water? Without a pallet to sleep on. Without the faintest glimmer of hope.

"*Daddy!*" LaMarcus yelled.

He slipped out of his wet backpack and broke loose from Dee's side, sprinting toward a lone figure standing in the middle of the boulevard, staring at the convention center in the rain. At the sound of LaMarcus's voice the man turned, and Dee could see his face buried inside the dark blue hood. It was Duval. He leaned forward and caught LaMarcus in a full run, the boy almost knocking him down. They hugged and Duval lifted his son as high as he could and they laughed and spun around in each other's arms and nearly toppled over into the wet litter heaped at their feet.

Dee and Ashley approached the man with less enthusiasm. Dee was happy to see her son laughing and wrestling his Daddy, and yet all at once it came over her, the many years of disappointment and second chances and broken promises. She wanted to hug Duval, and she wanted to slap his face. She couldn't reconcile her sense of relief with the anger and resentment of all the days and nights she'd raised these children alone.

Duval looked at her with his arm around their son's neck, turning on that devastating smile she'd once fallen in love with. But one of his eyes was swollen shut and his lip was split and his handsome features were notched and puffy. He was trying to game that smile on her, but parts of his face were too damaged to work.

"Hello, angel," he said to Ashley, extending a hand to her with LaMarcus wrapped around his chest. Ashley was slowing her steps, reluctant to get any closer, and Dee realized that the girl wasn't certain it was her father.

"It's him," Dee said. "It's your Daddy. You can go hug him."

But Ashley remained at her mother's side.

They drew closer now, close enough to smell him. Dee noticed the dried stains on his hoodie and the burn holes in his sleeves. He'd been through an ordeal of his own. "What happened?" she asked him in a quiet voice.

"It's cutthroat out there, baby," he said, looking north toward the Superdome and beyond. “I cain’t believe I found y’all. I really cain’t.”

“Actually, Daddy,” Ashley said without humor, “we found you.”

He smiled sheepishly and rubbed a hand across his wet bruised face. Something was wrong. Dee could read it in his eyes.

“Duval, where’s my father?” she asked him. “Where’s the boat y’all were bringing to take us home?”

# 45

Heavy oak limbs, two hundred years old, were lying across the streetcar tracks on St. Charles Avenue. The rain had stopped and they forged deeper into a jungle of wet green branches entangling the sidewalks and the avenue itself. LaMarcus and Ashley had stripped away leaves to make long stick weapons and were playing a game, hacking at the fallen debris in their path like explorers cutting through a dense rain forest with machetes. Dee was following behind them at safe swinging distance, still trying to piece together Duval's story. A young white woman trapped in her car. Pops's chest pains. The burning johnboat. An IV in a hospital corridor. Her father had told Duval to bring them to where the young woman's family lived on the corner of St. Charles and Arabella Street.

"Your Pops is probably there already," Duval had said, "waiting for us to show."

It tore at her to think she'd done this to her Daddy. She'd been too stubborn and careless to evacuate when there was plenty of time, and she'd dragged the poor man out of his peaceful home and put him through all this hell. He wouldn't blame her for any of it, of course, because he was her dear sweet Pops and a tough old Marine who'd give his life for her and his grandchildren. But she would never forgive herself for the trouble she'd caused.

"Hey, Daddy, are those army soldiers?" LaMarcus asked his father.

They were passing one of the tall graceful mansions on the avenue and a pair of armed guards was standing by a padlocked wrought iron gate. Duval recognized the dark uniforms and the

VIProtex patch on their shoulders. Private security, the same posse as that commando dude in the hospital, no doubt hired by the owner of this place to protect his property.

"You're walking in the wrong 'hood, people," said one of the guards, eyeing them with an AK-47 strapped to his shoulder. "Don't even think about squatting somewhere on this street."

Duval had to bite his tongue. He wanted to tell these Chuck Norris assholes to suck his long skinny black dick, but the children were with them.

"Go to hell, you racist peckerwood!" Dee said, and LaMarcus repeated, "Yeah, you peckerwood!"

Dee put her hand over his mouth and said in a low voice, "Mom gets to talk trash, child. You don't."

Duval thought maybe he should have said something to these assholes, man to man, for showing disrespect.

For block after block they worked their way through downed branches, the children slashing at them with their sticks. Ashley collected Mardi Gras beads that had been thrown into the trees in years past and were now strung like precious gems within arm's reach. They saw a group of solemn white people wandering around in a daze on the other side of the neutral ground and LaMarcus waved at them, but they didn't wave back.

Farther up the avenue they crossed paths with another pair of VIProtex security guards posted at a mansion gate. "*Hasta la vista,* Ah-nuld," Duval said to the guards, and Dee pulled him along by his hoodie sleeve. She didn't want him to get that other eye closed by a rifle butt.

Arabella Street was farther than Dee imagined, up near the universities and Audubon Park, and the children were complaining about the long walk and showing signs of fatigue when they smelled meat being grilled somewhere nearby. Dee noticed a white man smoking a cigarette on the cleared sidewalk in front of a mansion that occupied an entire corner of the avenue. He was a heavyset man wearing stylish oxblood penny loafers and a seersucker sport coat in spite of the stifling humidity underneath this gallery of dripping oak trees. His shoulders were slightly rounded and his hair was thick and gray, curling onto his collar, and he had the soft-skinned, jowled appearance of a New Orleans aristocrat with vaults of old money. He was enjoying a leisure smoke as he stared up at the broken limbs high above the streetcar tracks. Dee wondered when the security guards were going to step out from behind those tall hedges with their automatic weapons and tell them to move on.

"Our cat ran away," the man said with a friendly smile. He crushed the cigarette on the sole of his shoe and slipped the butt into his coat pocket. "The storm made him crazy, poor devil. My wife says she saw him way up in one of these trees."

"Hello," Dee said. "Is this the corner of Arabella Street?"

He nodded. "The street sign blew down. That and a piece of my roof and all the windows in the *garçonnière*," he said. He smiled at the children. "You kids hungry?"

Both of them spoke at once. "Yeeeahhh, we're starrr-ving."

He laughed. "Y'all come on in and get something to eat. We've got plenty. I put in a backup generator a few years ago and the darn thing actually works," he said. "Corinne's burning chicken and hamburgers on the grill. Come say hello. We've got about thirty folks staying with us right now, but there's always room for more."

Duval wasn't sure he wanted his kids to have any part of this. What if it turned out to be like that party last night in the Quarter? Bunch of sick twisted white folk sitting around a pool getting their freak on.

"Let me ax you a question," he said to the man. "Is there an older gentleman come by here maybe last night, this morning, looking for his family? Black man name of Hodge Grant wearing camo pants and a green T-shirt?"

The man squinted at him, thinking. "Doesn't ring a bell," he said. "But come on in and have a look around. He might be here. My name is Paul Blanchard, by the way," he said, extending his hand.

“Paul Blanchard?” Dee said. She recognized him now from photos in the newspaper. He owned one of the old family-run New Orleans coffee companies. “Are you the man they call Mr. Coffee?”

“I’m afraid I am,” he said with a courtly bow of the head. “If you like coffee, we’ve got a whole boatload.”

They heard the young woman calling before they saw her. “Daddy!” she said, her voice trilling somewhere behind the tall hedges. “Have you snuck off to smoke again? Mom needs you to come take a look at the toilets. They’re all backing up and the tap water is running brown.”

“Yo, that’s her!” Duval said, pointing at the pretty young woman approaching down a red brick path bordered with flowers that had been flattened by the storm. “The girl we pulled out of the car!” The last time he’d seen her, she was flopping like a fish on the deck of that Dorado motorboat and spitting up floodwater.

“Good Lord, I know who you are,” the man said, squeezing Duval’s arm. “You’re the ones who saved my daughter’s life.”

“Hey, *hi!*” The young woman greeted Duval with a sparkling smile. “You were the guy driving the boat. And this must be your family. I’m so pleased to meet you,” she said, coming toward Dee with her bandaged hands outstretched for an embrace. “Where is that wonderful Mr. Grant?”

It was midmorning when Alton Lee reached the outskirts of Lake Charles with sixty hungry and exhausted people on board the bus, most of them in some uneasy state of sleep. He’d driven down through the harrowing storm-battered darkness of old Highway 90, passing through the evacuated streets of Houma and Morgan City, ghost towns protected by prowling sheriff’s cruisers following the bus to make sure it passed out of their jurisdictions without stopping. The journey had been treacherous and slowed by fallen trees and downed power lines and sharp-edged sheet metal blown across the road. Even Lafayette looked dead. The man on the radio had said there was no point in stopping until Houston, because every shelter in southwest Louisiana was closed to more evacuees. But the needle had slipped below the *E* on the fuel gauge somewhere around Jennings, and Alton realized they would be lucky to roll into the next gas stop on fumes and a prayer.

It was one of those large sprawling gas stations on I-10 that catered mostly to cross-country diesel trucks. A lone eighteen-wheeler was pulling out as Alton steered the rattling yellow school bus up to the long row of pumps standing road-dusty and silent in the damp morning light. The trip had required every ounce of his concentration and he was bone tired and in need of a full night's sleep. Olive had done her best to keep him awake, talking to him over his shoulder from time to time while Jasmine dozed beside her and Baby Darius slept in her arms. Alton had closed his eyes more than once and the bus had drifted across the stripe, but no harm done. They had made it this far without rolling into a ditch.

He cut the engine and stood up from the driver's seat, working his neck, stretching his back and legs. "We need gas," he announced in a weak voice to the handful of passengers awake enough to hear him.

Across the aisle from his wife, the child named Edgar and the white college boy were bundled together in sleep. The young man opened his eyes and stared at Alton as if he didn't know where he was. "Are we there?" he asked, smacking his dry lips.

They hadn't exchanged a word about what had happened on the Crescent City Connection. Alton had stomped the gas like PJ had told him to do and they lurched ahead onto the dark deserted expressway. Tulane had heard the gunfire and crunching metal behind them and he'd stuck his head out an open window to watch the wreckage. He didn't want to think about what they'd done to that poor son of a bitch.

"Help me take up a collection, son," Alton said. "We need to buy some gas."

Tulane left Edgar asleep on the seat while he and Alton made their way slowly down the aisle, rousing people, asking for spare change. They raised nine dollars and seventy-three cents. Maybe enough to get them to Beaumont in this guzzling old beast, but not all the way to Houston.

"What're we going to do?" the young man asked Alton as they stepped down out of the bus. The morning air smelled like pine tar mixed with diesel fumes. It was good to be out of that funk-smelling swelter of bodies.

The store clerk was standing behind his counter, staring at them through a long tinted plate-glass window. "I'll talk to him," Alton said. "You stay here with the bus. Don't let nobody get off. We don't want to scare this pump jockey with all these nappy-headed New Orleans folk."

The clerk was a young Middle Eastern man with a well-groomed dark mustache and parted hair, and he wore a clean collared shirt with pockets on both sides. When Alton limped up to the counter, the clerk was watching news coverage of New Orleans on a small TV near the cash register. Alton watched it with him for a few moments in silence. He glanced over at the glass coolers and wondered if he could pinch off a little of that money in his pocket to buy a beer for the road. He would have to hide it. Olive would pitch a fit if she caught him drinking and driving.

"It's bad, you know," he said, watching footage of the flooding. "That's where we're coming from." He poured a handful of jingling change and wrinkled dollar bills onto the counter top. "This is all we've got, my man. But we need to make it to Houston."

He explained the situation. Sixty of them piled into the bus, mostly old people and children heading for the Astrodome. Would he be so kind—could he find it in his heart—to take their nine dollars and seventy-three cents and let them fill up at the pump?

"I'm very sorry, sir," the clerk said in his foreign accent. "I'm not authorized to do that sort of thing."

"Who can authorize this to happen?"

The clerk shrugged. "The owner, sir, is who I imagine. But he never comes to the station. I have met him only twice."

"Do you have his phone number?"

The clerk was reluctant to answer. He shifted his feet and stared at the floor. Glanced at the news coverage. Straightened packs of gum and Bic lighters arranged in a tidy countertop display.

"Listen, my friend," Alton said, laying his hands on top of the clerk's busy hands to get his attention, trapping them on the counter. "I've got sixty people on this bus, all of 'em tired and hungry and ready to go off. A couple of old ladies look like they need a doctor. I cain't predict what they'll do if we don't get back on the road to Houston real soon. If you don't give us some gas, we'll be stuck sitting around your store all day. We'll be sitting here when your shift is done and when you come back tomorrow morning. And we'll be sitting here when all the television stations show up to take pictures of a broke-down bus full of Katrina people begging for a little charity. Now don't you think you oughta call your boss and let me explain what we need?"

"Shall I phone the police, sir?" the clerk asked, withdrawing his hands. He was a well-educated gentleman with good manners, maybe a teacher or something like that back in his home country. His question might have been a threat. It might have been a genuine attempt to help.

"Why don't you call your boss and let me talk to him?"

The clerk hesitated, rearranging tiny bottles of cologne and a stack of Styrofoam cups. Then he looked up and noticed what Alton had just noticed. People were filing out of the bus, ignoring Tulane's attempts to reason with them. They were roaming around near the pumps, several of them ambling toward the store.

The clerk quickly searched for a phone number on a laminated page attached to the counter by a string. He made the phone call and apologized to his boss for bothering him at home. After a long nervous explanation into the receiver, his back to Alton, he turned around and handed him the phone. "Mr. LeBlanc would like to speak with you," he said.

Mr. LeBlanc sounded like a concerned citizen. A decent man. "Go ahead and fill up," he said. "I've been watching the TV for three days and I'm real sorry for what y'all are going through down there. We've had our share of hurricanes here in Lake Charles, too, you know. It could be us next time. Good luck and God bless you, sir."

Alton thanked the man and blessed him back and gave the phone to the clerk. The young man had a short exchange with his boss before hanging up. "Yes, sir," he said, and "yes, sir, very good. I'm sorry for the bother, sir." And then he laughed hard at something said on the other end of the line.

The clerk flipped a switch behind the counter and said, "Please, you may fill up, sir." He was still laughing at what his boss had said to him.

"Throw in a pack of Camels," Alton said with a wicked grin, nodding at the cigarette display. "And let me in on the joke."

The clerk hesitated, then tossed a pack of Camels onto the counter and pushed the loose coins and wrinkled bills back to Alton. Nine dollars and seventy-three cents. "He said not to take your money, sir."

"Awright, fine. What's so funny about that?"

"It's what he said after that, sir." He glanced out the window at the dozens of ragged people milling about. "Don't take it personal, please."

"Awright. I'm listening," Alton said, unraveling the pack of cigarettes. "What did the boss man say?"

"He said, 'Thank God for Houston.'"

Dee, Duval, and the children spent the rest of the day with the growing crowd stranded at the Blanchard home on St. Charles Avenue. Claire Blanchard, an attractive middle-aged woman with short salt-and-pepper hair and troubled eyes, opened her home to them. She took Dee upstairs to her dressing closet and found dry clothes for her, Bermuda shorts and a Mardi Gras T-shirt and panties and a bra that was a size too large but would work for now. It was the nicest thing anyone had ever done for her, and she teared up when she slipped on a pair of dry socks. She had despaired of ever wearing dry socks again.

They ate their fill of chicken and hamburgers grilled by a shrunken little cook named Corinne who smoked an extra long cigarette while turning meat in a cloud of charcoal smoke. Guests wandered freely about the grand old house, a motley collection of uptown wealthy white friends who hadn't evacuated and the Blanchards' domestic employees and their families and other black people who'd wandered down from the flooded neighborhoods above Freret Street, searching for help.

At one point, Claire Blanchard approached Duval with a stooped old nanny who must have been eighty years old. "Young man, let Rosetta take a look at your eye and lip," the white lady said. "They could use some attention."

Rosetta sat him on a toilet seat in a downstairs bathroom that opened into a large library full of books. He'd never seen a room like this in somebody's house. "You need stitches in this lip, child," she said as she held his chin in her trembling hand and swabbed hydrogen peroxide into the cut. "Butterfly bandage the best I can do for now. What kind of trouble you walk into?"

"Disagreement over a boat," he said, wincing from the sting.

"I'll find you an ice pack for that eye. You stay out of the disagreement business, you hear me?"

He smiled at her. "Yes, ma'am." He could hear his aunts telling him the same thing. He hoped those good women and his momma were someplace safe. Someplace far from this lip-splitting town.

Outside on the front lawn, eating pasta salad from a paper plate, Mr. Blanchard confided in Dee that his wife's mother was living out her final days in the terminal care unit of a hospital downtown, suffering from pancreatic cancer. "We were on the phone with her doctors all weekend and they assured us she was in good hands and that the hospital was equipped to handle a hurricane of any magnitude. We were foolish not to take her out of there," he said. "Now I wish to hell we'd done something. It's tearing poor Claire apart. I couldn't get through to the hospital's home office in Baton Rouge, either. I may have to hire someone to go down there and rescue her."

Duval was sitting on the grass nearby, pressing an ice pack against his swollen eye. The sky had cleared of rain, and sunshine blazed down on them. "Mistah Blanchard," he said, "I been at that hospital you're talking about. Things are messed up down there. The backup generators are flooded and . . ." He couldn't bring himself to tell the man what he'd witnessed firsthand. The body bags stacked in the stairwell, the awful smell. "Last I heard, they were flying helicopters in to carry people off."

"You were there?" Paul Blanchard said, his expression turning somber.

"That's the hospital where Pops is?" Dee asked.

"Is or was," Duval said. She hadn't said it out loud, but he knew she was blaming him for leaving her daddy by himself in that damned place. Why hadn't Hodge shown up by now? Duval had kept his end of the deal. Where was the old man?

He watched LaMarcus and Ashley and a handful of other children kick a soccer ball around a carpet lawn so smooth it reminded him of the golf greens he'd been chased away from in City Park when he was a boy. He laid down on the grass and closed his one good eye, and when he woke up, long shadows had stretched across the grounds in the waning afternoon light. He got up to flex his sore legs and search for more food and noticed Mr. Blanchard talking to a familiar-looking dude over by a washtub full of iced drinks. It took him a few moments to get a fix on that stringy-haired white boy. He was the one who'd been driving the Dorado ski boat when they rescued the Blanchard girl.

Duval stuck his hands in his pockets and jiggled the mess of keys Hodge had entrusted to him. They were still there, heavy as brass balls, reminding him what he'd promised. He walked over to the two men. "Yo," he nodded to the boat pilot. "S'up, man?" The guy was still wearing his soiled CVS uniform shirt. "You were the dude in the other boat."

"Good to see you, brother," the guy said with a big-hearted grin, giving Duval a fist bump. "I'm glad you found your family. Where's the older gent?"

"That's what I want to talk to you about. You still got that sweet-running motorboat?"

The young man grinned at Paul Blanchard. "We were just discussing that," he said. "It's stashed away so nobody will find it."

Duval said, "I don't have money to pay you, bruh, but I need you to do me a solid." He glanced over at Dee. She was sitting on the ground, clutching her knees, her thoughts far away. She was worried about her daddy and so was he. "I need you to take me down to the hospital where I left Hodge. There's a whole lot of water between here and there, and I ain't wading if I can help it. I could use a ride, my man."

Paul Blanchard was drinking something cold and clear in an ice-filled tumbler. He glanced past Duval to his wife, who was crossing the lawn to sit down next to Dee. "You must be reading my mind, young man," he said with a tired smile. "I was thinking it's time to get off my keister and do something about Claire's mother before it gets dark. Rusty here has graciously offered to take me down to the hospital in his boat."

Duval smiled at him, then at the dude named Rusty. "If it's no hassle, I'd like to hop a ride, Mistah Blanchard," he said. "It's something I got to do."

Paul Blanchard took his wife aside to speak quietly with an arm around her shoulders. That left Duval peering down at the mother of his children. He thought back to the early days before the babies, before he started getting some *strange*, before her unforgiving anger. He wished she'd stop hating on him and they could work this out, bring back something akin to friendship. But he knew he'd broken a good thing and there was no way to piece it together again.

"Me and Mistah Blanchard, we're going to the hospital in that dude's motorboat," he told her. "If Hodge is still there, I'll bring him back. Word."

She stood up and brushed the grass off her bottom. She didn't say anything at first, just stood watching LaMarcus kick the soccer ball over everyone's head into the tall hedge next to the wrought iron fence. "Let me go instead," she said.

He shook his head. "Stay with the kids," he said. "It's bad down there, Dee. I been there. I know where I'm going."

"What if he's not there?"

"Then he's on his way up here." Even with the butterfly bandage, it hurt him to smile through his split lip. "Just like your old man to show up while I'm out there up to my chin in gator piss."

She smiled weakly, then grew quiet again, lost in thought. "Be careful out there, Duval. I don't want anything to happen to you. LaMarcus thinks the world of you and needs a father. Ashley doesn't know it yet, but she needs a father, too."

Duval watched his son hustle after the soccer ball. He watched Ashley try to steal it from him. They were both strong and quick and smarter than he'd ever been. He was proud of them. Dee had raised two wonderful children all by herself.

"I'm gonna find their Pawpaw," he said, watching them laugh and fight over the ball. "For one time in their life, Dee, I'm gonna make this straight."

# 46

Floodwater had gushed through broken levees for three days, drowning neighborhoods and flowing down into the heart of the city. But the flood had stopped unexpectedly a few blocks above St. Charles Avenue, where it settled in shallow pools on streets and lawns. When the three men crossed Freret Street and encountered standing water, Paul Blanchard insisted on rolling up his trouser legs. The water was knee deep in the backyard where Rusty had hidden the Dorado ski boat under a pile of fallen branches and long jagged scraps of indoor-outdoor carpet. Like pallbearers escorting a coffin, they guided the boat northward until the floodwater reached their crotches, and then they used the small ladder to climb aboard.

Rusty steered them along wide Claiborne Avenue, which was navigable despite the bloated animal carcasses and trails of debris. Somewhere near Martin Luther King Boulevard they passed a sinking trash heap that Duval recognized as that old boatman's roped-together raft. But the plywood and aluminum siding had come untied and drifted loose from the beer kegs, and the tiki torch had disappeared along with the strange old man himself.

Duval didn't like the feel of this. He didn't like the signs. Daylight was fading and an eerie stillness had taken hold of everything, as if they were traveling down some sluggish brown bayou deep in the wetlands. There were no voices, no traffic sounds, not even the chattering of birds. Only their motor rumbling toward the elevated interstate and the silent downtown buildings as dull as gravestones in the dying light.

Just before they motored into the dark shadows beneath a cloverleaf of intersecting freeway ramps, Duval looked up and noticed dozens of hazy figures in white T-shirts staring down at them like Halloween ghosts. He waved, acknowledging their predicament. He knew they'd been stranded on that overpass for three days and had lost all hope. They leaned against the guard rail and watched the boat disappear into the columns and showed no inclination to address them or wave back.

When they finally arrived at the hospital's emergency entrance, Duval was struck by how high the water had risen since he'd last been here. The ambulance ramp was completely underwater now and he could no longer see the abandoned cars in the parking lot. "Go in through there," he said to the pilot, pointing toward the sliding doors that were jammed open to the outside world.

"That looks like the ER waiting room," said Rusty, his long thin strands of hair blowing in the air stream. "I can't take this thing into the frickin waiting room."

"Why not?" said Mr. Blanchard. "Pull right on through those doors, son. This might be the only time we're ever admitted to a hospital without filing paperwork."

Rusty slowed the engine, turned on the deck lights, and guided the Dorado quietly through the ER entranceway, forcing them to duck their heads. The boat's momentum carried them into a dark waiting area whose bucket chairs created a colorful plastic reef just below the water's surface. They were met instantly with a horrible stench that caused Mr. Blanchard to gag and cover his nose with a handkerchief. Garbage floated everywhere—food wrappers and spoiled fruit and drinking cups, mixed with medical supplies—swatches of gauze and surgical masks and empty syringes. A dead squirrel drifted in the soup with stiff outstretched paws.

"Jesus fucking Christ—if you pardon my *français*," Rusty said, killing the engine to avoid fouling the prop. He'd pulled his CVS shirt up over his nose, and his voice sounded nasal and far away. "A dude could get AIDS wading through this sewer."

Duval could see fear in Paul Blanchard's eyes. This was more than the uptown gentleman had bargained on. He closed his eyes and inhaled slowly, exhaled, struggling to keep his lunch down. "I had no idea," he said between pinched breaths. He was gazing into the darkness beyond the check-in counter. "Where is everybody?"

The place appeared even more abandoned than on Duval's first trip through these empty floors. Had the choppers finally come and taken everyone away?

"It's cool if you wanna stay in the boat, Mistah Blanchard," Duval said. "Give me a flashlight and I'll go scope out if anybody's here."

Paul Blanchard sat in silence on a deck chair. Sweat pimpled his forehead. "I'm coming with you," he said, removing his seersucker jacket and rolling down his trouser legs. He was sporting the kind of canvas deck shoes a rich guy would wear on a forty-foot yacht. "I've been here to visit Claire's mother. Once we get upstairs, I'll know the lay of the land."

They could hear an animal noise—what sounded like a growling dog—coming from somewhere down the dark corridor leading to the emergency rooms.

"Stay with the boat," Duval said to Rusty. "Somebody try to take it from you, book it on out of here. But don't go too far, bruh. You're our ride home."

Mr. Blanchard reached into his jacket draped over the chair and withdrew a small antique pearl-handled pistol that looked like it belonged in a museum case. "Here, Rusty, take this little Banker's Special. You may need it," he said. "It won't do me any good in deep water."

Duval braced himself for the shock and slipped over the gunnel into a nasty lukewarm slop that leveled off just above his waist. He was surrounded by floating trash—an empty blood bag, cereal mini-boxes, a bulb syringe, long coiling ropes of rubber tubing. God damn, he hated this. Mr. Blanchard was cautiously descending the small ladder, and when he slid into the water and his feet found the muddy bottom, he lost his balance and panicked, flapping his arms and splashing Duval's face. Duval tried not to think about the toilet water dripping down his nose as he seized the back of the man's shirt and steadied him. "Stick close," he said, pulling Blanchard along by the shirtsleeve. "There's a rent-a-cop up in here that might point his A-K at us."

They'd brought flashlights from the Blanchard home and aimed their crisp beams into the unlit corridor ahead. Thousands of white pages floated on the dark water, what appeared to be hospital records and forms. They waded past exam cubicles and deeper into the EMS surgery area, searching for the stairwell to the upper floors. The animal noise grew louder, sounding to Duval like an angry dog tearing at something mushy and wet.

"What the hell you suppose it is?" whispered Mr. Blanchard.

The sound was coming from one of the small surgery rooms at the end of the corridor. A violent gnawing sound, definitely an animal chewing on something, a grinding of gristle and bone. They saw they would have to pass the room in order to reach the stairwell. Duval was in the lead and approached the doorway slowly, gripping his flashlight like a hammer, hoping to skirt around whatever they were up against. He shined the light into the dark cubicle and gasped. "Muthuh-fuckuh!" he said, falling back a step and splashing into Mr. Blanchard. Their flashlights found the dog eating the bowels of a dead man lying on a surgery table, his hospital gown shredded and hanging off him in tatters. The dog raised its bloody muzzle and stared into their bright beams, snarling at them, barking, a mangy brown mutt baring bloody teeth, its hair matted with mud and leaves.

"Let's get the hell out of here before that beast decides we're dessert," said Mr. Blanchard, grabbing Duval's loose hood and pulling him away.

When they forced open the door to the stairwell, the stench was even worse, decaying flesh trapped in an enclosed space. They had to wade through a pontoon of leaking yellow biohazard bags before they reached the stairs. As soon as they climbed free of the putrid water, Duval felt it coming and bent over to heave everything he'd eaten today. He couldn't keep food down. And he couldn't get the image of that dog and the bloody corpse out of his head.

"Better to get this out of the way," said Mr. Blanchard, patting Duval on the back and stooping over next to him. The older man stuck two fingers down his throat and puked against the wall.

Duval led him up the stairs past the body bags and swarming flies to the fifth floor. This was where he'd last seen Hodge stretched out on a gurney with an IV in his arm. The stairwell door stood propped open by an office chair, and a scrawny street cat sat curled on its seat like an evil gatekeeper of all that lay beyond. Duval shined the light in its yellow eyes and it arched its back and hissed at him.

"This place gone jungle," he said, kicking the chair. The cat leaped down and ran off into the darkness.

As they entered the floor, they could hear a man talking somewhere down the long bleak corridor. "Thank goodness," said Mr. Blanchard. "Someone who can direct us."

*"The National Guard has finally started to arrive in significant numbers from around the country. Some would argue they're three days too late. Most of them have been deployed to the Superdome to maintain order . . ."*

Whoever he was, he was speaking with authority.

Duval's shoe slipped on something underfoot and he angled his light downward. He'd stepped on a folder of paperwork, scattering loose pages like the ones they'd seen floating on the water.

"Holy Jesus, Mary, and Joseph," said Mr. Blanchard, making the sign of the cross. He'd trained his flashlight on a long row of sheet-draped bodies arranged against a wall. A folder of medical records had been placed next to each body to identify who they were. "Nobody's going to believe this," he said. "Not up in America."

They walked down the grim corridor, passing body after shrouded body, some lying on mats, some on gurneys, others left on the bare floor. Duval wondered if Hodge was under one of these sheets.

*"For two days now, Army Corps helicopters have been dropping sandbags into the two-hundred-foot-wide breach in the Seventeenth Street Canal. The sandbags weigh three thousand pounds, but it looks like they're*

*dropping flour sacks into the Grand Canyon. We tried to find a spokesman who could tell us how effective . . .*"

It was a radio program. Garland Robinette on WWL. Someone had left a boom box in one of the patient rooms. Duval and Mr. Blanchard stood in the doorway, listening to the report. Late afternoon light glowed through the open windows. That gimpy street cat from the office chair roamed toward another cat sitting on a pile of trash and broken glass.

"Want me to turn it off?" asked Duval.

"No, leave it on. It helps a little. Whistling past the graveyard, I suppose."

The cats began to rub against each other and meow, their tails raised high. The other one wore a collar tag and looked as if its back had been scraped raw by a drawknife.

"Disrespect," said Duval, reaching down for a chunk of fallen plaster. "Damn cats got no business being up in here like this." He threw the plaster at them and they scattered.

Mr. Blanchard stared back into the dark corridor. "Your father-in-law," he said, raising his flashlight near his ear like a dart he might hurl into the shadows. "Where'd you last see him?"

Duval pointed with his light. "On that rolling bed right over there," he said.

Their flashlights danced across a sheet-covered figure lying on the gurney. An IV pole stood close by, next to an oxygen cart. "We've come to the hard part," said Mr. Blanchard. "How do you want to do this?"

Growing up in the St. Bernard Housing Project, Duval had seen a dead body now and again, but not like this. Bodies every whichway you turned. Dead people floating in their yards, slumped over in cars, stacked up in body bags. He didn't want to lift that sheet. But he didn't want this white man to think he was a coward, either. And maybe he had something to prove. This was why he'd crawled into a boat and come all this way, wasn't it?

"I got it," he said.

He stood over the draped body and tried to slow his quick shallow breathing. The narrow corridor was ripe with rotting organs and he couldn't draw enough good air into his lungs. He felt lightheaded, his hands tingling. If he couldn't slow himself down, his racing heart, his breathing, he was either going to pass out or puke again. Damn, he didn't want to lift this sheet. If it was Hodge, he didn't know what he would do.

"Do you want me to help?" Mr. Blanchard offered in a kind way.

"I got it," Duval said again.

He held his breath and forced himself to raise the sheet just enough to shine the light on Hodge's face. Only it wasn't Hodge but an old woman with an oxygen mask strapped across her nose and mouth. She was dead but her eyes were still open, staring up at him. He dropped the sheet and stepped back, his entire body trembling. There was something familiar about those eyes and the shape of her face. She could have been his mother.

"Is it him?" Mr. Blanchard asked, placing a hand on Duval's shoulder.

Duval shook his head. He couldn't find words. He needed air and rushed back into the room with the boom box radio and hung his head out a broken window, sucking in outside air five stories above the flooded streets. He could see people wandering on the elevated interstate. Hodge might be out there, he thought, rambling around half out of his head.

*"FEMA is saying it sent five hundred buses from Arkansas—with food, water, and medical supplies—but where are they? It's Wednesday afternoon and nobody has seen the FEMA buses yet. Sources close to Governor Blanco say she's going to issue an executive order to commandeer all the buses she can get her hands on. But the problem is bus drivers. There aren't enough drivers willing to drive into New Orleans . . ."*

"They may've put him on a helicopter." Mr. Blanchard was

standing in the middle of the room, listening to WWL. "Or he may've walked out of here on his own. You said he's a tough old Vietnam Marine. Those guys know how to handle themselves."

Duval turned from the window. "He might be under another sheet," he said, shaken by the thought of it.

"Well, there's one sure way to find out."

Duval stared at the tile. "I cain't lift up any more sheets, Mistah Blanchard," he said, still haunted by those eyes staring up at him. "Call me any name you want to, I just cain't do it, man."

The radio was sitting on a food cart. Mr. Blanchard walked over and turned it off. "We don't have to lift any sheets, son," he said. "All we have to do is look at the names on those medical records they left next to the bodies."

They set about their task with the somberness of army chaplains blessing the battlefield dead. There were fifteen bodies in all. They knelt beside each one and took turns reading the names aloud, so there could be no possible mistake. Joanne Porter, Wanda Jackson, Joseph Giusti, Hilda McAdams, Andre Louvier. After each name, Mr. Blanchard made the sign of the cross and prayed a Hail Mary in a low mumbling voice Duval could barely understand. He wasn't raised Catholic but he lowered his head with each prayer and in his heart he asked God to accept these abandoned souls into the Kingdom of Heaven.

When they reached the last hand-printed record—a seventy-year-old male with chronic asthma named Johnny Richard—Mr. Blanchard rose to his feet and said, "He's not here."

Duval sighed and laughed dryly and said, "Prob'ly back at your crib, finishing off them chicken wings." Hodge had made it out. He was certain of it. The old man was tough as they come.

They heard a tinkling sound moving down the dark corridor and both swung their lights like aimed pistols. That scraped-raw cat with the collar tag was on the prowl, sniffing at sheets, meowing faintly in the stifling heat.

"I had that old gat of yours," Duval said, "I'd put one in that little fucker's skull."

Mr. Blanchard pointed his light toward the exit door to the stairwell. "Will you accompany me to the twelfth floor, my friend?" he asked Duval. "That's where they're keeping Claire's mother. Terminal Care Unit." Sweat dripped from his thick gray hair, trailed down his face. It felt like they'd been working a ten-hour shift in a coal mine. "Let's hope conditions are more propitious up there," he said, his flashlight beam roaming over the sheeted bodies.

The climb up seven flights of stairs in the stinking swelter left Mr. Blanchard breathless and grabbing his knees in front of a door stenciled with the number 12. "Gotta get back to the gym when this is all over with," he said, huffing.

Duval worked the door handle and discovered it was unlocked. When they entered the dim-lit corridor, the hideous odor made Duval's eyes water. The Terminal Care Unit smelled even worse than the fifth floor.

"This isn't good," said Mr. Blanchard, pulling the wrinkled handkerchief from his pocket again and placing it against his nose.

They didn't need their flashlights. Patients' doors were left open and weak light from outside windows cast strange distorted shapes across the corridor. "This is her room up here," said Mr. Blanchard.

The bed was empty and stripped of sheets, the room vacant. He looked over the effects on a nightstand. "Yes, this is hers," he said, lifting a framed family photograph and smiling fondly at the picture. "Back when my mother was alive and the two families got together for holidays. Claire's family is Jewish and mine is Catholic. We were always celebrating something."

Duval watched him rummage through the closet. Her sleeping gowns were still hanging there, and a dress, a windbreaker. "Poor thing, they must have medevacked her out of here with only the gown on her back," Mr. Blanchard said. "It's going to be hell figuring out where they've taken her." He was holding a stylish dress the old woman would probably never wear again. "We should've come and got her over the weekend," he said with a catch in his throat. "Poor dear only weighed ninety pounds. She was too fragile to move and they told us she'd be all right up here. I should have listened to Claire. She wanted us to come get her and drive her to a hospice in Baton Rouge."

They wandered back into the corridor, silent and disillusioned and exhausted by all they'd encountered in this dark building. Mr. Blanchard carried the framed family photograph with him but didn't seem to know what to do with it. They faced each other in the shadowy light. Paul Blanchard was a kind man, a good man, and Duval wished he knew what to say to him. He was trying to arrange the right words in his head when he noticed a yellow piece of paper taped to a door farther up the corridor.

"Yo, what's that?" he said. Mr. Blanchard turned to see what he was looking at.

The sheet of paper was torn from a yellow legal pad and taped to the door with medical tape. It said DO NOT ENTER, hand-printed with a black marker.

A small chrome cross was fixed to the door, next to a panel of rose-colored glass. It must have been the hospital chapel. Duval tried to peer through the glass but it was nearly opaque. When he gave the door a slight push, a muffled voice said, "Cain't you read what the sign says, son? Don't go in there."

Duval didn't recognize him at first because of the respirator covering his nose and mouth. It was the old security guard named Tucker. His uniform shirt was stained with blood and dark sweat rings, his shirttail hanging loose, and he was carrying a scoped rifle like he meant to use it. There was a wild reckless look in his eyes that made Duval want to back away slowly.

"Remember me?" Duval said. Those hollow dark eyes were terrifying. Like it wouldn't take much to set him off. "I come up in here with an older gent named Hodge Grant. Old Marine with a bad heart. Y'all got to talking Vietnam days."

"I remember you, son," the guard said. He didn't seem like the same man. Something had hardened in him. "Got the hell beat out of you down on the ER docks." He examined Duval with those hard eyes and laughed a little crazy. "Looks like you're gonna be wearing them tattoos for awhile."

Duval turned and motioned to Mr. Blanchard. Maybe a rich white man could calm this crazy old dude down. "Me and this gentleman here are looking for our people," he said. "You know if Hodge got out okay? He ain't on the fifth floor, where I left him."

Mr. Blanchard introduced himself and Tucker lowered the rifle to shake his hand. "You the last man standing?" he asked the guard with a worn smile.

Tucker nodded. "They all cleared out," he said. "Choppers. Air boats. They took everybody they could. Axed me to come along too. I said no. Gotta keep my word. That's pretty much all I got left."

Mr. Blanchard explained that his mother-in-law was named Ida Benjamin and that she was a patient here in the Terminal Care Unit. "Is there a record of where they sent them all? Poor dear only has a couple of weeks to live," he said. "My wife and I—we can't let her pass in some strange place with people she doesn't know."

Tucker propped the rifle against the wall and removed his respirator. He hadn't shaved in days and a grainy white stubble was scattered like bird seed on his dark jaw and neck. He stared at the two of them for a long while, his face washed in sweat. "Wait here," he said before walking toward a custodian closet across the hall. He returned with two dust masks and handed them to Duval and Mr. Blanchard. "Best I can do for now. Put them on and follow me."

When they pushed through the chapel door, Duval understood immediately why the place had been marked DO NOT ENTER. It was the epicenter of the foul odor that had assaulted them in the corridor, and the masks did little to alleviate the awful smell. The odor would sicken the reporters who arrived a day later to take photographs.

Nineteen bodies were arranged like napping day-care children in the soft violet glow from a stained glass window. Tucker directed Mr. Blanchard to where Ida Benjamin was lying under a baby blue blanket, her serene face exposed to the light. Her son-in-law knelt down by her side and made the sign of the cross.

Tucker signaled for Duval to follow him. He crossed the chapel and raised a sheet to show Duval where he'd put Hodge after the doctors had lost their struggle to keep him alive. Duval peered down at the man's chiseled old face, asleep now forever. He would not forget their journey together and what Hodge had said to him that final time. *Go find your children and take care of them till they're old enough to be on their own. That's what a man does, Duval. It ain't changed in ten thousand years.*

"He passed sitting in a chair," Tucker said, removing his respirator. "Stubborn old warrior to the end. Trying to protect some dead lady he thought needed protecting. Wouldn't leave her bedside and it took us too long to get the doctors up here. I don't think he knew how bad off he was."

Mr. Blanchard was carefully stepping around bodies, making his way over to look at Hodge. He had removed his dust mask, too, and tears were flowing down his cheeks.

"He didn't suffer," Tucker said. "It was like he dozed off to sleep."

Duval didn't know how he was going to tell this to Dee. He didn't know what they would do with the body.

"We were soldiers once," Tucker said, still holding onto a corner of the sheet and staring down at him. "I promised my brother here I wouldn't leave him to the rats and I'm gonna keep that promise. I'm gonna stay here till somebody shows up with a long black hersh. I don't care if it takes six months, I'll be right here. Y'all go tell that to Brother George Bush and Mayor Nagin." He looked around the chapel. "Tell them to come get all these good folk and give them a proper burying. I ain't leaving till somebody comes in here to clean my people up and put a robe on them and make them ready to meet their Savior."

"Amen to that," Mr. Blanchard said.

Tucker turned to him. "I'm sorry for your loss, sir. Everybody in this town remembers Miz Ida Benjamin. White lady that took on the haters and opened up the schools to black chirren back in the day. We'll mourn that good woman, Mistah Blanchard. We'll praise her precious name."

The three men stood in front of the altar and held hands in a circle. It made Duval uncomfortable to hold a man's hand, but he had to let that go. Tucker recited the Lord's Prayer aloud and Mr. Blanchard prayed another Hail Mary, and when it was Duval's turn he didn't know what to do so he took off his mask and sang what he remembered of an old gospel song his mother and aunts had taught him when he was a child. A river song like Hodge had requested.

*One of these mornings, bright and fair*
*Wanna cross over to see my Lord*
*Gonna take my wings and fly the air*
*Wanna cross over to see my Lord*
*Get away, Jordan*
*Get away, Jordan*
*There's one more river to cross*

It was evening now, the third day. Light had softened to a faint violet hue in the chapel, and in the corridor the shadows grew bolder, as if the last candle on earth was guttering out in a dry wind. It was nearly dark as the boat carried them back to their families. The three men rode in silence, the air thick and still. A terrible stench rose from the sitting waters of the doomed old city, for the dead were still tethered to their trees.

# Epilogue

Four weeks later, Dee was still working through the bureaucratic paperwork, waiting to claim her father's body from the FEMA morgue in St. Gabriel, a small town downriver from Baton Rouge where Katrina victims were being stored and identified in an industrial warehouse. Hodge had already purchased a plot next to Dee's mother in the Garden of Memory Cemetery on the outskirts of Opelousas, and Dee was determined to bury him there.

On that Thursday morning following the hurricane, after a sleepless night at the Blanchard home, they were transported by the young man named Rusty in his neighbor's boat to the Jefferson Parish line, where the truck and trailer had been waiting for them, miraculously unharmed, in the Wendy's parking lot.

"You know how to handle this old hunka junk better than me," Duval had said to Dee, offering Hodge's mess of keys. The truck had roared to life like a belching tractor, and Dee drove them through storm-ravaged South Louisiana for four long hours with her quiet children beside her and tears running down her cheeks.

Duval stayed with them in the farmhouse for a month and slept on the patched old leather couch in the living room. He insisted on driving the children to their new school every morning. He mowed the lawn and tended the vegetable garden and helped around the house. He fed and befriended Hodge's half-blind old Catahoula hound. Dee sensed that something was different about Duval now. The hurricane had changed him, as it would change everyone who had survived that terrible ordeal.

Duval borrowed the pickup several times and drove back to New

Orleans to search for his mother and aunts. The Housing Authority had closed down the St. Bernard Housing Project, and eventually all the projects in the city, but he tracked down his mother's pastor, who told him the women were safe and living in the fellowship hall of a sister church in Marianna, Florida. Dee listened in on his phone calls to his mother every night and remembered the sweet young man of twenty she had met in the Dillard library.

"I'm coming to get y'all, Momma," he told her. "Just give it a little more time till the N. O. is in better shape. I'll have some money by then and come pick y'all up."

Dee didn't know where he was going to get the money. Or the wheels to drive to Florida. But he said it with such love and conviction that she hoped he could keep his promise.

For the first two weeks, Dee woke up every night in her parents' bed and cried over all she'd lost. Her Daddy, Tante Belle, the house in Gentilly with all their keepsakes and belongings. Everything was gone. Her job as a teacher's assistant, her evening classes to earn a teaching degree. And where were the children's schoolmates and their neighborhood friends? Every tie to their old life had been scattered in the floodwaters. Things would never be the same again.

The children were healthy except for a few mosquito bites, but Dee and Duval had to make regular visits to the makeshift clinic the city had set up for Katrina evacuees. Dee had developed a serious skin rash, and Duval couldn't keep food down. They both ended up taking antibiotics, but three months would pass before Dee felt like her old self again.

She used the computer at the local library to search for Tante Belle's nephew Preston and eventually located him at his cousin's home in Marshall, Texas. She told him what had happened to his aunt and they shared a long cry over the phone. She'd searched for Tante Belle's body at the warehouse in St. Gabriel when she was looking for her father, but she couldn't find any record of her. She suspected that the rescue workers had yet to discover her body in

Gentilly Terrace, and she offered to help Preston search their neighborhood as soon as it was safe to return.

One day a letter arrived in the mailbox addressed to Pops Grant. Dee recognized her brother's handwriting. The return address was marked *David Wade Correctional Center* in Homer, Louisiana. She had no idea where Homer was located until later, when she Googled it on the library computer and discovered it was in the piney woods not far from the Arkansas state line.

*Dear Pops,* the letter began. *I hope your health is good. And I hope Dee and her two kids are cribbing with you until N. O. is back up on its feet.*

He apologized for not staying in touch and said he'd run into a little trouble with the law again. He'd been awaiting arraignment in the Orleans Parish Prison when Katrina flooded the unit where he was jailed.

*Things got crazy, but I am OK. They sent me and some of my classmates up here until OPP can bounce back. I hope you find it in your heart to come visit me before too long. I know I messed up again and I am taking the weight for this. I dont blame you if your mad at me. But I would like some face time with you before they put me away where the sun dont shine. I miss you, Pops.*

And then he asked his father for a favor.

*Hard to explain, but I met a nice couple name of Alton and Olive Lee. They took some people to Houston in a bus. Do you think you could locate them some how and keep me up to speed on their where abouts? Theres 3 little children they are caring for, and I would like to know if the children are doing alright.*

He ended the letter by telling his father that he loved him.

*I am going to do better, Pops. I just need to work out this bid and then get back in the population. There is some things I want to do in this life and I cant do them inside.*

He signed the letter *Your loving son, Lucien "PJ" to the* G.

Dee cried when she read the letter. She cried when she was finally able to get through the corrections system and speak to her brother by phone. She cried when she told him that their father was dead. She promised that she and the kids would drive up to Homer and visit him at Thanksgiving.

Her new life in Opelousas was so filled with forms and document searches and bills and the daily routine of keeping the children fed and getting them off to school every morning that she'd almost forgotten about Robert Guyton. That's why she didn't recognize his voice when he called one evening in October.

"You didn't believe me when I said I would call, did you?" he said. She could feel his handsome smile on the other end of the line.

"People get caught up in something that shakes their world and they sometimes say things they don't mean," she said.

"I always mean what I say, Dee."

They talked for two hours about everything they'd been through. She told him about Hodge's death and about the father of her children sleeping on the living room couch. Nothing seemed to deter him. He invited her and the kids to supper on Friday evening at Prudhomme's Cajun Café near Lafayette. "Wear your dancing shoes," he told her.

Prudhomme's was a country roadhouse, Cajun style, with baby alligators swimming in an aquarium and their scaly old grandfathers stuffed and mounted near the cashier's counter. Robert Guyton and his eight-year-old daughter, Kedra, were waiting for them at a table surrounded by boisterous white people. When he saw Dee arrive, he stood up from his chair and smiled. He looked comfortable in civilian clothes, a Hawaiian shirt and jeans, his hair trimmed nicely and his face smooth shaven. He hugged Dee and the children and introduced his daughter. She was a beautiful girl with long beaded hair, and Dee could understand now why Ashley had caught Robert's eye. She and Kedra could have passed for sisters.

Onstage out in the dance area, a band of weathered old Cajuns wearing cowboy hats and suspenders were sawing fiddles and pumping accordions and hollering through every song. After much laughter and a lively supper of crawfish, shrimp, and red snapper, Kedra led

Ashley and LaMarcus off to the dance floor to teach them the Cajun two-step, leaving Dee and Robert to themselves and another round of Abita beer.

"How long do you think you'll be staying in Opelousas?" he asked her.

"We want to get back to New Orleans as soon as we can," she said. "But I don't know when my school will start up again. And I don't know if they can fix up our house. It was underwater, all but the roof."

"I suppose the right thing to say is I hope things recover quickly in New Orleans and y'all can get back to your life there. But to be honest, Dee, I like having you as a neighbor. I'd like to get to know you better."

She clinked the stubby neck of her beer bottle against his. "Let's take it slow and see how it goes, Robert," she said, feeling like a real woman again for the first time in months.

"How about we start out there on the dance floor?"

She looked over at her children, who were laughing and struggling to follow Kedra's lead. The dance floor was filled with ancient white couples who seemed to be gliding along in some faraway time.

"Not quite my flow, yo. They ever bumpin' some hip hop up in this place?" she asked with a ghetto-girl head wag.

He laughed and stood up and offered his hand. "Come on, it's a two-step," he said. "But we'll take it one step at a time."

A few weeks later, Duval found a paying job with a construction crew in the Lower Ninth Ward. During the days he tore out molded Sheetrock and in the evenings he volunteered with a charitable outfit to remove furniture and refrigerators from flooded houses. He began to stay the entire week in New Orleans. His old crib in Gert Town was destroyed, so he lived in a tent city in a school parking lot with young volunteers from around the country. New Orleans was a ghost town, at least where he was staying. The nights were long and dark. More than once he woke in his tent in a hot sweat, shaken by the same nightmare. His mother's eyes were staring up at him from under that lifted sheet.

He returned to Opelousas on weekends to spend time with LaMarcus and Ashley. Dee didn't know how long this routine would last, but she was always grateful to see him. Ashley had begun to speak to her Daddy again and tease him playfully. "Now that you're a carpenter, Daddy—when we all move back to New Orleans," she said one day, "why don't you build a house with a swimming pool so we can swim whenever we want to?"

Two weeks before Christmas, Duval had saved enough money to rent a car. He drove to Marianna, Florida, a quaint little Panhandle town with a tall Confederate monument on the town green. His mother and aunts wept and hugged him and patted his cheeks, his momma crying, "My boy, my boy. I knew you would come and get us." He had patiently filled out the paperwork for the two FEMA trailers waiting for them back in New Orleans. He had come to take these good ladies home.

# Acknowledgments

First and foremost, I thank my son, Danny, for his assistance and companionship during the research and writing of this book. In the early months after Hurricane Katrina and the breached levees destroyed New Orleans, I drove through the empty streets of the city while Danny, in high school at the time, took notes as we absorbed what we were seeing. The city was virtually abandoned, except for "the sliver by the river," and we encountered no traffic, or pedestrians, or signs of life in most of the neighborhoods. I also want to thank Malik Rahim and my old Stanford friend Don Paul for showing us the devastated Lower Ninth Ward and the houses left in ruin. Don also read the manuscript of this book with great care and offered outstanding advice.

I consulted with several friends whose homes were damaged and their lives disrupted by the hurricane. Especially helpful were Tana and Rene Coman, Stephanie Bruno, and Gerry Vetter, who returned to his neighborhood by boat and provided me with amazing anecdotes and floodwater depth charts of the entire city.

Several friends and fellow writers were kind enough to read the first draft of this book and give me encouragement and invaluable feedback: Jim Magnuson, Jan Reid, Annette Carlozzi, Geoff Leavenworth, Kathleen Orillion, Dick Holland, Karen Davidson, Gary Phillips, Michael Hurd, and Lynda Gonzales. My son, Danny, also proved to be an insightful editor and critic. Jan Reid very generously recommended the book to TCU Press.

My agent, Bill Contardi, was a steadfast and patient advocate throughout the process of attracting a publisher, and we could not have found a better publisher than Dan Williams and his staff at TCU Press. A special thanks to Kathy Walton for her judicious editing.

Three of my very good friends and fellow writers passed away while I was writing this book—James Crumley, Fred Pfeil, and Max Crawford. I will always hear their literary voices and strive for the excellence they brought to every sentence they wrote.

Photograph by Charlie Palafox

Thomas Zigal is best known for his Kurt Muller crime series set in Aspen, Colorado. His novel *The White League* is the first in his New Orleans trilogy. He has published short stories, essays, and book reviews in literary magazines and anthologies for nearly forty years. He grew up in Texas, resided in New Orleans for four years, and has lived in other cities all over the country. He now lives in Austin, Texas, with his wife and children.